BURDENED BONDS

HANNAH HAZE

Front cover designed by Covers by Christian

Edited by Buckley's Books

 Formatted with Vellum

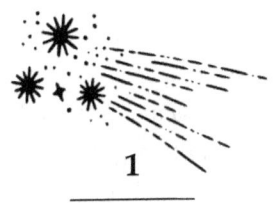

1

S tone

I RUN in the direction of her dorm, even though I know she won't be there, even though I can feel she's gone; my bond strained and stretched as if she's far far away.

But that can't be right. That can't be possible. Something has happened and I need to find her.

My feet hit the gravel path as students race around me, ducking for cover, seeking safe refuge, calling out to one another. Above me, the huge silhouettes of dragons swoop eastward and westward, north and south, great balls of fire roaring through the air, scorching everything in their paths. The sky blazes a multitude of colors too, magic colliding and exploding with such force I swear any minute the fabric of the heavens themselves will rip and tear away.

I keep running, ignoring magic that swoops past my

head, magic that explodes on the path around me, magic that smashes into buildings and sends rubble flying.

I keep running, the dark dorm building that is hers soon emerging from the gloom.

And then I skid to a halt.

A man lies motionless and still on the path in front of me, his eyes open and lifeless, gazing up at the riot of colors in the sky, the lights reflected back in his blank pupils.

As I venture closer, I see the dark shadow wrapped around his neck, his hands still clasped there, see the purple hue of his face, the strained expression frozen in time across his features. Strangled, strangled with magic.

The man is Marcus Lowsky.

I know his face, even if it's aged, even if there are more inks scrawled across his skin, more lines of time etched into the flesh. We walked the same streets as kids. We trod the same paths. He was a cruel bastard even back then, although a mere shadow of the man he became.

I stare down at his face. Who the hell killed him? Not anyone from the academy. The magic lingering around his neck is dark, nothing anyone in the academy would use. Unless ...

Rhi?

The man wanted to kill her. Did the bastard come close?

I glare down at his lifeless form and then I spit on his face. I consider giving his corpse a kick for good measure, but then I hear voices in the distance and footfall on the path. I look up and find three of Lowsky's men, their wolf tattoos clear on their skin, sprinting towards me. They halt just as I did when they spot the dead man on the path.

"He's dead," I yell at them. "Lowsky is dead."

They hesitate in indecision. One hauls magic at me halfheartedly, and then they're running away, yelling the news to their comrades.

I watch them go and then I turn my attention to Rhi's room, entering the dorm and finding her door ajar.

I've stood outside her room before, but I've never entered. It feels strange to do so now without an invitation, like an invasion, but what choice do I have? I need to find her.

The sight of the shabby room has my stomach turning. I hate the stupid social politics of the academy. I always have. It seems brutally unfair that some students can live in such fucking splendor while others live in such squalor. Is it necessary? Really necessary to rub the noses of those who have nothing in a daily reminder of their relative obscurity?

Her room is seriously crappy. Sure, it's no better than the room I had myself back when I was a student in the academy, but I feel more angry about it. Rhi deserves to live in a fucking palace like a princess, not a cellar like fucking Cinderella.

The room is empty. I search under the bed and inside the wardrobe anyway. My eyes lingering over her desk, her notebooks, her scribbled handwriting, her clothes hanging untidily in the cupboard.

She's not here. She really is fucking gone.

I stumble out of the dorm and automatically I sense something has changed.

The sounds of battle no longer boom through the academy, the sky is no longer ablaze with fire and magic, and the smell of fear and death and dying no longer permeates the air.

I pull out my phone as I pick up my feet again, but there's no coverage. The network is down. I curse under my breath, racing back along the pathways, back towards the mansion.

As I career around the corner, I'm in time to see the great dragons launch up into the sky together. I lift my hands, bracing myself, ready. The soldiers and men who attacked us have scattered, but I assume this is simply a temporary reprieve, a chance to gather their forces before striking us again. Around me other academy magicals do the same – a handful of teachers, a few of the students, York herself in her ripped and charred ballgown.

But there's no strike. No attack. The soldiers have gone and the dragons lift into the night in formation, high above us, soaring not in the direction of the city but out towards the west.

I tip back my head, mesmerized by the sight despite everything, the great creatures truly graceful in flight, as if they weigh nothing at all, as if they aren't vicious killing machines. As I watch them go, one of the riders out front turns his head and peers down at the ground, his eyes a glowing golden even over the distance. For a brief moment of time, our eyes meet, our gazes lock and my magic crackles.

I flex my fingers, ready again for the strike, but again it doesn't come. The man simply shifts his gaze back to the west and sweeps his arm over his shoulder, signaling for the other riders to follow him.

"They're leaving," York says, clearly as puzzled as I am.

"For now," I say. "For now."

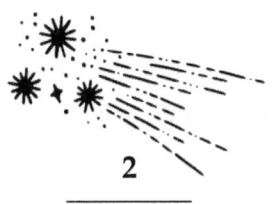

2

R enzo

I LIFT my little rabbit into my arms and carry her upstairs to her old bedroom. The room's been trashed and, although someone else has tried to neaten it again, it's not good enough. I tut like an old woman and lower her carefully onto the mattress, wrapping her up in the measly blankets and shushing her all over again.

Whatever it is that's gripped my little rabbit won't shift, not with coaxing and not with force. Half the problem is, I don't know what the hell is wrong. Something to do with that Kennedy boy. The one who walks like he's got a rod stuck up his ass, his nose in the air.

Did he curse her? Except I can't feel any dark magic lingering on her skin, dancing through her veins. The only magic I can feel is weak. Not like my rabbit at all. I don't like it.

I rub my knuckles over her cheek, telling her all over again that she's safe. Then I busy myself, using my magic to tidy the room, cleaning away all the debris and broken junk, driving away the dust and the grime, working hard until it looks like a fucking palace, gleaming and all.

The entire time, her little pig lies by the side of the bed, facing his mistress, chin resting on his trotters, eyes locked on her pale face. Occasionally his eyes swivel to me, checking what I'm doing, but I think we've come to an understanding, me and him.

"We can't stay here," I tell him, but he doesn't respond, eyes staring straight ahead.

It isn't like I want to move her either. Not when she's like this. Not when I don't understand what is wrong. "It isn't safe here." I punch my fist into her cushion. I think that's how the hell you're meant to do it. Make it all soft and fluffy for her, then I slide it under her head. She's sleeping but not peacefully. Her lips move in silent whispers, her eyes swing behind their sockets and her brow is damp with sweat, her precious body shaking. "It isn't safe," I say again, more to myself than him now.

I don't know how hard she fought last night in the academy. I don't know how much of her powers she revealed. I don't even know if there are people out there who already know about her, know how special she is. But if they do – if they know who she is – they'll be looking for her.

It's too difficult to sit still. I need to be doing something. Something more than pacing her newly gleaming little room.

I remember the herbs sitting in rows in glass jars along the kitchen window sill. I remember them hanging from the ceiling. It's what people do, right? When someone's sick, they brew them a healing spell. Fuck me if I know what one of those is. But I guess I've never needed an instruction manual or recipe book before – couldn't read them half the time anyway.

I place my cool palm on her warm brow, tell her I won't be away long, then creep downstairs, cursing every damn loose floorboard and noisy door. The kitchen's flooded with hazy light; the window yellow with the rising sun, golden dust hanging suspended in the air.

I open each jar, snap off twigs from the herbs, crush the leaves between my fingers and sniff. Memories sail through my head, sweeping me back to another time and another kitchen, potions simmering on the stove. I find a big bad pot like she had, haul it up on the cooker and add what smells nice, what feels nice, what hums through the air that it's going to help my little rabbit. My eyes stray up to the ceiling. She's lying right above me. I can sense her right there, the thing in my gut ever tugging me her way.

The potion simmers. Tiny bubbles form on the surface, popping and remolding. Steam and smoke and aromas cloud the kitchen. The windows mist, hiding the coming day.

I switch off the stove, dip my pinkie into the scalding liquid and lift it to my tongue. Doesn't taste too much like shit and it sends a warmth sailing though my body.

It's the best I can do. All I can do for her right now. Make her comfortable. Wait for it to pass. Hope it fucking does.

She's still restless when I return, the blankets all a tangle round her body. She looks like a fly caught in a web. I free her, smooth the cover flat. Then I sit down on the bed, right above her head, and comb my fingers through her hair. It feels like silk. Like water.

It's what I remember my mom doing once, when I was small and my head hurt so much I thought it was going to fucking burst. She wrapped me up in my bed, stroked my head, sang me lullabies. Yeah, it wasn't all bad. There were bits like that too.

I hum one of those tunes now. Something old, something that's lasted longer than people like us. A song they'll keep singing when we're gone. It seems to pacify her. She stills, her breathing deepens. My heart stills too. For a moment, I watch her. The way her shoulders lift and fall with each breath. The way her lip quivers when she sucks in the air. The way her blood leaps beneath her skin. She's so delicate. It would be so easy to hurt her, to break her, to ruin her – just like that bastard Marcus did.

I have to be careful with her. Extra extra careful baby steps, Barone.

It's so fucking different from everything I've done before. It's alien. Like picking up her knife in my wrong hand. Like trying to speak backward. Like trying not to think of her.

But practice makes perfect, right? That's what they say. And they can't say I don't practice.

Holding my breath in my chest, I rest my hands on her shoulder and roll her ever so gently, a little at a time, so she won't feel it at all. The pig eyes me with suspicion and I can't help winking at him, something which makes him snort. Finally, she's propped up against me and I reach for the cup with my potion, press it against her lips, wet them.

"Drink, little rabbit," I say. "Drink for me. Just a sip."

Her pink tongue slides from her mouth and dips into the liquid and I could fucking scream with joy. It would be fucking stupid though. So I keep quiet, let her drink a little. When she's had enough, I lay her back down, shuffling her along until there's enough space for me too. Then I slide alongside her, letting her little body roll into mine and wrapping her up in my arms.

I mustn't squeeze too tight, mustn't pull too hard.

Gentle, gentle.

Her head fits beneath my chin, her soft hair tickling against my throat and her breath flows across my skin like wind on the plain. As if she's trying to breathe life into me. Is that what this is? Have I always been dead? Dead inside, right? Am I finally coming to life?

The song withers on my lips as I listen to the song of her instead. The rhythm of her breath, the beat of her heart. Swinging back and forth between the two.

I'm tired. It's been a fucking long day. I can feel sleep sucking me under.

"I did some digging, little rabbit," I whisper to her. "About your mom." The pig lifts his head and glances at me. "Yeah," I say, my eyes drifting shut. "Seems the professor isn't the only one who's good at learning stuff."

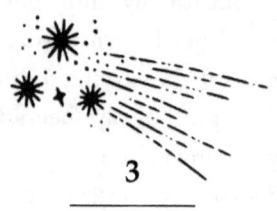

3

S pencer

WE TRAVEL in silence with all the lights of the truck we've commandeered cut out. The battle may be over, but we don't know what lies out there in wait for us or whether another strike may be weaving its way towards us at this very minute.

Tristan lies cocooned in my arms. He's waning, with every minute that passes slipping away and I curse under my breath and tell the professor to put his goddamn foot on the gas. Rhi's friend glances at Tristan's ashen face and then my own, then rests her hand upon my arm. So recently transformed from wolf form, her touch makes me flinch, my body sensitive, tender. But I know she means well, and though I want to scream at her too, I bite my tongue. It won't do any good. We need to deliver Tristan to his family, and then we need to find Rhi.

The concerned expressions etched on the enforcer and

the professor's faces tell me they have about as much idea about where she is as I do. But at least she must be alive. The enforcer is her bonded mate. If anything had happened to her, if she were ... I screw up my eyes. He'd know. He'd feel it. Fuck, would he feel it!

There must be a way to find her. There must be.

The beast inside me is silent and I'm surprised by it. I expected him to be raving and riling, straining to be released. Desperate to find her, tearing down walls, thundering across the countryside. Shit, hitching a lift on the back of a dragon just to get to her. However, although he's as aggravated as I am to find the girl, he isn't fighting this course of action. For once, we're in agreement. We need to save Tristan Kennedy, although I suspect our motives for doing so are different.

We hit a series of bumps in the road, our bodies buffeting about, Rhi's friend falling against the boy next to her – her date – as he grabs for the handle hanging from the vehicle's roof, then we veer around a corner and the big houses of the capital's expensive suburb comes into view. They're mostly untouched – only the buildings in the city's center are captured in flames – and I wonder how many of the great families are holed up inside, sheltering, and how many were out fighting for our freedom. I think of my own mom, my own dad, far from here. Are they safe? Shame swims through me, making me wince when I realize it's the first time tonight I've thought of them. All my focus has been on Tristan and Rhianna.

There are no other vehicles on the road, the tree-lined streets deserted, and we soar along out to the mound, out to the Kennedy place, its large iron gates standing guard against the world.

For a moment, I expect them to remain like that – closed

– barring our entrance, but the magical charm kicks in and they part for the heir of the family and his kin.

Stone skids the truck to a halt in front of the mansion's steps and I stare up at the house. All the lights are out. But that's not unusual. It was never somewhere that screamed life and party and all that crap. It always gave me the fucking creeps.

The man in black opens the door for me, offers to take Tristan, but I refuse. He's my friend. I found him. I'm not letting him go just yet. Not until I know he's safe.

I ignore the niggle at the back of my mind, the one whispering to me, telling me how ill he looks, how close to death he must be. I ignore the whiff of death I keep catching in his scent as well. Refuse to goddamn acknowledge it. I won't let him die. Not him too.

Not him too! As much a brother to me as my own was.

The others trail behind me as I race him up the steps, the great doors drawing open as I near, and the figure of his mom stepping out into the night, her face as pale as her son's, her hands shaking.

"Tristan?" she asks with trepidation, peering at the body in my arms.

"Yes, Ma'am," I step forward, half expecting her to shrink away, "Tristan."

"Bring him inside," she instructs, glancing at the others crowding around me. "Azlan," she says, addressing the enforcer, "your father and uncle have gone to the council building."

The enforcer is already turning on the steps, descending three at a time. "I have to go," he calls out.

"You're going to join them?" his aunt asks.

"No, I have to … Rhianna …"

"Azlan?" Tristan's cousin appears in the doorway beside her aunt. "Azlan, what's wrong?"

The man in black freezes, then turns again, racing up the steps. His sister runs to meet him, flinging herself into his arms as they wrap each other in a tight embrace.

"Ellie, you're okay?" he asks, releasing her.

"Yes, but ..." she trails off as she sees her cousin for the first time. Her gaze jumps back to her brother in alarm. "Rhi?"

The enforcer's jaw hardens and he shakes his head.

Ellie gasps, her hands flying to cover her mouth, her body shaking, but then Stone lays a hand on her shoulder, scowling at his friend. "Missing, Ellie. Not ... not ..."

"We have to go find her." The enforcer's jaw is hard, his eyes steely.

Rhianna's friend steps forward. "You know where she is?" The enforcer's entire body stiffens further. He shakes his head. "Then you need to stay here – all of you – and fix Tristan first."

My friend is weakening with every wasted moment arguing like this, he's slipping from us.

Tristan's mom senses it; her face is white with alarm. She takes my wrist in hers and pulls me through into the house and into the grand dining room, leaving the others to bicker on the doorstep. The long dining table occupies nearly all the space, its surface polished to perfection. So polished I can see my face reflected back up in it, bloodied, dirty, covered in soot.

"Lay him down," she says.

"Here?" I say. The wood is hard, solid, cold.

"Yes," she snaps with a little impatience, rolling up the sleeves of her cream blouse and pocketing her rings. "Ellie," she calls and the young woman comes scurrying inside. Tristan's mom waves her hand. "Fetch me my things."

Ellie nods, then sprints away and Tristan's mom looks down at her son, resting her palm tenderly on his golden crown.

"Tristan," she whispers, but even his mom's voice isn't enough to rouse him. He lies there unresponsive, unmoving, his magic a mere whisper in the air. "You tried to heal him?" she asks me, eyes still fixed to his face.

I shuffle forward. "I tried. I ... I couldn't. There was something ... something ..."

"A curse most likely," she says, and the slur I so often hear in her voice is no longer present. For once her voice is clear and focused, her eyes too. "Dark magic."

"Crimson?" I ask.

She peers into her son's eyes, her hand still resting on his forehead. "No, it's not crimson magic, not scarlet. It's not as ancient as that," she says, her eyes closed, "but its intentions are dark."

"Can you ..." I swallow.

"Heal him?" Her eyes snap up to mine.

I nod. She doesn't answer and her niece returns with a large wooden box, the others sidling into the room after her.

"You decided to stay?" she says, her stiff words directed at Azlan.

"For now," he answers.

"That girl has been nothing but trouble," she mutters.

"That girl is your son's fated mate," the professor spits.

What?!

I take a stumbling step away from the table.

Her fated mate!

What the fuck?

Is that true? It can't be, can it? And yet ... and yet ... The memory of the two of them together in the meadow comes crashing back into my mind. Was it right there in front of my eyes all along? Plain to see?

I wait for the beast to spit and howl inside me. But he's quiet. As if this earth-altering piece of news was already known to him. Had always been known to him.

But this can't be right!

I am certain of two things. Tristan Kennedy hates Rhianna Blackwaters. Rhianna Blackwaters hates him back. They can't be fated mates.

But then I think of that day in the meadow again; their magic playful, joyful, twining and spinning around one another. The girl laughing so freely it made my stomach flip.

I remember Tristan's obsession too. As raw and all-consuming as my own. Maybe I knew. Maybe I knew it all along, but chose my damn hardest to ignore it. Like everything else about her.

I scrub my hand over my face, feeling the soot and the dried blood on my skin.

There's a stunned silence. Everyone as shocked by this piece of news as I am. Or maybe not everyone. The girl's friend, Winnie, seems unperturbed, and Tristan's mom ... I observe her face. The news does not seem to have shocked her either. Did he tell her?

She says nothing, waving her hand over the box, polished like the table and decorated with an ivory inlay of twisted flowers. I remember Tristan once telling me his mom had been a talented magical back in her youth, top of her class, just like him. My own mom had once hinted at it too. It's what Tristan had surmised had interested his father in her – beautiful and powerful. She's always been beautiful, but I could never see that power or that talent. She looked tired to me, nervous. She always smelled of fear.

The box's lock clicks and she lifts the lid away. Inside are tiny bottles and paint brushes and it looks almost like the tools of an artist and not of a magical. They are also old and dusty, clearly untouched in many years.

Tristan's mom runs her fingers over the bottles tenderly, as if they are dear friends. Ones she's been long separated from.

"It's a curse," she says. "But what kind I can't be certain." She looks up at the professor, lurking in one corner and scowling. "Phoenix?"

His body jerks as if his thoughts were elsewhere, but then he steps forward. He peers down at her son and rests his hand on my friend's forehead like his mom had done. His brow furrows in concentration.

"Ahhhh," he grunts, "it's a dark curse, a bitter one – malediction or execration maybe."

"That's what I thought." Tristan's mom frowns too. "But I need to know the exact curse if I'm to remove it."

There's silence.

Ellie fidgets on her feet, wringing her hands. "Surely, you can ... we can't let him–"

"May I try?" Rhianna's friend steps forward hesitantly. She's still wearing a ball gown, ripped and torn to shreds, and her hair hangs in a tangled mess around her crown.

"And you are?" Tristan's mom asks.

"Winnie Wence."

"And you think you could–"

"Winnie's one of our most talented students," the professor says, and my gaze flicks to Rhianna's friend. Is she? I hardly ever noticed her until Rhianna showed up. She never spoke in class, rarely stepped forward to demonstrate her powers.

"Please," Tristan's mom says with a pain I feel right in the center of my chest.

Winnie steps to the side of the table, Stone withdrawing to make room for her. She glances down at Tristan. Even with the color drained from his face and the life seeping away from his body, he is still beautiful, like a marble statue, perfectly crafted. She brushes the hair from his brow and rests her own hand there far more gently than Stone had.

She closes her eyes.

I scrub my hand down my face again, gaze flicking between her and my friend.

"Well?" I snap impatiently after what feels like forever.

"I don't think it's any of those curses." She grimaces, her voice shaking when she speaks again. "I think ..." she swallows. "I think it's a pernicious curse."

There's a collective intake of breath.

"It can't be!" the enforcer says firmly. His sister's body shakes silently and tears slide down her face.

Winnie steps away and Tristan's mom rushes back to place her hand where Winnie's was.

She closes her eyes, mouth moving with words I don't hear.

"Those curses," Winnie's boyfriend whispers. "They were used by ... by ...magicals from the West."

Winnie nods. "Those soldiers, they were from the West, weren't they?" Her eyes are full of fear and they swivel between me and the enforcer.

"The attack came from over the border." I confirm. "They had dragons. We were taken by surprise. We couldn't stop them."

"Where the hell did they get dragons?" Stone mutters to his friend, shaking his head.

But the enforcer's attention is locked on his aunt and his cousin. "Pernicious?" he says.

"Yes," Tristan's mom says. "Winnie is right. It is a pernicious curse."

Ellie's tears fall harder and she turns away.

"Then there's nothing that can be done," the enforcer says with that steeliness in his tone once again.

My knees buckle. My heart cracks.

"No, Azlan. There is something that can be done."

"Aunt!!" Ellie says, spinning back around and reaching for Tristan's mom. "You can't!"

"What?!" I ask them, but they don't hear me. "What?!" I ask, turning to Stone and then Winnie.

"The only way to remove the curse," Winnie says, her voice so quiet I barely hear it, "is for another magical to take it from him. Another magical who shares his blood." A tear slides from her eye and she brushes it away with her fingers. "The stronger that blood connection, the more chance of a successful removal. But it means ..."

I glance back at Tristan's mother, already pushing up the rolled-up sleeves of her designer blouse. "The curse would infect the other person instead."

"Yes," Winnie says. "It would kill them."

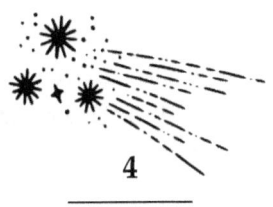

zlan

"AUNT," I say, grabbing her arm as she pulls stoppers from three vials of potion.

She shakes off my hold, a look of determination cemented on her face. "What do you expect me to do, Azlan? Sit back and watch my own son die in front of my eyes?" She tsks with her tongue.

"But Aunt," Ellie protests, the tears coming thick and fast down her cheeks.

"I know what it will mean. I've made my decision. There is no point arguing with me and every point in helping me. He was always better than me, far better than his father. He needs to live," her steely voice falters, a sob gurgling in her throat, before she regains herself and continues, "he has to live."

I stumble back from the table. I thought I knew my aunt.

I thought I knew my family. Selfish, self-serving, cruel. I always lumped my aunt in with her husband. A cold, close-hearted snob. Concerned only with herself, her looks and her position in society.

Pain stabs through my heart. I've never doubted myself and my decisions. I have always been sure of myself, in my beliefs, in my abilities, in my cause.

But how wrong I have been. How fucking wrong. Rhianna. Tristan. My aunt. Fuck, even what I've always believed about our republic and the threat in the West. All of it lies in tatters. Our capital lies in ruins, burning and smoldering out there in the lightening dawn. And my mate, my girl, my Rhianna, out there somewhere without me.

I search for her through the bond, reaching for her automatically, innately. I can feel her, faint and distant, her emotions and feelings making no sense to me. I call to her. Fuck, I scream with all my might. But I receive no response, no reply.

Where the hell is she? What the hell has happened?

My gaze flicks back to my cousin. My aunt is treating the wound, dabbing the potions into the mangled flesh, Stone, Rihanna's friend and Ellie all working together, whispering the healing incantations, all their faces pale with fright, the tears still trickling from my sister's eyes.

Is he really her fated mate too? Three of us? Stone, Tristan, me.

Can that really be?

Fated mate pairs are rare. Quadruplets? It's not something I've even heard of. As if reading my thoughts, my aunt murmurs, her eyes closed, "The fated mate bond has been sealed between them."

"Wh-what?" I say. Sealed?

"Very recently. It is brand new," she says. "You must be

ready. When I release the curse, you must be ready to help him. The pain caused by their separation will be immense. You must give him something for it."

"There is nothing for that kind of pain," Winnie says. "The only way to release the bond is through ... you know ..." she trails off, her cheeks glowing a bright red.

"And here I was singing your praises, Miss Wence," Phoenix says. "Where on earth did you get such inaccurate information?"

"Erm," she chews her cheek, "the internet."

Phoenix sighs with exasperation. "How many times have I told you students in class? The internet is not a reliable source of information." Winnie's entire face flushes red. "You have triggerwot in the house?" he asks Ellie. She points to one of the vials in my aunt's box. "Then we'll be ready to help him."

The Moreau boy shuffles on his feet beside me. Someone has wrapped a blanket around his shoulders and he clutches it with both hands, eyes locked towards his friend. I blink, scratching my head. Only now contemplating the strangeness of his appearance among us. I left him at the border days ago. How the hell is he here? How the hell did he get here?

I go to ask him. And then I stop, remembering his secrets, remembering all his secrets. He loves Rhianna too. Loves my mate. Or is it more than that? Is this strange fucked-up tangle of fate more twisted, more perverted, more damn complicated than any of us ever contemplated?

More pain spirals through my chest. I think of Rhi, how new all this has been for her, how confusing. How often I've seen her lift her chin in defiance, square her shoulders when really she's scared and frightened. Did she know about Tristan? Has she felt the pull of the bond towards him? And how the hell did that make her feel?

There are so many things I still don't know about her and so many things she has yet to discover about me, so many secrets we've been keeping from one another. Guilt swirls with the pain in my chest. She never told me about the bond with him. Never asked me about it. Was she scared of me? Of my reaction? Fuck! Fuck!!

There's a moan from the table and I snap my eyes back that way. My cousin looks as much like a corpse as he did moments ago, but the noise came from his mouth, his eyelids flickering ever so softly. My aunt holds his hands in hers, muttering words I've never heard before, and the tang of dangerous magic tarnishes the air.

I dart forward and grab Ellie by the wrist, yanking her away.

"Get back," I shout at her.

"Wh-wh-what?" she says, gaze fixed on our aunt and our cousin.

"Ellie get away!" I pull her right back against the wall, shielding her body with mine. The curse is dangerous and dark and I can feel it hissing in the air like a live snake, angry and vengeful and ready to strike. "It could latch on to you!" I yell. "Phoenix, Winnie, get the hell away."

The two of them jolt at my words and hurry back, as the ground beneath our feet shakes, the air vibrating with violence as if a wind has broken through the windows and sweeps through the room. The magic hisses more loudly, our hair beginning to flap around our faces, the lights flickering on and off.

My aunt grunts, her face purple with concentration, her hands clutching at her son. He jerks, jolts, his body lifting and then slamming down on the table. She sings the spell, bellowing it, and yet the wind that whips around the rooms is so strong, I hardly catch the words. I cling to Ellie, push my own magic forward, creating a shield I hope will protect us both.

Tristan's eyelids snap open and his eyes roll around in their sockets. His body convulses and judders. But my aunt holds him tight, refusing to let go, battling with the magic that's singeing her hands a deathly black, forcing the curse from his body.

"Is it working?" Ellie whispers from behind me, clinging to my hand as Stone swears and Winnie buries her face in her boyfriend's chest.

My aunt's voice becomes high pitched, louder still, sparks flicker from her fingertips and her eyes glow an icy blue, her hair dancing around her head.

The hiss of the curse winds higher and higher and the magic in the air turns so electric I feel it crackle painfully against my skin. The wind whips and snaps, the entire room shakes and I dive to the ground, taking Ellie with me, covering her head with my arms. The pressure is so fierce I think my skull might crack, and I yell at my aunt to stop.

But then there's a flash of light, so blinding, so white, it wipes away all other colors. I close my eyes, shield my face and Ellie's.

And then quickly as it came, it's gone. The wind drops. The room still. The light hazy with dawn.

A scream of agony rips from Tristan's throat and before I can stop her, Ellie's darting from my hands and forcing the triggerwot between his lips. The scream morphs to a long drawn-out moan, that withers away to nothing as his rigid body softens.

Tristan pulls himself up to sitting, blinking rapidly, peering through the smoke that lingers in the air. He's weak, his arms trembling. His eyes swim in and out of focus until finally his gaze alights on his mother and he's on his knees on top of the table, reaching for her in the next moment.

"Mom?" he cries, the pain in his voice more unbearable to my ears than that scream.

She's slumped in a chair, her breath feeble and rattling in her chest, a dark shadow crawling across her skin.

"Mom!" he shouts, skidding off the table and landing beside her, taking her bony shoulders in his hands. "What's wrong? Mom?"

He shakes her, but she simply gasps for breath, her own gaze not leaving his face.

He swings his head around, noticing the rest of us for the first time, all of us but Ellie hovering on the floor, knocked off our feet by that blast of magic as the curse left his body and entered my aunt's.

His eyes land on Stone. "Professor! Professor! Help me! My mom ... help me!" Stone's own gaze drops to the floor. And Tristan, wild, desperate, hunts for someone who can aid him. His eyes connect with mine.

"Az–"

"There's nothing we can do, Tristan," I say, standing to my feet. Ellie rushes to Tristan's side. The tears descending her cheeks in violent sobs that rattle her entire body. "It's a pernicious curse. Your mom took it from you to save you."

"No!" he says, shaking his head. "No!" he repeats, his gaze back on his mom, horror and pain – so much pain – crashing across his face. "Mom, no!" he chokes out. "No!"

She's struggling for breath, the dark shadow tight and dark around her throat. Somehow, she manages a smile. It's weak, but more honest an expression than anything I've ever seen on her face before. She lifts her hand, resting it against his cheek.

"My beautiful boy," I read on her lips.

"Mom, please," Tristan says, shaking her with less force now.

"Be careful, Tristan. Of your father."

"Mom. Don't. Give it back to me. It was mine. My time. My death. Not yours. Not yours!"

She smiles warmly and I can see how proud she is of her son.

"I love you," she says, and then her eyes drift shut, the last breath whines out of her throat and her body slumps.

"No!" Tristan screams, cradling her lifeless form. "NO!" He repeats the word over and over again, each one more faint than the last. But then his jaw hardens, his eyes too, and loud, angry, erratic spells crash from his lips, his magic flickers in the air. It's weak, depleted, useless. Most of it drained by the battle, his injury and the deadly curse. "My magic," he moans.

Ellie wraps her arms around him, tugging him gently away from his mom.

"She saved you, Tris," she whispers to him. "She gave her life for you."

"Why?" he whines uselessly. "I don't deserve that."

"Because she loved you."

Rhianna's friends approach the slumped body of my aunt and gently Winnie lifts her into a more comfortable position, a more dignified one, so that if anyone walked in now, they might guess she was simply napping in her chair.

"She shouldn't have ... she shouldn't ... why? How? How the fuck did this happen?" Tristan says, his face as tear-stained now as my sister's, tugging at the strands of hair on his head.

"You were hit, badly wounded in the attack in the hall," the Moreau boy says. "Remember? I tried to heal you but I couldn't. You were ..." he holds his friend's distraught gaze, "you were dying. There was no other way to save you."

Tristan storms around the table, fury raging across his face. He knocks his hand hard against his friend's chest. "You should have found a way. You should have stopped her."

"Tristan," I say firmly. "There was no other way."

"It should have been him, not her," he screams. "Not her. She deserved better. She deserved more. He made her life a misery."

He doesn't say who he means. But I can guess.

"She loved you, Tristan," Ellie says.

He buries his face in his hands, rocking his head from side to side. His shirt is ripped and singed and soaked red with blood. He's lost his shoes and his hair is black with soot.

He groans like a wounded animal, snot and tears streaming from his chin. Then he snaps his hands away and looks around at us all wildly, his eyes streaming with pain. He spins around, his gaze spiraling over the six of us circling him. And then he jolts to a halt.

His face cracks in even more pain, as his body snaps taut like a wire yanked tight.

"Where's Rhianna?"

5

R^{hi}

"TRISTAN!"

I blink open my eyes, sitting bolt upright in my bed. The movement and an intense agony in my gut make me woozy, and my vision and the world spins around and around before finally righting themselves.

I blink again. The daylight filtering through the window is not bright but enough to make my eyes ache. Outside, the wind sweeps through the meadow and the distant trees moan.

The pain in my gut is intense, an ache throbs dully in my head and my body is stiff with sleep. Have I been sick? Did I go to bed with a raging headache and stomach and only just wake up?

Gingerly, I pull the bedsheets back, searching my

bedroom for Pip, about to call out for my aunt, to tell her I feel a little better now, when a voice fills the room.

"Little rabbit?"

I jolt.

It's a man's voice – a deep, rough voice. It's not my aunt's.

For a moment, panic swoops through my body and then in the next, everything comes flooding back to me – my aunt, the man in black, the council, the academy, the attack, my fated mates.

"Little rabbit?" the voice says, much more quietly this time, with more trepidation and a hand rests hesitantly on my shoulder.

I flinch and dive from the bed, spinning to face the man sitting behind me and scurrying across the room until I hit the wall, my arms outstretched in front of me, ready for an attack.

Renzo Barone – the hitman sent by Marcus Lowsky – Marcus Lowsky who tried to kill me.

The man examines me, his mismatched eyes racing all over my face.

"Looks like she's feeling better, little man."

Little man? My eyes drop to the side of the bed, where Pip is up on his trotters, examining me too.

"Pip," I yelp, "Pip get over here now!" I wave at him frantically, wanting him as far away from that psycho as it's possible to be.

Pip grunts and ignores my command, peering over his shoulder at Renzo and grunting a second time.

"Yeah, still a bit confused."

"Confused?" I snap, "what the hell? – where the hell? – what the–"

Renzo raises his arms and I gasp, my magic sparking on my fingertips ready for his assault. But he simply smirks, lifting his hands right above his head and stretching, the vertebrae in his backbone cracking, and his dark t-shirt lifting, flashing me a strip of his toned abdomen, covered in a crisscross of inks.

That familiar hook in my abdomen tugs in his direction and I scowl. Familiar it may be, but it feels different too, all mixed up and confused. My bond is buzzing with energy and tension, straining. But it's also sore and painful. I scowl harder, my eyes dropping to my own stomach, until the thud of feet on the floor has me looking the psychopath's way again.

He rests his elbows on his knees and his chin on his balled hands.

"What do you remember?" he asks patiently, undeterred by the way my fingertips are hissing with magic.

I peer at my pig, who's lowered himself back down to the ground and waits for my answer.

What the hell is going on?

My head pounds and spins and I'm dazed and confused.

This is the man who tried to kill me. Yet, Pip doesn't seem to care and, if I'm honest, the man's presence doesn't scare me like it once did. A memory flickers through my mind, of the woods at the academy, of my knife. Then another of Marcus Lowsky writhing on the floor, and this man, Renzo Barone, sweeping me away.

My brow wrinkles. I shake my head.

"I remember ... the academy. I remember the ball. I remember ..." I shake my head. Is that right? "Dragons?"

"Yeah." Renzo grins widely. "Dragons," he says, his voice full of awe.

I lift my hand to my head, touching my forehead, trying to reassemble all the loose memories in my head, order them into something that makes sense.

"We were attacked. I was fighting ... fighting with ... Tristan." My bond sparks. Renzo sits up straight. I strain to remember and then I gasp, my hands flying to my mouth. Pain spirals through my body, and I sink to my knees moaning. "Tristan ... Tristan ... he's ... oh god, no ... he's ..."

Renzo swings his legs. "Nah, I don't think he is."

I shake my head, tears bubbling in my eyes. "No, you don't understand. I saw ... I saw him get hit." A sob tears from my throat. "By a bolt meant for me."

"Little rabbit," Renzo says, more firmly this time. "He ain't dead."

Pip squeaks his agreement, trotting over to me and climbing into my lap, licking at my face.

"Not cool, little man," Renzo says with disdain, "I've seen where that tongue's been." I hear the man stand, the bed creaking, and then his feet on the worn carpet as he stalks towards me. He crouches by my side and slides a forefinger under my wet chin, lifting my face to his.

"He isn't dead. I think he was very, nearly, pretty dead," I sniffle, "and that's why you've been so damn ill. But you're back with us now, so he must be safe."

"What?" I say, his eyes – one brown like bark, one green like the grass – swimming through my tears. The man is insane. It's what I've been told. It's what I've witnessed. And his words make no sense to me. Tristan nearly died and that made me ill?

"I think," he says, slowly, like he's explaining something to a confused child, "Tristan boy got hurt, very badly hurt, and it sent you, his fated mate, into a malaise. One you'd still be lost in if he were still ill, if he were dead. But seeing how you're making a lot more sense to me, and to little man, than you were an hour ago, I'm assuming, he's out of danger or healed or something." He shrugs.

"We're not fated mates," I say automatically.

"Yeah, you are," he says, pinching my chin. I swipe the back of my hand over my face, wiping away all the salty tears. His words have calmed me and I wonder if there are any truth in them.

"We're not bonded," I tell him and the corner of his mouth twitches as he notices I'm not denying the fated mate part anymore. "We never sealed the–"

"Bond? Yeah, I think you did." He quirks an eyebrow. "If you're worried that I'm going to be jealous about you fucking other–"

"I'm not sleeping with Tristan Kennedy!" I snap. "And why would I care what you thought?"

"I don't get jealous." He peers into my eyes. "It's not something you need to worry about."

"I haven't slept with Tristan Kennedy!" I repeat, louder and with more force this time. We've kissed once – for about precisely ten seconds – and he fingered me once in that moment of madness in the classroom. Neither of those were enough to seal a fated mate bond. The assassin might have guessed right about the fated mates part but he's wrong about this.

"Huh," Renzo says, rocking back on his heels. "You must have done it some other way, then?"

"What?" I say, my cheeks heating. If he means the fingering ... He can't read my thoughts like Stone, can he?

"You must have sealed the bond through some other means."

Really? Is he right?

I concentrate in on the sensations deep inside my gut, where my bonds lie. It doesn't feel like it did before. There were two bonds, strong, connected, vibrant. And now, now there are three ...

But if that were true – if we had somehow sealed the bond – wouldn't I be in agony right now, the way I was with Azlan whenever he first left the room. And sure, my stomach hurts a bit, but not like that.

"If we were newly bonded mates, I'd be writhing around in agony right now due to our separation."

"You were," he says, "I made you a potion for the pain."

I shake my head. "There's only one way to remove that kind of pain and it involves ..." I trail off, my cheeks sizzling.

"Fucking? Ha!" Barone says. "Is that what the enforcer told you? He's more deviant than I gave him credit for."

"He didn't ... it's just something I know."

He shrugs. "I made a potion. It made the pain go away."

I peer down at my stomach again, even more confused than when I first woke up three minutes ago. I'm in my old house. I have no idea how we got here and no idea where everyone else is. I reach for my mates through the three bonds, trying to find them, trying to connect with them, but the distance is too far, the bond too strained, stretched thin.

I huff in annoyance and rub at my stomach.

The man crouching opposite me watches the movements of my hand.

"It must have happened in the battle," I say, sniffing, "the sealing of the bond." I remember combining our magic, fighting together in unison, our magic so powerful it blazed and roared. So entwined and interwoven it was indistinguishable. When he was hit, it felt like I had been. It felt like my soul had been wrenched from my body.

I feel the ghost, a memory, of that pain now, and I wince.

"Okay, little rabbit?" he asks, alarm suddenly marking his features. "You thirsty? Hungry?"

It's all a blur after that moment, after Tristan fell to the ground. I don't remember what happened next, what I did next. The next memory I have is lying on the ground, staring up into the sinister face of Marcus Lowsky, of thinking I was going to die, and then of this man saving me.

Renzo Barone.

"I'm thirsty," I admit.

He nods, stands to his feet and walks over to my desk. A tray rests on its surface with a cup, a bowl, a glass and a jug of water. He pours me some of the water into the glass, the liquid tinkling against the surface, and then he hands it to me.

I take it, staring into its clear depths. I hesitate.

"You've been drinking my broth the last few hours – not a euphemism." He chuckles. "Bit late to worry about me drugging and poisoning you now."

"What broth?" I ask with suspicion, taking a cautious sip of the water.

"Something I brewed for your discomfort. You seemed," he frowns, "in pain. I didn't like it. He didn't either." He points towards Pip, sitting and watching us both.

"And how long was I out?"

"Several hours." He turns his back on me and spins his finger in the air above the cup, the liquid inside swirls and bubbles and then he hands it to me too. "Drink this. It'll help you regain your strength. We got to go."

"Go? Go where?"

He shrugs, shaking his hand for me to take the mug. "Fuck knows. Away from here."

"I'm not going anywhere."

He frowns harder at me. "Yeah, you are."

I laugh flatly. "Errr, no, I'm not."

"Little rabbit, I know what you can do." His unusual eyes twinkle. "You're fucking powerful. You were safe when they thought I'd killed you. When they thought you were dead.

But now they know you're alive. Now they've seen how special you are too. And I'd bet you my knife, they're all looking for you."

"Who?"

"Does it matter?"

"Of course it matters."

"Everyone."

"Everyone," I say in annoyance, ignoring his outstretched hand and the cup of broth, "really helpful."

"You have powers a girl like you shouldn't have. That makes you interesting, dangerous, useful. To the authorities, to the Wolves of Night, to the other gangs, to whomever Lowsky was working with in the West."

I sit up straighter. "What do you mean?"

I guess he reads my curiosity and decides to use it to his advantage.

"I'll tell you all about it," I nod, "once you've drunk that broth and we're on the road."

"I'm not drinking it."

He holds it up and takes a gulp himself, his face screwing up in disgust. "Fuck, that tastes bad."

"You're really persuading me."

"Yeah, but look." He holds out his free hand. "No boils, no rashes, and I'm not convulsing, not dropping down dead. It's safe, just tastes like donkey balls."

I pull a face, one he examines.

He dips his head so we're eye level and the hook in my stomach hums, pulling me his way. "You're still weak, little rabbit, and you need to be strong. Drink this. I swear on your pig's life it's going to help you, not harm you."

"On my pig's life?"

"Yeah, I like him."

I snort and then watch in shock as Pip sidles up to the man and lets him tickle his ears.

"This is so fucked up," I mutter, taking the cup from his hand and wondering if I lost my senses in the battle, if I went into some crazy-ass dream after what happened to Tristan, one from which I'm yet to emerge.

But crazy dream or not, I don't think Renzo Barone is going to hurt me – not yet anyway. And as I have no idea what's happening back in Los Magicos, as I have no idea where my mates and my friends are – I think I have very little to lose by drinking something that might benefit me.

I take a sip, Renzo's face lighting up as I do, and then I take another and another. It does taste revolting, but it also has a warmth seeping through my body, fortifying me, removing the aches and the pain and helping to clear my head.

"This is good," I tell him.

His chest practically puffs with pride. "You think?"

"Yeah." I take another gulp, my magic pulsating through my veins. "Several hours?" I ask him.

He nods.

"And do you know what's happening in Los Magicos? Who those men were? The ones with the dragons? Are we win–"

Renzo frowns and shakes his head. "Too many questions, little rabbit."

I tilt my head and examine him like he's been examining me.

"Do you know what happened after we left Los Magicos?"

"No," he says and pulls his phone from his pocket. "There's no signal out here. And anyway, the thing died a while ago. You don't have any chargers in this house."

"We never had a phone," I explain, then remember the cell phone Trent gave me. The last thing I remember wearing was that ball gown from Tristan – a lump forms in my throat that I swallow away. My phone had been in my purse but god knows where that went.

For the first time, I glance down at my body and register the outfit I'm now wearing.

Not a ball gown any longer.

Pajamas.

"Did you undress me?!" I shriek, leaping to my feet. A smirk forms on his face. "Fuck, did you ... did you touch me?!" I wrap my arms around my body, feeling violated and nauseous.

He looks down at Pip, annoyance and anger on his face, and I step forward, concerned he's going to strike out at my pet.

Pip squeaks up at Renzo and then at me.

"If you're implying ..." he says, his voice tight and dangerous.

"You undressed me," I snap. "You took my fucking clothes off."

"It's what you do when someone is unwell," he explains. "You put them in something more comfortable."

"Sure," I say with sarcasm, remembering that I hadn't even been wearing a bra under that dress. Realizing I'm still not wearing a bra.

I wrap my arms more tightly over my chest.

"I was trying to take care of you," he mutters, staring at the ground sulkily.

I decide to change the subject.

"How did we get here from Los Magicos?" That too is a blur. I remember Marcus Lowsky falling and then Renzo, Pip in his arms, above me. The next thing I remember is waking up in my bed just now. If I was as unwell as he claims, I wonder how the hell he carried me through that battle, how he wasn't stopped by Stone or Azlan, how he managed to bring Pip and me all the way to my old house, and all so quickly.

"Magic," he says, looking up at me.

I remember him vanishing from the woods in the academy.

"I don't understand."

"It's something I can do," he says, fiddling with the rings on his fingers. "Slip from one place to another."

"Slip ... what does that mean?"

He glances up at the ceiling. "If I concentrate real hard, I can hear, I can hear the vibrations of time and space around us. They're like strings, each vibrating to their own note. And if I concentrate even fucking harder, I can bend those strings and slip between them. Move from one place in time and space to another."

My brow crumples. The broth has helped, but I'm still dazed, struggling to follow his words.

"You can travel through time, go back in time?"

"Huh," he says, glancing back down at me, "I never tried that." He grins. "Bet that would be fun."

"So what do you do?" I ask in annoyance.

"Mainly travel from A." He walks to one side of the room, winks at me and then disappears from sight completely. I stare at the empty space and in a blink of an eye he reappears at the other side of the room. "To B."

"You can make yourself invisible?"

He shakes his head. "I jumped. From one side of the room to the other."

"And you jumped us from Los Magicos to my house, to here?"

"Yep."

"Then jump us back," I say, stepping towards him. "I need to find my mates and my friends and–"

"No."

"No?" I say with indignation.

"We're not going back to Los Magicos. It isn't safe for you, little rabbit."

I scoff. "How do you know? You have no idea what happened after we left."

"Doesn't matter. I'm not taking you back."

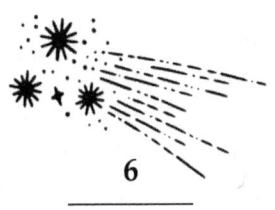

6

T ristan

"WHERE'S RHIANNA?" I repeat when no one answers me.

"We don't know," Azlan says, staring into my eyes.

"You don't know?" I spit. "You don't know?!"

"She disappeared in the midst of the battle," Rhianna's friend, Winnie, explains.

"You let her disappear?!" I hiss at Azlan, stalking towards him. "Why weren't you watching her, guarding her, protecting her?"

Azlan squares up to me. He's lost his dinner jacket, his shirt is ripped, and he's covered in cuts, bruises and soot.

"You want to explain to me, Tristan, why you all of a sudden have an interest in the welfare of my mate?"

I stare right into his dark, angry eyes. "Because she's my mate too."

"Yeah," he says, "your mate too. Something you never thought to tell me." He takes a menacing step closer to me.

"Azlan," Ellie gasps.

"Does your father know?"

"No," I say, not backing away.

Azlan glares at me. "You've treated her like shit." He turns his head and glares at Spencer. "You've both treated her like shit. I should beat you both to a fucking pulp!"

"You weren't exactly the perfect gentleman yourself," the professor says quietly from behind him.

Azlan glares at me harder still. "What happened to you? You used to be a nice kid. Then you grew up into this stuck-up asshole."

"Me, the asshole? You're the one who turned his back on his family. Who left his own sister all on her own to endure the shit our fathers hand out."

"Tristan," Ellie gasps.

"I look out for Ellie," Azlan says. "And I've been looking out for Rhianna. Which is more than you can say."

"Oh really? Because I seem to remember it was me that just took that fucking curse for her. Who saved her."

"But how about all the other bullshit you put her through? You think I've forgotten how you spoke about her to me?"

"I've been trying to put things right," I mutter. "I've been trying to make things up to her."

"Huh," someone snorts, and both Azlan and I turn our heads to stare at Rhianna's friend, her arms crossed, an extremely unimpressed expression hovering on her face. "And doing a pretty pathetic job of it," she says. "Honestly, both of you should have been groveling at her feet, begging her forgiveness and pledging your undying love to her. She is amazing and you," she points at us both, then points at

Spencer and Stone too, "*all* of you have been giant, massive, humongous, unbelievable dickheads." I go to protest but she shoots me a warning look and I clamp my mouth shut. "Too busy with your own self-importance to realize just how amazing and wonderful that girl is."

Winnie's boyfriend scratches his cheek then nods his head. "Rhi really is awesome."

"I know that," Azlan snaps.

"Then what the hell are you doing standing around bickering? Why aren't we out searching for Rhi right now?"

"We?" the professor asks.

"If you think I'm going to stand back while my best friend is missing, you are sorely deluded, Professor Stone."

"I like her," Ellie says.

"Because she's also awesome," Trent says. Winnie nods with defiance.

"So what's the plan?"

"I'm going to go out looking for her," Azlan says, already turning towards the door. "Are you coming, Phoenix?"

"Don't you dare," Winnie says, wagging her finger in his direction.

He turns, slow and sinister. "Don't I dare what?" he says with a face full of thunder.

"Wander off," she says, looking just as stormy.

"Wander off?" he spits.

"What did I just say? You've been acting like dickheads. All of you. You need to snap out of it and get your act together for our girl."

"That's what I'm doing!"

"No, you're not. You're going off in a huff."

My huge cousin growls at Winnie Wence but Winnie Wence, to her credit and my surprise, holds her ground.

"You need to work together, *we* need to work together.

Fate made you Rhianna's mates for a reason, and I'm guessing that's because you are clever, talented and power-ful. You need to combine those talents and powers, and use them to find Rhianna, because she's special and it won't be too long before bad people figure that out and come after her."

"Bad people like your father," Azlan says to me.

"Bad people like the fucking chancellor," I snarl back at him.

"It doesn't matter who the bad people are, what matters is that Rhi is safe!" Winnie says with exasperation.

"Winnie's right," Ellie says. "You shouldn't be at each other's throats like this. We've ... we've already lost someone dear to us tonight," she rests her hand on my shoulder, "let's not lose another."

Azlan peers at his sister and his demeanor softens, his shoulders slackening. "Okay, we can try to work together. For Rhianna's sake," he adds, throwing me a dirty look.

"Good," Winnie nods, "I think we should start with a bit of honesty."

"Honesty?" I say. "I thought we were looking for Rhianna."

Winnie looks around at us all. "I'm serious when I say Rhi's special, and not just in the I-love-my-best-friend way. Fated mates are freaking unheard of these days. To have one fated mate is rare. But to have four!"

"Four?" I say, peering at Azlan and then Stone. "There's another–"

"Me," Spencer says, stepping out from the shadows. He's naked except for a blanket wrapped around his shoulders and his body is even more busted up than Azlan's. "Rhianna Blackwaters is my fated mate."

"Fucking hell," Stone says, flinging his hands in the air. "You have to be kidding?"

Azlan ignores him, simply glaring at Winnie. "You knew about this?"

"Sort of," she says, looking less confident than she did a few minutes ago.

"Rhianna knows about this?"

"Sort of," she repeats.

"Sort of?" Spencer says.

"We talked about how she felt the pull towards you and Tristan. She was really confused about it. Especially considering the way you were treating her."

"Assholes," Stone growls.

"You were no better, Professor."

"Wait?" Spencer says to Stone. "You're her fated mate too? But you're her professor. That is seriously ..." Stone scowls at him and Spencer trails off.

"Four mates?!" I say. "Four? What the hell does this mean?"

And how the hell do I feel about it? I knew about Azlan. I knew about Stone. But Spencer too. The way I feel about this girl is like nothing I've ever experienced in my life before. I'm aware I'm obsessed, infatuated, fucking insane about her. But can I share her? Share her with three other men? Would I want to?

I stare down at the floor. I'm in my socks. My shoes are missing, the floorboards hard beneath the soles of my feet.

Yes. The answer is yes. I could do anything for this girl. I would do anything. I've already given her my life. Anything else seems inconsequential.

I raise my gaze back up to Spencer. He's watching me with trepidation.

"Why the hell didn't you tell me?"

"*You* didn't tell *me*," he points out.

"I didn't know what to make of it at first. I was too caught up worrying about myself and my reputation to realize–"

"Just how amazing she is?" Winnie snarks.

"Yes," I say, meeting her eyes. "Yes."

"And what's your excuse?" Winnie turns and directs her attention at Spencer.

"Excuse? I don't have an excuse."

"You left the academy. Left your mate. You good as rejected her."

"She's better off without me. And I didn't reject her. She rejected me. She had her chance to stop me and she didn't."

"Are you surprised after the way you treated her? And what do you mean you're not good enough? You think any of these clowns are good enough for Rhi?" she says, sweeping her arm around us all.

Spencer peers at me, then Azlan. "I'm a danger to her."

"I think Rhi has done a pretty good job of handling you, Spencer Moreau."

"You don't understand," he says sulkily.

"Try me," she says.

"I think you should," Azlan says. "If we're going to work together to find Rhi, she's right. We need to be upfront and honest."

Spencer works his jaw as if he finds it difficult to say the words. "I'm a werebeast."

Ellie gasps and Trent curses under his breath.

Winnie Wence, however, strides towards him and thumps him hard on the chest with her fists. Spencer doesn't even flinch.

"You attacked her! You attacked Rhi! It was you!"

"I didn't attack her. It was the beast, and he wasn't going to harm her."

"Wasn't going to harm her?!" Stone spits. "You know how many grazes and claws marks I had to treat on her body?!"

"We're one being," Spencer says. "If I'm her fated mate, then so is he, and he would never harm his mate. In fact, we hitched a ride on the tail of a fucking dragon to ensure we got back here to protect her."

We're all silent taking in this piece of information. Then finally, the professor huffs out air through his teeth.

"Is there anything else? Any other bits of information or secrets that we need to know about? Kennedy – do you have a second dick for instance?"

"Only one on his head," Winnie mutters.

"Rhianna can wield crimson magic," I tell them all.

"Wh ... holy crap!" Winnie gasps. It's one bit of information it seems her best friend hasn't shared with her, although neither Stone nor Azlan seem shocked by this news.

"That's ... are you sure?" Ellie says, alarm in her eyes.

"She blasted me with it," Spencer says. "I'm sure."

"Who is this girl?" Ellie whispers under her breath.

"And where the hell did she go?" I mutter.

We're all silent a second time until Trent fidgets on his feet.

"Has anyone tried her phone?" he asks cautiously.

Immediately, Stone, Azlan and Ellie are pulling their cells from their pockets. I don't know where the hell mine is and I'm guessing both Spencer and Winnie have lost theirs too.

"There's no signal. The tracking device on her phone isn't working either," Azlan growls, practically crushing the device in his fist.

"Towers are probably down," Stone says. "First thing an attacking force would do would be to kill all communication networks."

"She probably doesn't even have her phone on her," I say. "How the hell could she just vanish? Can't you feel her through the bond?"

As I say those words, I unconsciously feel for her myself and the sensation I meet in my gut has my legs buckling. It's different from before. The bond is different. Despite how fucking weak I feel, the bond is alive – strong, vibrant, buzzing with energy. It's as if ... as if ...

But when? How?

The others are muttering around me but I don't hear the words. All my attention is now focused on that bond in my gut. The one that ties me to my mate, the one that despite its strength and energy feels stretched thin, like she's far, far away. Too far away, unbearably so. I need her here, by my side, in my arms.

Stone glances at Azlan. "I don't know about you, but one moment I could feel her close by – I knew she was there at the academy – and the next she was whipped away."

"You think she was bundled into a vehicle?" Spencer asks.

"Or on top of a dragon?" Trent points out.

"No." He scratches his fingers through his beard. "It wasn't like that. It was more sudden, more brutal. Like she'd been torn away."

"What the hell does that mean?" I say.

"She was at the academy one moment, and in the next she was somewhere else." The professor's fingers freeze in his beard and his eyes widen with horror. "Like she'd moved through space and time."

Alarm flashes across Azlan's face too.

"What?" I say. "What?"

"There's only one person we know with the ability to do that," Azlan says.

"Renzo fucking Barone," the professor growls. "He's taken her."

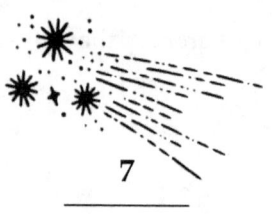

7

R enzo

MY LITTLE RABBIT is not happy. She took a lukewarm shower under the dribbling faucet and now she's rifling through her wardrobe, clothes flying in all directions, mumbling curse words as the little pig squeaks around her ankles.

She says she doesn't give a shit if I take her to Los Magicos or not. She's going anyway.

Yeah, she's not. I won't let that happen. We need to disappear somewhere we can't be found – where no one out to snatch my little rabbit away from me can find us.

"How you going to get there?" I ask her. I'm sitting on top of her desk, hands tucked under my knees, legs swinging backward and forward. Her motorbike's a burned-out shell in the back yard and I'm pretty sure there's no bus service out here in a shithole like this.

I like watching her, especially now she's full of life again.

I like it even more when she's mad at me. It makes me fucking hard when she glares at me with those pissy eyes like she could scratch mine out.

"I don't know. I'll walk if I have to."

"That'll take you – what? – a month?" Is that right? I could never do the math. The numbers bounce around even more than the letters. "You have enough supplies for a month? Can you carry them all?"

She spins around, her arms full of clothes. "Fuck off!" she snaps.

"I'm just pointing out the flaws in your plan, little rabbit."

"There wouldn't be any flaws if you just took me yourself."

"Not happening."

"Then I'll be walking."

I sigh. "Along the highway?"

"Probably. Maybe I'll hitch a lift."

"There'll be patrols out on the main roads. Gang members, soldiers."

"Then I'll take the back roads," she says, flinging the clothes into the only bag she could find, an old string shopping bag from the kitchen.

"Yeah, there'll be patrols on those roads too. I'm telling you, little rabbit, people are going to be looking for you. We need to be smart about this." I tap my index finger against the side of my head.

"There is no *us*!"

I know she's mad at me right now so I let that fly.

I jump down from the desk and stalk towards her. She doesn't scurry away like she did when she first woke up and she doesn't flinch either. She lets me come right up close to her, not moving at all, tipping back her head to look up into my face.

I like her eyes. The color that rings the dark depths of her pupils are clear. It reminds me of honey. Sweet sticky honey. Full of sugar. Making your tongue buzz. I like the way I can read them. I've never been able to do that before. But her eyes tell me when she's mad, or afraid, or happy. It makes things a hell of a lot easier.

"It's time for us to go," I tell her.

"I told you there is no us. And unless you're going to ..." she waves her hand about, "me back to the capital, I'm not coming with you."

It's cute she thinks she has a choice in this. But I'm determined to keep her safe, so she doesn't.

"There are two ways we can do this. Both involve us getting the hell out of here and as far away from Los Magicos as possible." She scowls. "So which way do you want to do it? You can take my hand and let me lead you where we need to go. Or would you prefer the old fashion way? You know, involving me knocking you out and slinging you over my shoulder."

"There's no way in hell–" she begins and I guess that means it's the second option.

Before she has time to react, I flick my finger against her forehead and immediately the lights go out, her legs crumpling underneath her. I catch her in my arms before she hits the floor.

The pig's not happy about it, he snorts angrily at me as I collect up some other useful bits and pieces for our trip, pouring out the potion I brewed into an old thermos flask. Then I shift her over my shoulder as promised, pick up the shopping bag from the floor and head out the front door.

I could use my abilities to shoot us somewhere far away from here, but truth be told I'm tired on account of all the caring and nursing duties. Plus, shooting us out of Los Magicos was the only time I've taken someone with me like that. It was a risk. One that could have backfired, seen us separated. I could have lost her in the folds of time. She could have gotten hurt.

I don't want to take that risk again. Not unless I really, really have to.

Unfortunately as I step out of the house with my little rabbit slung over one shoulder and her pig under my other arm, I see I'm going to have to take the risk far sooner than I expected, because streaming into the meadow are a group of soldiers. Soldiers from the West. Seems I was right. Lowsky may be dead but there are still people out searching for her.

Unless they've come for me.

I shouldn't dismiss myself so quickly.

I have a reputation.

I grin at them.

"Is it me you want or the girl? Or perhaps it's the pig?"

"Hand her over Barone," one of them shouts. "And you'll be rewarded."

"How much?" I ask.

He mutters a figure. The number has my mind spinning. It's big, a hell of a lot of zeros all bouncing around. I whistle.

Someone could disappear with that kind of money, sail across the ocean and live in luxury for the rest of their days. They could live like a prince.

"It's all yours," he says. "Just hand her over."

"Nah," I say, and then I shoot the three of us the hell out of there.

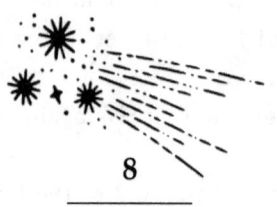

8

S tone

"THERE WERE members of the Wolves of Night at the academy tonight," I say, "fighting against us. I found Marcus Lowsky's dead body right by Rhi's dorm."

"Lowsky's dead?" Azlan asks me.

"Yes," I say. "And Barone had to be there too."

Spencer shakes his head in response to my words and my eyes trail over his form. A werebeast? Him? How the fuck did I never spot that? Why the hell did York never tell me?

I look for signs of it now. A hunch to his posture, a wolfish gait to his movement, the hint of wolf about his face. I don't see any of it. He looks like any normal man – just like the rest of us.

"The men that attacked the academy weren't from the

gangs. They were fighters from the West. I saw them come over the border with my own eyes."

"And I saw the markings of the Wolves of Night on the bodies of the men I was fighting," I tell him.

"They must have been fighting in allegiance, together," Winnie says.

We all turn to look at her.

"You think the Wolves of Night have joined forces with our enemies in the west?" Azlan says. She hesitates, then nods. "Why?"

She shrugs. "Money?"

"Where do you think Barone will have taken her?" Tristan asks. The golden boy isn't looking so golden anymore. His face is grief stricken, his clothes torn and drenched in blood, his crown of golden hair matted and black with soot.

"Back to the Wolves of Night compound," Azlan says with more confidence than I feel.

"If they really are working together," I say, "he may have handed her over to the West."

Azlan grunts. "Possibly, but we start at the compound. If she's not there, then ..." He trails off.

If the West has her – a girl who can wield crimson magic – a girl fate has bound to four powerful mates – what the hell will they do with her?

"We can cross that bridge when we come to it," Winnie says in agreement with my friend. "Do you know where the compound is?"

"Yes," Azlan says. "Out in the wastelands. Not far from where Rhi was living."

"That's two days' drive away!" I say in despair, starting to pace. Two days to reach her! Two days in the hands of that psychopath! "He's probably torturing her as we speak!"

"We could take my car?" Winnie says.

"Your car?" I say. Has the girl lost the plot? We need to find a way to get there quickly–

"Where is it?" Azlan asks.

Winnie grimaces. "Back at the academy."

Azlan thinks for precisely one second. "Let's go!"

"We're going all the way back to the academy for a car?" I say. "Doesn't your uncle own about twenty cars?"

"This car's special." Winnie grins. "It's been modified. It'll get us there in half the time. Maybe quicker with a bit of help."

I stare at Winnie Wence. Until she ended up roommates with Rhi, she'd hardly said boo to a goose. Now I'm discovering she has an illegal car that she's been housing on school grounds.

"Let's go then," Azlan grunts. We all nod our heads stepping towards him. All except Tristan. He stays exactly where he is.

"I need to ..." He glances towards the dining room. "I need to wait for my father. I need to tell him ..." He trails off.

"About your mom?" Ellie asks, and he nods.

"So you're not coming?" Azlan spits.

"I will come. I'll catch up with you. I'll find you."

Azlan snorts. "Sure you will."

"I want to find her just as badly as you do." Tristan scowls at his older cousin. "I want her safe. But ... but ..." His eyes flick to the dining room a second time. "I owe it to my mom to break the news to my dad."

Azlan gives his younger cousin a hard stare. "Your dad is–"

"I know what my dad is, Azlan. I'm not doing it for him. I'm doing it for her. I can't just leave her body," he swallows,

"I need to know he'll take care of things. Of her. That he'll give her a proper burial."

Ellie rests a hand on his arm.

"Fine," Azlan huffs. "You can keep an eye on Ellie."

"What?" Ellie says, outraged. "I'm coming with you."

"You're not. You're staying here. This house is probably the safest place in the republic right now."

"That's what they said about the academy," Trent mutters.

"You don't know his uncle," I mutter.

"I'm not staying here. I'm coming with you," Ellie insists, striding towards the door. Her brother intercepts her, landing his heavy grip on both her shoulders.

"You're not. You're staying here with Tristan where it's safe." Ellie goes to argue again, but then Azlan leans in to whisper in her ear and her steely disposition melts into something softer, her eyes darting to their cousin. She nods.

"How will we keep in contact?" she asks.

We all look at each other. I guess we've relied on mobile phones for too long. All of us struggling to come up with an alternative method of communication now the towers are down.

"I have some old walkie talkies back in my room," Trent finally offers.

Tristan peers up from his thoughts. "I think I may have an old one from back when I was a kid."

"Go find it," I instruct him.

"And use the fifth frequency," Trent adds.

Then Azlan's already through the door, not hanging about for any more discussion. The rest of us hurry after him. As we step outside, I realize there are still no sounds of battle booming across the sky, no more magic exploding overhead. Does that mean it really is all over?

"What the fuck is happening out there?" Spencer says, staring out towards the burning buildings of the capital. "Is it over? Did we win or did we lose?"

It's a fucking good question, one I realize we're fools if we don't try and answer. If we're going searching for Rhi, if we're going to rescue her, we need to understand what we're facing, who these enemies are and whether we have been beaten by them, or whether we beat them.

"I'm going to go and find out," I say, changing direction, away from where the vehicle is parked on the driveway and towards the huge garage where I know the Kennedy family keep their collections of precious cars and, more importantly, fast motorbikes.

"What are you talking about?" Azlan says, clearly pissed. "We need to find Rhi."

"And that's going to be a lot easier if we know what the hell is going on, Azlan."

Ash from the city flitters on the cold wind around us and the air stinks of smoke.

"Fine," he says, "but I'm coming with you. You three," he glares at Spencer, Winnie and Trent, "can go fetch the car."

Spencer opens his mouth to protest just like Ellie did two minutes ago, but my friend can be fucking intimidating at the best of times; faced with the kidnap of his mate, he's downright terrifying. "You need to take care of Winnie Wence."

"Or you won't be able to find my car," Winnie reminds him.

Azlan shakes his head. "Because this girl is important to Rhianna."

Winnie squirms with embarrassment but she also looks at my friend with a little more admiration than she did earlier this evening when she was calling us all shitheads.

"Go!" Azlan barks. "We'll meet you at the Baker crossroads on the edge of the city."

"But you don't have a radio," Winnie points out. "How will you contact us if anything happens to you?"

Azlan, my best friend and the authorities number one enforcer, smirks. "Nothing's going to happen to us."

And then he's whistling towards the garage, beckoning out a motorbike for each of us.

As WE SOAR along the suburban streets of Los Magicos on our Kennedy motorbikes, I wonder what the hell we may be letting ourselves in for.

Barone wasn't wrong. Apart from that recent battle with the assassin out there on the streets by the docks, my life's been cushy and easy. Sure, the young people at the academy can be pains in the ass, but they're not trying to break my neck or blast a hole in my skull. The only real challenge I've faced has been avoiding the unwanted advances of over-excitable girls.

But life wasn't always like that. Once a thwack round the ear hole, a slap to my cheek, a fucking thrashing, was a daily occurrence as I was moved from one foster home to the next. My time as a student at the academy, despite the hard physical training and the occasional scrap with another kid, was a blessed relief. A moment to catch my breath before we were sent to the border for our service.

And now, here I am soaring straight into the midst of who knows what and all for that girl. That girl I love so fucking much I don't know what I'll be capable of when we meet the man who's taken her.

For now, though, I need to focus on the task at hand.

Find out what the hell is going on without getting ourselves killed.

Usually, with my best friend riding by my side I'd feel pretty damn confident that the odds were in our favor. But I can tell he's as unhinged as I am, and I fear neither of us is capable of making the correct or sensible decision right now.

The closer we near the center of the capital, the more damage there is to the city. But it's not as bad as I feared, not as devastating as I imagined. In fact, the wreckage is contained and limited, most of the damage directed at the council building, now a smoldering shell, its glass dome shattered, its great white pillars cracked and broken, the flag that once flew from its top tattered and black, buffeted by the blowing smoke.

It's eerie. There are no soldiers here any more, no battle raging. The fighting is over. The streets are deserted.

Azlan points towards the council building and we fly that way, finding the gates are no more, the metal melted and disintegrated into the ground, the grand front doors blown in and the interior dark despite the gaping hole in the building's roof.

"Where the hell is the chancellor?" Azlan growls. "Where the hell is my father and my uncle? Where the hell is *everyone*? This doesn't seem right."

"It feels fucking bizarre. You think they surrendered?" I ask. Is that why the attacking forces retreated at the academy? No need to keep fighting if our nation had already capitulated.

"No," Azlan says. "They'd fight to the bitter end."

As we sit debating, a senior commander comes marching through the battered doors of the council building, flanked by a troop of soldiers, all armed. They're dirty and battered, their uniforms hardly discernible, and it takes me a moment to deduce that they are not the enemy. They are men from our side.

The commander spots us at the same time as his men, and they all raise their weapons.

"Hey you there! Enforcer," he yells, "all men have been commanded to report in for further instructions."

"Where are the attacking forces?" Azlan yells back.

"Retreated," the soldier says, puffing out his chest. "Right back to the border."

I glance at Azlan.

Is that true? They took us by surprise, bypassed our forces at the border on fucking dragons. They've left the council building utterly destroyed. Their forces overwhelmed the academy. Why the hell would they retreat? They were on the verge of taking control of the republic.

I'm guessing my friend also smells a rat.

"Let's get the hell out of here," he growls.

I smirk at him. "Wait just one moment," I whisper, then turn my head in the commander's direction. "Who's ordered all men to report in? The chancellor?" I call to him.

"The chancellor has been arrested. The Lord Protector is in charge now." Lord Protector? I glance at my friend in alarm. "We've been instructed by the Lord Protector to assume anyone who disobeys an order is an enemy of the republic and to arrest them. We can answer your questions later."

"Who has given that order?" I try next.

"Put your hands up or we'll shoot!" he yells.

"Enough talking," Azlan says, sweeping his hand through the air and sending an explosion of magic crashing towards the men. It explodes all around them, swallowing them up in a cloud of smoke and dust and we don't delay any longer, we hit the gas, and skid away. Bullets and magic alike hurtle around us, whistling over our heads, one brushing my shoulder, another my cheek.

"Shit," I groan. Does this make us fucking fugitives? And who the hell is the Lord Protector?

I yank harder on the accelerator as we weave through the city. In the distance, we spot a line of men made up of city officials and two of the chancellor's enforcers marching behind a group of security forces. I wonder where they are being taken and why.

My chest tightens.

Guilt.

Am I doing the right thing? Leaving these magicals – our countrymen to their fate – while I head off to rescue my girl? Is that the right thing to do? But, unlike my friend, I've never been a hero, never pretended to do the right thing. Until Rhianna, the only person I cared about – the only person's welfare and preservation that concerned me – was my own.

Now I have Rhianna. And I don't care if it's morally corrupt, I don't give a shit if it's selfish, I'm going to help her at the expense of every other person in this whole wide world.

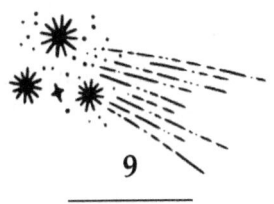

9
——————

Tristan

ELLIE THRUSTS A GLASS of something into my hands.

"Drink this," she says and I blink, pulling myself out of my dark thoughts. I'm sitting in an armchair in the den with no idea how I got here, Ellie's kind face hovering in front of mine. "It'll make you feel better."

It's eerily quiet out there now. No more booms and blasts of exploding magic. Does that mean it's over? Does that mean we won? Or did we lose?

"What is it?" I ask, my voice hella croaky. "A potion?"

"Alcohol," she says, smirking, "I broke into your dad's liquor cabinet."

I sniff the amber-colored liquid. Bourbon. "Fuck, Ellie. This is probably from his priceless collection."

Ellie shrugs, sinking into the armchair next to mine and

holding a glass of her own up in the air. "To your mom," she says, before taking a large gulp.

I hesitate, then lift my glass too. "To mom," I say, peering into the liquid and then taking a long draw. The alcohol stings the back of my throat, but it's welcome, helping to pull me even further from the darkness I'd been falling into.

"Do you know what you're going to say to your dad?"

I drag my hand over my face. No. No, I don't. And I'm beginning to think I did the wrong thing waiting behind to talk to him when I should be out searching for Rhi.

My dad has never shown any affection to my mom, not that I remember anyway, but I have to believe he cared for her, even if it were just a little. It only seems right that I am the one to break the news to him, rather than letting him find her cold body. However, the idea of telling him his wife is dead, dead because of me, has the darkness threatening to steal me again.

"I'll find the words once he's here." And I'll make sure he's prepared to give her the funeral, the burial, she deserves. Even if I won't be around to attend – news, I won't be sharing.

I peer at my wrist watch. Where the hell is my father? And how much longer will he be? I want to be away, out searching for Rhi with the others.

"Are you going to tell him about Rhianna?" my cousin asks as if reading my thoughts. She's as aware as I am that he isn't going to like the news. It was one thing Azlan – his wayward nephew – bonding to an unregistered girl from the wastelands, but his only son? His heir?

It'll also spark his interest, arouse his suspicions. A girl with not one but two Kennedy mates. He already suspects there's something unusual about her. Now he'll be determined to find out what.

"No, I don't think that would be a very good idea. I'm going to break the news about mom and then I'm leaving. I need to help the others find Rhi."

Ellie swirls the liquid in her glass. "Why were you so mean to her, Tristan?"

"My mom?" I don't want to think about her. We moved her to the bedroom together, laying her out on her bed as if she'd just taken one too many of her pills, and once she'd slept them off, she'd be awake again. Back with us. "I tried to be a good son. I tried to protect her from him, like she tried to protect me."

"Tristan, I don't mean your mom," she says gently. "I mean Rhianna, your mate."

I fold over in my chair, scrubbing my hand in my filthy hair, the glass shaking in my other hand.

"You have no idea what it's like to come face to face with your fated mate, someone destiny wants to bind you with for eternity, and know nothing about them, nothing at all. Not even their voice, not even their name. It was ... it was a shock."

"One most people would find incredible, Tristan," she says, with a little more firmness this time.

"Most people haven't had their life mapped out in front of them from the day they were born. Most people don't have expectations, the burden of their family, resting on their shoulders." I peek up at her through the curtain of my hair. "I knew from the moment I met her – Rhianna – that my life was going to change. And I guess I was ..."

"Scared?"

I snort.

My cousin rolls her eyes. "Oh because no one in the Kennedy family ever gets scared. Or at least they'll never admit to it because that would be admitting weakness.

And one thing this family has to remain at all times is strong." She slides her glass onto the coffee table. "Well, let me tell you something, Tristan. I was absolutely petrified just now, scared out of my mind that we were going to lose you!"

I can feel the corners of my eyes dampen with tears and I wipe them away with my fingers.

"But your mom, she sacrificed herself for you, and you know what that means now, don't you?"

"What?" I say.

"You have to do better. Better than you have done in the past. You have to be a better person, Tristan. For Rhianna, for Azlan, for the people in this family that matter, probably for this entire country."

"I'm not sure I can be." I'm not made that way. I was molded by a cruel man with only his purpose in mind.

As if reading my thoughts for a second time, my cousin says, "You're not your father, Tristan."

And as she says those words, we hear the front door slam back and we both know it's him, like he's arrived just so he can argue against that very damn point.

We look at each other, the color the liquor had brought to Ellie's cheeks draining away.

I down the remainder of mine, slam the glass down and stand to my feet. Ellie does the same and we climb the stairs back to the main entrance of the house together. My feet are heavy and loud on the wooden steps and I have the peculiar notion that I'm a condemned man, approaching the gallows, ready for his fate, for his doom. I shake the notion away, push the door open and find my father in the hallway, tugging off his leather gloves, his black cloak already discarded on the floor.

He spins around at the sound of the door, hands raised,

ready to strike, then seeing it's only me and Ellie lowers his arms.

His shirt is torn at the shoulder, the skin underneath singed and there's a gash across his forehead, his usually slicked-back hair loose over his brow.

"So you're alive then?" he says, sounding neither pleased nor distressed by this news.

"Only just," I say.

"You're lucky to have made it out," he says, threading a finger through the rip in his shirt and touching the burned flesh below, healing it quickly. "I hear that the academy fared much worse than the capital."

"Is it over?" I ask him, searching his face for clues on the outcome of the attack.

"Yes, for now it is over. The forces from the West have retreated."

"So they *were* forces from the West?" I ask him, sensing Ellie quivering behind me. I'm not ready to deliver my bad news, not ready to face his rage just yet.

"Who else would they be?" He smiles.

"Where have you been?"

"Fighting. Where you should have been too, instead of cowering here at home with your mother."

The mention of her has my gaze dropping to the floor, an action my father reads as shame.

"Always a coward," he spits.

The accusation hits me square in the chest, has anger flaring in my veins. He can call me a lot of things. But not a coward.

"Unlike you," I hiss, raising my gaze to his. "So brave, so powerful." My father looks at me with amusement. "Yet here you are, already fled from the fighting, back to your impregnable home."

He shakes his head. "You really understand so little about politics and the ways in which this world operates. I had such high hopes for you, Tristan, and yet every day you disappoint me."

The anger inside me flares more viciously. Ellie's fingertips brush against my back as if she's trying to calm me. I swallow, swallow down all the rage, even though it scrapes at my throat like I'm swallowing a thousand knives.

"Mother is dead," I tell him.

I expect some kind of reaction. A flinch. A look of regret. A howl of pain. Something to tell me he cared about her, something to prove all my suspicions about his indifference are wrong. But all he does is nod and stride towards his study.

"Did you hear me," I say, more loudly this time, striding after him, "mother – your wife – is dead."

"I heard you the first time."

"And don't you even want to know how it happened?"

"Tristan, we are at war," he snaps, opening one of the tall wooden cupboards that nestle in the room's paneling and pulling objects from its inside. "The council has been destroyed, the academy attacked, our borders overrun. I don't have time–"

"She's dead!" I yell at him. "Gone!"

He freezes, then spins, his eyes cruel and angry. "And did you not hear me, boy! This is war. Not some silly dueling match. No more pretending. People die in wars. Many people already have and more will follow."

"She was your wife. Don't you care even a little bit?"

"What I care about is seizing this opportunity and making it ours. So instead of standing there and bawling like a little child, go clean yourself up. Our guests will be arriving any moment now."

I should go, turn around and walk away, pretend I'm doing as he says and walk straight out the door, taking my cousin with me.

But my insides are raw and painful, the hurt too great, and I cannot find the usual disinterest and boredom I use to mask my feelings. I can't tamper them down. I can't control them. It hurts too much. My mother gone. My mate missing. My heart ripped into shreds.

I race at him, pushing him hard on the shoulder. "Your wife. You're meant to care. You were meant to love her. To protect her." I push at him again and again, my magic slashing at his skin. "And all you ever did was cause her pain."

"Enough!" my father yells, slamming his own magic into me, so hard I'm thrown backward, skidding across the floor and crashing into the far wall.

Now I should leave. Now I should go. No good will come of this. No good at all. He never cared for her or me. And I can't make him care now.

But I'm too raw, all my emotions hurtling and colliding around my body, making my magic hot and dangerous. And I've had enough. Enough of his games, and his schemes, his cruelty and his punishments.

I blast magic across the room and into my evil, twisted father. A man I've never liked. A man I've always struggled to love.

My magic is low, but not as much as it should be, and I know that's because I have her magic in my veins now too, joined, fused, molded to mine. I have a piece of her power. A piece of her soul. A piece of her heart.

The impact smacks into my father, knocking him onto his knees. And now there's emotion on that blank face of his. Shock.

"You dare to strike at me?" he snarls, firing magic that sizzles and hisses my way. I block it with my own, lifting my arms to shield my face from its heat and when it fizzles and dies around me, I send another bolt at my father and another. Angry, raging magic so frantic, I barely see what he manages to block and what hits him. Then he strikes back at me, chains and ropes lashing at me, attempting to curl themselves around my arms and legs, my waist and my neck. I swipe them away, cutting through them with my magic.

I'm stronger than him. Better than him. And I'm no longer a slave to his will.

But I'm wrong. The injury has weakened me, so has this separation from my fated mate, and he is more conniving. He is more cunning. One of the ropes latches onto my neck and squeezes, squeezes tighter than it ever has, so that immediately the air is cut from my lungs and my brain. I gasp feebly for air, scrabbling at the ligature, dark blotches spreading across my vision.

"I understand you're upset," my father says, stalking towards me. "But there's no time for these juvenile outbursts. This is the opportunity we've been waiting for, Tristan, one that will see our family rise high above the rest. One that will see us wield more power than we've ever had before. So put your feeble mother out of your mind. Because now is the time to seize that opportunity."

"If she was feeble, it's only because you made her that way, reduced her to that," I scream, the words taking the last of my breath and then I blast through his rope, through his magic, pulverizing him into the bookcase behind him, the books tumbling from the shelves and his weapons crashing to the floor.

Before he can react, I'm up on my feet, blasting more magic his way as I back out of the room.

"I'm leaving."

"You can't leave!" my father roars from his study, blasting magic at me.

"Watch me," I snarl, turning to grab my cousin's hand and take her with me. But, as my body spins around and my eyes connect with hers, I freeze.

There's a knife, one of my father's weapons, hovering right in front of my cousin's throat, barely an inch from her flesh, ready to strike. Her entire body shakes and her eyes widen with horror.

"No, son," my father says, striding from his study. "It doesn't work like that. You don't get to leave this family. You can't turn your back on us."

"This has nothing to do with Ellie. Let her go."

"It's okay, Tristan," Ellie whispers, her voice shaking. "Go!"

I shake my head, desperately searching for a way that I can leave and bring her with me.

My father slams his hand on my shoulder, his fingers cold and tight.

"I don't think either of you understand what's happened tonight." He lets the knife inch closer towards Ellie's throat. "Our great republic nearly fell to the forces in the West. It was only through luck and pure determination that we evaded their attack and pushed them back beyond the borders. But things will have to change now. The chancellor has proved his incompetence. This country needs a new leader. A stronger, more ruthless one, one who can destroy our enemies and keep us all safe from harm."

"And let me guess," I hiss, "that leader is you."

My father laughs, that cruel, nasty sound that makes me shudder. "But of course."

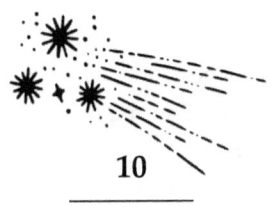

10

S pencer

WE MEET no traffic on the road, no fucking dragons overhead and the fighting in the capital appears to have died away completely. Soon, the academy comes into view, the sun rising behind the mound and silhouetting the remnants of the destroyed mansion, its turrets toppled, its roof caved in, its walls charred.

It has a lump forming in my throat. This was my home. And now it's destroyed. What else has been shattered?

Trent parks the vehicle behind a hedgerow in a field near the bottom of the hill and we climb up towards the academy. The fighting may be over but we are unsure who or what we'll find at the academy. Whether they'll be friend or foe. So we hug the tree lines and the hedgerows, the bright daylight making our presence far more conspicuous than we'd like to anyone on the lookout. However, finally we reach the meadow and the only way onwards is to break our cover.

"I could cast a fog?" Winnie suggests, "something to conceal us?"

The day is frigid and cold and perhaps a mist lingering over the meadows would not be out of place, but its sudden appearance would be.

I shake my head. "We go quickly and we stick together. If we get split up, we meet back at the hill where we left the vehicle."

They both nod, obviously happy to follow my instructions; all that time as dueling team captain obviously paying off. We keep our heads down and race across the meadow. Strips of the grass have been burned away, the earth scorched and ash blows across from the campus and into our faces, the stench of soot irritating my nose, the beast inside me snarling.

We cross the meadow without detection and hit the perimeter of the gymnasium. The dueling pitch has been uprooted, the stands caved in but the gymnasium itself has escaped untouched, only the walls discolored by the soot swirling in the air.

Winnie gasps as we swing around the building. From here we see the shell of the mansion, much less of it standing than I'd realized. The other buildings – the magical labs, the greenhouses, the student dorms – are all in tatters.

"There's nothing left," Winnie says, hands rising to cover her mouth.

"Come on," I say, tugging on her arm. We don't have time to hang around staring. We need to fetch that car and go.

We hug the walls and make our way along the paths.

But we soon realize there's no need. The battle is truly over. The fighters from the West gone. Instead, students and teachers are picking through the rubble, leading injured people away and tending to those yet to be moved. Intermingled among them are reinforcements from the republic, inspecting the damage and handing out orders.

"It seems safe," Trent says, "I'm going to head back to my room to pick up those radios. I'll meet you back here." He squeezes Winnie's hand, then races off before we can stop him.

Winnie and I continue along the path, swinging around another corner and walking straight into Summer fucking Clutton-Brock.

She's dressed in a velvet academy sweatsuit, her hair tied up neatly, her face doused in makeup. She does not look like a girl who just stepped out of a fucking battle. She looks like she's been to the salon.

Her violet eyes alight on Winnie and then on me and then she screams so fucking loud I think I actually burst an ear drum.

"What the fuck," I mutter, attempting to push past her.

She scuttles backward, continuing to scream her dumb head off, except now she's waving a painted fingernail at the two of us too.

"Help! Help me! It's the werebeast," she yells as loud as she can. "It's Spencer Moreau, the werebeast!"

"Shut the fuck up," I growl at her, but her screeching has already attracted the attention of others. People lift their heads to peer our way and footsteps march towards us.

"And Winnie Wence," she continues, "best friends with that girl who attacked me with crimson magic!"

"I told you, shut up," I growl menacingly at her, but she

doesn't, continuing her damsel-in-distress act, even though her eyes are twinkling with malevolence.

"Remain exactly where you are and lift your hands in the air." I turn my head and see a group of the republic security forces strolling our way. York lingers behind them.

"What?" I say.

"You heard us. Put your hands in the air. Both of you."

What the hell? I peer towards York, but she simply averts her gaze to the ground.

"Why?" I say, swinging my gaze across all the faces now staring at me, most – unlike fucking Summer – with real fear in their eyes.

"We've been ordered to arrest any magicals who pose a threat to the republic," he says. "Now do as I say, lift your arms and remain still. There's no need to make a scene."

I peer over my shoulder at Winnie.

"Spencer," she says nervously.

I tune into my senses. Count the number of scents. Twenty. There's at least twenty of these security agents scattered across the academy grounds.

Could I fight them off? Could my beast? Possibly but then there are the teachers and the students – my so-called friends – too and fuck knows whose side they'd pick.

I stare into Winnie's frightened face and I think of Rhianna. Alone, in danger, probably even more frightened. I don't have a choice.

"I'm going to distract them," I tell Winnie. "You grab that car and get the hell out of here."

Winnie shakes her head. "That isn't going to work and I'm not leaving you."

"It is," I say with a grin, losing the shirt someone had thrust at me back at Tristan's place. "And I'll catch up with you."

"What are you doing?" the security jerks yell. "I told you, remain still." A warning shot whistles over our heads and Summer screams again.

"Spencer," Winnie says, "Rhi will never forgive me if something happens to you."

"Winnie," I say, still smiling at her even though I'm sure it no longer reaches my eyes. "We both know that's bullshit and we both know she will be fucking devastated if anything happens to *you*. So go now, while there's still time. We need that car!"

I don't wait for her to argue anymore, I toe off the too-tight borrowed sneakers and start to run in the opposite direction to the security forces, magic already pummeling after me.

They want me, they can damn well come and get me.

I streak along the paths, students and teachers scattering out of my way, the sound of heavy boots chasing after me.

As I careen around the corner of one of the dorms, I come face to face with a security agent and slam magic into his shocked face. A man behind him calls out, his magic shooting past my head. I fling the first man in front of me, using him as a shield and firing at the second.

"He's here!" he yells to his comrades. "Over h–"

He doesn't finish his words. I slam my fist into his mouth and he collapses to the ground. I throw the body of his comrade on top of him and, leaping over them both, race around the corner.

"Yeah, here I am you fuckers. You want to come and get me?"

I meet more of them around that corner, five perhaps and more running in my direction. I just hope it's all of them, that Winnie has made it down to the parking lot. I keep my ears trained for the sound of an engine as I blast my magic at the security agents firing on me. But all I can hear is the whistle of magic as it soars past my head, exploding on the path behind me. I swerve one blast, block another, send a third hurtling back the way it came. I'm better at this than them. Stronger, more skilled, better trained. But there are more of them than me and twice magic strikes me, scorching my thigh and my shoulder.

I hiss with the pain and keep fighting, making as much noise as I possibly can. Keeping them busy, aware they are coming closer to me, closer and closer, despite the first few agents falling to the floor.

Where the hell is that girl? Where the hell is that car?

I start to despair, convinced she must have been captured, convinced I will be too. The agents form a ring around me, trapping me against the wall of the gymnasium. Still, I fight. Firing magic with increasing desperation as more and more magic hits my body, bruising my skin and singeing my flesh. Another agent falls and another, but the ring around me grows tighter and tighter, and I don't know how much longer I can hold them off. Then finally – finally – there's an almighty crash, the roar of an engine, and a beat-up car comes hurtling through the parking lot doors.

The agents spin. They shout. Some start to direct their fire that way. The car swerves and careens, attempting to avoid the onslaught of the magic. A fire bolt hits the roof, a blast digs a crater into the path ahead.

She's not going to make it. She's not going to get away.

I yell at the agents, try to attract their attention back to me. More magic hits my body and I howl in pain, a howl that splinters right down to the bones of my body and I know what I have to do. I charge, pumping my arms and my legs, straight towards the ring of agents and as I do, the beast takes over my body – a body that cracks and creaks, lengthening and stretching, reforming, so that by the time I'm on the agents I'm more beast than man.

The car screeches away as the beast snaps his jaw through throats, breaks bones with the force of his body, sends men falling to the ground. He fights and fights, his jaw soaked in blood, the scarlet liquid dripping from his mouth.

But it's no good. There's too many of them. Too many soldiers. The ring tightens and tightens still. He howls in pain as magic hits every part of his body and soon they're on top of us, holding us down, weaving tight magical chains around our body. And soon we can't move at all.

Caught.

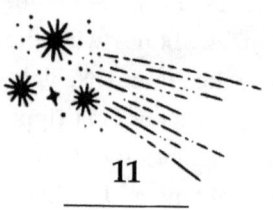

11

A zlan

"WHERE THE FUCK ARE THEY?" I mutter. It's midday. The weak winter sun is as high in the sky as it's going to reach, its thin rays barely penetrating through the smoke that still drifts in the air.

It tickles the back of my throat and I cough.

"You wanna go without them?" Stone asks, peering at his watch and then back down the road. We've tucked ourselves down an alley between two of the buildings that hug the crossroads out here on the far side of the city. But there's still a risk we will be spotted again – we've already evaded three attempts to capture us.

Have the others faced similar obstacles? Were they not so lucky?

This plan was probably a stupid one. That car may be

useful, but probably not worth getting ourselves captured over securing.

I should have insisted we stayed together. When we find Rhianna, when we ensure she's safe and sound, she's going to want all of us. All her mates and that best friend of hers too. I have a feeling she's going to hold me responsible for their safety and she's going to be pissed at me if I've lost one or two of them.

"Five more minutes," I say to Stone. "We give them five more minutes and then we go."

Those five minutes crawl by. I want to be away. I want to be active, doing something, even if all I am doing is closing the distance between us. My bond aches for her and I can't stand to be this far away from her.

My gaze swings between the empty road and the ticking hands of my wristwatch. Even out here on the edge of the city, these streets are usually bustling with traffic and people. But today, people have locked themselves away in their houses, hiding, sheltering, tending to their wounds.

The seconds creep by. I strain my eyes into the distance. Nothing.

I roll up the sleeves of my tattered shirt. I wish I had my fucking cloak.

"Let's go," I tell my friend, wheeling my motorbike out onto the road and jumping up on the saddle. He does the same and we're motoring away in the next moment, both alert, both watching the road in front of us and behind, plus the goddamn sky above us too.

We've been riding for barely ten minutes when Stone calls out.

"There's a vehicle coming up fast behind us."

"Shit!" I say, turning my head to peer back down the

road. I can't tell if it's friendly or hostile. My guess is the latter.

I signal to Stone to hit the gas, and push the motorbike to go fast, so fast the vibrations from the engine make my bones rattle and the wind assault my face, the soot in the air making my eyes stream.

"They're closing on us!" Stone yells.

I swing my gaze left and right, looking for a way off the road, an escape. There is none, we're caged in by a fierce drop on one side and a tall barrier on the other. We have no choice, we're going to have to face whoever's coming our way.

I signal to Stone again and we slow the bikes. He draws up alongside me.

"We going to see these fuckers off?" he says.

"Yes," I answer, lowering the stand of my bike to the floor and readying myself.

The vehicle screeches closer, a puff of dark smoke trailing along behind it and the nearer it gets the less sure I am that it's an enemy.

"What the hell?" Stone mutters. "That car is seriously fucked up. It looks like it's hardly hanging together."

My shoulders relax. I lower my arms.

"It's Winnie," I say. "Winnie's car."

"That's the car?" Stone says as we watch the tin can draw closer. "That's the car you want us to ride out to the waste-lands in? Are you fucking insane?" He strides back towards his bike, kicking the stand away.

"It's the fastest way," I tell him as the car jerks to a halt in front of us.

"That thing will fall apart before it's left the outskirts of Los Magicos and we'll be a goddamn easy target if we come under attack."

"Stone," I say more firmly, striding towards the passenger door, and flinging it open. "Get in!"

Stone mutters every curse word known to man under his breath and with a massive scowl on his face that makes him look like a five-year-old in a sulk, climbs into the back seat. I take the front one and slam shut the door.

"You were leaving without me?" Winnie says, in an accusing tone.

"Yes," I answer, "we didn't know if you'd made it and we couldn't afford to hang around waiting any longer. The republic forces are back in control of the city but rounding up men for interrogation. We didn't think it wise to hang around to answer their questions. Especially when it's unclear who is in charge." I peer towards the back seats. "Where's Moreau? Where's Trent?"

Winnie shifts her gaze towards the windscreen and shakes her head. "Trent's okay, I hope. But when we arrived at the academy, there were the republic's security forces there too and they tried to arrest me and Spencer. I got away. They took Spencer."

"And how about Tristan and," I swallow, "Ellie. Have they made contact on the radio?"

"I didn't get a chance to hang around for any radios," Winnie says. She peers out at the road. "Do you want to go back to the mansion?"

I shift my gaze to the windscreen too, staring out at the road ahead. That seems like an impossible choice. My sister could be in trouble. But so is my mate. I've vowed to myself to protect and look after both of them. And while my bond and my heart are pulling me towards the wastelands, that doesn't mean my heart isn't also pulling me back towards the mansion.

"Ellie's with Tristan," Stone says. "Whatever has happened to them, he'll look after her."

"He just almost got himself killed," I huff. "In fact, if it wasn't for my aunt, he would be dead."

"I hate to admit it about the asshole," Winnie says, "but he's skilled and powerful. He's won the academy's Principal Prize and the Excellence in Magic Award the last two years running."

"And was more than influential in helping the academy win the Transatlantic cup," Stone adds, somewhat reluctantly.

"I think the professor is right," Winnie says, already hitting dials on the dashboard. "Your sister and Tristan have each other. Rhi has no one and every minute we waste, god knows what that psychopath is doing to her."

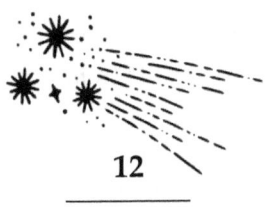

12

R enzo

It's dark by the time she comes around and we're deep in the heart of the forest, south of her home. The ground is hard and cold, the first breath of winter whispering in the night's air. A fire crackles in front of her, the orange of the flames flickering over her face, keeping her warm.

I blow into my stiff fingers, watch as her eyelids slowly flicker open, excitement jumping in my veins. She's more fun awake than asleep.

This time when she regains consciousness, it's not like before. This time realization hits her brain almost immediately, and she snaps up, my leather jacket sliding off her shoulders.

"You fucker, you knocked me out!" Her brows pull low and wrinkling her forehead.

"You weren't cooperating," I tell her, rubbing my fingers together.

"And that's how you operate, huh? Every time someone disagrees with you, you knock them out."

"Nope," I say, flicking dirt from under my fingernail. "I kill them."

She jolts, then sits up straighter.

"So I'm lucky? Every time *we* don't agree on something, you'll simply render me unconscious so you can get your own way?"

I shrug. Seems as good a plan to me as any other. But one I'm gathering she doesn't like.

She throws my jacket down to the ground in irritation and peers around into the darkness.

"Where are we and where's Pip?"

I point to my lap where her little pig is resting his head.

"Pip!" she snaps. The pig's head jerks upward. "You can't be serious?"

"He agrees with me. He doesn't think it's safe to return to Los Magicos."

"He's a pig," she says, her bottom lip protruding slightly, begging me to come bite it. "And not a very smart one at that."

"Huh," I say, rubbing my knuckles against the little man's head. "I might be wrong but I'm not sure that's a very nice thing to say."

She gapes at me, her mouth now hanging open. "You tried to kill me. Do you think that was very nice?"

"You tried to kill me back."

"I was defending myself!" She rolls up onto her knees and jabs her finger my way. Is this foreplay? Because it's turning me on. "Plus, you also just knocked me out without my permission. Do you think *that* was nice?"

I scratch my cheek and make a wild guess. "Err, no?"

"No, it was a complete dickhead move to make."

"There are people out hunting for you. I don't want them to hurt you," I tell her for like the twentieth time. My little rabbit is smart. Smarter even than the pig. I don't understand why she doesn't get this.

"You *think* there are people hunting me. You don't know that for sure."

I huff, pick up one of the sticks I gathered for the fire and toss it into the flames, watching as they curl around the wood, engulfing and smothering it completely.

"Little rabbit," I say, deciding it might be time for some truths, "I don't think I've been the only one looking for you."

She eyes me, fiddling with the zipper on my jacket that now lies by her feet. "You haven't," she agrees.

I push the pig from my lap. Hot fire licks through my body.

"Who else?" I ask. "Who else has been looking for you?" How close did they get? Did they lay hands on her? Did they hurt her?

Her hands stroke the leather of my jacket in a way that makes me fucking shiver.

"The chancellor."

"The chancellor?" I say, sitting back. That wasn't what I was expecting. The thoughts crash together in my head and then my eyes flick back to hers.

"Because you were an unregistered."

"Because of my mom."

"Ahhh," I say. "Your mom."

I guess I say it in a way that piques her interest, because she shuffles forward on her knees, closer to the fire, closer to me. The light from the flames dances across her skin, turning it golden.

"Why did you say it like that? Do you know something about my mom?"

I could tease this out, dangle this in front of my little rabbit and make her leap and jump and stretch for it, struggling to clasp it between her paws. I like teasing. I like torturing. I like making people suffer. It's so ... entertaining.

But with her, it's different. With her, every fucking thing is different.

As much as the scowl and the hissy eyes are a turn on, I want her to be pleased with me. I want her praise, her thanks, her adoration. Mostly I want her. Want her close like she was in the bed, her warm body lying flush against mine, and I suspect I'm only going to get that in two ways. By force or by pleasing her. Force would be my normal preferred choice of action, obviously. But she's strong, stronger than she was, and there's a chance I might not be successful.

Then there's this strange desire – one I've never felt before – the desire to have her touch me back. And I don't just mean her mouth around my cock. I mean, really touch me.

And so I'm straight with her.

"I told you I'd find out about your mom and I did."

"Wh-why?" she says, lifting her hand to stroke her pig as he comes sidling up to her.

Why? That wasn't the response I was expecting. Then again when is the response ever the one I was expecting? People are fucking complicated.

"I like helping you. I like caring for you." I want you to want to do those things for me.

The wrinkle reappears between her brows.

"Why?" she repeats, this time her voice a whisper, her body very still – a frozen, frightened rabbit. What is she frightened of? The truth?

Yeah, I'm guessing I'm not anyone's first choice for a fated mate.

"You're smart, little rabbit, and I think you know why."

She stares into my eyes and it makes my heart pound. Bang bang bang.

But she doesn't answer me. She's not ready to admit it. That's fine. The thing about being an assassin is you have to be patient. You have to wait for the right moment to strike and kill. I don't have much patience for most things. But the important things. The things that make my heart pound like that – yeah, I can be endlessly patient for those.

"What did you find out about my mom?" she asks me instead.

I shake my head and pull out her knife – his knife – from my pocket, laying it flat on my palm and watching the flames flicker across the blade this time.

"It wasn't your mom I found out about, little rabbit. It was your dad."

13

R^{hi}

THE FIRE FLICKERS BETWEEN US, the crimson flames reflecting onto the shining blade of my knife.

"My dad?"

Renzo crooks his finger and beckons me closer. The hook in my stomach responds, attempting to pull me his way. I stare into his face and down at the knife and for once I relent to my bond, walking around the fire and taking a seat on the ground beside the man who has tried to kill me more than once.

He holds the knife out to me.

"I went looking for answers about your mom, like you asked me to." Asked him to? I never asked him to... "Ignoring the answers resting right here in my palm." He tuts at himself.

"It was my dad's knife," I concede. The only connection to him I ever owned apart from my blood and my DNA.

"You know anything about him?" he says.

I shake my head. "Until recently nothing but his name. Caspian."

"That wasn't his name," Renzo says and I can't help frowning as I gaze back into the fire. Pip's watching us from the other side, his face only just visible through the flames, embers pirouetting into the black of the night.

"The chancellor said he was a dark magical from the West. But the chancellor is full of bullshit and I don't know whether to believe him or not."

"Can you see magical fingerprints, little rabbit? Can you read them?"

I peer up at the madman's face. "Can you?" I ask. Was he the one who read my fingerprints on this knife? Did he tell Marcus Lowsky that I was the one who killed his brother?

"Yes," he says, "one of my many talents." He offers me the knife. "But you try, little rabbit."

I stare down at the blade, my own reflection staring back up at me. It makes me jolt. I look a mess, my face pale, my cheeks sunken, dirt in my hair.

The knife glistens in the fire light and I long to hold it again. Is it strange that I've missed it? Strange how safe it made me feel? Renzo once said it was no ordinary knife and if it belonged to a dark magical, perhaps he is right.

I take it anyway, unable to resist the urge to wrap my fingers around the cool handle once more. I close my eyes and search for the fingerprints. It's much easier than it was in Stone's classroom without all the noise and magical interference. Out here in the forest with no one but Renzo, me and Pip it's much easier to focus my mind and search. A face emerges from the gloom of my subconscious. A young woman, the expression on her face startled, her hair dark, her eyes clear. The woman is me.

"I see myself," I tell him.

"Yeah," he says, amused. "You did kill Joey Lowsky after all. But search a bit harder, little rabbit, further back."

I scrunch up my eyes and do as he says. Pushing the image of myself to one side and gripping the knife more tightly, willing it to show me who else has wielded this blade.

At first nothing happens and I wonder if Renzo's simply crazy or I am unable to do this. But then, just like before, a face emerges from the gloom, blurry and murky at first like an out-of-focus photograph. Then gradually, gradually, the features sharpen, the colors intensify.

A man. The same man from the locket.

I snap open my eyes in frustration.

I already knew this knife belonged to my dad. This hasn't told me anything new.

"My dad," I tell Renzo, flinging the knife to the ground.

"So you know who he is?"

I shake my head in irritation. "I told you, my aunt said he was called Caspian. The chancellor said he was a dark magical. That's all I know."

The assassin watches my face, his eyes swinging from side to side. "Ahh you don't recognize his face."

I chew my lip. "What do you mean?"

"Little rabbit, I do. I know that face. And his name was not Caspian. And he wasn't any ordinary dark magical."

"Who ... who was he then?"

"Little rabbit, your father was the ... Black Prince." He grins at me like he just delivered the most precious of gifts straight into my hands. I stare back at him blankly. He waits. I continue to stare at him.

"Ahhh," he repeats. "You don't know who that is."

I kick at the earth, dirt hitting the flames with a hiss. I'm so fed up with everyone knowing more than I do.

"No, I don't. Who the hell was the black prince?"

Renzo picks up my knife from the ground, brushing dirt from the blade.

"Do you see pictures in your head, little rabbit?"

I sigh. I want answers but straight answers from a man like Renzo Barone are impossible. I've seen how his mind wanders, flicking from one thing to another like an erratic fly. If I want my answers, I'll have to be patient.

"Like dreams you mean?" I ask him.

"Yeah." He digs the point of the knife into the ground and spins it on its point, the crimson from the fire flashing over us as it does. "I was never any good at reading or writing. But pictures, they've always been so clear to me. There are the pictures I can see with my eyes – the ones that are really there – and then there are the other pictures. When I was a kid, I used to try and capture them." He snatches the knife, halting its spin, and scratches a line into the earth. Then another and another. "But it made my mom mad. She didn't like paint on her walls and all that shit. But I still see the pictures – like when you're away from me, I can see your face – clear as day in my mind."

"I used to have these dreams," I tell him, "when I was young – they were so real, so vivid."

He nods like he understands, continuing to scratch at the ground.

"Look," he tells me and I gaze down at the marks he's made on the ground. Only they aren't marks. It's a picture. Of a man's face. My dad's face.

Renzo waves his hand above the picture and it lifts into

the air, filling with color and depth and movement, like a cartoon.

"How are you doing that?" I say in awe.

"Magic," he answers like I'm dumb. "Like I said, I'm no reader. But the old man who lived next door to me when I was a kid used to tell me stories and they painted pictures in my head. Ones I've never forgotten." The man in his picture wears armor black as night, his hair is dark too like mine and he's striding towards an army of men. "So, little rabbit, do you want me to tell you the story of the black prince?"

I drag my eyes from the moving picture and back to Renzo's face. His miscolored eyes sparkle in the firelight.

"Yes," I tell him, "I want to know."

The picture hovering in front of our eyes dissolves and a new one forms.

"Then let's start from the beginning," Renzo says.

The picture moves and it's like watching a movie, an animated one, one come to life in front of me, and the voice narrating the story isn't the assassin's, it's an old man's, the old man that told him the story, and now tells me the story too.

The story of the Black Prince.

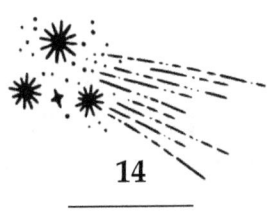

14

T he story of the Black Prince

IN THE BEGINNING there was darkness. A bottomless, impenetrable darkness that hung over the lands and took the shape of monsters. Great beasts that terrorized and plagued the people.

Magicals were fewer then – and because the darkness was magical and uncontainable – feared.

The monsters hunted the people. The people hunted the magicals.

And so it continued. On and On.

Until Fate intervened, bonding a young woman with five mates. Powerful and brave. Together, they drove the darkness away and were rewarded with the rule of the land. Magicals were no longer feared. They were saviors.

But though the monsters were gone, new monsters had

taken their place. The darkness now lay in the hearts of men and a new terror reigned.

The old magical kings ruled as tyrants. Taking what they pleased, doing as they wanted. The great magical families fought to possess the throne. The country was always at war, the people always hungry. They longed for peace. They longed for something better.

In the end, they rose up.

The dark magicals who had used their magic to enslave and abuse were pushed back, further and further and the western border was formed. The magicals that remained pledged to establish a better land, a better world: the republic. The council was formed to rule in peace and harmony, the powerful magical families working together under the leadership of an elected chancellor.

But though the darkness had been driven away, it lingered out there, just beyond the border.

The threat from those disposed to the West remained and the council, wanting to keep its promise to the people, decreed that all magicals should be registered and a protection force – an army – be formed to protect the new republic from attack.

Decades passed. The academy was formed to train the next generation of magicals in battle. The threat from the West never diminished, but it never grew either.

That was until the black prince.

They say he was descended from dragons themselves. They say he had unknown powers – that he could turn day to night and night to day. They say he could wield crimson magic as if it was nothing but child's play.

The forces in the West had been fractured and splintered. They had spent as much time fighting one another as they had the new republic. But the black prince was ruthless and cunning, murdering his enemies, slaughtering anyone who stood in his way, until eventually the magicals in the West fell under his command, united by his fist. He formed them into an army with the intention of overthrowing the republic and reuniting the two countries. Ruling them both.

His attacks on the republic were stronger, more ruthless than anything that had come before. There were tales of dragons, of ancient magic, of new sinister curses. For a time, the republic struggled to keep him at bay. It looked as if the republic would fall.

And then as quickly as the black prince had risen to power, he fell, disappeared, vanished.

A dark cloud dispersed by the wind.

Some say he was killed by his own men, some by an assassin from the republic, some that he succumbed to the charms of a siren.

But he was gone and the threat from the West fell with him.

15

R^{hi}

THE ANIMATED pictures fall away and it's just me and him, the fire and Pip once more.

I swallow. The pictures may be gone but they remain dancing in my mind. This man, powerful and dangerous, determined to rule both lands.

"You really think he was my dad?"

The assassin picks up a stick, snapping it in half between his hands and letting one end catch alight; he twists it in the flames, watching as the fire consumes the wood.

"I'm no scholar, little rabbit. But I remember things. Things like faces."

"But you don't know for sure. You could be wrong. It's not like you ever met him. You just have this picture in your mind."

"I guess that picture came from somewhere, though, didn't it? An illustration. A photo."

I chew on my lip and stare down at my hands. I can feel the magic tingling in my nerves. That light, airy magic that's always been there, and that dark, more sinister magic too. The magic that wants to tear everything and everyone apart. Does that come from him? My dad?

Was he really this black prince – if such a man even existed? Or is this a clever story created by a crazy mind?

I wish I had my locket. I wish I could open it right now and stare down at the picture. The one of my mom cradling a tiny baby in her arms, that man by her side. Were they in love? Was I created from that love? Or was he only ever using my mom as a weapon, like the chancellor did, like the council.

"This is why we have to get the hell away," Renzo says, the flames racing closer and closer to his fingers as he grips the stick. "If they suspect you are who you are, then you're too fucking dangerous to let wander about ... the black prince's daughter."

"Do you think ... do you think I'm like him?" Dark, dangerous, evil.

The flames lick right against his fingertips and he turns to look at me, excitement flickering across his face.

"I think you're fucking incredible, little rabbit. I think I'd follow you anywhere, do anything for you. I've never met anyone like you before."

"You mean ... the crimson magic?" I say with a disappointment that surprises me. The man is sick and twisted and I can't forget the way his face had lit up when the scarlet magic had sizzled on my fingers.

"Everything about you. The dark and the light. The shadows and the blaze. The way you get real mad at me, the way you scream, the way you're always fighting." His eyes swim down my form. "I've never wanted to consume anything as badly as I have you."

The intensity of his gaze and his words make me shiver and he tosses the remainder of the stick into the fire making the flames burn higher.

"You know that's never going to happen," I tell him, despite the hook pulling me violently towards him, despite the way my skin tingles as his arm brushes against mine, despite the way the firelight makes him look almost breathtaking.

Maybe I shouldn't admit this to him. Maybe I should be a hell of a lot smarter, stringing him along so that'll he'll continue to help me, so that he won't fucking kill me. The truth could make an already unpredictable and dangerous man even more so.

But to my surprise, he simply says:

"Why not?"

"Because," I say, peering out to Pip for help, "you tried to kill me."

"Tsk," he says. "Some people would call that foreplay, little rabbit. In fact, if you want, we could play a little game of chase now. You run and I'll catch you." His eyes darken and I shiver again.

It's not exactly surprising that I'm attracted to him. The man is hot, his face sometimes boyish, sometimes frightening, his body solid and strong, his eyes strange and mesmerizing. If it wasn't for all the other stuff, I doubt I'd be resisting the pull of the bond at all.

But fate is wrong about this one. Hell, fate has been one fucked-up bitch about most of my mates. But this one ...

"You're an assassin, Renzo," I tell him firmly. "You kill people. And that is ... that is ..."

"A job."

"It's sick and evil and wrong."

"You've killed people."

"In self defense. I don't do it for money," I scowl at him, "for the thrill of it."

"The man in black kills for a living."

"That's not the same thing."

"It isn't?" he asks innocently, his face all puzzled. "Why not?"

"He's doing it for the authorities. To keep the republic safe."

"Little rabbit," he says, sounding annoyed now. "I know you don't believe that bullshit. Me and him, we're no different. We're both huntsmen. We just have different bosses. Or we did. I think I just killed mine." He chuckles.

"See – that's what I mean!"

"Hey, I killed him for you."

"Did you kill Andrew Playford for me too?!" I cry.

He examines my face. "Yes?" I frown at him. "No?"

"I don't want you killing people for me. You have to stop doing that."

He shakes his head. "No fucking way, little rabbit. I'll kill anyone that lays a finger on you, anyone who tries!"

"Urgh!" I jump to my feet in frustration. "I don't want any more blood on my hands."

But I guess that choice is not my own, because I've no sooner said the words, than my senses are tingling.

"Magicals," I whisper to him. "I can feel them. That way." I point through the trees.

Renzo's on his feet in a flash. He waves his hand, and the fire dies with a hiss, plunging us into darkness.

"Which way are they moving?" he whispers as Pip brushes against my ankles.

I tune into the sense.

"Towards us," I say with alarm. "Do you think they saw our fire?"

Renzo scoops Pip up in one arm and grabs my upper arm with his free hand, his fingers tight and firm and causing electricity to dart across my skin despite our current proximity to danger.

"I can kill them," he whispers, "or we can hide, little rabbit. Your choice."

"Hide!" I tell him. "We don't even know who they are. They may be no threat to us at all. We can't just kill them."

Renzo huffs in frustration like a kid who's just been told he can't play with his ball, then drags me along behind him. For such a large man, he moves silently, barely making a noise as we tread over dead leaves and branches and further into the forest.

"They're still coming," I hiss at him, peering over my shoulder and through the darkness, trying to make out who the hell is following us.

Renzo picks up his pace and drags me down to crouch behind a bush. It's lost its leaves with the coming winter and it doesn't shield us as well as it could, but in the darkness it should do.

We wait and soon we hear the snapping of branches, the rustling of leaves, then the whispered voices of people. I strain my eyes, trying to make out who it is out here in the woods.

Renzo bristles beside me as they come into view, his entire body is tense, his magic straining to be released in the air around me.

I rest my hand on his wrist, hoping to convey to him that we should stay still, not attack. His body relaxes ever so slightly and I can feel the thump of his pulse beneath his skin, the fine bones and taut sinew.

I brush the pad of my thumb over the veins that run beneath the surface of his skin as I watch the people emerge from the gloom. Not soldiers, people. Two, maybe three, families, I'm guessing. Three women, one man, a gaggle of children. All of them carry bags on their backs or their shoulders, wrapped up in warm winter coats, scarves and hats. The children whisper nervously among one another, their hands clasped in each other's, while the adults swing their gaze through the trees, backward and forward, searching for danger.

I hold my breath. I don't think they're any threat to us – in fact Renzo is probably far more of one to them than they are to us – but they're mere feet away and I'd rather not take the risk.

The man whispers to one of the women and they peer in our direction, my eyes almost locking with the woman's through the branches of the bush. But then she points to the south and they trudge off in that direction.

When they're far enough away, I release my breath, but I hang on to Renzo's arm until the families are lost in the dark.

Then I turn to him.

"I don't think they were searching for us. I think they were fleeing the fighting."

His eyes are fixed on my face, so intense my cheeks heat in the cold air. Then slowly his gaze falls to where my hand clasps his wrist. The electricity, passing through our skin, crackles so loud I swear I can hear it and my bond hums in response, his magic brushing up against mine and making every nerve in my body hum too. I go to snatch my hand away, but he captures it, holding it in place.

"Don't let go," he whispers, "it feels so good, little rabbit."

And I shouldn't obey his order. I should zap him instead and pull my hand away. Yet, it does feel good, so good.

He strokes my knuckles with the calloused pads of his fingers – rough yet soft, soft yet rough. A sigh escapes my throat.

"Touch me more," he says with a growl that should frighten me. He's like a wild animal. Not one I can tame. If I touch him like he asks, I risk losing a finger, risk losing my throat. "P-p-p-please," he adds and I wonder if he's ever used that word before in his life.

I lift my other hand slowly through the cold air, so cold it nips at my nose and my toes, lift it up towards his face. He stops breathing and stares into my eyes and I remember the first time we met, when he bound me with his magic and looking into his eyes had felt like falling. I experience it all over again, the ground disappearing beneath me and my body falling, falling, falling.

He swallows, the lump in his tattooed neck rising and falling too.

What the hell am I doing? I think as I reach closer, nearer, feeling the heat of his skin before I touch his cheek. Rough and soft. Soft and rough. Beneath my fingertips. I wait. Wait for the attack, for the pounce, for the strike, and when none comes, I stroke my fingers along the groove of the scar that marks his cheek, feeling where the flesh split open and weaved back together, thinking how clever that is, cleverer than any magic, our bodies knowing what to do without us asking, my fingers stroking over his cheekbone, knowing they should, following the pull of my bond and not my commands.

His eyelids drift shut and the pulse in his wrist flutters.

I follow the curve of his cheekbone to the edge of his face, following it down to the edge of his jaw, the skin here sharp with stubble. I let my fingers crackle through it, pinching his chin like he'd done mine, staring at his lips.

I want to kiss him and the idea both excites and disgusts me. How can I want to kiss a murderer? How can I want to press my mouth to a man who's stolen the breath of so many? Why do I want to touch him at all?

My bond spirals in my stomach, but it's not the only sensation residing there, there's nausea too.

I go to pull my hand away, but then he says:

"No one's touched me like this before."

And I know what that feels like. What it's like to be alone. To have no one. And I keep my hand right where it is.

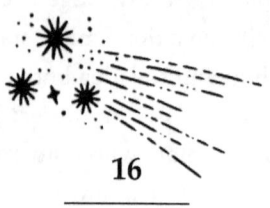

16

A zlan

THE JOURNEY IS NOT a comfortable one. Stone wasn't exaggerating. The car is a rust bucket, a rust bucket that hardly fits my large frame. I am crammed into the seat, folded in half with my knees scraping the underside of my chin, feeling every bump and crater in the road. Every so often I glance in the rearview mirror to be met with my friend's unamused expression.

It doesn't help that the girl is a really shit driver. Not that she seems to notice her own limitations, oblivious to our winces and sucked-in breaths, and politely declining every offer I make to take over behind the wheel.

Halfway there I decide I need something to distract me from the near misses and my increased agitation about both Rhi and Ellie. I flip on the radio and scroll through the stations. I'm met with a hissing noise at every frequency.

"They're all down," I say. "All the stations."

However, finally we hit on one lone station, one I bet is situated somewhere as far away from the border and Los Magicos as you can get. It plays old country songs and when one comes on that I remember my mom singing, I sit back and close my eyes, hoping it might calm me the shit down.

Towards the end of the song, however, when the guitars are fading, the song cuts dead and a loud voice blares across the frequency instead.

I snap open my eyes.

"Citizens of the Republic. Yesterday at twenty-one hundred hours forces from the West invaded our lands and attempted to topple our government. They were fortunately thwarted, although not without the loss of lives and some destruction to our great capital." I sit forward in my seat. It isn't the chancellor speaking. No, it's my goddamn uncle. "No doubt we were betrayed by traitors within our midst, citizens who aided and abetted our enemies. As such, a state of emergency has been declared, and the council has chosen to install me, Christopher Kennedy, as temporary Lord Protector of our nation. I will not rest until our enemies – the weeds that grow hidden among us – have been hunted down, tugged out by their roots and utterly destroyed. Rest assured, no such attack will ever be allowed to happen again. You will find me a ruthless tyrant when it comes to our enemies and a fair and just ruler to all those faithful to our republic."

I sniff. Fair? Just? He'll hunt down every dissident, every opponent he can and obliterate them. There will be no fairness, no peace. There will only be tyranny and fear.

"It doesn't make any sense," Stone says in irritation. "Who the fuck led the attack and why the fuck did they back off?"

I shake my head. I don't know. Since the fall of the Black Prince two decades ago, the forces in the West have been split and fractious. Different leaders have risen, fighting amongst themselves. No one has wielded enough power to lead an attack like the one last night. If they really did …

"Maybe this has nothing to do with the West after all," I say, "maybe this was a coup."

"Moreau insists forces attacked from over the border."

I shrug. "My uncle could have planned it to look that way."

"Do you think they'll reinstate the cell network?" Winnie asks unsurely. "I really need to check that Trent and my family are okay."

I snort again and Winnie peers at me with distress.

"I'm sure they will," Stone says, obviously wanting to placate our driver. But he knows it benefits my uncle to keep communications down. He'll want everyone scurrying around like headless chickens in the dark. Makes it easier to swoop down and pluck off his enemies one by one.

We're all quiet for the next hour. The scenery beyond the window is one blurred line of color as we hurtle along at unrecognizable speeds, but I catch glimpses: houses, forests, the mountains in the distance. The fighting didn't reach this far. In fact, out here, you could believe that last night didn't happen at all, that nothing has changed.

Another half hour passes, the sun sinking behind the horizon and the car beginning to slow.

"We're here?" I ask Winnie. We're deep in the wastelands now. The authorities' grip here has always been weakest, the gangs ruling in effect. Lowsky's compound lies in the heart of the forest in front of us. It's not somewhere I've ever ventured before.

"I've taken us to the point you instructed."

"Right," I say, "Stone and I are going to go on foot from here. You need to keep yourself and this car hidden until we return with Rhi."

"Foot?" Winnie says.

"We don't know who's out there. Lowsky's men may be out patrolling. Fuck, there may even be soldiers from the West or my uncle's men. We'll be less conspicuous this way."

"You're not going without me," Winnie says, already unclipping her seat belt.

"Miss Wence," Stone says, leaning forward in his seat. "You need to guard this car. We may need it as our getaway vehicle."

"I'm coming with you," she says, ignoring her professor.

"Miss Wence, you are not. Let's not beat about the bush. This is going to be dangerous and you have no combat experience."

"No combat experience?" Winnie huffs. "What was I doing then when the academy was attacked?" Stone goes to answer her question, but she cuts right through him. "Plus you said yourself, I'm a good magical."

"You are," Stone says. "You're also important to Rhi and seeing as we've already managed to mislay two of her fated mates today, we're not losing you too."

"Which is why I should come with you."

"No," I say firmly. "You're staying with the car."

"And what the hell am I meant to do if you don't come back?"

"If we're not back by daybreak, you get the hell out of here."

"And go where? Those men at the academy tried to arrest me."

"Back to your family."

She looks at me, a hard look a mere scrap of girl like her

has no right to make, and then throws that same hard stare Stone's way.

"Fine," she says, "but I don't like it. And if you need me to come rescue you–"

I snort. Her rescue us? Less than likely.

Winnie points a finger at me. "Then you send up a flare. The colors of the academy crest."

I have no intention of doing that. Stone's right. We have a duty to keep this girl safe and we've already risked her well-being bringing her this far. Still, I nod my head, just to avoid an argument.

"Find somewhere to hide the car," I say, tugging on the door handle and climbing out of the vehicle.

I wait for Stone to join me and then we head off, leaving the road and plunging into the trees.

"You know where you're going?" Stone says.

I close my eyes, take a deep inhale searching for scents on the wind, hunting for traces of magic. I catch a hint of both. Southeast.

"This way," I tell him and he follows me through the woodland.

The trail grows stronger the further we travel, and twice we're forced to lay down low among the dead leaves to avoid passing patrols catching sight of us.

It's Lowsky's men. No soldiers here. But something is wrong. I can tell by their skittish behavior, by the unease I smell in their scents.

Have they heard that Lowsky's dead? Is that what's bothering them?

Or, if they were working with the forces in the West, as we suspect, do they fear retribution now the invasion has failed? Are they alarmed, like the rest of us, at my uncle's sudden rise to power? The chancellor was ruthless with no time or patience for the gangs but he was a mere pussycat compared to my uncle.

From a distance we follow three gang men as they trample through the forest, muttering to each other in concerned voices and soon we see the high fences of the compound in the distance.

From what I can make out, it's not as well-fortified as I'd expected, a few gang members lolling around the entrance and a few circling the perimeter.

"This doesn't seem right," I muse.

"What doesn't?" Stone asks, crouching beside me.

"Why are there so few of them? Why aren't they properly organized?"

"I'm telling you, Az, Lowsky is dead. Their leader has gone. They probably don't know what the hell to do."

I rub at my chin, watching the men. They look unsettled.

"How about Rhi?" Stone asks. "Can you feel her? Can you feel her close by?"

I shift my focus away from the men and their scents, and focus in on that feeling in my gut, my bond. I can feel her more than I could and can feel her mixture of emotions, turbulent as always. I wish I was more adept at reading them. I wish I could tell if she was hurt, afraid, in danger. But maybe women have always been a damn mystery to me, and maybe, despite our bond, despite fate's intentions, I understand Rhianna even less than most.

I don't say any of this to my friend. Instead I say, "She feels closer."

"Yes," he says, screwing up his face. "But close enough? Shouldn't we be able to feel her more if she were this close? Maybe she isn't here after all."

"Stone," I say in frustration. "This is the only lead we have. Fuck, you're right, she might not be here. But I'm going to find out for sure. And you can come with me or not."

"Is that your plan?" a voice says from behind me and I nearly jump a mile out of my skin as Winnie crouches down in the undergrowth with us.

"I told you to stay with the car," I growl.

"And I decided that was dumb and that if we're rescuing Rhi, then I'm helping."

My worn patience finally breaks and I snap up to standing and stroll through the thinning trees towards the gates.

Phoenix mutters another long string of expletives and jogs to catch up with me, Winnie right behind him.

"So I assume we're going through the front door," he mutters.

"I've never been one to sneak in the back," I say, "it isn't my style."

He shakes his head at me, this time muttering that I'm an idiot.

Yeah, I probably am. Walking straight into the lion's den is probably damn foolish. But I'm going to do it anyway.

17

R^{hi}

"I NEED to get back to Los Magicos," I tell him. He wants us to go on in the direction of the mountains. He thinks it will be safer there and the run-in with the families has made him even more skittish than he was. "I need to get back to my mates. I need to get back to my friends. I need to get back to school."

"If it's still standing," he scoffs.

"That's the point. We don't know. We can't wander about in the wilderness forever."

"Not forever, little rabbit, just until everything calms down, blows over."

I rest my hand on my hip. "Okay, enough of the bullshit. Let's be frank here for a minute. Are you holding me captive?"

"You're free to go," he says, shrugging.

"And if I do?" He shrugs. "How far will I get before you drag me back?"

"Depends how much of a fight you want to make it." His eyes light up. "I love a chase, little one. Do you want to run and I'll catch you?"

"No," I tell him firmly, "I want to go back to Los Magicos."

He ignores me and collects up our stuff – the string bag I filled with supplies, his leather jacket and Pip. Then he strolls off into the darkness whistling to himself as Pip squeals in protest and I chase after them both.

I am not winning in this situation and I need to be smarter about this.

The forest is dark, even though the canopy is leafless and the sky visible above us. It's stacked with heavy winter clouds, no moon or stars to light our way and Renzo clicks his fingers and creates a ball of light to help guide us through the thick undergrowth.

"Are we walking all the way through the night?" I moan.

"It's fucking freezing," he says, "so unless you want to get naked and huddle up with me, we need to keep moving."

I pull my coat more tightly around me, balling my cold hands in my pockets and trying my damn hardest not to imagine what it would be like to get naked with this man.

I can still feel the presence of those magical families on the periphery of my senses, but they're far away now and I'm not worried until a loud scream screeches through the trees, bouncing off the trunks and disturbing the sleeping birds that flap up into the air in alarm. The noise is followed by bangs and more screaming.

I freeze and look at Renzo.

"Those children!" I cry and then I'm picking up my feet and running in their direction.

"Little rabbit!" Renzo yells. "Little rabbit!!" He's after me in a flash, catching my arm and yanking me to a stop. "What the fuck are you doing?"

"They're under attack," I pant. "We have to help them."

Renzo's face contorts like I've just asked him to walk over hot coals and shoot himself in the head. "*Help* them?"

"Yes, can't you hear?" I yank on his grip, the screams becoming more desperate. "They're under attack. We need to help them."

I yank again but all it achieves is a tighter grip on my arm. "No, we don't."

"Renzo Barone, stars help me, if you don't let go of my arm right now, I will be the one knocking *you* unconscious!"

"Fuck yes," he says, his eyes wild.

I growl at him. "I freaking mean it, Renzo!" And to my utter surprise, he lets go of my arm immediately. For a moment, I just stand there stunned, but then there's another scream – this one undeniably belonging to a small child – and I'm running again in the next, Renzo close behind me.

We crash through the trees. The screaming has turned to sobbing, and a desperate lump forms in my throat.

What the hell is happening? What the hell will we find?

I run hard and soon we can see them in the distance, the scene lit up by hovering balls of light. Four new men stand in front of the families, they have a hold of two of the women. The man from before rests on his knees, blood dripping down his face, and the children are huddled together, crying. I gasp, picking up my pace, but Renzo is faster. He thrusts Pip into my arms and races ahead.

Magic flashes in the darkness. There's more yelling and screaming. I see the family fleeing through the trees and when finally I reach the place they'd just occupied, I find

Renzo facing off against the four men. I sprint to his side, dropping Pip to the floor and raising my arms.

"Who's this?" one of the men says with a curious grin. "Who've you got with you, Barone?"

"No one," Renzo says, pushing me hard on the shoulder away from him; so hard I almost stumble to the ground.

"A girl?" The smile on the man's face widens and his gaze flicks to his companions. "Not *the* girl. Are you bringing her in? You know the reward for her has quadrupled." He meets the eyes of his friends. "Maybe we could take that reward for ourselves."

"She's not the girl."

I straighten up. The balls of light have extinguished and I'm forced to squint through the darkness at the men. They don't look like the soldiers that ambushed me at the graveyard or those that attacked the academy. No, they look like the men who surrounded the man in black all those months ago. Lowsky's men. The Wolves of Night.

"Then who is she?"

Renzo opens his mouth like he's going to answer their question, and the men almost lean forward, eager for his answer. But he doesn't speak, instead he sends a barrage of magic crashing unexpectedly their way.

The men swerve, block and duck it, firing their own magic back at us.

"Don't hit the girl!" the first man says. "She's wanted alive and unharmed now."

His words only seem to make Renzo madder. He flings magic at them, wild and crazy, and this time it's too erratic for them to dodge. One man's hit in the chest, falling to his knees. Another cries out as a bolt knocks into his hip.

"Hand her over, Renzo," the first man says. "You're

outnumbered. You're not going to win this battle. Hand her over and we'll let you go!"

"Let him go?" another of the men hisses. "Are you crazy?"

"How about *you* turn around and leave," I call out and the attention of all the men is drawn back to me, "and we won't hurt you?"

The second man laughs.

"We're not letting them go," Renzo growls. "We're going to kill them."

"I don't want to kill them," I growl right back.

"We're going to anyway." He grins at the men and I'm not blind to the way his eyes twinkle with relish.

"We are not killing any more people!"

"Are you done?" the first man asks. "And might I point out that you are outnumbered. The only ones doing any killing here will be us, so if you want to avoid that, Renzo, you'll hand her over."

Renzo chuckles like that's the best joke he's heard in years. "You have no idea who you're dealing with," he says, tears running down his cheeks as the amusement rocks his body.

"We do, Renzo Barone. We know you well enough," the first man says with even more irritation.

"I'm not talking about me, knuckleheads. I'm talking about her." He turns and looks at me, winks and then sends another blast of magic hurtling the men's way. This time even more powerful.

I tut at him, but when the fire is returned four fold, hitting his body, making him stumble backwards, blood mixing with the tears on his face, I'm forced to step in. I send a flurry of my own magic back. Not strong enough to kill, but enough to have them pacing backwards.

"I'm giving you a chance," I call out. "A chance to walk away. This doesn't have to end in violence. No one has to get hurt."

Renzo scoffs and spits blood onto the forest floor. "So you'd let them walk away, would you? What do you think they were going to do to that family, little rabbit?" he asks me. "Invite them round for tea?"

I know he's right. Of course he is. I just ... I just don't want to ...

"What were you going to do?"

The second man sniggers, cruelty painted clearly across his face.

The first man ignores him. "They're fugitives. Potential criminals. We were going to take them in for questioning. We weren't going to hurt them. And we won't hurt you either, little girl. So if you're really keen to avoid someone getting killed," he motions his head towards Renzo, "then come with us now."

"And where will you take me?"

"We'll hand you in to the authorities. Seems you're wanted. Although who the fuck knows why."

"The authorities?" I say glancing at Renzo. Does that mean the invasion by the West failed? Are the authorities still in charge?

As if reading my thoughts, the man adds, "There are new authorities in charge now." The fourth man has stumbled back onto his feet and all four stand ready to attack us. "So, what's it going to be?"

"Fuck this!" Renzo says and before I can stop him, he sends a powerful ball of fire directly at the men. It's so fast, so powerful, the four men have no time to respond and they're consumed by the flames in a matter of seconds. They scream, a noise that has me turning away and covering my ears. The heat from the fire fierce on my back.

The flames crackle. The screaming dies away and in another second so have the flames, the cold air returning in its place.

I remove my hands from my ears. I'm too scared to turn around, too appalled to look at what must remain of the men. Instead, I glance at Renzo. His eyes remain fixed that way, a fascination dancing in them.

"You shouldn't have done that," I say, scooping Pip up into my arms. "There was no need."

He jolts out of his trance and his gaze snaps my way. He looks at me with as much fascination and curiosity.

"You know there was no other way, little rabbit."

"There was. If we'd–"

"You think they wouldn't have done the same to us?"

There's blood still seeping from his hairline down his face and he blinks as it smudges into his eyes.

I start walking, through the trees, and when I'm far enough away from what's just happened, I flop down onto the cold earth of the forest floor and bury my face in my hands.

I don't know what to do.

This man is a psychopath – and as much as I'd like to deny it, pretend it wasn't the case – it's clear he gets a kick out of killing. But then not everything he says is madness. Those men – what would they have done to those families – to that man, to those women – stars– to those children?! What would they have done to me?

And he's right about people out looking for me too. Those men confirmed it. The price on my head has quadrupled. Quadrupled! So am I right to be hiding out here with him, hoping my mates find me? Or should I be out searching for them?

I just don't know.

The thought of them hurt, injured, in danger, has my body shaking and I instinctively reach out for them through the bond. I can sense them over the distance – alive – trying to reach me too, stretching and straining to find me. It's unbearable and my body shakes all the harder.

"Little rabbit?" the man who's just added four more kills to his name says behind me. "Those kids are safe. Isn't that what you wanted?"

I wipe my face with my hands, and peer up at him.

I can read the genuine puzzlement in his features. He's trying to understand me. I wipe the back of my hand under my nose. Good luck to him because I don't even understand myself.

I sniff, and pull myself back up onto my feet.

"Yes, you're right. It is what I wanted." I nod, scraping my hair back from my face. "Thank you. Thank you for that."

His eyes travel all over my face, trying to read my expression. Then he cocks his head.

"I think you need some sleep, little rabbit."

As soon as he says the words, I realize how right he is. I'm exhausted, utterly shattered, emotionally, mentally, physically. All I want to do is lie down, close my eyes and sleep for a hundred years.

"You said it was too dangerous to sleep out here in the forest," I say.

"It is," he says, "but there's somewhere ... come on."

He starts to walk. He no longer has my bag – we lost that in the dash through the trees – and my pig is lying patiently by my feet waiting for me to make a decision. I peer in the opposite direction. I don't have to follow him. I could go my own way.

He keeps walking, silently, barely making a sound, not looking back to see if I'm following.

"What do I do?" I stare down at Pip, who stares right back at me. His dark eyes jet in the gloom. He doesn't answer me.

This is my decision. Not his. Not Renzo's.

I close my eyes and it's my bond that answers me, tugging me in the direction of the assassin.

I open my eyes and glance down at my stomach and for once I decide to follow fate's command.

"Come on," I say to Pip. He doesn't move and for the first time I register that something isn't right. I crouch down beside my pet. He's breathing rapidly, his little rib cage falling and rising at a frantic pace and his entire body shaking.

"Pip!" I scream.

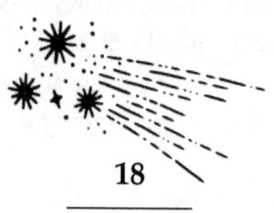

18

R enzo

I HEAR my little rabbit scream and I'm bounding through the undergrowth towards her without a second's thought. I find her crouching on the ground, her little pig laid out in front of her wheezing and shaking.

"Pip," she sobs, her hands fluttering all over him in indecision. "What's wrong? I don't know what's wrong with him!"

I examine the animal. His eyes are glazed, his jaw grinding in pain.

"D'you get hit by some magic, little man?" I ask him and my little rabbit glances up at me in alarm.

"Hit!" she gasps. "Shit! Pip!" She grabs a hold of the sleeve of my jacket, pulling on it. "He's so tiny. He can't … what should we do?"

"Little rabbit," I say, waving my hand above the small

pig, trying to determine what's wrong with him. "Calm the fuck down."

"What's wrong? What's wrong with him?"

I wish I knew the fucking answer. But I've spent my life harming not healing and fuck me if I know. Something tells me imparting that piece of information to my little rabbit is not going to help our current situation.

"Yeah, he's been hit by a spell," I say confidently, ignoring the pathetic look the pig throws me.

"Is he ... is he going to be okay?"

"Just fine," I tell her, lifting the little man gently into my arms. "Just going to need a bit of time to work the stuff out of his system."

"Oh Pip," she says, resting her palm on his brow. "Is there anything we can do to help him?"

Her voice sounds less panicked now. She fucking believes me. Guess I should feel guilty or something, lying to her like that. If the pig dies, she won't be happy. But instead, I have to suppress the corners of my mouth from pulling upwards. She believes me, my little rabbit – though I bet she'd deny it – she trusts me.

"He needs rest. Come on. Let's get moving."

I stride back the way I came, my little rabbit hip hopping beside me like I'm the Pied fucking Piper.

The little pig's body is hot in my hands. He's burning up with a fever. She uses her magic to blow cool air over him as we walk, whispering soothing words in a voice that makes my skin fucking tingle.

"How old is this pig?" I ask her, staring down into its feverish face.

"Pip?" She screws up her face thinking. "I don't know ten, eleven, maybe twelve years old. I remember I was small when my aunt found him wandering the forest on his own.

Deduced his mom had abandoned him, the runt of the litter. He was too adorable to leave, so we kept him."

"Huh," I say.

"What?" she says, stroking the pig's cheek like she'd done mine earlier behind the bush, something I want her to do again. Over and over again.

"Ten's old for a pig, right? Little man doesn't look old."

"No," she says, "unlike the rest of us, Pip never seems to age, lucky rascal."

"Huh," I say again, looking down at the small pig in my arms.

He doesn't look like a wild pig to me. He doesn't look like an old pig either. The pig manages a feeble grunt as if telling me to leave well enough alone.

We walk some more, right to the edge of the forest and the foothills of the mountain, ignoring the paths and climbing the first slope as day breaks behind us, our shadows endlessly long on the ground in front of us.

"Are we nearly there?" she asks, her eyelids heavy.

"Nearly, little rabbit. Look there it is."

She lifts her gaze and finds the shepherd's hut nestled in the crag of the mountain, invisible from the sky and to anyone walking from any other direction than the one we're walking.

"It's safe?"

"I think so," I tell her. The shepherd that used this hut is decomposing under some rocks in the stream in the valley over yonder. No one's claimed the hut since he met his untimely end. And by end, I mean me.

Still, my little rabbit approaches the wooden building cautiously, searching with her senses for anyone nearby and even though she senses no one but us, she pushes back the door like someone might jump out and pounce on her.

The hut isn't exactly some five-star hotel. Its one room houses a single wooden bed, its mattress stuffed with straw, a chair, and a shelf with a kettle, a cup, a plate and some dried meat in tins. I lay the little pig out on the end of the bed and my little rabbit pulls one of the threadbare blankets over his quivering body, whispering to him some more until his eyes drift shut.

The place smells of rotting wood and damp. That's never bothered me before. But I want her touching me again and I don't know if she will when the place smells like shit. It's why I'm guessing girls like candles. I remember Marcus was always lighting the things whenever he had some girl round sucking his dick.

I wish I had one now. I'd light it. Ask her to touch me again, touch me a whole lot more, suck my cock.

It's a hell of a lot warmer in here than it is outside but she adjusts the blanket under the pig's chin anyway, then peers up at me.

"Are you sure he's going to be okay?"

"Positive," I say.

Her shoulders sag and she smothers a yawn.

"Time for bed, little rabbit."

"It's morning," she says.

"Yeah. Best to travel at night and sleep in the day. Lie down now and go to sleep."

She peers around the tiny hut. "Are you going to rest too?" I nod my head and she narrows her eyes. "There's only one bed."

"Yeah," I say. "There is."

"We're not sharing a bed," she tells me, already toeing off her boots and curling her feet up onto the mattress.

"Yeah," I say. "I figured as much." I tug one of the blankets onto the floor and lay it out alongside the bed. Then I kick off my own boots, shrug off my jacket, and lay it over my shoulders, lie down and stare up at the ceiling, tucking my hands behind my head.

I hear my little rabbit fuss about on the mattress, then finally lie down herself. I glance over at her. She's curled on her side with her hands tucked under her cheek. Our gazes connect and that sensation in my stomach goes batshit crazy.

I stare back up at the ceiling. What the fuck is wrong with me? I want to consume my little rabbit so badly, it's fucking killing me inside. When I want stuff, I take it. I could take her now. Sure she'd kick up a fuss, probably zap me a hell of a lot with her magic. Hell, she might fucking kill me before I even got started. But that would be half the fun of it, right? That *is* half the fun of it, right? When they scream and make a fuss?

Fucking and killing. It's not a lot different. That's why they call it *la petite mort*, right?

But this little rabbit isn't the only one confusing the hell out of me. I'm confusing the hell out of myself.

I'm different. I've known that as long as I've understood what the word meant. It may bother the fuck out of everyone else, but it's never bothered me. So I don't do what I should. So I don't act like I should. Yeah, I'm pretty sure my brain doesn't work like it should. So fucking what?

But this, this is different. Because I'm lying on the floor instead of climbing on top of the girl I want to fuck.

"Renzo," she says into the silence. It's the first time she's used my name like that. It has my head snapping her way. "Thank you for Pip, for those families, for … for those men."

I stare at her. "You know I'd do anything for you, little rabbit. Anything at all."

"I asked you not to kill those men."

"Ahhh," I say, my cheeks tugging upwards. "If you ask me to do something fucking stupid, something that's going to get you hurt, then I'm not going to do it." I shrug and her own cheeks tug up into an expression that makes her look a thousand times prettier.

"I've never had this compulsion before," I confess. "You're the first person I've ever wanted to do anything for."

"Marcus Lowsky?" she points out.

"Not the same." I wet my lips. "He wanted me to kill you and I didn't want to do it. So I didn't. Funny, because there were other times he asked me to do things I thought were fucking stupid, I did them anyway."

"I guess you didn't care enough about those things."

"You think I care about you?" I ask her.

A pink color spreads across her cheeks. Even prettier. "Do you?" she whispers.

"I ... I'm not like other people, little rabbit. I see how other people are. They get all scared, all angry, all sad. I was born all wrong. I don't work like other people do." She holds my gaze. "You care about your mates?" I ask her. "The enforcer, the professor, that stuck-up kid?"

"Yes," she says.

"What does that feel like?"

Her eyes flick upwards and she's silent for a moment. "It feels like ... the room lights up when you're with them. Like everything is brighter, more colorful and your heart beats so fast you can hardly breathe. And you want to be with them all the time, so much it hurts to be apart." She chews on her lip. "But mostly you want them to be happy, to be safe. That's more important to you than your own happiness, your own safety."

I nod, turning over her words in my head. "Then I do

care about you, little rabbit," I conclude. "Because that's how it feels."

The corners of her lips tug upwards again. "You're so fucking confusing," she mumbles.

"What's confusing about this?"

She doesn't answer and I reach up and grab her hand from under her cheek, her breath hitching as I do. I take her hand and lift it back to my face.

"I like it when you touch me, little rabbit," I say, and the darkness of her pupils swims wide.

"I like touching you," she murmurs.

"You do, do you?" I say, my voice darker than her eyes. I shift up onto my knees and tug my shirt over my head. "Then touch me some more, little one," I tell her.

19

R hi

I STARE at his bare chest, muscular, solid, covered in scribbled tattoos and unhealed scars. It's chaotic, mesmerizing, totally suited to him. He reminds me of the back of my notebook, doodles scrawled all over the pages.

Shifting to the edge of the scratchy mattress, I let my fingers trail down from his face to his chest. Mostly the scribbles are dates and places and I don't want to think too hard about what those must mean, but in among them there are pictures. A tiny moth by his right hip, its translucent wings fragile on his olive skin. On his right side, there's a cobweb as intricately weaved as the real thing, a spider lurking in its center ready to strike. And right in the middle of his chest, between his pectoral muscles, to the right of his thumping heart, is a crow, mid flight, its black eyes locked straight ahead.

I touch them all, trace the dark lines of the inks, feel the warmth of his skin and the solid strength of his muscles. Muscles that twitch with my touch.

My own heart beats a little faster, my bond flutters in my stomach and I can't deny the way my skin heats.

He hums with satisfaction and I press my whole palm against him, my touch more firm, sweeping my hands over the ridges of his muscles and the grooves of his scars, over his shoulders and up into his dark hair.

The hum morphs to a growl, his eyes turning sinister. My heart beat leaps to my throat. He's so dangerous and yet vulnerable too. Wild, yet starting to be tamed. I think he'd let me do anything to him and to test that theory I scrape my hands down his chest, leaving red marks in their wake.

"Fuuuuuccccckkkk," he growls and then he's captured my hands again, leading them down the grooves of his tightly packed abdomens, lower to the waistband of his jeans. Here he lets go, and with his gaze locked on mine, undoes the buckles of his belt and the buttons on his fly.

My heart beats frantically now, my bond needy and incessant. I'm not sure if I could pull away even if I wanted to. Even though I know I should.

He takes my hand again and leads it down inside his pants, coiling my fingers around his cock, hot and stiff and jerking against my palm.

"Little rabbit," he says, his voice like poison in my ear, smooth and deadly. "You know how to touch me here, right?"

"Y-y-yes," I say and I stroke my fist along the thick length of him, twisting when I come to the head. He shuffles his jeans and his boxers down his hips, freeing himself and gazing down at where I'm holding him.

"Fuck, that looks good, little rabbit. My cock in your paw."

I rub my fist back down to his base and then along to the head again.

He sighs and throws back his head, exposing his throat to me, showing just how much he trusts me.

"You can go harder," he murmurs. "No need to be so fucking gentle."

I shuffle right to the edge of the bed and hold his cock more firmly in my hand, an ache beginning to pulse between my legs.

His eyes flick to look at me, and without warning, he grabs a hold of me and pulls me down onto the floor with him.

I increase the rhythm of my hand, closing my eyes and feeling him pulse beneath my fingers. And then I feel his teeth at my throat.

Have I been a fool? Is this where I finally meet my end? With his cock in my hand and his teeth in my throat, ripping it out?

But he does no such thing. He rakes his teeth down the column of my neck, firm enough to smart, his nose pressed against my skin, trailing after, inhaling my scent, and then he's licking his wet tongue up the scrape he's made, soothing it better, murmuring nonsense words I don't understand.

I sigh, the sensation making my bond giddy and my panties wet. My grip loosens, my rhythm stutters. He growls his displeasure, nipping the point where my neck meets his shoulder. A warning.

I swallow, and continue, continue until I feel his cock jerk once, twice in my hand and then he's spilling his seed

all over my fingers, thick white ropes of it. The salty mascu-
line smell of it punching the air.

"Fuck, little rabbit, fuck," he says, leaning over me,
caging me with his body, staring down into my face with so
much heat, I start to pant. I wait, too frightened to scuttle
away, too hot to want to. What the hell will he do next? And,
as if reading my mind, he says, "Going to touch you back
now."

I close my eyes. This is so wrong, so twisted and sick. I
shouldn't want his hands anywhere near me. But it's what
fate wants. And she must want it for a reason, right? She
must have bound us together for a purpose. I can't believe
it's random – the man sent to kill me, the man destined to be
my mate.

And so I trust in her again, letting him push me back
against the blanket and the hard floor. Let him undo the fly of
my jeans, let him shimmy them all the way down my legs so
I'm lying there in just my top and my panties. There's still
time to stop this. Still time to tell him no. But again, I forget all
the nagging doubts, all the reasons this is suicide, and focus
in on that feeling thrumming deep in my gut, purring with
excitement as he licks his tongue all the way up the inside of
my leg until his nose is nuzzling right into my pussy lips.

"You're going to be a good little rabbit for me now, aren't
you? You're going to let me touch you. You're not going to
make a fuss. You're going to let me hear you scream."

Fear brushes over my skin, but I'm so wet now, there's no
denying how much I want him to touch me, how much I
want to scream for him.

He peers up at me from between my thighs, his pretty
mismatched eyes glinting in the pale light. Then he lifts his
hand to my mouth, tracing his fingers under my chin and up

to my mouth, touching my lips before thrusting his fingers inside my mouth.

"Suck," he commands and I do as he says.

His eyes twinkle with that excitement, then he removes his fingers and yanks away my panties, staring down at me all bare and wet for him.

"Never seen anything so pretty," he murmurs. Then he's thrusting those same fingers deep inside my pussy. I guess I'm pretty turned on, swollen and sensitive, because it feels divine, my hips rising and my elbows giving way beneath me. His gaze sweeps up from my pussy to my face and remains locked there as he massages his fingers inside me. "Tell me what you like," he says, those eyes flicking over my face. Something I'm understanding means he's struggling to read me, unable to understand me.

"Like that," I pant. "Like that."

"You want it hard?" he says, rubbing me with force. "Or soft?" He decreases the pressure.

"Both. All of it."

He nods, his expression serious. He's taking notes.

"And this," he asks. "This is the spot?"

He hits the point inside me that has me crying out, my hips lifting again and my hands scrabbling in the blanket. "Uh huh." I manage to blurt out.

"Hmmm," he says as my pussy flutters around his fingers. "What else do you want, little rabbit? What else do you need?" His eyes are burning hot and all the shame I should be feeling is swept away in my undeniable desire for him.

"Here," I say, parting my pussy lips and showing him with my hand where my clit lies. "I need you to touch me here too."

He examines the place. "Show me how. Show me how you want me to touch you."

I swallow and then ring my clit with my finger as he massages deep inside me. The combination of the two actions has me soaring upwards.

He studies the movements of my finger with an intensity I find mesmerizing. I can't drag my gaze away from his face.

Moans start to fly from my mouth, my body writhing on the blanket. I can feel the orgasm inside me building and building.

"I'm going to come," I tell him.

"Fuck, yes, as loud as you can, little rabbit. I want to hear you scream so fucking badly."

He pushes my hand to one side and presses his thumb to my clit. I'm so overly sensitive he shoots a bolt of electricity straight through my body and I cry out.

He growls, his face wild with excitement now. He flicks me again with his thumb and I scream a second time, my hips rising right off the floor.

"Little rabbit!" he moans. And then he's flicking me hard and fast, his finger moving inside me too, and I lose all control, all reason. The orgasm building inside me is powerful and all-consuming and when it comes, I think for a minute he's shot us through time and space again, because I forget where I am, who I am, why I'm here. For a brief moment, the world disappears and all I am is feeling, swimming through my body, lifting me up and spinning me around. I'm lost like that, drowning in clouds of bliss, and then I float back down to earth, panting as I flutter open my eyes and find him looking straight into them.

"It felt good?" he asks me.

I giggle as I catch my breath. "Yes, just a bit."

He frowns. "Only a bit!"

I giggle again and rest my hand on his cheek. "It's just a way ... it was good, really, really good." I sigh, ecstasy still humming in every one of my nerves.

"Then I'm going to do it again." He rings my sensitive clit with his thumb and I know it isn't going to take a lot to have me screaming again. But once was enough, right? I should put a stop to it now. I succumbed to this. Now I should regain my senses and push his hands away.

I'm weak and foolish though. His touch feels too, too good. And I'm not sure I ever want him to stop touching me even though I have no idea where this will lead.

Could I seriously accept him as my mate? Would the others accept him? I can't see it somehow. Azlan would kill him before I'd even got a chance to explain.

But what will happen when I tell him this isn't permanent? That this doesn't mean we're going to be together?

These are the serious questions I should be asking myself. Instead, I'm swept away again and then I'm falling asleep beside him on the floor, the blanket tangled up around us.

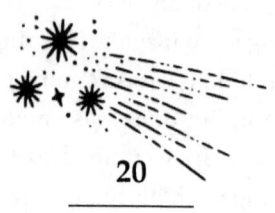

20

S pencer

I EMERGE FROM THE DARKNESS.

Pain.

So much pain. In my leg, in my arm, spearing through my jaw, thumping in my head.

I can't breathe. I can't think.

It hurts. Hurts so much.

The darkness envelops me.

✳

THE DARKNESS FADES. I don't know how much time has passed. The pain hits me again.

Hard and violent.

The darkness races up to meet me again. Promising me sanctuary, escape.

Its tentacles wrap around me, pulling me into the abyss.

This time I resist, pulling against it, even though my body screams with the pain.

I force my eyes open. Only one obeys. Light hitting my pupil like a dagger through the eye. I wince and despite the overwhelming urge to shut it again, strain it open.

I try to lift my right arm but it refuses.

I try the left, first feeling how my other hangs at a grotesque angle from my shoulder, then the way the left side of my face is a puffy, wet mess.

With effort, that has nausea stinging my throat, I peer down my body. I'm naked, covered in blood, my leg twisted and broken.

My vision swoops and this time I can't fight the darkness as it yanks me back down.

THERE'S A VOICE, permeating my sanctuary of darkness. I pull myself back to consciousness, to the here and now.

The voice is louder now, but it takes everything I have to deduce the words.

"Stand up, mutt. They want to talk to you."

I drag my working eye open. A blurry face leers above me.

"I said, get up."

Something hard collides with my ribs and adds to the pain.

More darkness.

But it fades much quicker now. Someone is shouting at me, pulling me to my feet, the pain so vivid I can no longer escape it.

I feel for the beast inside me. But he's silent. I can't find him. Is he out cold too?

What the hell happened?

"Spencer Moreau?"

My good eyelid flutters. I strain to see.

A hand slaps me around the face. My eye pulls into focus.

It's a soldier holding me up. One dressed in the republic's uniform. A man I don't recognize. He's not the man shouting.

I swivel my eyeball, even that movement sending pain spiraling through my head. My gaze is hazy, perhaps untrustworthy, because I swear the man standing next to him is Tristan's father, Christopher Kennedy.

"For goodness' sake," he tuts, "give him some pain relief or we'll never get any straight answers out of him."

"And his injuries, Sir," the soldier says, peering at me with clear disgust. "Should we heal those?"

"He's a mutt. A curseded. Leave him as he is."

"F-f-f-f-fuck you," I stutter, my lips bruised, my tongue heavy.

The soldier scowls at me, draws back his hand and I'm plunged straight down into the abyss.

NEXT TIME I emerge from the gloom, I'm alone again and the pain isn't intense. It's still there, hovering in the background, but it isn't as bad. I can breathe. I can think.

The swelling on my face must have subsided slightly because I can open my wounded eye a little.

The room I find myself in is dark and dank, no windows to the outside world, the walls stone and damp, the air freezing cold. A dungeon, I'm guessing, or a cellar. Am I still at the academy, down in the basement of the ruined mansion? Or am I somewhere else entirely?

I shift my head, even though it has pain shooting down my neck. There's one heavy door on the far side of the room. Shut. There's no one else here. The soldier and Christopher Kennedy – was that really him? – gone.

I assess the damage to my body. The rest of me is just as busted up as it was. A broken leg. A dislocated arm. Fuck knows what to my face.

I search for my magic, determining if there's any chance I could fix this damage. But I'm low, the tank almost empty, barely enough to light a bulb. I also find metal cuffs wrapped around my wrists, my arms chained to the cold wall I'm slumped against, and as I swallow I realize, there's another metal cuff, around my neck.

A collar.

The beast stirs angrily inside me. He's awake now too. I consider shifting our forms. He'd have the strength to bust through these chains, I'm sure. But even as I think it, I sense he's as weak, as bruised and battered as I am. He was the one that endured this beating after all.

I pull feebly on the chain with my good arm. It's not only my magic that's weak. I am too.

Why the hell am I here? Who the hell has chained me to this wall? And what the hell do they want?

I try to think of some way out, some way to escape. I doubt very much that remaining here is going to end well for me. But my head aches and it's hard to assemble the thoughts in my mind; any glimmer of an idea quickly flickering away, my efforts to grab it and make it stay too slow.

I close my eyes. I'm so damn tired and though the pain is weaker, it still has my stomach turning and my jaw tight.

What's the point in remaining awake? There's nothing I can do but wait. Wait for them to return.

It's the sound of heavy boots that wakes me next, followed by the drawing back of heavy locks and the creaking open of the door. A soldier peers through the gap, then swivels his head to talk to the person behind him.

"He's awake."

"Be careful then. He's fucking strong."

"And chained to the wall," the soldier in the doorway says. He swings the door back and they both walk through. The second man lingers by the far wall as if he doesn't trust these chains to keep me bound. I doubt they would usually, but in my current state he has nothing to worry about.

I glare at the two men as the first one stares down at me with a vicious grin.

"On whose orders are you keeping me here?" I snarl.

"The Lord Protector's."

I frown. My head smarting with the effort to think. Lord Protector? Who the hell is that?

"If my mother knew–"

"Your mother?" The first soldier chuckles. "You mean the mutt's whore?"

I smart at the insult, tugging on the chains that bind me, even though I have no strength to give this man a beating.

"She's dead, little pup. Along with your mutt of a father."

"D-d-dead?" I stutter, the word sticking in my throat. My mom. My dad. Dead? That can't be true. This fucker is bull-shitting. Trying to provoke me.

"You're lying," I growl.

"I'm afraid not," another voice says, before Christopher Kennedy steps into my cell. His voice is calm yet sinister, and the cold look in his eyes, the calm expression on his face, makes me shudder. "I sent a group of agents to arrest them both and unfortunately they chose to resist. Most unfortunate. They were killed in the resulting struggle. You have my sympathies."

He looks anything but sympathetic. In fact, he looks freaking elated, and what feeble magic I have sizzles on my fingertips.

"On what grounds were they arrested?"

Christopher Kennedy steps closer until he's looking straight down his crooked nose at me.

For a moment, I wonder how he and Tristan could ever be related. His father's face is always twisted with displeasure. His features sharp and hard. His eyes cold, his demeanor colder still.

"It seems we've had enemies hidden among us. Traitors working with the dark forces in the West. Traitors who helped them launch that attack – an attack we only just averted by the skin of our teeth."

"My parents are not traitors."

"Were," Christopher Kennedy corrects. "And they were. All werebeasts are traitors – abominations to our kind. The chancellor was a fool to ever let you live among us." He sneers at me. "I am no such fool. I will not allow it."

"What the f–"

"You'll be remaining here, Moreau, locked up where you can not harm our people, where you cannot consort with our enemies."

"Remain? You can't do this."

"I can," he says. "I'm in charge now."

"But Tristan – he'll tell you – I'm no enemy, no spy, no danger."

"No danger?" he scoffs. "You attacked seven of my men who were simply trying to detain you."

"They attacked me," I growl.

"But I also hear you attacked a pupil at the academy. A poor defenseless girl."

"I ... I ..." My gaze drops to the floor in shame.

"See, you are a danger. Probably even to yourself. Here is where you belong and here is where you will stay. Be thankful you haven't met the same demise as your traitorous parents."

Shame mixes with the pain and bile rises in my throat. Is he right? Is this where I belong, locked away where I can't hurt anyone?

"Why did you attack Rhianna Blackwaters, Moreau?"

"Wh-what?" The bile sinks down my throat, and I look back up at his face. Calculating now.

"Pig girl – I hear that's what you students call the girl." I flinch. "You attacked her several weeks ago. What provoked you?"

"It wasn't me," I say feebly, "it was the beast." The beast bristles inside me as if outraged at my betrayal.

"This is the pathetic excuse the chancellor gullibly swallowed for all these years. You're one and the same – both dirty, deranged mutts," he spits. "Why the Blackwaters girl? You were at the academy for three years and she was the only one you ever exposed your true nature to."

"I can't pretend to understand the mind of the beast. We are not the same. We are different."

"Nonsense!" Christopher Kennedy shouts, making the two soldiers in the cell jolt. "There must have been a reason. What is it about this girl? What is special about her?"

"She isn't special. She's a nobody from–"

Christopher Kennedy scoffs. "I've heard that before and I don't believe it. Tell me the reason."

I glare up at him and don't say a word.

He examines my stubborn face. Does he believe me? I

doubt it. He must know his nephew is bonded to her. Does he know about her other mates too? About the professor? About his son?

"If you refuse to tell me, Moreau, then we'll have to find a way to loosen your tongue." He nods to the first soldier, who steps forward cracking his knuckles.

He grins at me, his stupid face flashing with malice.

Then he draws back his fist like he did before and hits me square on the chin. My head flies back with the force of the blow and I feel the bone crack, see stars dart across my vision. The pain splinters through my skull, igniting all that pain from before.

I take a deep inhale, then rock my head forward. I spit blood out onto the floor and glare up at the soldier rubbing his bruised knuckles.

"You get a kick out of beating a bound man?" I ask him. "You want to unchain me and make this a fair fight?"

"I get a kick out of beating a monster like you," he spits and then he hits me again. And again. And again.

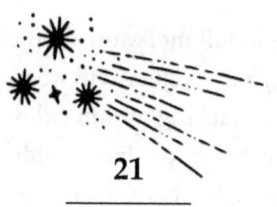

21

T ristan

MY FATHER WANTS to retain a semblance of normality, convince all the people – magicals and normals alike – that nothing has changed and anything that has is for the better. The chancellor may be locked away in a cell somewhere, along with other 'enemies' of the state, but things will continue as they always have. Only now, under the Lord Protector's care, we'll all be safer.

Does anyone actually believe that bullshit? Or are they just too spineless to complain, to protest, to ask the obvious questions?

It doesn't matter. He wants me back at the academy and Ellie back at her father's house. I have little choice but to obey. He's having me guarded around the clock by the best of his men, and while I'm sure I could out-power them one-on-one, I face little chance one-on-four, especially when I'm still recovering, still building back my powers, still weakened by my separation from Rhi.

Perhaps when I'm back at the academy, I'll have more opportunities to slip away. More chances of finding out what's happened to Azlan and the professor, to Spencer and Winnie. To Rhi. I can feel her through the bond, distant, and though I strain with all my might to get a better read on her emotions, on where the hell she is, it's useless.

Yes, the academy is the best place for me. The separation from my mate has me feeling half mad; pain I can't understand lingers in my gut and the temptation to do something stupid, to tear down the world just to get to her, is severe and ever-looming. Acting normal – like I don't give a shit about anything – like I'm not dying inside because of this separation – is becoming harder and harder. Especially under my father's watchful eyes. At least at the academy, it won't be him watching me.

He has his men drive me back to the academy – one sitting either side of me in the back seats, as if they half expect me to jump from the speeding car. It's mighty fucking tempting. But I remain where I am, my nails digging deep into my palms, so fucking deep I'm drawing blood. I watch as the hill comes into view, the academy resting on its brow. Work to rebuild has already begun, scaffolding ringing what remains of the burned-out carcass of the mansion.

Once again, my mind is drawn to those dragons. Where did they come from? And more importantly where did they go?

It makes no fucking sense. The Western forces were winning, they were beating us. They had dragons for fuck's sake. Why did they retreat? There was no reason, no need. They could have overtaken the republic completely.

I'm beginning to suspect that nothing was as it seemed. That those soldiers weren't from the West at all. That the entire attack was all my father's doing. His chance to grab control.

It's a thought that's still niggling away at me as the car comes to a halt outside what remains of the mansion and one of the men opens the door, sliding out and then waiting for me to do the same. He stands guard beside me as the principal comes hurrying across the gravel towards me. She looks immaculate as always, dressed in her usual tweed suit, but there's something different about her demeanor. She seems skittish, nervous, she twists her hands against her skirt and she offers me a look of consolation.

"Mr. Kennedy, I'm so pleased to have you back but so very sorry to hear about your mother. She was a," she hesitates, "wonderful woman."

"Thank you," I say, "she was."

"Well, returning to the academy – to a sense of normalcy will help, I'm sure. Although, as you can imagine, we are all shaken." She lifts her hand and rests it on my shoulder, then turns to the guard by my side. "Mr. Kennedy will be safe from here. The Lord Protector has increased security at the academy. We are in no danger." Her eyes flick behind me and I twist my head to find a pair of soldiers patrolling the boundary of the academy.

Are they here to keep danger out or me in?

The guard gives the principal a courteous nod before returning to the vehicle. And the principal gently nudges me to walk around the perimeter of the ruined mansion.

"We're hoping it will all be repaired in a couple of months. Good as new with some added security measures your father has devised included. In the meantime, we've erected some temporary classrooms and a canteen." As we walk around the building work, I see tents scattered across the grounds including a giant marque I'm guessing is the new food hall. "Luckily, your dorm building encountered very little damage and it was repaired as a priority. I'll let you return there now, Tristan, and get yourself settled. Dinner will be served at the slightly early time of 7:15pm from now on to allow for your father's daily broadcast afterwards." She balks slightly, her eyes dashing to mine in alarm. I pretend I haven't noticed. "Mandatory attendance, of course."

"Of course," I say smiling, waiting as she turns and returns in the direction of the building works. When she's out of sight, I pick up my feet, racing along the academy pathways, passing students who gape as I pass them, crashing through the dormitory doorway and up the staircase.

I halt at the door, lift my fist and pound on the wood.

At first there's no answer, and I pound harder, louder this time, the door shaking in its frame. Another minute passes and then it draws back and Summer Clutton-Brock stands in the doorway.

Her hair is shorter than the last time I saw her – the night of the ball – skimming her chin, and her skin looks so pale it's almost translucent – none of that usual bronze tan all the cheerleaders sport.

Her eyes land on me and several emotions flurry over her face – shock, jubilation, fear.

Yeah, she should be fucking scared. She should be fucking terrified.

She regains a hold of her emotions, pulling her face into one of excitement.

"Tristan! You're back. I'm so fucking pleased. The last few days without you have been–"

I shove her backwards and into her room, slamming the door behind me.

"You broke it. You broke the fucking binding promise."

The smile on her lips wavers ever so slightly.

"What? What are you talking about, Tris? I never broke any–"

"You did. I felt it. I told you I'd know if you broke it."

"I didn't break any stupid promise," she says, the smile turning sour.

I grab her by the throat and slam her into the nearest wall. She scrabbles at my fingers and I squeeze, squeeze until she's gasping for air.

"You think I'm stupid? An idiot? Is that it, Summer?" Her face turns bright red, her long fingernails scratch at my skin. "You broke it. We both know it. So who the hell did you tell?"

She scowls at me and sends a sharp zap of magic right into my gut.

I grunt, the pain making my eyes water, but I keep a hold of her throat, shaking her this time.

"Are you deaf?"

She blasts more magic my way, much more forceful this time, blowing us apart. I stumble backwards, watching as she gasps for air. Then I'm on her again, this time twisting her around, and banging her face-first into the wall.

She grunts, then scrabbles to break free, blasting magic my way which I bat away like it's an annoying fucking mosquito.

"Unless you tell me, right now, I'm going to fucking kill you, Summer Clutton-Brock."

"You can't!" she screeches. "You can't treat me this way. Your father promised to protect me. He promised you wouldn't be able to lay a finger on me."

"So it was him you told?" I laugh. "You really are fucking stupid, aren't you, Summer? You believed what my father told you? You trusted him? You should know Christopher Kennedy is a lying snake, one that will sink his poisonous fangs into you the first chance he gets."

"You're wrong, Tristan Kennedy," she taunts. "He admires me. He values me. So you'd better start treating me with respect."

"You have to earn respect," I snarl.

"Get your hands off me right now. I've already alerted campus security. Your father abhors violence towards women. His men will beat you to a pulp – just like your disgusting mutt of a friend."

"What?" I say, letting her go and stumbling backwards. "What did you say?"

She twists around, hugging her body to the wall, a cruel smile spreading across her lips – one I've seen directed at her victims many times before, never at me.

"Daddy didn't tell you? Your friend," she spits out the word like Spencer was never anything to her, "has been locked away – like all his kind – locked away where they can't do any harm. Frankly, I think they should be exterminated. It's what I told your father."

"Stars help me, Summer Clutton-Brock. I am going to kill you," I hiss, raising my hands, ready to strike her. And it's in that moment, with dark intentions – sinister, evil ones – swimming through my veins that I first feel it. Something dark in my magic. Something ... scarlet.

Crimson magic.

A *touch* of crimson magic. Not mine. Rhianna's.

So this is how it happened. How we sealed the bond. When we were fighting side by side, her magic entered me – and mine? Did mine enter her?

The thought of it has me shivering from the top of my head to the tips of my toes.

In the distance, I hear heavy boots on the staircase. Summer wasn't lying. Campus security is on its way. Would they really lay a finger on me? Tristan Kennedy – the Lord fucking Protector's son. I don't know. I don't know what to believe anymore. The world has turned upside down. Everything I thought I knew unraveling before my eyes.

My mom dead. Spencer locked away. Rhianna gone.

"You're too late, Tristan Kennedy," Summer says with glee.

I peer down at my hands. Crimson magic? Could I wield it? Do I want to wield it? Because if I did, would I be any better than him? Would I be just like him?

I glance back up at Summer and something glints around her neck. A necklace. No. A locket. Piglet's locket.

I stride forward, the bravado vanishing from Summer's face as she cowers away from me. I grab a hold of the chain and yank it clean away from her neck.

Then I get the hell out of there before I do something I'll regret.

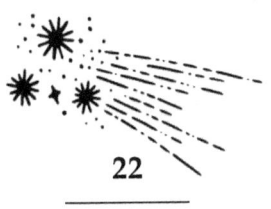

22

A zlan

I STRIDE STRAIGHT UP to those compound gates and it takes them several slow minutes to work out who I am and why the hell I'm here. I'm still dressed in my fucking suit. No cloak today.

"The enforcer!" someone yells. And then all hell breaks loose, magic shooting in all directions. I deflect and batter it away, not even breaking stride as I blow the compound gates clean away, and walk straight through into the heart of the Wolves of Night's lair.

I'm angry. I've never been so angry and it's hot and scalding and raw in my veins; my magic feeling stronger, more deadly than it ever did before.

Several men rush at me at once but I send them all scattering like dominoes and I keep walking, aware of Winnie and Stone deflecting and firing magic behind me.

I swing my gaze around. Where is she?

I grab the next fucker who comes for me by the scruff of his neck, and lift him clean off his feet.

"Where is she? Where's the girl?"

He looks at me with utter confusion.

"Girl?" he repeats. "There is no girl."

He's lying. She has to be here somewhere.

"Where's Barone? Where's Renzo Barone?"

"Barone?" He looks just as confused. "Missing. He hasn't been seen in days."

"And where was he last seen?" I yell at him as magic whistles right above our heads, making the hair on his head swoosh backwards. Another follows on its heels, narrowly missing the man's ear.

He gulps and attempts to struggle free.

"I asked you a question," I say, shaking him so hard his bones rattle.

"At the attack. At the attack on the academy."

So he *was* there. We were right.

"And where is he now? Where did he take her?"

"Who?" he says, looking utterly confused.

I throw him to the floor and he hits it so hard, he's knocked unconscious.

I survey the rest of the men. Scraps and scrabblers. This isn't the heart of the Wolves of Night. These are the remains.

"Who's in charge?" I yell out, sweeping my arms around and disabling all the magic in the fingertips of the few magicals lurking among the gang members.

It's easy, like whipping candy from a baby, my magic so much stronger, it's laughable.

Desperate looks flitter among the gaggle of men – chickens with their heads cut off. Without their leader they don't know what they're doing.

I turn to Stone and Winnie.

"We need to search this place. We need to be certain she's not here."

"Azlan," Phoenix says, taking a hold of my arms. "I can read these men's minds."

Right, mind reading. I'm a fucking fool. "And?"

He shakes his head, pain in his eyes. "She's not here. Barone's not here either. They haven't been here at all." He lowers his voice to a whisper. "Barone hasn't been seen nor heard from since the attack on the academy."

"You think he's dead?" I ask him, watching the desperate men.

Phoenix shrugs. "No. I still think Barone has her."

"Then what are you fucking standing there for, Phoenix," I snap. "Read one of these fucker's minds and work out where he's taken her."

Phoenix gives me a look that says he'd like to strangle me, but answers my demand calmly. "You think I haven't done that already? Not one of these men here knows a thing about the assassin, other than he's off his fucking rocker."

I groan, and scrub my hand against my eyes. It makes sense. The assassin has always operated as a lone wolf. No friends, no family, no associates. It's one of the many reasons it's been so hard to track him down.

"It's okay," my friend says. "We'll find her."

But I'm not so sure, a sense of desperation grips me around the throat and I struggle to breathe. Every time I attempt to reach her, I fail. She's too damn far away and not knowing – not knowing she's safe is like torture.

I stomp back the way we came, halfway through the broken gateway, when Stone calls out to me.

"Azlan, wait!"

"What?" I call back. I can't bear it. Can't bear the possibility, the suspense.

He doesn't answer me and I peer over my shoulder to find Stone towering over a kneeling man, Winnie hovering at his shoulder.

"Something about a girl," Stone says, eyes fixed on the quaking man. "I saw something in your mind about a girl. Tell me or I'll force it out." He grins. "Probably taking most of your senses with me. Do you fancy being a quivering, mumbling wreck for the rest of your life?"

The man stares up at him, confusion on his face.

"If you're looking for her, you already know."

"Know what?" Phoenix says as I storm towards them.

The man eyes me nervously. "Haven't you heard? There's a new bounty on that girl's head. That's the one you're looking for, right? The one that killed Lowsky's brother. They want her captured and brought in alive."

Phoenix glances at me. His face is as stone-like as his name but I read the concern in his eyes.

"Who?" I grunt. "Who's offering the reward? The," I cringe, "Lord Protector?"

"I hear there's more than one offering such a reward."

"Who else?" Stone asks.

"I don't know. It's just a rumor I heard from some of the other men. I don't even know if it's true."

Stone stares straight into the kneeling man's eyes and I know he's checking to see if the man is lying or not.

"Where are those men now?"

"No idea. They left."

"Why?"

"Probably out searching for the girl too."

"What ... what reward are they offering for her capture?" Winnie asks from behind me.

The man mutters a figure.

Winnie gasps and that concern in Phoenix's eyes turns to alarm.

We're not the only ones who are going to be out looking for her and that reward is a very strong incentive for all the lowlifes and scumbags out there. Our urgency to find her just racked up tenfold.

✴.

"WHY THE FUCK hasn't she tried to contact us?" I say with irritation as we make our way back to the hidden car, taking a round about route through the trees, even though the members of the Wolves of Night seem to possess no desire to attack or engage us. In fact, they seem mighty happy to let us leave.

"The communication lines have been down," Phoenix points out.

"They're back up now," I say gruffly.

"Yes," Phoenix says patiently as if talking to a particularly obtuse child, "but she could be dealing with two situations. She may have realized that there are people out hunting for her, in which case getting on the end of her cell and broadcasting to the world her location would be stupid. Who knows who might be tracking her phone." He looks at me pointedly, reminding me that, yeah, I'd done exactly that myself. "Or," he swallows, his face distorting, "she's being held captive and has no way of getting to a communication device."

"She could still try to reach us through the bond," I say sulkily, kicking at the dead leaves on the ground.

It's damn cold out here in the wastelands, and my toes and fingers are frozen stiff.

"Azlan," Stone says, this time with a little more frustration. "You can feel how great the distance is. For all we know she may be trying to reach us, like we've been trying to reach her, and failing."

"Those men hadn't seen her or Renzo," Winnie says, from my other side. She's been silent since we left, obviously mulling things over. "If he's handed her in, collected the reward, wouldn't we have heard? Wouldn't those men have heard?"

"We don't even know who *is* looking for her," Phoenix points out.

"My uncle – my uncle will be looking for her," I say with certainty. The man is shrewd. He'll have figured things out by now and he'll be keen to investigate the girl and her capabilities, her powers. He'll want to know if she's a threat or something he can use to his own advantage.

"Christopher Kennedy?" Winnie asks.

"The Lord fucking Protector himself," I say with disgust.

"If he had her, Tristan would know and he would have let us know."

"Tristan can't be trusted," I say.

Winnie considers this for a moment. "I think he can be. I think he wouldn't want Rhi to fall into his father's hands."

"You didn't see how lovesick the guy was acting these last few weeks, Az. I think Winnie is right."

I'm not so sure but I listen as Winnie continues thinking aloud.

"So if Barone hasn't handed her in–"

"He's probably torturing her somewhere," I snap.

"No, I think St ... Professor Stone may be right. I think she could be on the run, hiding from those who are chasing her."

"Miss Wence," my friend says with a genuine smile.

"While I'm honored with the level of respect you continue to show me, I think it time we dispense with the formalities, you may call me Stone. Or perhaps you'd prefer the nickname you and Rhianna devised for me?"

Winnie's cheeks pinken in the cold.

"What was it?" I say.

"Where would she go?" Winnie asks, clearly changing the subject. "If she were on the run, where would she go?"

We're quiet again as we consider this, the frozen leaves crunching beneath our boots.

"The only place she knew other than the academy was her home," Phoenix says.

"She wouldn't be stupid enough to return there," I say. "It would be too dangerous. Too many people know it was her home."

"Didn't she already go back there once?" Phoenix points out. "Even with an assassin on her tail."

"She had her reasons," Winnie says in her friend's defense, "and we dealt with said assassin, thank you very much." Winnie glares at us both. "I think we should go back there."

"I'm telling you, it's too dangerous. And she won't be there."

"And I'm telling you, it's the only potential lead we have. And even if Rhi isn't there, there might be other clues – hints of other places she knows, people she may have gone to for help."

"There are no such people," Phoenix says. "She was all alone."

We walk on. The forest is quiet. The ground hard. The air turning more and more frigid.

All alone. She was all alone. I've spent much of my adult life alone, hunting, chasing, pursuing. It's been a lonely job but I've always had Phoenix and Ellie to come back to. I've never been properly alone in the world. I can't imagine what that must have felt like, how she must have felt.

It makes the guilt for the way we treated her ten times worse.

Well, she's not alone anymore. She has us and we're going to find her.

"Okay," I say at last. "We'll go check out her house."

23

R^{hi}

I'M RUNNING, running as fast as I can, my chest heaving as I gasp
for breath, my arms and my legs aching, my throat raw and dry.
I keep running, keep pushing onwards. I need to get there. It's
important that I do – vital.

I need to reach the beast. I need to find it. It's injured, hurt,
dying, its life source draining away. Only I can heal it. Only I can
save it.

It's important that I do. Fate is insistent. It's my destiny to
save the creature. I cannot fail.

I WAKE UP WITH A START, my heart racing, my body bathed in
a layer of cold sweat, the strange dream still vivid in my
mind.

An injured creature. I had to save an injured creature.

Immediately, I'm up on my knees, and scrabbling along the floor until I find Pip laid out on the bed.

"Pip?" I say, resting my hand on his little body. "Pip?"

His eyes open a little and then drift shut again. His skin is hot, his body quivering.

What the hell is wrong with him? I stroke my hand down his body.

In my dream I needed to heal a creature – a beast. Was it Pip? Have I neglected him? Did I trust too much in Renzo's opinion? Should I be trying to heal him now?

I close my eyes and feel through his body with my magic. I can feel no injuries, no wounds. All I feel is the remnants of magic – is that the magic that struck him? I try to tug at it, to pull it away, but it's as if it's welded to his very soul, weaved into his very bones.

"Oh Pip," I say, resting my forehead against his. I've always taken him for granted. Always. He's always been with me, by my side, giving me courage when I've lacked it, support when I've had none, a friendly face when I've needed one. I can't lose him. I can't bear to lose him.

"Is he no better, little rabbit?" Renzo says, from somewhere behind me. It's dark in the little cabin and the temperature has dropped. I shudder, wiping away tears from my eyes.

"No better. He's never been sick before. In all the years we've had him. Not once."

"Never?"

"Unless, you count the times he's scoffed himself silly and made himself vomit. But I don't think that counts." I manage a smile, swiping away at another tear.

Renzo comes to kneel beside me and looks down at the

pig. "He doesn't seem any worse, little rabbit, and that's a good thing."

"Is it?" I say, hopefully, one minute eager to reject any advice from this man, now happy to latch onto it.

"Yeah." He strokes Pip's ear.

"I dreamed I was meant to save him. That I was meant to heal him."

"I told you, little rabbit, you just got to give him time."

"You don't understand," I say, shaking my head. "It seemed so real."

"Dreams always do."

"But mine ..." I peer at the assassin through the darkness. He's dressed in just his jeans, his hair ruffled, his eyes sleepy. He looks more boyish than ever. "My mom was a seer."

"Yeah, I heard that," he says. And somehow I'm not surprised. "You ... you think this was the same, little rabbit?"

"I used to have these dreams when I was little. They'd seem so real. And sometimes they'd ..." I stare down at Pip, watching as his frail ribcage lifts and falls.

"Come real."

"Yes. But then they stopped. Just like that. And I never had another – I didn't really dream at all."

"Until just now?" he asks, intrigued.

I shake my head. "I dreamed of you. Several months back, I dreamed of you. I dreamed you were trying to strangle me, to squeeze the breath out of me."

Renzo chuckles. "Fuck me, I'd love to squeeze that throat of yours, little rabbit." He leans and whispers into my ear. "You know it would make everything feel even fucking better."

I twist my head and peer into his eyes. I think I could be

tempted to do all manner of dangerous things with this man.

But the dream buzzes around my head, pulling at my attention.

"What if I am seer – like my mom? What if this dream meant something? What if I am supposed to heal Pip and I can't?"

Renzo settles backwards, crossing his legs and resting his chin in his hands. "Tell me about the dream. Tell me all about it."

I close my eyes. I can see it vividly in my head, just as clear as that film he'd conjured into the air. I watch it play out against my eyelids, describing it to him in detail. When I'm done, I open my eyes, and he leans back.

"Pip's no beast, little rabbit. I don't think that dream is about him. You've tried healing him. So have I. He's sick. He's going to get better. And that dream–"

"It wasn't just any old dream!"

"Maybe," he says. "But what it means isn't clear. Not yet."

I feel a little comforted by his words but the dream still consumes my thoughts. I want to talk it through with Stone, with Winnie, heck even with Azlan. I miss them all and the separation from my mates is painful, even with the draught Renzo's been giving me. Are they feeling that too?

Is Tristan?

I lay my hands on my belly.

The pain when Azlan and I were apart after we first bonded was unbearable – so strong I felt like my entire body was being subjected to the cruelest form of torture. That pain didn't fade until we started to sleep together. Is Tristan enduring that right now? Is he okay? A guilt about it swims through my body. Tristan hasn't been good to me. He's treated me like shit. He's spoken to me like I was a piece of shit. But he also saved my life – sacrificed his own for mine. No matter how hard I try, I can't feel as angry at him as I was. I can feel myself softening.

"Renzo," I say. "I know you want to protect me. I know you want to keep me safe. But I'm safest with my mates. I think you know that really and I need to get back to them."

"There are bad people out there hunting for you, little rabbit."

"There have always been bad people hunting for me. And I spent the first twenty years of my life hiding away from them, running away. I … I can't do that any longer. I need my mates. I need my friends."

The assassin is silent. He tilts his head from one side to the other as if weighing up the decision in his mind.

"I didn't think fate gave a shit about me. I didn't think anyone did," he says without a trace of self-pity, "that was unless I was trying to kill them." The right side of his mouth lifts. "Then they cared about me a lot. But fate, nah! I thought she'd cast me to the curbside long ago. Didn't give a shit. I was wrong. She gave me you. Gave you me. She has something in mind for me. I don't know what that is any more than I know what your dream means, little rabbit. But I'm thinking I'm destined to follow you so that's what I'm going to do. You want to go find your mates, then that's what we'll do."

"You're going to come with me?"

"Need to keep you safe, little rabbit. You have a habit of hopping straight into trouble."

"Yeah," I say, "I do." I smile at him, but it soon fades. "You know they'll kill you?"

"Who?" he asks, his eyes flashing like he likes that idea.

"The man in black, Stone. Probably Tristan and Spencer too."

"I'm like a cat. One of those mangy street cats. I have nine lives. You don't need to worry about me."

"So you'll take me to Los Magicos? You'll transport us there?"

He shakes his head. "Too dangerous." I start to argue but he points at my pig. "I don't think the little man could handle it."

"So how will we get there?" I say with frustration. "You said there'd be soldiers out on all the roads."

"We'll go the long way. Over the mountains."

"Over the mountains?" I stare at him in disbelief. He really is crazy. "That isn't even possible."

"Little rabbit, you really do underestimate me." He leans forward and, before I know what he's doing, he pinches my chin between his finger and thumb and stares into my face, his only millimeters from my own. "Everyone always does," he says, and then presses his mouth to mine and kisses me.

The two of us have thrown our lot in with fate now. Both trusting that she knows what the hell she's doing. And so, when the assassin kisses me – hard and incessant, seeking out my tongue with his – I kiss him back. Just as hard, just as incessant, just as needy.

We pack a few supplies from the hut into a rucksack, take some of the warm clothes stuffed in a tiny chest of drawers, wrap Pip up into a blanket and set off into the night, me desperate to start moving, Renzo adamant it's too dangerous to stay in one place for more than one day.

It's far colder outside than it was in the little hut, the sky heavy with a blanket of cloud and wisps of snow fluttering around us. I wrap the scarf I took around my head, my eyes tearing as a wind sweeps through the foothills of the mountains, and peer up at the peaks.

Out here in the open, my head is much clearer, not clouded by the proximity of Renzo or the masculinity of his scent. And I wonder again if I'm doing the right thing. If I'm trusting the right person. The mountains loom above us, tall and menacing and I can't see how any person could possibly scale them. Then again, Renzo Barone is like no other person I've ever met. He sees things in a different way, I'm learning that. He looks on challenges that others have labeled impossible, crazy, suicidal, and sees opportunity. Fun, even.

We follow what I think must be paths cut through the scrub by mountain goats. They weave up the hillsides, only wide enough for us to walk one behind the other and soon we're trudging through snow, more of it blowing in our faces and catching in my eyelashes. To my surprise, despite the bitter conditions, our progress is fair, and before long we're high above the land below. I stop to catch my breath and gaze down through the falling snow. The valley and the land – the few buildings that bedeck them – are small and tiny like pieces on a chessboard. As if I could reach out and pick them up with my hand.

Renzo places the sleeping Pip, wrapped in a bundle of blankets, on the ground, and comes to stand behind me, wrapping his arms around my middle and resting his chin on my shoulder.

"You see all that, little rabbit, I think it could all be yours." I frown, unclear what he means. "I think you could have it all if you wanted to."

"I ... I don't understand."

"It never occurred to you, little rabbit?"

"What?"

"You're special. The black Prince's daughter. Maybe you're the one who should be ruling this country. Not the chancellor. Not the authorities. Not Lowsky or those jerks from the West. You, little rabbit."

I frown harder and push him away. Is this why he wants me? The real reason?

"With you by my side, I suppose. Ruler of all the land."

"Yes, little rabbit. We could rule it all," he says, not hearing the sarcasm in my voice.

"And my other mates?"

"You're angry?" He attempts to grab my hand.

"It doesn't matter," I say, with irritation, reaching down to pick up Pip. "Let's keep moving. It's freaking freezing out here."

I hug my coat around Pip and hold him close to my body – partly to ensure he's warm and partly because he's acting like a mini hot-water bottle.

We climb some more. The terrain becoming steeper and more craggy, large, jagged rocks frame our path, the snow deeper, my breath hanging in clouds in front of my face. I can see the peak of this first mountain above us, the ridges of it sharp against the sky like the tooth of a predator piercing the silver clouds. It makes me shudder, but we don't stop. Soon we're scurrying over and down the other side, the valley and the land lost behind us, and we enter the heart of the mountains, more peaks rising up in front of us.

Renzo tugs a bottle of water from his bag and insists I drink, before taking a swig himself and then pouring a little into Pip's mouth. Pip wriggles in my arms, his eyes screwed shut, but he gulps it down. I murmur some words of comfort to him, kissing his head, as that strange dream rumbles around my mind.

And it's in that moment that a roar pierces the silent night, so loud, so fierce, it shakes the ground beneath our feet.

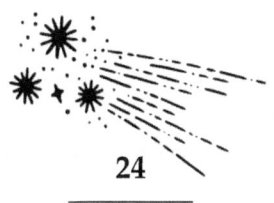

24

S tone

I KNOW AS SOON as Winnie's tin-can of a car screeches to a halt in the meadow that Rhi isn't there and I flop forward and bury my head in my hands. This is fucking hopeless. We're fucking hopeless. What kind of fucking useless fated mates are we if we can't even find our girl?

"She's not here," I say to Winnie, because Azlan must already know.

"Okay," Winnie says, nodding, her hands still poised on the steering wheel. "Okay. Well, we knew that was most likely going to be the case, but it was worth a try and I say we still search the place."

I lift my head from my hands and attempt to peer out of the window. It's covered in a layer of thick grime but through it I can just about make out Rhi's house, the one she was living in when we found her. I only caught a glimpse of it that day but it definitely didn't look like this – the front door kicked in, the windows all smashed, the walls marked with soot. It looks like someone tried to burn the place down. Anger spirals through my veins. What bunch of fuckers did that to her home? I doubt they've left anything intact, anything behind.

"I think we're going to find jack shit in there," I say, but Winnie's not to be deterred. She's out of the driver's seat and already striding to the house.

"Woah, there, Miss speedy pants," I hiss, jogging to her side and grabbing her arm. "Less haste, more speed, okay? There may be some ... unsavory types lurking inside."

"In there?" she says with skepticism, pointing to the wreck of the house. She has a point. It isn't exactly the ideal hang-out spot.

I probe for any whirring minds lurking inside and I find nothing. "I can't hear anyone," I tell my friend. "You wanna check?"

I keep a hold of Winnie's arm and let Azlan pass through the doorway first. We hear his heavy boots stomping through the building and then he calls out, "All clear."

Winnie yanks her arm from my grip and hurries inside and I shove my hands in my pockets and follow after her.

I'm intrigued to see where Rhi lived. The girl is still a goddamn mystery to me – so many things I don't know about her. I'm sure this house will reveal all sorts of things to me. But I'm also reluctant to step inside. Someone has violated her home, and it's like they've violated Rhi herself. It makes me feel sick.

Inside the place is a mess. It's clear someone did try to burn the place down and failed, or perhaps they lit a fire that got out of control. The living room is a charred mess, nothing having survived the flames. The rest of the place, though trashed, has fared slightly better. Winnie disappears up the staircase and I find Azlan standing in the kitchen, cans, boxes and packets strewn all over the floor.

"She was here," he says with certainty.

"How can you tell?"

"Her scent."

I shake my head, disappointed. "She came back here a few weeks ago, remember?"

"No," he says, his eyes gleaming with a renewed hope. "It was more recent than that." He closes his eyes and inhales, his broad chest expanding as he sucks in the air. "Only a few days ago. She can't be far from here, Phoenix."

I scoff. "Azlan, she's with Barone. He could have taken her anywhere he wanted."

My friend's shoulders sink in disappointment. As he opens his eyes, Winnie enters the kitchen.

"Anything?" I ask her.

"It looks like someone was staying in her bedroom. The bed looks slept in."

"Azlan thinks she was here a few days ago. But she's gone now. And where ..." I trail off.

"Shit," Winnie says, the first time I think I've ever heard miss-goodie-two-shoes curse. She up-rights one of the toppled kitchen chairs and sinks down onto it, pulling a jar filled with herbs towards her and shaking them in her hands. "We must be missing something. There must be a way to find her. You're fated mates for goodness' sake." She slams the jar back down on the tabletop. It skids along the surface, toppling over and rolling towards the edge. I catch it before it falls off the table and place it down more carefully on the top.

"Tambric spice," I say, "wouldn't want that exploding into the air."

"Tambric spice?" Winnie says, her eyes leaping to mine, then the jar and then back to mine again.

"Yeah," I say. "One of the foster dads I stayed with used to rub it into our skin if we," I scowl, "misbehaved."

Winnie winces. "That's awful."

"Yeah," I say, eyeing the content of the jar with disgust.

"But it can be used for other stuff too, right? I'm sure I read ..." She pulls out her phone from her pocket, then curses again. "There's no internet signal out here."

"Don't tell me, you want to log on and check your social media?" I say sarcastically. "You think Rhi's posted her whereabouts?"

"No!" she says. "I wanted to check something. I'm sure I read something about Tambric spice and fated mate bonds."

I stare at her, open-mouthed, then grab the jar and lift it to my face.

Tambric spice! Fuck, yes. I read that too in one of those many, many, many fucking text books, journals and periodicals I read on the subject.

"It can be used to enhance a fated mate pair's ability to communicate over distance. It can strengthen the bond," I say, staring at the dried leaves. A purple color I've loathed ever since that fucker rubbed the stuff all over my back. It's hard to like a color when it's caused you so much pain.

"Are you sure?" Azlan says, stepping towards me. He looks dubious as he takes the jar from my hand.

I rub my temples, straining to remember that page, to see it in my mind's eye. "I think so."

Azlan hands it back to me. "You think so," he says flatly.

"I'm almost 100 percent sure."

"Almost?"

"Pretty certain."

"Pretty?"

"I remember reading it," Winnie says, "when I was helping Rhi with her," she waggles a finger at Azlan, "problem."

"Can you remember how to use it?" I ask her.

She considers this, then shakes her head with disappointment. Azlan huffs in irritation and I don't blame him. Every time we seem to gain a step forward, it ends up being a false lead. We have Tambric spice. We think it could help us. We can't remember how the fuck to use it.

"We could experiment with it?" Winnie suggests.

"I'm guessing you've never had an encounter with the stuff?" She shakes her head. "Trust me," I say bitterly, "it isn't something you want to be experimenting with."

"Crap." Winnie chews on her lip. "I can see the stupid page in my head. I can remember where the damn recipe sat, right over there in the top right-hand corner. I just can't ..." Her eyes flick up to me. "But you could."

"I could, what?"

"You could read it."

"What?" I say, sounding just as annoyed as Azlan.

"You could read the memory in my head, couldn't you? You could see it and read the instructions."

"Reading memories isn't as," I exhale, "pleasant as reading real-time thoughts, Miss Wence. For you, I mean. For me ..." I shrug.

"How unpleasant?"

"Like having your tooth pulled. Without magic to numb the pain."

Winnie sits up straight in her chair. "I'm no wimp, Professor. I have the worst period pains you can imagine–"

"Okay," I say, waving my hand, definitely not needing to hear about that.

"I'm not afraid. And frankly, I'd walk over burning coals and drink poison for Rhi. She saved my life."

"And mine," Azlan says quietly.

Winnie nods. "So, a little discomfort while you scrabble about in my mind is worth it if we can find her and bring her home."

"All right." I place the jar back on the table and roll up my sleeves. "Azlan, I'm going to need you to make a note of what I find. I may only catch a fleeting glimpse and it may not be long enough for me to memorize it."

Azlan swings his gaze, before opening drawers under the countertops. He retrieves a pen, and licking the nib, tests it on a scrap piece of paper he scoops up from the floor.

"Ready?" I ask Winnie. She nods. "Azlan?"

"Ready."

"How long ago was this memory?"

"Back when Rhi was in the hospital."

I rest my fingertips on Winnie's forehead and close my eyes, letting my mind wander into hers. First, I'm presented with a picture of myself, leaning over her and then her whispered thoughts. She's more nervous about how painful this might be than she was letting on, but there's a determination there too, and I can read how much she cares about Rhi, something that lifts the girl even further in my estimation. Rhi's been damn lucky to have a friend like Winnie – a friend who believed in her from the start – unlike us shitheads.

I push that thought away and focus in on the job at hand, brushing past the present and deeper into Winnie's mind, sinking into her memories.

The first few relate to our altercation at Lowsky's compound and the night of the attack. I skip those, plunging deeper, trying not to look at several that involve her and her boyfriend getting naked.

Beneath me, I can hear Winnie wince, sucking in breath, her brow crinkling beneath my fingers. I need to hurry the fuck up.

There are plenty of memories of Rhi in Winnie's head and it breaks my fucking heart to see Rhi opening her heart to her friend, confused, hurt, saddened by our actions. I scroll through them until I find Rhi lying out on a hospital bed, her face pale as snow, her leg all bandaged. I never saw her then, never saw how bad she looked. It has me sucking in breath through my teeth.

"Phoenix?" I hear my friend ask from far, far away. But I'm here now, scanning through all the pages of printed-out information Winnie had read for her friend. Pages and pages and pages – and then there it is. The article on uses of Tambric spice, an entire section dedicated to fated mates. I read it out quickly to Azlan. I can already feel Winnie's mind fighting to eject me, can sense her body weakening beneath me. I need to get out before I cause her any damage. I read it aloud with such speed I'm not sure if Azlan will even understand and once I'm done with the final sentence, I pull myself out. Stumbling away from Winnie, my hands falling to my sides.

I'm panting. My head aching. My vision spinning.

I squint my eyes and peer at Winnie.

"Are you okay?" I ask her. She's slumped in the chair, her brow sweaty, her skin green-tinged.

"Not my best, but I'll live." She eyes me. "You didn't go snooping in there did you?"

"Miss Wence," I say, laying my hand over my heart. "You have my word." To be honest, I have no desire to admit to what I glanced. Nope not going there at all. Winnie Wence is far kinkier than I'd given her credit for.

Winnie massages her temples. "Did you get it down?" she asks Azlan.

"Yeah, I got it," he says, reading through what he's written.

"So," I say. "Does it seem like something we could do?"

"I don't know. How good are you at brewing a potion?" Azlan asks. "Because I could never do that shit."

I frown. It's not exactly my forte either. Who wanted to waste time slaving over a simmering cauldron at the academy when there were far more exciting forms of magic to learn? In fact, it was barely taught.

"Not great," I admit.

"Well, you're lucky I tagged along then, aren't you?" Winnie says, holding her hand out to Azlan. "Because my grandma can brew a wicked potion and she taught me everything she knows."

Azlan passes her the slip of paper and she scans her gaze down the scribbled words, a little frown that worries me forming between her brows.

"Ahhh," she says.

"Ahhh?" I repeat. "What the hell does that mean?"

Winnie peers up at me with her don't-get-fresh-with-me expression. "It means this is one tricky potion. In fact, it's not the kind of potion a person can brew alone. I guess it's not surprising – we're messing with ancient magic here."

"We can help," Azlan says sternly.

"Ahhh," Winnie says again, "no offense but it needs more experienced hands."

Azlan frowns and peers down at his hands. "My hands are experienced."

"Oh I'm sure they are," she mutters under her breath.

"We need someone who knows what they're doing. My grandma."

"Your grandma?" I say, scratching my fingers through my beard. "Winnie, every moment away from Rhi is like hell. Every moment Barone could be–"

"Stone," she says, "I know. But this isn't something we can afford to mess up. This is ancient magic we're talking about, the fated mate bond. I'm pretty good at brewing potions but this is beyond my capabilities and I'm not prepared to brew something that ends up damaging Rhi," she tilts her head, "and the two of you," she adds reluctantly. "My grandma can do this. We can leave in the car right now. Sure, it'll take us a little longer but it'll be worth it."

I scratch my beard some more and peer over at my friend. "What do you think?"

"I think we don't have a lot of choices."

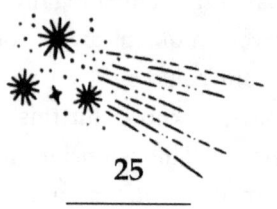

25

S pencer

THE BEAST PULLS me into consciousness. There's someone else in the cell. Not a guard. Not Christopher Kennedy. This man's scent is strong and wolfish.

Another werebeast.

I know it before I drag my eyelids open and through my blurry vision, see the other man chained to the wall opposite me.

His skin is brown, although not as dark as mine, his tangled hair almost black. It hangs in a matted curtain over his face, his head dropped forward so I can't see his features at all. However, it's clear he's older than me by ten, fifteen years at least. He's unconscious, his ragged clothes soaked in blood, his feet bare and cut to smithereens, his left arm broken.

Through the haze of pain, I watch him. He's alive; his chest expanding and deflating feebly and the occasional groan rumbling in his throat.

I can tell he's a werebeast by his scent but I look for other signs too. Is there a way to know? The build of his body, the configuration of his face. I don't see anything obvious, but as I examine him, he begins to stir.

I've never met another werebeast outside my tight family circle. Of course, I know they exist. But my mom has kept us away from them.

His eyes flicker open and with a great effort he lifts his head and peers through the gloom in my direction.

"Spencer Moreau," he says, his voice raw with pain. "I thought it was you."

"D-d-do I know you?" I ask.

One corner of his busted lip curls upwards. "I doubt it. Your family's always been too good to socialize with the likes of me."

I stare back at him blankly unsure what he means.

"My family is dead."

The man stares at me with little emotion. "Be thankful you had a family to begin with. Be thankful you aren't dead with them."

I scoff. There have been moments, moments when the pain has sucked me into its dark, dark depths where I've longed for death, prayed for it, anything to stop the agony.

"Why aren't you dead?" the man asks, wincing sharply as he shifts his body. "Why aren't we all dead?"

"All?" I say. "There are others?"

The man smiles, the teeth he has are scarlet with blood.

"I was one of six they captured. There are more in the cells down here."

"Six?" I say, amazed. That many.

"My pack," he says, for the first time the bravado fading in his eyes, sadness lurking beneath. "Three killed."

"I'm sorry," I say and he lifts his eyes from the ground to look at me.

"Your sympathy means little when you have done nothing to help our cause over the years, Moreau."

"Cause?"

He spits a mouthful of blood onto the hard ground and glares at me. "Maybe you are more of a pup than I realized."

I don't have the energy to rile at the insult. It sails right over my head. Everything hurts too much to care what some stranger thinks of me, not when I think so little of myself. But I am intrigued. Packs? Cause?

"I've never heard of weres living in a pack before," I admit. Although maybe pack is just a fancy way of saying family.

"Some of us have refused to play by the authorities' rules and restrictions," he hisses. "Some of us have chosen to live our own way, even if it's branded us exiles and criminals."

I stare at him. Is this true? "And why have I never heard of this?"

He snorts. "You expect me to believe you haven't?"

I growl at him, my beast for once stirring inside me. The other man examines me.

"Your parents were collaborators–" I start to argue, but he ignores me, plowing onwards regardless. "Happy to live in luxury while the rest of our kind suffered."

"It wasn't luxury," I mumble. "They suffered too."

I think of my dead brother. Of my dad, lost to madness by his grief, rarely returning to his human form, and my maman trying to hold the family together. I think of the scars on her body.

"It doesn't matter now," the man says, the fight deflating from his voice and his head dropping forward, his chin resting on his chest. "They're going to kill us all."

"I can't die," I whisper, more to myself than him.

"We all have to die, Moreau."

"I have a fated mate."

The man chuckles, lifting his head to peer at me. "Sure you do. We all have people we love."

He peers towards the door.

I shake my head, pain shooting up my neck and searing into my skull. "I don't know about love," I mutter. Do I love her? Am I – a monster, a beast – even capable of love? "I do know she is my fated mate."

"You? A were? Why would fate give you a mate?"

"I don't know. But I'm not the only one."

The man's face crinkles in confusion. "You know of other weres with fated mates? I've never heard of that."

"No, not weres. My girl, my mate, she has others. Four in total. Four fated mates." I wonder why the hell I'm telling him this. He could be a spy for Christopher Kennedy, a clever way to extract information from me.

I close my eyes. Idiot. Stupid idiot.

I hear the man laugh, a laugh that descends into a coughing fit. The sounds making my ribs hurt.

"You're mad," he whispers eventually, "mad."

"Yeah," I answer. "Perhaps I am."

Why would fate want me as a mate for her? A useless mutt. A curseded. Chained to a wall, defeated and broken. No use to her. No use to her at all.

"Jacob. You didn't ask," the man says, "but my name is Jacob."

I open my eyes and meet his and I realize there is the clue, the giveaway, deep in his eyes, I can see his beast lurking there, right below the surface. "Don't tell them," he says. "Don't tell them about the girl."

"Don't tell who?" I ask.

But his eyes are drifting shut and soon he's lifeless again.

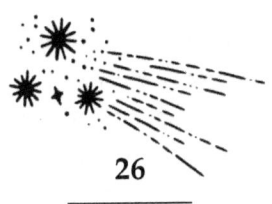

26

A zlan

SOMETHING'S CHANGED since I was last here. Something about this suburb is different. I can smell it in the air. I can see it in the empty streets and the twitching curtains. I can feel it in my bones. Fear. People are afraid.

Perhaps that isn't surprising. The republic just came under a deadly attack. One that nearly saw our country fall into enemy hands.

But I don't think it's the threat from the West these people are afraid of.

"How safe do we think it is here?" I ask Winnie as she pulls the car up into the driveway of her grandma's little bungalow.

"Here?" Winnie giggles. "My mom used to send me and my sisters here in the summer holidays. Trust me, nothing ever happens here. It's the dullest, most boring place in the world. In fact, Nonny is the most interesting thing about this place."

I peer at those twitching curtains and I'm not so sure. We are fugitives of the republic now, wanted by the Lord Protector. I wonder if anywhere is really safe.

Winnie's grandma appears to share my reservations because she's hurrying out the front door and down the pathway and when she spots Stone and me lurking in the car, instructs Winnie to park up in the garage. Winnie does as she's told and once we're safely inside, we climb out of the car and follow Winnie's grandma through an internal door into the house. Birds tweet from a room off a hallway and an old cat curls itself around my ankles as we're led to the kitchen at the back of the house.

Once inside, Winnie's grandma inspects us with suspicion. She's an older woman with short, spiky hair and big oversized glasses that magnify her shrewd eyes.

"I've already had agents from the authorities knocking on my door asking questions about you, Winnifred. They've been to your mom's house too. You know she's out of her mind with worry. We all have been."

"I'm sorry, Nonny," Winnie murmurs, fiddling with the hem of her shirt and looking mighty guilty. "Sorry I haven't been in touch. It's been difficult."

Her grandma reaches up and pats her cheek. "But you're okay? Not hurt?"

"I'm fine."

"Then don't stand there like a wombat, give me a damn hug."

Winnie wraps her arms around her grandma immediately and the old woman squeezes her back, whispering words in her granddaughter's ear that I don't hear. Winnie kisses her cheek and then they separate.

"Now," Winnie's grandma says, "I know who you are." She glares at me. "But who are you?" She points to Stone.

"This is Professor Stone, Nonny, from the academy. This is Rosa," she tells him, "my grandma."

"He doesn't look like a professor," she says with suspicion and I can't help a guffaw.

"Yeah, I get that a lot," Phoenix mumbles.

"He's another of Rhi's mates."

"Another," the old woman says, her eyebrows rising. "And where is Rhianna exactly? You do know she's wanted by the authorities?" she eyes me and Stone, "you all are."

"We don't know where she is," Winnie explains. "She went missing the night of the attack on the academy. The enforcer—"

"Azlan," I say.

"And Professor Stone haven't heard from her – neither have I – and they haven't been able to reach her through the bond. She's too far away."

"Are you sure ..." the old woman gives her granddaughter a sympathetic look, "that Rhianna is alive?"

"Yes," I say firmly. "We can feel her."

"Just not strongly enough to track her down or communicate with her."

"Which is why we're here, Nonny. We need your help."

"Mine?" The old woman looks taken back. "The authorities' number one enforcer and a professor from the academy need *my* help."

"Yes, Nonny."

"Well," she says, resting her hand against her chest. "Well ..." then her eyes narrow, "what with exactly?"

"Rhi may be in danger—"

"I imagine with half the country after her she probably is. What exactly do the authorities want with her?"

"The girl has unusual powers," I tell her, deciding honesty is the best way to win the old woman onto our side and get her to help us. Hopefully, it will be the quickest way too, because every ticking second is agony. "And the Lord Protector knows that I am her fated mate. He may know she has other fated mates too."

"Others?"

"Four, Nonny. Like in the fairytale of Queen Æðelflæd and her five knights."

The old woman sits down hard on a chair resting in the corner of the kitchen, swiping her glasses off her nose with one hand, the other still lingering against her chest. "This girl, you don't think ..."

I frown. "Think what?"

"Four mates!" The old woman shakes her head. "I've never heard of such a thing. Not in real life. Only in fairy tales as Winnie says. What powers does she possess?"

I glance at Phoenix who keeps his mouth shut.

"No, no, don't tell me," she says, raising her hand, "perhaps it's best I don't know. If those agents come knocking again, it's probably better I know as little as possible."

"You wouldn't tell, Nonny."

"No, Winnie, darling, but they were a tad," she smiles flatly, "forceful."

Winnie gasps and I ball my hands into fists. The chancellor had his flaws, but that would never have been allowed under his rule. My uncle really is a piece of shit.

"Will you help us?" Phoenix asks her. "I understand if you'd rather not. I understand we're putting you in a difficult position."

"Nonsense." She waves her hand through the air. "Of course, I'll help you. Rhianna is Winnie's friend and besides, I like that girl. She has spunk."

"She's certainly had a lot of spunk," Winnie mumbles.

I glare at the girl and she looks away from me, her cheeks heating.

"What exactly do you need me to do? It's very flattering for an old woman like me to be asked for help but I'm not exactly sure how I can help you." A yappy dog trots into the room and jumps up onto her lap, and she strokes her hands through his fur.

"We need you to brew us a potion, Nonny."

"Winnie, of all my grandchildren, you are the best potion brewer. I don't see why you need my help."

"I do. It's complex, really complex."

"Ahhh," the old woman says with some suspicion, "what exactly does this potion do?"

"Strengthen the fated mate bond – making it possible to communicate over vast distances."

The old woman stares into my face. "We're talking about manipulating ancient magic here."

"Yes."

"That's dangerous."

"Which is why we need your help, Nonny."

"Are you sure you want to do it? I'm flattered you think I'm capable but I'm no academy professor."

"I'm sure," I say. "We've been separated from Rhi for long enough. We need to find her."

The old woman tickles her dog under its chin and considers our request. "Okay," she says at last, "do you have the recipe?"

Winnie tugs the piece of paper from her pocket and her grandma hooks the glasses hanging around her neck onto her nose and reads the words.

"You have the Tambric spice?" Winnie nods. "Hmmm. This is tricky, very tricky."

"You think you can brew it?" Phoenix asks with a note of desperation.

"With Winnie's help, I think so." She pushes the dog gently from her lap and stands up. "We'd best get started. Most of the folk around here are blind as bats but someone may have spotted you arriving and if they did, there's a chance they've already shopped you in to the authorities. We may have limited time to make the potion." She turns to her granddaughter. "Fetch my cauldron – the silver-plated one." She turns to us as Winnie scuttles from the room. "And you two," she says, "will be our assistants."

"Assistants?" Phoenix says with obvious disgust.

"Yes," she says with a twinkle in her eyes. "Don't expect to stand around while us women do all the hard work. Those days have long passed. You can start by brewing us a pot of tea. Kettle's over there."

WINNIE'S GRANDMA is true to her word. For over an hour, she has Stone and me fetching and carrying for her, using our magic to chop up ingredients, and providing her and Winnie with ample tea and snacks. There's little time to stand and watch but in the moments I do, I can see her murmuring with her granddaughter as they hover over the silver cauldron, adding ingredients slowly, stirring occasionally and consulting not only the notes I'd made but an array of ancient-looking recipe books too.

The small kitchen soon fills with clouds of billowing steam – steam that morphs in color from white to pink to purple as they add their ingredients and the pungent smell of Tambric spice leaves is inescapable. My eyes water and the fumes tickle the back of my throat, making me cough.

"We're nearly done," Rosa says, not looking up from the bubbling liquid. She beckons me closer and I peer down at the concoction. It's a rich plum color and thick like treacle. "Just one last step left and this is the trickiest part." She dabs the back of her hand against her clammy forehead. "I'm going to need your help."

"What do you need us to do?"

"We need to add a little of your magic – both you fated mates. Winnie and I could do it, but I think it will be most effective if the magic comes from you two."

"Okay," I say. "How?"

Rosa smiles. "Be patient. I'm getting to that bit." She stirs the potion and a puff of steam billows into the air. "I need to add the last ingredient and as I do, I need you both to add a drop of your magic." I step forward and she lifts up her hand. "But not just any old magic. Magic soaked with love."

"Love?" I say flatly.

"You do love the girl, don't you?" I shuffle from one foot to the other, then nod. "Then you take a little of that love, you mix it with your magic, and you add it to the potion. The potion needs to know your intentions are pure. It needs to know you are using it with your loved one's best interests at heart."

"A potion can't think," I mutter. This sounds like the kind of woo woo bullshit Ellie dabbles in.

"That shows how much you know, young man," Rosa says sternly. She tuts. "You men are always so quick to dismiss potions in favor of fancy-pants magic. And frankly, it's stupid. A well-brewed potion can be just as powerful as magic wielded by the most accomplished magical."

I hope she's right. I hope this is going to work because I'm fucking desperate here.

"I don't know how to add love to my magic," I say gruffly.

The old woman hooks off her glasses and steps towards me, resting her palm right above my heart. "Love resides in your heart. When we're in love, our heart is over-brimming with it. It's damn hard to miss. You say you love Rhianna, then you must feel that love right here."

I glare at her. All I feel is my heart pounding with irritation against her hand.

She tuts. "Close your eyes." I hesitate, then do it. If it means finding Rhi, I can swallow my skepticism and my pride and embrace the woo woo. "What do you feel?"

"My bond," I say, that shimmering, powerful sensation residing in my gut. Not my heart.

"Yes, I imagine that's pretty overwhelming. But let down your guard, Mister Tough Guy. Let down your guard and let your feelings out. Let yourself truly experience your feelings for your fated mate."

I let out a breath and try. I try my damn hardest. At first I think I'm going to fail. I'm so used to locking away my feelings. It's something I've done all my life. Feelings weren't allowed in a family like ours – especially after my mom passed. Those barriers I've erected to stop myself from feeling all the pain and heartache, all the fear and guilt, are strong and well fortified. But they're not going to stand in the way of me finding my fated mate. And so I crash through them, letting all those hidden feelings come flooding out. I brace myself, waiting for the pain, the heartache, the fear, the guilt, and it's there, of course it is, but those feelings are drowned by the vast volume of love that comes pouring out too.

Love. I knew I loved her. But did I truly know how much? Did I allow myself to acknowledge it? Because to love is to risk losing, is to risk that pain and heartache. It's what

Phoenix feared so much when Rhianna first entered our lives.

But I've come to learn those fears were foolish. I'd risk it all for this. I'd risk everything for her.

"You feel it?" the old woman asks me, her hand pressing against my ribcage.

"Y-y-yes," I say my voice caught in my throat.

"Then coat your magic in it and get ready." I feel her step away. "Are you ready too, Professor?"

"I am."

"Winnie," she says, "get ready with that spoon. On the count of three ... one ... two ... three!"

I send a drop of my magic spiraling through the air and splashing into the potion. There's an almighty bang, the force of it making me stumble backwards, the kitchen full of smoke.

I cough, waving it away from my face and peer towards Rosa and the potion.

Winnie is picking the old woman off the floor. Her face is black with soot and her short hair standing on end.

"Are you all right, Nonny?" Winnie asks anxiously.

"Perfectly fine, Winnie, don't fuss," she says, batting her granddaughter's hands away. She peers down into her cauldron and a wide smile spreads across her face. "Looks like it worked."

I sigh with relief, glancing at Phoenix who's smiling too.

"Can we use it straight away?" I ask her.

From down the hallway, the birds start to tweet again and the dog races from the kitchen yapping away. Rosa peers after it, the smile slipping from her face.

"I think you'd better take it to go," she says, "there's someone coming."

27

R^{hi}

"What the hell was that?" I gasp. "An earthquake? An avalanche?"

The assassin looks over his shoulder at the distant mountains, in the direction from which that noise came.

"I don't think so."

I stare off in that direction too and suddenly I'm overwhelmed by that feeling of déjà vu. This is like my dream. Just like my dream. I was running through the mountains, under the falling snow towards the beast in need.

A violent shudder races down my spine.

Fate. Destiny. It's calling me. Leading me a certain way.

But do I want to go that way? What will I find if I do? What kind of burden may be laid upon my shoulders?

"What's up, little rabbit?" Renzo asks, observing me.

And I realize I'm too damn curious not to go. I need to find out where this dream ends. If it was just a dream – the similarities to our here and now purely coincidental – or whether it was a glimpse of the future? Like the ones I used to have as a kid. Like the ones my mom endured.

"Which way do you think that came from?" I ask him.

He swivels the rings on his fingers. Then tilts his head to the south. "That way."

Yes, that's what I thought too.

I start walking, another groan, the earth trembling, causing me to pick up my pace. It's not the sound of sliding snow, or the ground splitting. It's the sound of an animal. A fuck-off big animal by the sounds of things. A beast for sure.

"Little rabbit, that doesn't sound friendly." Renzo pants from beside me. "I think we should be running in the opposite direction."

"No," I tell him, "it's like my dream. We have to go this way."

We skid down a hill, passing the skeletons of mountain goats as we do, the dark sockets of their eyes staring up at us as we pass.

I don't want to think about what killed these. I don't want to think about that at all. Because if I do, I'll stop running altogether.

"Little rabbit," Renzo says, glancing at the gnawed bones, "I'm all for a bit of fun. But this–"

"Are you scared?" I challenge him, as another of those monstrous groans tells us we're drawing closer. I swing my gaze around, trying to work out where that sound is coming from.

"Of what?" he asks.

"I don't know. Being mauled, being eaten, dying!"

"Nah," he says without the merest hint of bravado, over-taking me and running between an outcrop of rocks. I follow him, squeezing through the narrow gap, the stone scraping at my body and when I emerge through I find myself in a crevice, somewhere the snow has been unable to penetrate, Renzo stopped right in front of me.

"What?" I say, trying to push my way past him. "What is it?"

He blocks me from passing. "Stay back, little rabbit," he hisses.

"What is it," I say with irritation, pushing at him harder. Despite my attempts, I fail to move his solid body at all.

"Little rabbit, it's a dragon."

I gasp and for one whole minute I stand there, clutching Pip to my chest utterly flabbergasted. Then the beast roars, the blast of sound so fearsome, my hair is swept back from my face and I close my eyes.

"I think we should go, little rabbit. I'm not sure we're welcome here."

"Renzo Barone," I say, zapping him with my magic. "Let me pass. Let me pass right now or–"

He steps aside and I move forward, catching sight of the dragon for the first time.

It's gigantic. Twice the size of any of the dragons that attacked the academy, and, unlike those other dragons – all a sluggish green color – this one is beautiful, its scales a glistening rusty gold.

It lies curled up, its wings tucked in, although its head is raised and staring right at me. Its eyes are not beady like that glass dragon hanging in the council building. These shine black and beautiful. It stares right into my eyes as if challenging me to look away, as if judging my mettle and my worth, and my magic tingles in my fingertips.

I remain completely still, somehow sure this is the right thing to do.

"Let's go," Renzo hisses.

Carefully, I shake my head and after a minute the dragon turns its head away, lapping its tongue over its chest. It's then I see it is injured. A gaping wound on its chest and another on its side, one leg twisted. I also see the metal collar it wears around its neck, the scales chafed away. There are other cuffs too – one encircling each of the beast's ankles.

This is no free dragon. It's a captive one. But if so, where is its owner and what is it doing here, high up in the mountains?

"It's hurt," I tell Renzo.

"She," he tells me.

"She?" I say, "how can you tell?"

"Just can," he says, moving closer to me. "I have a feeling, little rabbit, that an injured dragon is even more deadly than a normal one. And this one is fucking big."

"I need to heal her," I say, laying Pip gently on one of the rocks on the ground. "That's what my dream was about. I'm meant to heal her."

"You ever healed a dragon before?" Renzo asks.

"Well, no," I admit. "It's not exactly something we've been taught at the academy. But I'm pretty good at healing humans now," I say, thinking of Winnie. "How different can it be?" Renzo stares at me. "Until the attack on the academy, I'd never even seen a dragon before. I thought they were extinct."

"That's what people said. But people talk shit," he says.

I take a step forward and immediately the dragon snaps her head around to glare at me warily.

"Little rabbit," Renzo warns.

"If she wanted to kill us, she'd have done it already."

"You don't know that. She might like to play with her food."

I ignore him, staring back into those raven eyes. "I'm not going to hurt you," I tell her, watching as her ears swivel on the sides of her head. "I'm going to help you." The dragon turns its head again and licks at the wound. "Yes," I say, "yes, I can heal that."

The dragon makes a moaning noise that rattles through her body, much quieter than before, then rests her head down on the ground, gazing at me with those eyes. I can tell the creature is in pain. I can read it in her features.

I've nursed sick and injured chickens before plus a squirrel that got caught up in the chicken wire. This dragon may be hundreds of times bigger than those creatures but I think I need to treat her like any other wild animal.

I lift my hand out in front of me and wait. Cautiously, the dragon lifts her head.

"Little rabbit," Renzo hisses beside me.

"Trust me," I say with probably a lot more confidence than I truly feel, "this is going to be fine."

He harrumphs in irritation and the dragon's gaze flicks to him before returning to me. She brings her face closer to my outstretched hand until her nostrils are mere millimeters away. My hand looks like a mere pimple against her vast size and I should feel afraid. I should be quaking in my boots. But I'm not. Fate has brought me here. If fate's brought me here to be eaten by a giant dragon, burned to a crisp, then so be it.

The dragon growls very very softly and I'm contemplating that one of those options might be my fate after all, when the creature inhales, sucking in my scent and making my hair rustle around my face.

Then she lays her head back down on the rocky ground and I release my breath, Renzo swearing behind me.

I take a step towards the dragon, then another and another. She watches me move closer, but she doesn't appear to mind and soon I'm standing right beside her with a much better view of the wounds. It's not as deep or as fatal as the wound I healed on Winnie. It's not as deadly as the one Tristan took to his body, the memory of it making me wince – but it is weeping, and closer now I can see a great tear in one of her wings. She can't fly, with her broken leg she can't walk. And that wound will slowly turn septic and eventually kill her.

"She's beautiful," Renzo says, coming to stand beside me again.

And she is. Even in her injured state she is truly magnificent.

"I'm going to touch you now," I tell her, raising my hand towards her.

"Careful," Renzo advises.

I edge my hand closer. The dragon's eyes stare fixedly on my hand. I move it closer still and then closer some more until I'm hovering my hand right above her scales. Then with a steadying breath, I touch her.

Immediately she's snapping up her head again and growling but I hold my ground, refusing to move and fixing on her with a determined gaze.

"I'm going to help you." Her scales are cool to the touch and I don't know if that's the way this giant lizard should be, or whether her injuries have caused her temperature to drop. The scales themselves are not rough as I expected, but to my surprise they're like the softest of leather.

I close my eyes and allow my magic to seep slowly into her body, soothing, numbing magic that has the dragon sighing in relief, her taut body relaxing under my touch. Her body feels different to bodies I've healed before, different from Pip's, and it's not just the sheer size of the creature. It's something more. There's magic in her body, and it seems to respond to mine, to recognize mine. It's familiar, similar, moving to my command.

"She's big, little rabbit. Healing her is going to take a big chunk of your magic."

I shake my head. I don't think it will. I search out the wound on her body first and get to work knitting together the scales, mending the ripped tissues and blood vessels. Her magic responds, following mine and doing the same.

"It's working," Renzo says.

I move on to her leg. Her thigh bone is snapped clean in half. I wonder what happened to her. Did she crash into the mountain? Was she wounded in that battle?

I concentrate on fixing the bone. Despite the size of that wound, the bone is much harder to mend. I need to line it up, ensure it's straight and bone proves harder to encourage to grow. Soon, my eyes are screwed tight and there's sweat on my brow despite the coolness of the air.

"Easy," Renzo whispers, his hand resting on my shoulder, his presence, his magic giving me the renewed strength I need to continue. I don't know how much longer I work, but eventually I'm satisfied and fall back, panting, Renzo catching me in his arms.

The dragon stares at me and opens out her torn wing, fluttering it.

"Yeah, yeah, give her a break," Renzo growls, and the dragon folds in its wing and drops her head to rest on her front legs.

"I don't need a rest," I insist, reaching out to touch her again.

"You do," Renzo says, taking a hold of my wrist and dragging me back to where we've left Pip and our bags. He pulls out the water bottle and one of the dried bits of meat, and insists I drink and eat. I flop down on the floor and start to chug down water.

The dragon watches me and then something catches her attention. Pip. She shuffles forward, leaning her head towards my pig, her eyes alert and ... am I seeing that right? ... hungry!

I jump to my feet and lift my hands.

"He's not on the menu," I warn her. I don't care how big this dragon is, how beautiful she may be, if she tries to torch Pip, then I am going to blast her with every ounce of power I possess.

Pip lifts his head feebly and blinks his eyes, jolting slightly when he finds a giant dragon bearing down on him. He grunts and then to my surprise, lifts his snout towards the dragon. The dragon responds, lowering her head closer.

My magic sparks on my fingers and my heart leaps clean out of my chest and into my throat.

"Pip!" I hiss.

This isn't a friendly pup. It's not a smart-assed chicken. It's a dragon. Beside her, Pip looks like a speck of dust.

He doesn't seem to hear me, or maybe he's just being his obstinate self and ignoring me altogether, because he lifts his head higher still and presses his snout against the dragon's nose. The dragon focuses her eyes and Pip does the same.

"Are they communicating?" Renzo asks.

Either that or kissing. Or perhaps the dragon is determining if Pip's tasty enough to eat. I take a step towards them, ready to intervene. But I've no need, Pip lowers his head and the dragon curls up again.

What the hell was that? I shake my head, wondering if I'm still caught in that dream. If I'm not really awake at all. But then Renzo nudges me to eat up as if nothing just happened at all, as if my pet pig didn't just get flirty with a dragon the size of a castle.

When Renzo's satisfied that I've eaten and drunk enough, he flops down on the ground beside me.

"You gonna fix her wing next?"

I peer over at the tattered thing. I know it's going to be even more challenging to fix it than it was her leg. In fact, I'm not confident I have the skill (or the patience).

"I'm going to give it my best shot," I tell him, taking another gulp of water.

"And then what? Are we gonna keep her?"

I spit out the water I'm drinking. "Keep her?" Not in a million years had that idea occurred to me. Keep a dragon? The dude is more insane than I realized.

"You already have a pig as a pet," he points out. "That isn't exactly conventional, is it?"

"Yes," I screw the cap back on the bottle. "But Pip is small and portable and not that much trouble – usually. This dragon is not, given she'd even consent to come with us."

"She would. She's tame and probably trained. She belonged to someone."

"Someone who kept her chained up!" I say, with a frown. "Someone who didn't look after her properly. Someone who was whipping her," I say, pointing to the lacerations on her sides I'm sure were caused by a whip and not the accident that caused her other injuries.

Renzo's eyes travel over those whip lacerations.

"So you're going to let her go?"

"I haven't really thought that far ahead," I say, rubbing at my head. "But I don't think it's a case of 'letting her'. She should be free."

Renzo shakes his head, a grin hovering on his lips. "And they say I'm mad."

"What's mad about that?" I say defensively.

"A dragon roaming free! I mean, don't get me wrong, little rabbit, I love it. But you always seemed the sensible type to me."

I doubt a sensible woman would have gotten frisky with a known psychopath only hours before. Nope, I lost my senses long ago. I am probably as mentally deranged as he is.

"I'm going to let her go."

"She'll probably just fly back to her owner. That's what abused things do – humans and creatures. It's hard to break free." I turn my head from the dragon to the assassin. How does he know that? Is he talking about himself? Or someone else in his life?

Sometimes it's so easy to forget that this man has a taste for blood. When he talks to me like this, he can seem like anyone else – even if his thoughts are a little rambling.

Was he born with a taste for blood? Would he have been that way no matter what? Or did something happen to make him that way?

I think of the man I killed in the woods. Of the choices I've made. If I hadn't had my aunt looking out for me – loving me – would I be a different person altogether?

I stand up, brushing the dirt off the seat of my pants and, with a deep inhale, walk back towards the dragon. As I approach, she stretches out her wing again, as if reminding me that I haven't fixed it yet. The first rays of morning light are filtering down into this crevice and it catches on the fragile fabric of her wing, lighting it up in a rainbow of glittering colors, so beautiful, it catches my breath.

"Yep, I'm going to deal with that wing next." Although seeing it in the light makes me nervous about it. It's so much more complex than I realized in the darkness and it's kind of surprising that a creature so menacing and so large could possess something so fragile. However, if I don't try, she can't fly, and even with her fixed leg, I suspect she'd be trapped down here.

I take the broken wing in my hand, spread it out and examine the tissue. It reminds me of a butterfly's wing or perhaps a moth's – if butterflies and moths were the size of small buildings. I debate how I'm going to handle this and in the end the only idea that comes to me is to use the same technique my aunt taught me to darn socks. And, yeah, we darned a lot of socks. Hopefully, fixing this wing won't be much different.

I close my eyes again and with my magic follow the pattern of the tissue, knitting new tissue and then finally binding it all together. It takes me more than an hour, the sun rising from behind the mountain and into the sky above us by the time I'm done. Then I tackle the broken bone and ligament in the wing. It's snapped or cracked in several places and the process of fixing it is just as hard as it was with the leg. I'm shaking with exhaustion by the time I tackle the last part, Renzo hovering around me clearly distressed.

My magic is waning in my fingertips and I'm utterly exhausted, but I keep going until that very last fine bone is mended. Then I collapse on the floor in a panting heap.

"You okay, little rabbit?" Renzo asks, handing me the water bottle once again. I take it from him but my arms are shaking too hard and I don't have the strength to lift it to my parched mouth. Renzo takes it back from me and pours water between my lips, most of it dribbling down my chin.

I swallow the liquid. "I'm fine."

He goes to inspect the mended wing, stroking his hand over the thin tissue. "You did a good job."

"You think it will work?"

As if the dragon thinks that question is directed at her, she stretches out her wings and flaps them through the air. I hold my breath, half expecting the thing to rip in half again, but it holds, the air beating around us.

The dragon makes that rumbling growl in the back of her throat, puffs of smoke issuing from her nostrils and then she lumbers up onto her feet. She tests her weight gingerly on the mended leg, and then finding it strong, leans her full body weight onto it, curling and stretching her razor-sharp talons. On her feet, the dragon seems even bigger, towering above me, Renzo and Pip, and the daylight has every one of her rusty-gold scales shining like polished shields.

She lifts her head, gazing up at the sky, smothered in thick winter clouds above us, and then peers back down at me.

She meets my eyes, roars and then shakes her head, the metal chain rattling, the sound echoing off the rocks.

And I know what she's asking.

I raise my trembling hand, but Renzo bats it away.

"I'll do it," he says, and the metal collar and the four metal cuffs spring open in unison and clatter to the ground.

The dragon looks at us both, stretches out her magnificent wings and this time beats them through the air with such force both Renzo and I are thrown backwards. I wait for her to lift up into the air and soar away. Instead she lowers her head to the ground and snorts.

"What's she doing?"

"I'm no dragon whisperer," Renzo says, "but I think she's inviting you to jump on board."

I stare at him in disbelief. "Seriously?"

"Either that or she's going to eat you."

I clamber up onto my feet and step closer.

"Are you sure?" I ask her, even though I have no idea if she even understands me.

The dragon snorts, and ripples her scales.

"You want to ride her?" Renzo asks.

I look over my shoulder at him, like, duh. Of course I want to freaking ride her.

Carefully, conscious that she may still be sore, I reach up above my head and take a grip of the top of her neck. I attempt to drag myself up, but I'm weak and I don't have the strength. Then I feel a pair of strong hands clasping around my waist and lifting me upward. With his help, I slide on top of the dragon's neck, swing my leg over and shuffle backwards onto her back. I wait for her to move. She doesn't. She remains in that position, this time eyeing Renzo.

"I think she wants you on board too."

"Fuck! You think?" he says, his face filling with boyish excitement.

"Either that or she's going to eat you," I say with a grin so wide my cheeks are hurting.

He jumps up onto the dragon with ease and I expect him to plant himself firmly in front of me, taking control. He doesn't, he shuffles himself behind me instead, settling down so his body is pressed right up against mine, his hands back on my waist. I'm not sure he needs to be quite that close, or hold me quite that firmly, but it sends my bond wild and so I don't complain about it.

The dragon lifts her head, peering upwards a second time, and then flaps her wings. Beneath us, her muscles ripple and flex and then we're lifting off the ground. At first she's working hard, her wings beating with force as she raises us vertically through the gap in the crevice, but as soon as we're into the open sky, she spreads her wings as wide as they will go and then we're soaring, flying over the snow-capped mountaintops.

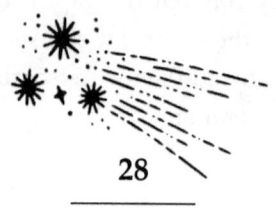

28

S tone

Rosa hooks an empty jar off a shelf, dunks it into the bubbling liquid and secures the lid. Then she's thrusting it into her granddaughter's hands and pushing us towards the doorway.

"Go!" she hisses, "I'll keep them distracted for as long as I can."

"Come with us," Winnie says, grabbing the old woman's arm.

"No, Winnie, there isn't time."

"Then I'll stay. I'm not leaving you alone to face those bastards."

"Winnie Wence, I am perfectly capable of looking after myself. Just because I'm an old woman, doesn't mean I don't have a few tricks up my sleeves–"

"But Nonny–"

"Winnie," Rosa says, staring deep into her granddaughter's eyes and squeezing her hands between her own. "This girl is special, we know that. And maybe she's the one to end these dark days we're facing. You need to find her."

"Stone and Azlan will find her. I need to stay with you!"

"Those two couldn't find their tits from their elbows." Azlan bristles at the insult. "They're going to need your help." She pushes her granddaughter towards the hallway. "Go, darling before it's too late."

"I love you, Nonny," Winnie says, throwing her arms around her grandma.

"I know you do and I love you too."

She peers at us over Winnie's shoulder, motioning towards us and I take Winnie's elbow and gently pull her from her grandma and towards the interior garage door. In the doorway, I pause, and turn back to Rosa, already shuffling along to her front door.

"Thank you," I say.

"Don't screw this up," is all she says and then the door is closing and we're diving into the car once again.

"They could be waiting for us outside," Azlan tells Winnie as she settles behind the steering wheel. "You're going to need to floor it as soon as I blow the garage door away."

"Okay," she says, blinking tears away from her eyes and turning the key in the ignition, setting her jaw in a steely lock of determination.

"Are you ready?" She nods, setting the stick into reverse. "Phoenix?"

"Born ready," I say.

"On the count of three – three ... two ... one!"

Azlan blasts magic behind us and the garage door is ripped from its hinges and flies away. Immediately, Winnie hits the gas, shooting the car backwards out of the garage and onto the street. She screeches to a halt, and for a fleeting moment I see the shocked faces of several agents from the authorities before all hell breaks loose. Winnie yanks on the stick, we fly forward, just as the agents hurtle magic at us and Azlan and I hurtle it right back at them. Sparks hit the car, a window smashes. Winnie keeps right on driving, careening us down the street. I lean out of the window and shoot blinding magic at those bastards, hoping to take all of them out. Hoping that means Winnie's grandma might stand a chance of running away after all.

Then Winnie's hitting buttons as we zoom away, so fast the agents have no chance of catching us.

"Any suggestions where we go next?" Winnie asks.

"Cross country," Azlan instructs her. "There're too many pairs of eyes – too many spies – out here in the towns and the suburbs." Winnie hits more buttons and half an hour later pulls us up in a turnout.

We sit there, all catching our breath, and then I lift the jar of potion from my lap.

"I say we don't waste any more time and take this damn potion."

Winnie swivels in the driver's seat. "You need to drink at least a cupful." We all gaze at the jar. There's only enough for one.

"Shit!" I say.

"You take it," Azlan tells me.

"No," I say, shaking my head. "It should be you. You bonded with Rhi first. Your bond is probably stronger. Besides which, you're a much better damn magical than I've ever been."

"Bullshit, Phoenix," Azlan says. "It should be you. You're better with your words–"

"Me?" I say, laughing out loud in disbelief.

Azlan glances at Winnie. "Well ..." she says, chewing her cheek, "neither of you are exactly Shakespeare, but I'd say Azlan is right. You are capable of stringing more than two words together into a sentence."

"And you understand her far better than I do," Azlan adds.

I scoff again. Understand her? Sometimes perhaps, most of the time she drives me round the bend – defying me, acting irrationally, failing to think things through, acting like a damn brat.

Fuck, I really, really miss that woman.

"Fine," I say, not prepared to waste any more time arguing. "Is there anything in particular I need to do?"

"Nope," Winnie says, "just drink it."

I unscrew the lid and the stench of Tambric spice hits me square between the eyes, making me splutter. I hate this smell. I really hate this smell. It reminds me of things I've chosen to forget. I try my damn hardest to push those memories to one side and lift the jar to my lips. I've failed to ask Winnie about the potential side effects of this potion. Will it have my mouth blistering? Will it be so painful I'm screaming?

I peer down into the thick, gloopy mixture. It doesn't matter. I'd swallow scorpions for that girl. I'd eat glass.

I bring it to my lips, and tip it into my mouth. It tastes rank – sour and bitter – and my immediate reaction is to spit the revolting thing out. But I force it down, feeling it tingle against my throat as I swallow. Then, trying my best not to smell and taste the stuff, I take another mouthful and another until I'm flinging my head back and tipping the very last drop down my throat.

Swiping my hand across the back of my mouth, I burp

and screw the lid back on the empty jar, tossing it onto the seat beside me.

Both Winnie and Azlan are staring at me expectantly.

"Well?" Azlan says, "did it work?"

I examine my body, searching for signs that it has. All that feels different is a mighty sense of sickness residing in my belly. My bond feels no different.

"I don't know."

"Shit!" Azlan mutters.

"You haven't tried yet," Winnie points out with a roll of her eyes. "Nonny is a superior potion brewer. It's going to work."

I bring my fist to my mouth, smothering a second burp and then I settle back in my seat and reach for Rhi through the bond.

Immediately, it's like I'm being whisked through the air and that sick feeling gets a whole lot worse.

Rhi? I call out, crossing my fingers and my toes and even my goddamn balls that this is going to work. *Rhianna, are you there?*

Static. Like an untuned radio.

My shoulders sag. It hasn't worked.

Stone? Stone? Oh my god. Is that you?

Fuck, yes, sweetheart. Yes, fuck, it's me.

I snap open my eyes. "It's worked," I say, grinning my head off, tears of relief pooling in my eyes. "It's working."

"Where is she, Phoenix? Where the fuck is she?"

Azlan looks as if he'd like to crawl over the seat, grab me by the collar and shake me senseless.

Stone? Stone? I can hear you. Are you there?

I'm here, sweetheart, right here. Are you safe? Are you in any danger?

I'm fine, Stone. Just fine. Are you? Is Azlan? Winnie? The ... others?

I'm here right now with Azlan and Winnie. We're all just fine. I don't tell her about Tristan Kennedy and Spencer Moreau. *Where are you? Can you tell me where you are?*

Where am I? I hear her laugh though the bond, vibrant and wild and carefree. *I'm flying on the back of a dragon.*

I stare at Azlan. Yeah, I don't get this girl at all.

A dragon ... sweetheart? Has she lost her senses? Has that bastard hurt her so badly she's lost her mind?

The next few sentences come flying across in a speedy blur of excitement. She was climbing in the mountains, trying to get back to Los Magicos, to us. She found a dragon. An injured dragon. She healed the dragon and now she's flying it.

I rub my temples.

"What?" Azlan says anxiously. "What's wrong? Where is she?"

I shake my head at him and press my finger to my lips. He scowls at me but I don't care. I'm trying to make sense of this.

Why are you in the mountains? There's a pause in our communication. *Rhi? Rhi?*

There are people hunting me, Stone.

I know sweetheart. They're hunting us too.

Over the mountains seemed the safest route.

The safest route? She has lost her senses, that confirms it. It's winter. The mountains are treacherous at the best of times but in the heart of winter? What the hell is she thinking?

I tried to reach you. There's sadness in her tone now. *I've been trying for days.*

So have we, Rhi. So have we. But we're going to come and

find you now. Right now. Although how we're going to find her in the fucking mountains, I have no clue at all. *Just give me a landmark, a reference and we'll be there.*

There's more silence. Is she thinking? I go to check if she's still there and then she answers.

Crow's Peak, she says. *We'll meet you at Crow's Peak.*

And then, although I can still feel her, far more strongly than before, the communication connection breaks.

I stare straight ahead of me, stroking my fingers through my beard.

"Phoenix!" Azlan snaps. "What the fuck?"

"She's not alone," I tell him, eyes flicking to him.

"Barone," he says, his face darkening.

"Barone," I repeat.

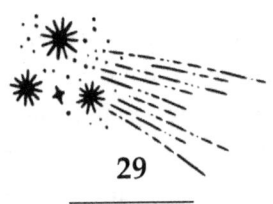

29

T ristan

I SIT at the desk in my old room, legs jiggling, staring down into the open drawer. Fuck, I want a joint. Fuck, I want one so badly. But I need to keep my head clear. Getting high right now, while it might calm all this raging anxiety in my body, may soothe the pain in my gut, is not going to help me think. And I need to think.

I rake my fingers through my hair.

I need to find my mate. I need to know she's safe. I need her with me. And not because of the unbearable pain in my gut, but because of the fucking ache in my heart.

But she's not the only one I need to find.

Was Summer talking bullshit? A load of crap simply to push my buttons? I've only been back in the academy 24 hours and the girl is worse than ever. Like she owns the school and everyone in it. And fuck, maybe she does, because it's not only Johnson kissing her ass now, all the fucking teachers are, including York herself. In fact, if I didn't know better, I'd suspect they're afraid of her.

I don't know what kind of pact she's made with my father, what bargain she made, but she obviously thinks it's a good one. One that gives her power over even me.

I slam the drawer shut and jump to my feet.

I've always been confident in my decisions and my own abilities. Yeah, maybe at times I've been over-confident – fucking cocky. I've never doubted myself before. But now, now I don't know what to do for the best.

Fate wants me with Rhianna. *I* want to be with Rhianna. But then there's Spencer. Doesn't fate want him with Rhianna too? Won't she need him as much as she needs me?

Is that how this works? And if that's the case, shouldn't I be trying to find my friend, trying to help him? If that's even possible.

I rake my fingers more firmly through my hair, tugging at the roots.

Should I talk to Summer again? Should I try to sweet talk more information out of her? Or should I reach out to my father, pretending to be supportive of his plans in the hope he'll supply me with information?

I decide a safer bet is York. She's never particularly liked me – I'm sure of that – despite the fact I've been her best student these last few years. She's always tolerated me. Plus, given the current circumstances and who my father is, she may be reluctant to tell me anything helpful at all.

I walk along the path towards the laboratories where York has set up a temporary office. There are few students out and those that are, clutch their books to their bodies and keep their gazes trained to the ground. Everyone is afraid.

It's hardly fucking surprising. The authorities' security agents are patrolling the grounds and this afternoon two more students were pulled from our magical history and politics class for questioning. It's rare anyone returns from such questioning and unclear where the hell those students go, although my father's daily announcement yesterday gloated about the continuing number of traitors the authorities are finding and arresting.

What makes you a traitor is unclear. Although I suspect disapproving of my father is the foremost crime.

Lessons are in full swing – not that I've bothered to attend – and as I pass Dr. Johnson's classroom I can hear Summer pontificating in her high-pitched whine. The stupid girl is obviously unconcerned by the fact two of her posse are among those who have disappeared in the last few days.

How the hell did I put up with that girl for so fucking long? How did I ever think a girl like Summer was superior to a girl like Rhianna? Was I fucking stupid?!

I shake my head at my own idiocy and stop outside the principal's new door. I raise my fist and debate whether I'm doing the right thing. Unsure a-fucking-gain.

The decision is taken out of my hands.

"Come in, Mr. Kennedy," the principal says from behind the door, even though I haven't knocked. I push open the door and step through into the old lab. The tables and chairs have all been stacked in one corner, leaving only one behind in which the principal is sitting, papers, that have obviously been salvaged from the wreck of the mansion, stacked by her feet. "What can I do for you?" She removes her reading glasses. "I understand you haven't attended any of your classes today, not even gym class."

"I'm not interested in using real, harmful magic against my classmates without the proper protections."

"Your father believes such adjustments are needed in our teaching practices in order to ..." she smiles flatly, "toughen up our students. He is quite certain if such teaching techniques had been in place before the enemy forces attacked the academy, they would not have been able to overrun the school."

So I didn't imagine that? We were losing the battle – we were vastly overpowered and overrun. I still don't understand why those forces withdrew, how the authorities managed to regain control despite the council also falling. It makes me all the more suspicious of my father.

"I don't agree with everything my father believes in."

The principal stands up and walks to the window, her hands clasped behind her back.

"A very dangerous position to hold, indeed," she says so quietly I barely hear her. "Even for his son."

Am I wrong about this? Are the principal and my father allies? I always thought her to be an independent woman who didn't bend to the rules and stood up to the chancellor when the occasion arose. Am I wrong?

"Everything seems dangerous these days."

There's a ceramic laboratory sink in the corner of the room and the tap drips into the basin. It's like the quiet beat of a drum. Somehow ominous and it makes my skin prickle.

"So you're not here for information on your fellow students? I thought perhaps your father had sent you. Although, what more he could possibly hope to glean, I don't know. I understand Miss Clutton-Brock has become a very useful source of information to him."

"No doubt." I hesitate. Then decide I'm already in up to

my neck. I don't have a lot to lose. And fuck it, I've been an arrogant selfish asshole all my goddamn life, and it's about time I did something about that. Like Ellie said, time to be a better person. For Rhi. For my mom. "Actually, I *am* here to ask you about another student. But it isn't for my father."

She twists around to face me and pierces me with her glare. "Who?"

"Spencer Moreau."

She looks a little surprised. I bet she thought I would ask about Rhianna. I bet my asking her to the ball didn't go unnoticed.

"Spencer Moreau is no longer a student of this academy. As you well know, he left before the attack on the academy."

"Yes," I say, stepping towards her. "But do you know where he is? What's happened to him?" The principal continues to stare at me, her mouth closed shut firmly. I plow on regardless. "Summer – Miss Clutton-Brock – seems to believe he's been locked away." I lower my voice, even though it's no longer a damn secret. "That all werebeasts have been."

"Yes, that is what I've heard too."

"There have been no announcements about it. Nothing in the press."

"I assume your father has no need for all his activities to be reported, nor all his decisions to be announced."

"This is meant to be a democracy!"

"This was never a democracy, Mr. Kennedy. I'm sure you are aware of that."

"Do you know where Spencer is? Where he's being kept?" The principal's brows leap up in alarm. "I want to see him ... he's ... he's my best friend."

The principal returns to her chair and sits herself down.

She looked nervous yesterday, today she looks tired and older than she did. "You're not the first student I've had in my office asking questions after their friends. I had a girl in here sobbing only an hour ago. What am I meant to say?" Her face contorts in pain and she spreads her hands out, palms up on the tabletop.

"Please, if you know where he is, can you just tell me?" I place my hands on her desk and lean forward.

She twizzles her hand in the air and the Bunsen burners lined up at the back of the room all light up and the tap turns on full force. It means when she speaks again, I struggle to hear her over the noise of the burning gas and the pouring water.

"I can't be certain, but I've heard rumors the werebeasts under arrest are being kept in the swamp fortress." I nod and stand up straight, about to turn and leave. "Mr. Kennedy, you didn't hear this information from me."

I look at her with my practiced bored-ass expression. "What information?"

She smiles. "Be careful."

＊

I DECIDE to leave after dinner. While nobody may care if I skip classes, my absence at dinner will be noticed – not least of all by the royal fucking queen bee herself. And I don't want her reporting that to Daddy's little helpers. Maybe even to Daddy himself.

I sit with what remains of the dueling team. Dan's in the clinic recovering from a ruptured spleen – the college infirmary destroyed along with the rest of the mansion. Zach and his family are said to be on the run. And Maddock went in for questioning yesterday afternoon.

The mood is somber – although Josh tries his best to throw a few wise cracks around. Most of them fall flat and in the end we eat in silence, forced to listen to more of Summer's endless chattering.

I don't have an appetite. The constant pain in my gut has wiped away any desire to eat, so I swivel my fork through the stew and wait for the minutes to pass.

At eight o'clock exactly, my father's now nightly broadcast is projected onto the far side of the canvas wall, his face staring out at us all. Most of the students visibly cower away, some staring down at their plates. Not Summer, she sits up straight, clapping her hands with glee as if we're about to be treated to an evening of cabaret.

My father's announcements travel straight over my head and I barely register any of the words about new measures, tighter restrictions, more arrests. Instead, I stare straight into his harsh eyes, convinced he's staring right back at me, convinced every warning he issues is directed at me personally.

My ears only perk up when he flashes the faces of several fugitive magicals he says are wanted by the republic. Among them are Piglet, her roommate Winnie, and my cousin himself. The rest of my father's words are lost to the shocked gasps and murmured whisperings of the students in the dining hall as well as Summer's cold cackle.

"Oh my God, Pig Girl! I knew she was trouble. I've been saying it for months. That girl is clearly deranged. I'm so glad the Lord Protector has seen it and is going to deal with her at last. She should never have been let into this school."

She tosses her hair, then twists her head to peer over at me, her smile not only cold but sinister.

I stare right back at her with such fucking hatred, I'm

surprised my magic doesn't spring straight out of my fucking eyeballs and annihilate the little bitch.

Unfortunately, I have far too much control and blasting Summer into a thousand tiny pieces isn't going to prove helpful, even if it would give me a ton of fucking pleasure.

I swing my jacket off the back of my chair and onto my shoulders. Then I shove my chair backwards roughly, the legs scraping along the ground and cutting through all the chatter. Every student in the dining tent turns to look at me as I stand to my feet. There's a hushed silence as if they're all waiting for me to do or say something.

"That girl is worth one hundred thousand of you," I tell Summer and then I leave before she can throw some retort back at me.

As soon as I'm out of the dark path, the winter's wind howling through the campus, I regret that remark. It may be true – hell, probably everyone but Summer knows it's true – but there's no doubt it will be reported back to my father and I don't need him on my case. I don't need him asking me any more questions about Piglet. Yeah, it's time to leave.

I check there's no one following me on the path behind me, and then I let myself merge into the darkness, disappearing into the shadows where I belong. Invisible, I should be able to slip unseen past the guards. However, I suspect there are trackers among them – magicals with the ability to sense the presence of other magicals – unseen or not. I can't leave by the front door. I'm going to have to go out the back.

I gaze up at the ghostly trees of the forest, their branches rattled together by the wind, swaying like ghouls. There're all sorts of tales about the forest – about what lies in its heart. It's said to be impassable – a natural protection for the academy, far more effective than any guards or security force.

It's said to be impassable to any ordinary magical. But I'm no ordinary magical. Maybe that's fucking arrogant. It's also true.

I zip up my jacket, lift up my collar, lower my chin and head under the trees.

I'm going to find Spencer and then together we'll find our girl.

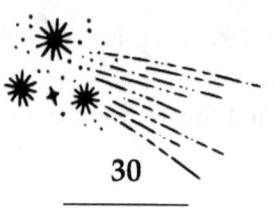

30

R enzo

WHEN I WAS A KID, I wanted to be a bird. I spent a fuck load of time trying to turn myself into one. My mom said it was dumb. Flying away? From all that shit? It didn't seem dumb to me.

One time I got far enough that I sprouted feathers all along my fucking shoulder blades. It looked awesome.

Didn't work though. I didn't lift one inch off the ground. All it did was make my mom's face ugly and then she set to screaming. Said I was a freak. Plucked every single one of those feathers out.

Fuck that hurt. Probably more than all the knives plunged into my gut, magic crashed against my body, nails dragged down my cheeks, teeth sunk into my skin.

I gave up after that. Thought my mom was right. Flying was stupid. I was fucking stupid.

Yeah, she was wrong. She was wrong about a lot of things.

Flying is ...

Flying makes you feel like the king of the world. Makes you feel like you own the fucking heavens. Flying lifts you above the ground with all its pain and its torture and its confusion and takes you right up into the clouds, coats your face in a fine moisture that tastes like dew on your tongue, paints rainbows in front of your eyes, takes you through and up to where the sun was hiding all along.

And flying with *her*, flying with my arms wrapped around her waist, flying with her body pressed up against mine is ...

Little rabbit screams as we plunge back through the clouds again. But it isn't one of her terrified screams, or one of those screams she makes when I wind her body up tight and then let it go. It's a scream like kids make when they're happy. I can feel it in her magic, her body vibrating with it under the grip of my hands.

"This is incredible," she gasps, wiping the fine cloud droplets from her eyes. But I don't think incredible gives this feeling true justification. This is freedom. Another life altogether.

"You're a natural at this, little rabbit," I say into her ear.

"Me?" she laughs, "I'm not doing a thing! It's all her."

I don't know about that. The dragon reads the girl's desires, taking her where she wants to go, like they're talking to each other without saying any words.

"I could stay up here forever," she sighs, as the dragon catches a current and we skim below the clouds, riding the breath of the wind.

"Let's," I say. "Let's stay up in the sky forever and never go back down to earth."

She laughs again like I was joking. Then she shakes her head. "I need to get back to Pip. I need to ..." She hesitates. Then leans down, lying against the dragon's neck, resting her cheek against her scales and gazing down at the ground below us. "Can you even tell where we came from?"

I peer down at the land below, so small I could smash it with the heel of my boot.

"No," I say, even as I spot the gap in the rocks.

Unfortunately, little rabbit is eagled-eyed and spots it too. "There!" she cries, pointing below us. "But how the hell do we–"

She doesn't finish her words, the dragon is already swooping down, spiraling through the air, making me fucking dizzy, until we're right above that crack in the rocks.

"We'll never fit through!" little rabbit cries, closing her eyes. But the dragon masters it with ease, gliding through the gap and landing on the rocks below like she doesn't weigh a fucking thing.

The little pig's still laid out on the rock. He lifts his head and makes a feeble squeak.

"We're back," I tell him, sliding off the dragon's back reluctantly and landing with a thud that shakes the ground.

I hold up my hand to my little rabbit and, without a hint of a pause she takes it, sliding from the dragon herself.

Little rabbit isn't afraid to touch me anymore. The idea doesn't repulse her. It makes that thing in my gut spin like a whirlwind, has the cold blood in my veins warming.

She lands on her toes, and bounces straight up into my arms, flinging hers around my neck.

"That was so incredible. My heart's beating a million miles per hour," she sings right by my ear.

I squeeze her tight, liking the way her soft body feels pressed up against mine, and she throws back her head and looks up into my face. Hers is all bright and I think she's happy, really, really happy.

And so I do that thing I've only ever done once before. Something I've never wanted to do until her.

I bring my face right up close to hers. I can smell her skin, feel her breath, see all the colors in her eyes. Then I press my mouth against her, my lips against her lips. They're tender, and wet, making me think of how my fingers felt inside her, making me hard. Fuck, this always looked boring. Kind of tame. Never thought it would be erotic like this.

She moves her mouth against mine and fuck that feels good, ignites all these sensations in my body, in my magic. I hold her tighter and move my mouth hard against hers, hungry against hers. I want to devour her. I bite at her lips, nibble on her tongue, plunge mine deep inside her mouth.

Her body melts against mine. Her breath turns panty.

And then the spell breaks. Just like fucking that. The dragon rumbles. She pulls her mouth away from mine, then her body. Then she's letting go of my fingers.

She steps away from me, and lavishes all her affection on the giant beast instead, stroking her palms over the creature's gleaming skin, laying her hand on its snout, whispering words of praise.

I glare at the stupid animal. Not only am I competing with a pig, I'm now competing with a fucking dragon. How come little rabbit, doesn't stroke me like that, doesn't whisper nice words to me? Is it because I can't fly?

The little pig makes another of those feeble snorts.

"Yeah, you were out for the count yesterday," I say to him, "don't pretend you witnessed a thing!"

"What?" my little rabbit says, hand still resting just above the dragon's nostril.

"Nothing," I grumble, wondering what I have to do to get her to touch me like that again.

"We have to go," she tells me, giving the dragon one last pat, before walking towards the pig and our discarded bag.

"Are we taking her with us?" I ask, thumbing towards the dragon.

"No, I told you already."

"But, little rabbit, flying her was ... awesome." I gaze into the little rabbit's eyes and they sparkle with excitement. "Think where we could go on her back. You wanna get back to Los Magicos, we'd be there in an hour."

"Change of plan. We're no longer going back to Los Magicos." She slings the bag over her shoulder and picks up her pig. "We're going back down the mountain."

I scratch my head. I worked for Lowsky and his family for a long time. Once those guys made up their minds, there wasn't a fucking dragon on a rampage that could shift it. Little rabbit changes her mind like the wind changes direction. It makes me fucking dizzy. Fuck, I love it.

"You going to tell me why?" I say.

She looks at me and then the dragon, then shakes her head. "No."

I kick at the earth. "I could force it out of you."

She rolls her eyes. "You try and knock me unconscious again, I will–"

"I wasn't thinking of that."

"If you hurtle magic at me, I'll–"

I look at her darkly, letting my gaze meander down her lithe body. "I have other ways of torturing you now." She swallows and that fucking dragon rumbles again.

I throw her a dirty look over my shoulder. She's lucky I don't throw a bolt of magic. But she's too beautiful to destroy – not when my little rabbit has worked so hard to fix her up.

She's also deadly. Just like my little rabbit.

"She'd be an effective weapon against your enemies," I tell my little rabbit, although I'm also making my case to the dragon. Someone fucked her up. Someone put her in chains. I bet she has enemies like the rest of us.

"She wants to go," Rhianna says, "she deserves to be free. A creature like her shouldn't be kept as a pet."

I look at the woman before me. I had illusions about making her my pet. I am stupid after all. Because she's right and because she's like the dragon. She can't be owned. Not by me.

The dragon snorts and clouds of black smoke billow from her nostrils, then she spreads her wings again and rises up into the air. We watch her go, flying through the crack in the rocks and then up into the sky. She soars in a circle, golden against the dull clouds and then she's gone.

"There's every chance someone else will catch her," I say.

Rhianna shrugs. "It's beyond our control."

She squeezes through the narrow passage in the rocks and then we follow the meandering path through the maze of skeletons. We're halfway through when I tell her to stop, taking the bag from her shoulder and the pig from her arms, and then her hand in mine.

It takes us the rest of the day to retrace our steps and descend the mountain, the sun falling behind the peak and casting us in shadow, the light and the warmth fading away.

I don't feel the chill though. I'm buzzing, fucking buzzing, bouncing on my toes, swinging her hand in mine, whistling under my breath.

I rode a fucking dragon.

Little rabbit let me kiss her.

I think of all the things I've done in my life. The first time magic sparked in my fingers. The first time I made someone hurt. The first time I watched someone die. The first time I stole a life.

Those were good days. Some of the best.

They pale in comparison to this day.

Who fucking knew making out would be better than torturing a man to death? Fuck me – that is a surprise.

Little rabbit seems happy too. Her magic all sparkly and fizzing. But the lower we get, the closer we come down to earth, the more it fades along with the light. Her hand cools in mine. Her body stiffens. Her gaze flicks around us.

I'm shit at reading people. But with her it's different. There's something wrong. Is she worried we're going to be attacked?

"What's up, little rabbit?" I ask her as the night paints the sky black above us.

"This thing between us ..."

"The sex?"

"We haven't had sex. We're not having sex."

"We're going to have sex, little rabbit."

"If we have sex ... I'm not talking about sex!" She looks up at me with eyes full of fear.

"I won't hurt you," I tell her. "I know I said I would, but things are different now. I want to make you feel good. I like making you feel good."

She stops. "You promise?" I open my mouth to answer her but she laughs and looks away to the ground. "Why am I even asking you? You'll only tell me what you think I want to hear."

I take a step towards her. "Have I ever lied to you, little rabbit?"

Her brow creases. She's thinking. She shakes her head.

"Do you believe in fate?" she asks me.

"I've never really believed in anything before, little rabbit. Not the gods, not the stars, not fate. Not family or friends. Nothing. But I believe in you, little rabbit."

"Oh shit," she says, "I want to believe you."

I shrug. "Then do." She looks up into my eyes. The world tips on its axis. I see the future and the past deep in her pupils. I feel fate pull me towards her.

"Don't let me down," she says earnestly. And I'm going to kiss her again. Maybe pull her to the ground and make good on that promise to fuck her. But before I can, a voice calls out in the night.

And I'm dropping the pig and the bag and ready to strike.

It's dark. The sky hidden beneath clouds. I can't see a fucking thing. I send a flare of light up into the sky as the voice shouts again.

"Rhi!"

Before I can stop her, my little rabbit steps forward, waving her hands above her head.

"I'm here!" she shouts. "Right here!"

The mountainside flashes with white light and below us I see who she's waving to.

Her friend, the professor and the man in black himself.

Just fucking perfect.

31

R^{hi}

TIME DISTORTS and the next events occur as if I'm watching them in slow motion.

One moment we're cloaked in darkness, hidden from all around us, the next light streaks across the mountain and everything is cast in a startling brightness.

I see Azlan, Stone and Winnie on the slope beneath me. I see the exact moment they spot me on the hill above them. I see them wave. I see Winnie start to run. I see Azlan's face flood with relief.

And then I see the moment all three spy the man beside me.

Renzo Barone.

Winnie halts. Stone lifts his arms. Azlan growls.

And then the flare puffs out and we're all plunged into blackness again.

"You could have warned me," Renzo mumbles in the dark beside me and then a bolt of magic comes hurtling his way. He ducks and the thing skims right above his head, lighting him up in a hue of blue.

"Stop!" I scream, "Azlan stop!"

Another stream of magic crashes in Renzo's direction, and I use my own to block it and send it fizzling to the ground.

"For fuck's sake, I said stop!" I shout louder still, struggling to hear myself above the noise of more magic.

"Am I allowed to fight back?" Renzo asks, sounding bored.

"No!" I tell him. "Just ... just behave."

"Fuck me," he mutters, swerving to the left as a ball of fire almost melts his cheek.

I growl. I knew this first meeting was going to be difficult. I knew Stone and Azlan would take some talking to, some persuading. I didn't think they'd try and kill him quite so quickly.

"Azlan! Stone! Stop, please! We need to talk!"

I deflect more of their magic, Renzo crouching and forming a shield as a barrage of coordinated magic hurtles his way.

"Are they always so difficult?" he says, looking like he may actually be enjoying this.

"Yes," I say through gritted teeth, "and in case you forgot, you did nearly kill me."

"Shit, yeah, I did!" he says grinning. "You should be honored, little rabbit. That's practically a declaration of love from me."

Remembering how fucking painful that was, I consider sending my own bolt of magic his way, but before I have a chance, a speeding bolt hits Renzo smack on the right shoulder and sends him flying to the ground. He lies there panting, a wound the size of my fist visible through his scorched jacket, and grins up at me.

I roll my eyes, spin around and send a smack of thunder crashing through the air, enough to send Winnie, Azlan and Stone falling to the ground as well.

Then, with my hands on my hips, I stride down the hill towards them.

"Did you not hear me?" I yell. "I said stop!"

Before I can say more, Winnie jumps back up to her feet and flings her arms around me, squeezing me so tight I can hardly breathe.

"Rhi, you're okay?" I can hear tears in her voice and I laugh, pulling away to look at my friend. I can't help smiling into her worried face.

"Of course, I'm okay."

"He didn't hurt you? He didn't ... Oh stars, I've been so worried about you and–"

But I don't hear the rest of her rambled words because Stone is pulling her off me and wrapping me in his own arms.

"Thank fuck," he mutters, hugging me against his chest, one hand pressing the back of my head, the other the small of my back. I bury my face into my mate's jacket and inhale his scent, overwhelmed to be back in his arms. He kisses the crown of my head and I shake, relief suddenly flooding through me. There was a little part of me, a secret part I tried to suppress, that wondered if I'd ever see him again.

The relief lasts precisely one second and then I remember my other mate. Azlan.

I peek out from Stone's jacket and see that mate, not striding towards me, but up the hill with a murderous look on his face.

I wriggle free of Stone and chase after him.

"What are you doing?" I cry, struggling to catch up with him.

"What else? Going to finish him off."

"No, you're not," I say. I don't think he even hears me and I pick up my pace, racing to catch him. I grab his arm, just as he halts.

Renzo is sitting cross-legged on the ground, Pip curled up in his lap.

"Hey man," Renzo says, "what's up?"

Azlan growls and lifts his hand but I catch it in mine and yank it back down.

"Rhianna," he hisses, "let go of me. I'm going to kill him."

"No, you're not," I say, stepping between the two men.

"Rhianna!" he growls, sounding more like a rabid wolf than a human man.

"You're not going to kill him. You're not going to hurt him. I won't let you."

Pain washes across the man in black's face. "Rhi, he tried to kill you – he nearly killed you! I held you in my arms and felt you slipping away. Do you have any idea how that felt? Do you think I'd stand here and risk him doing it again?"

"You're going to have to, Azlan."

"Rhianna, I don't know what he's told you. What he's said. But this man is a killer. A known psychopath," he says as Stone comes to stand alongside him.

"Azlan, you've killed people. I've killed people," I say, repeating the assassin's argument.

"Don't tell me, sweetheart," Stone says, crossing his arms over his chest. "You've succumbed to Stockholm Syndrome."

"This isn't Stockholm Syndrome, or whatever ..." I wave my hands in frustration. "This is me asking you not to kill the man who saved me at the academy, he brought me somewhere safe and has been looking out for me ever since."

"Him?" Stone says, staring down at Renzo with obvious disgust.

"Me, Prof.," Renzo says grinning up at him in an infuriating manner that is most definitely not going to help our cause.

Stone turns his head and addresses his friend. "Definitely Stockholm Syndrome. Or possibly a bad knock to her head."

"He could have warped her memories. Fooled her into thinking–"

"I am in complete control of my senses!"

"Clearly not," Stone says, "otherwise you'd have killed that man yourself, instead of letting him molest your pig."

"Hey, hey," Renzo says, frowning, "me and the little dude do not have that kind of relationship. I'm much more interested in molest–"

"Yes, thank you," I say, feeling a headache building behind my eyes.

Winnie appears alongside the others and assesses us all wearily.

"What's going on?" she asks.

"Rhianna is having some kind of mental breakdown," Stone mutters.

"Does he always talk to you like this?" Renzo says menacingly.

"Yep," I answer.

"I wasn't the one who nearly killed you," Stone snarls.

Azlan growls again and takes a menacing step forward, one I'm forced to block with my body.

"I'm no clearer," Winnie says.

"Rhianna won't let us kill the assassin."

Winnie rolls her eyes. "Your boyfriends are really dumb." I smile at her, relieved by the knowledge that Winnie at least will be on my side, no matter how crazy-assed that side is.

"Mate, not boyfriend," Azlan spits.

"Well, in that case you should know her better by now. Rhi isn't going to let you kill anyone on her behalf. Gently torture perhaps. Maybe a little maiming–"

"–I like her," Renzo says.

"But no killing."

"Exactly," I say.

"So I have your permission to torture him?" Azlan says, cracking his knuckles.

"No!" I say, "Winnie was joking." Both Azlan and Renzo look disappointed. "We're not going to hurt each other."

"Looks like I already did," Stone says, peering proudly at the injury on Renzo's shoulder.

"We're going to talk like civilized human beings."

"He isn't civilized," Azlan sneers.

"Urgh!" I say throwing my head backwards.

"Maybe you should just hear Rhi out," Winnie says. "We've been separated for days. You've no idea what she's been through and she has no idea what we've been through."

My gaze skips to my friend and she smiles at me weakly.

"What happened?" I ask.

"You go first," she says. "Tell us what happened."

I start from the beginning. From the moment of the attack at the academy. Of fighting alongside Tristan, of seeing him fall. Of losing my mind and then falling into the hands of Lowsky. Of Renzo saving me, nursing me and then knocking me fucking out. Of the attack in the forest, of our climb up the mountain, of our discovery of the dragon.

I skip over our stay in the shepherd's hut and Renzo eyes me with curiosity.

When I'm done, Winnie's mouth is hanging open.

"You rode on the back of a dragon? Oh my stars! What was that like?"

But Azlan is less concerned with the dragon and more so with the men that attacked us in the forest.

"Who were they?" he asks me.

"Lowsky's men," Renzo says, then shrugs. "Or not anymore. Lowsky's dead."

"You killed him?" Stone asks.

"Yep."

"Good."

"And the men in the forest," Renzo adds.

Both Azlan and Stone nod reluctantly.

"Why did they attack you?" Azlan asks.

"They weren't attacking us at first. They attacked a couple of families fleeing through the forest."

"And you intervened," Stone says flatly, shaking his head like I'm stupid.

"You'd have done the same," Winnie says. And we all know she's right. Stone may act the asshole with the hard outer shell. But underneath, he's soft as butter really.

"They knew who she was," Renzo says from the ground. "They said the reward for her capture has quadrupled."

"My uncle," Azlan sneers, "the new Lord Protector is after her."

"I don't think he's the only one," Renzo says, stroking Pip's head.

"What makes you say that?" Stone asks.

"The men at her house—"

"The men at my house?" I say.

"Yeah, the ones who came for you when we were leaving." I stare at him flabbergasted. He never mentioned them before. "They weren't from the authorities, or the gangs. They were from the West."

"The West?" Stone stares at me. "Why would men from the West want Rhianna?"

"Same reason your uncle does, I presume," Winnie says.

I peer at Renzo, wait for him to say more, for him to reveal–

"What?" Stone says. "What was that?"

I spin my face around to face him. "Nothing."

"You're a horrible liar. That wasn't nothing."

I glare at him and dare him to press me. He doesn't, he simply shakes his head.

"So what now?" Winnie says. "We can't go back to Los Magicos. I'm sure the capital is going to be full of the Lord Protector's spies and you – as well as us – are on the most wanted list."

"Congratulations!" Renzo says.

Winnie looks at him like he's mad, which he probably is. "And now it seems that the West may be after Rhi too. So what are we going to do?"

They all begin to debate this. Renzo wants us to go hide out in the mountains. Stone thinks we should leave the continent. And Azlan wants to try and reason with his uncle. They go round and round in circles, and all I really want to do is ask after Tristan and Spencer. I know Tristan's alive. I can feel him through the bond. But Spencer? I haven't seen him since the night of the attack on the academy. Is he even alive?

Something, however, keeps me from asking. Tristan may be my mate, but his father is now Lord Protector and after my head. Tristan has always considered me to be below him, not good enough to be his mate. He told me so himself. Okay, so he had a temporary change of heart, but now his dad's running the republic, it's likely he's returned to his original way of thinking. He's certainly not here, is he?

And as for Spencer ... He left the academy. He chose to turn his back on the bond.

Maybe I'm a fool to think of either of them at all.

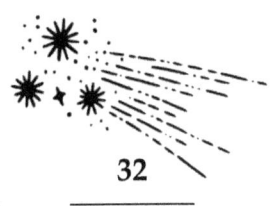

32

Spencer

"Is she pretty, your mate?"

It's darker than usual and I struggle to see the other man's face through the gloom.

I wet my lip, the metallic taste of blood dissolving onto my tongue.

"Yeah, yeah, I guess she is."

He lets out a weak chuckle. "Sounds like you really believe that."

I frown. "She is pretty," I say with more conviction. "Maybe not in the conventional way. She's no blonde bombshell. But ..." I still can't see his face and maybe that makes it easier to tell him the truth. "There were times I'd catch myself staring at her and I'd realize I'd been holding my breath the whole damn time, because ..."

"Yeah, I know what you mean. My Daisy, she could do

that to me too. In her human form she was stunning, would have heads turning everywhere we went. But in her wolf form," he chuckles again, "fuck me, she was terrifying. Fierce and strong and unstoppable. Freaking terrifying."

I think of Rhi, chin raised in defiance, eyes spitting with insolence. Maybe that's what I found most beautiful about her. Maybe that's what pulled me towards her. Her inability to back down, to give up, to refrain from fighting.

"And she wasn't ashamed, you know, of what she was," the were continues. "She wanted me to love both her forms and I did."

"Weren't you frightened? That you'd hurt her? That your beast would?"

"No, we would never hurt her. We loved her. Both of us. She was ours."

"I'm scared I'll hurt her. That he'll hurt her."

"What does he feel about her?"

I sift through my memories, through those glimpses of the beast's emotions. "He wants to make her his."

"Then why would he hurt her?"

"He attacked her."

"And he hurt her?"

"No, no ... he wanted to devour her."

"He sounds like every other beast, head over heels for a girl."

I sniff.

"Wh-what happened to your girl?" I ask, almost scared to hear the answer.

He's quiet for some time and then he whispers into the darkness. "Killed, when they came for us. Killed."

"I'm sorry."

"I should have done more to protect her, to save her," he

says and, though I can't see them, I can hear the tears in his voice.

"I'm sure you tried," I say feebly, not knowing what else to say.

"And maybe it was for the best," he says even more quietly, "I couldn't bear the thought of her here suffering like this."

"No," I say. We're silent again for some minutes, both thinking.

"Tell me more about her, your girl," he says.

I screw up my eyes. It's painful thinking about her, thinking I might never see her again. It makes my heart ache more than all the rest of the pain put together.

"Please," he says, "give me something to distract from this pain." And I think it's the pain of losing his girl he's talking about, not the physical wounds.

I blow out air through my teeth. "She came from the wastelands," I whisper, "an unregistered."

I tell him everything in the quiet of the cell. I tell him it all. The way I fought the bond. The way I treated her. The way I left her.

When there's no more to tell, the cell is silent again and I don't know if he's drifted back into unconsciousness. Or maybe he's so disgusted with me, he no longer wants to talk with me.

I close my eyes, willing sleep to suck me back under, and that's when he speaks.

"We all make mistakes. Especially when it comes to the ones we care about," he says. "If you get out of here, if you ever find your way back to her, you have to make it up to her. Fate rarely gives us someone to love, to belong to. You shouldn't throw that chance away. You should grab it with both of your hands."

In the darkness, I hear him wet his lips.

"Moreau," he whispers, "there's a prophecy. Do you know the one?"

I frown, wondering if the pain is making him delirious.

"A prophecy? A prophecy about what?"

"A new Queen Æðelflæd."

My frown deepens. I recognize the name, but I struggle to remember it.

"They say a girl will come – powerful like the queen – the queen who had five fated mates. And she will free us all."

"What are you saying? You think that's Rhi?" I say with derision in my tone.

"I'm just an old, broken were," he says, "what the hell do I know?"

I shift on the hard ground, more pain shooting through my body. "It sounds like an old story to me," I mutter.

"Maybe," he says, his chains rattling, "but what if it's not?"

33

R^{hi}

IN THE END, we come to a decision that no one is particularly happy with but no one openly hates, and we all bundle into Winnie's car; me sandwiched uncomfortably between Stone and Renzo. Being physically squeezed between the two of them is not even the most uncomfortable part, it's the way they glare at each other over my head.

Am I stupid for bringing Renzo along? Is there really any hope of us all getting along in one big happy family? Then again, do I have a choice? Fate seems determined and fate is one stubborn bitch.

"What's wrong with Pip?" Winnie asks as we start our journey. My pet is laid out across my lap, still unresponsive and still ill-looking.

"He got struck by magic when we were attacked in the

forest," I tell Winnie, resting my hand on Pip's quivering body.

"Oh my goodness!" Winnie shrieks, spinning around in her seat and causing the rest of us to yelp, Azlan diving for the steering wheel.

"Eyes on the road," he says sternly.

"Ooops, sorry," Winnie says with some awkwardness. She focuses forward, peering at me in the rearview mirror. "It doesn't look like he has any obvious injuries."

"He doesn't," I say. "And we've both tried to heal him," I add, glancing towards Renzo. "But he's been like this since he got hit."

Stone scoffs. "You tried to heal him?"

"Yes," I scowl at him. "There's nothing obvious to fix. Just some lingering magic in his body that won't shift."

Stone shakes his head with his usual level of disappointment and gingerly lays his hand on Pip's stomach. "When was the last time this thing took a bath?"

"This 'thing'," I snap, "smells a lot better than you do, Professor."

The professor sniffs his shoulder. "You may have a point. It's been a few days since I've had the pleasure of a bathroom." He leans and sniffs me too. "Seems you haven't either." I sniff myself and grimace. "Let's hope there's a bathroom at our destination."

He closes his eyes and pretty soon his brow furrows. I don't have to be a mind reader to know he's having about as much luck curing Pip as I did.

"What do you think?" Winnie asks him after a few minutes.

"No injuries but some residual magic that's making him sick."

"That's exactly what I said," I say, pushing his hand off Pip.

"Can you remove it?"

"Errr," the professor turns to stare out of the window, "no."

I sigh. Although, it's nice to be proved right for once when it comes to Stone, it would be far nicer to have Pip back to full health. I don't like seeing him like this and I miss his company.

As Winnie drives us, she fills me in on everything that has happened since the academy attack – Stone and Azlan butting in occasionally to add some details. I audibly gasp when she tells me what happened to Spencer at the academy and lean forward to rest my hand on her shoulder when she tells me about Rosa.

"I'm sorry, Winnie," I tell her later when we finally arrive at our destination. It's a deserted mansion in the heart of the prairie lands, somewhere Azlan was sent to apprehend unregistereds several years back. He's confident it's well hidden and almost certainly unoccupied. Still, he has Winnie park under the boughs of a willow tree and sets off on foot by himself to be sure. "This is all my fault."

Winnie shakes her head and takes my hands in hers. "Don't say that, Rhianna Blackwaters. It's not your fault at all. Did you attack the academy and the city? Did you place a wanted reward on our heads?"

"No, but if it wasn't for me, you would be at home with your family and your boyfriend–"

"Rhi, if it wasn't for you, yes, I'd be at home, cowering and afraid. But you give me hope."

I give her a quizzical look, unsure what she can mean by that, but before I can ask her, Azlan has returned and, leaving the car hidden under the willow, we walk on foot to the mansion.

It stands smack in the center of the land, prairie fields falling away all around it, and looks like the type of house a child would draw. Perfect rectangle, triangular roof with chimney pots, large door right in the middle, neat windows all around. However, it has the look of a house that hasn't been lived in for sometime. In the early morning light, I can see the windows are covered in grime, a creeper has grown out of control, curling right up into the roof tiles and the door hangs crooked.

"You take us to all the best places, Az," Stone mutters as we enter into the main hallway, coughing and spluttering because of all the dust spiraling in the air. It smells too, of damp and creatures.

"Renting a room at a five-star hotel in Los Magicos wasn't exactly an option," Azlan says. He swings open a door, behind which lies a dining room with a long table and many chairs, some toppled to the floor. "Let's sit down and formulate a better plan. We can't stay here forever."

I shake my head. I'm shattered, barely managing to stay upright, and swaying on my feet. "Not now," I say, yawning. "I've been awake for more than 24 hours and I need sleep."

Azlan looks like he might argue, but Winnie hooks her arm through mine and leads us towards the grand staircase, swirling her hand in the air to remove all the dust and the grime as we walk.

"Me too," she says. "I'm whacked. Let's all get some sleep. The plan we form will be a better one if we all have fully functioning brains."

We all peer at Renzo, who's fiddling with the ancient-looking light switch on the wall. "What?" he says, sensing us all staring at him.

"Nothing," I say with a smile.

If my mates were hoping they'd get to sleep with me, they're beaten to the punch by Winnie. She drags me up the stairs and into the nearest bedroom, one with a huge four-poster bed that could definitely fit me, Stone and Azlan on the mattress.

"I know you're probably biting at the bit to bang those boys," Winnie says, as we hover in the doorway. "But do you think just for tonight, we could be together?"

"Winnie," I say, hugging her. "I am not some nymphomaniac–"

"Debatable," she murmurs.

I elbow her. "I can go one night without ..." I lift an eyebrow. "Besides, sometimes a bit of anticipation is a good thing, right?"

"Definitely," Winnie says, flopping herself down on the mattress.

"And anyway, I am way too tired for any banging." Which isn't quite true. I'd be more than happy for either of my mates to throw me down onto the nearest horizontal surface. But Winnie has already sacrificed an awful lot for me and has been by my side from the beginning. I owe her my time and attention.

I go to lay Pip out on the floor of the bedroom, but Winnie snatches him off me and settles him at the end of the bed.

"I thought you were a strict enforcer of the no pigs on the bed rule," I say to her.

"He's sick!" she protests, although I think she's missed him as much as she's missed me. Let's be honest. Probably more.

I head to the door to say goodnight to the others and find Azlan lurking in the doorway.

"You're sleeping in here?" he asks.

"Yes, with Winnie."

He looks mighty disappointed, and I almost feel sorry for him, my own resolve fading. His eyes travel over my face and he grabs my hand, pulls me out of the room and slams the door behind me. Then he pushes me up against the closed door and kisses me, his hands tangled in my hair, his mouth hungry and incessant. His kiss makes me even more unstable on my feet. In fact, my knees begin to buckle and my head swims. I don't know if I can be the good friend I want to be and keep my promise to Winnie.

However, the sound of footsteps on the stairs has him pulling away, my bond mighty unhappy about it.

"I'll sleep in the room next to yours and Phoenix will take the room on the other side. Any problems," he eyes Renzo as he comes to join us on the landing, "you yell for us. Even if it's just a feeling of unease. Okay?" I nod and he kisses me again, this time more briefly. "Go get some sleep." He opens the door behind me. "You can take one of the bedrooms down the hall," he tells Renzo.

"Nah, I'm going to sleep outside her door."

I roll my eyes, placing a hand on Azlan's arm because I can tell he's steaming again. "You can't sleep outside my door. It's a hard floor."

He shrugs. "Doesn't bother me."

"There are beds down the hall," Azlan says firmly.

"And I don't want to be down the hall," Renzo says, as firmly. "I need to be near little rabbit, in case something happens."

"Little rabbit?" Azlan says, his face distorting with disgust.

I sigh and decide to leave them to it, stepping back inside the bedroom and shutting the door behind me.

Winnie's lying on the bed next to Pip, her hand resting on his stomach.

"When are you going to tell Stone and the ma– Azlan?"

"Tell them what?" I ask, tugging off my jeans and my sweater. Winnie's conjured new covers for the bed and a smokeless fire in the fireplace. It's pretty toasty in the room.

"About Barone?"

I frown. "What do you mean?"

She beckons me over and I slide under the covers, Winnie coming to curl up beside me. "About him being one of your fated mates," she whispers.

I jolt and stare at her.

"Wh ... I ... how did you know?"

She taps the side of her head. "Not just a pretty face, you know."

"Well, duh, I've been telling you that for months. But seriously, Winnie, is it that obvious?"

Winnie adjusts the pillow under her head. "I always suspected there'd be a fifth fated mate. Five all together."

"Why?"

"Because of the fairy tale. The tale about Queen Æðelflæd." I haven't been able to stop thinking about that tale as well. It seems so relevant, like it must mean something. "Five seems to be the most powerful number of mates. I think you were destined for that number, Rhi."

"That doesn't mean Renzo is my mate, Winnie," I point out, even though the sensation in my gut is undeniable.

"True." Winnie hesitates, clearly debating whether to plow on. "Renzo Barone is a psychopath–" I go to argue, but she raises her hand to silence me. "I'm sorry, Rhi, but he is." I shift on the bed. I was convinced he was too – utterly convinced. Now I wonder if he truly is. Or is that just wishful thinking on my part? "He doesn't care about anyone but himself. But he seems to have formed an attachment to you. I mean, he's sleeping outside your door."

"Still doesn't confirm anything, Winnie."

"I also don't think you'd let him tag along if he wasn't a fated mate. He did try to kill you." My best friend looks deep into my eyes. "So is he, Rhi?"

I flip onto my back and stare up at the canopy of the bed. Strange symbols have been carved into the wood and the drapes are embroidered with golden threads.

"Yes," I say. "Yes, he is." Winnie is quiet and her silence makes me anxious. I turn my head back towards her. "Winnie? This is fucked up. What am I going to do?"

"Have you, you know, sealed the bond yet?"

I shake my head, although I can't help my cheeks heating – something my eagle-eyed friend spots. She prods my cheek. "Can I assume you've come close?"

"Not that close." I cover my face with my hands. "Do you think I'm a deranged slut?"

Winnie giggles. "Not at all. He is kind of hot, in an unstable, totally insane kind of way."

"I'm beginning to find the instability and insanity sort of endearing," I confess.

"Hmmm," Winnie says. "Maybe Stone is right. Maybe you did bang your head."

"Winnie!" I cry. "Seriously, what am I going to do? Five mates? Most of whom hate each other. This is a disaster!"

Winnie shakes her head. "I don't think so." I give her a dubious look. "Okay, it isn't … *ideal*. But if fate chose Renzo Barone for your mate, fate has a reason."

"Maybe fate just has a thing for hot assholes," I mutter.

"Lucky you have similar tastes, then." I pinch her and she grabs my hand. "But, honestly, Rhi, I think he's your mate for a reason. I think they all are. I can't tell you what that reason is. I think it's something we have to figure out."

"I'm going to have to tell them, aren't I?"

"Uh huh, preferably before they kill each other," she says, peering towards the door behind which we can hear a kerfuffle. "Besides, Stone and Azlan already know about Tristan and Spencer."

"They do?" I say, my eyebrows leaping up my forehead. I swallow. "How did they take the news?"

Winnie shrugs and I groan.

"Okay," I say, resolutely, "I'll tell them. Only not tonight. Tonight, I need sleep." I bunch the cover up around my body and fall promptly asleep before Winnie has even extinguished the lights.

I WAKE WITH A JOLT, bolt upright in the bed, my body caked in sweat and shaking, the world spinning and Winnie shaking my arm. A second later three men, in various states of undress, come crashing through the door.

"What's wrong?" Azlan says, arms raised and ready. "What happened?"

"Nothing," Winnie says, stroking damp hair back from my face. "Just a bad dream."

"A dream?" Stone says, his jaw tightening. "What kind of dream?"

I peer at Renzo, lingering by the door. "The same one as before. I'm running to save a beast. An injured beast. One I have to save. Only I wasn't running up the mountain this time. I was somewhere else. Somewhere dark and," I shiver, "sinister."

"A beast? What beast?" Winnie says.

"I don't know. I can't see it. I don't know what it is. I just know it's hurt, injured, and I have to save it." I stare round at Stone and Azlan. "I had the same dream last time I slept. And it's like ... it's like my dreams used to be."

"A premonition," Stone whispers.

"Yes, but why has this dream come again? I healed the dragon. We watched her fly away."

"Maybe that wasn't the beast you were meant to heal," Winnie suggests.

"Then what beast am I meant to heal?"

"Spencer Moreau," Azlan says, and my eyes leap to meet his.

Spencer!

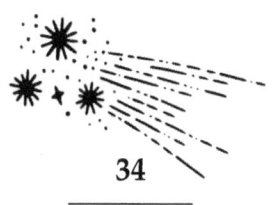

34

T ristan

I CREEP THROUGH THE FOREST, the trees becoming denser and denser the deeper I walk until I'm squeezing between tree trunks, leafless branches scraping at my shoulders and my face. It's eerily quiet. Perhaps it's because the birds have flown south and the other animals are hidden away hibernating. Or maybe it's the oppressive nature of the forest.

There are rumors among the students that the forest is haunted, haunted by ancient spirits that feed on the souls of trespassers. That's the reason the forest is impassible. That's the reason no one comes in or out.

That also sounds like bullshit to me. There are no such things as spirits.

Then again, there were meant to be no such things as dragons. And that turned out to be bullshit too.

The temperature this far into the forest is several

degrees cooler than it was out on the campus and my breath hangs like a ghost of its own in front of my face, the cold wind like icy fingers stroking at my skin.

Yeah, okay, it's creepy.

I try not to think about it, plowing onwards. I've turned off my phone – I don't want to be tracked – which means I've had to resort to old-fashioned methods of navigation. I hold a compass I stole from Johnson's classroom up to my face. By my reckoning, if I keep heading northeast, I should reach the other side of the forest. Then I'll have to circle back around the base of the hill, hoping no security forces are patrolling there, and head out into the lanes. There's an old motorbike out in one of the fields – one Spencer crashed on a night of craziness a year ago. We never bothered to try and fix it or to drag it back to campus. I'm hoping I'll be able to revive it back to life.

That's my plan, anyway. I admit it's not the best. I could find myself lost in this forest. I could find myself caught. The motorbike may no longer be there after all this time. Or perhaps I won't be able to make it start. It's the best I have for now, though, so I'm sticking with it, even as the wind wails through the branches overhead and has me reconsidering my life choices.

I try to ignore it and the sinister sensation that there's someone out here in the forest with me, my skin creeping. This is how it must have felt for Piglet that time I followed her into the forest. Only that time there had been someone there with her. Me.

This time I'm imagining it. Imagining the sound of whispered voices and the brush of fingertips against my skin, of my mom's voice in my ear.

"Tristan."

I spin around. The trees are so close now, so crowded, so

clustered together and drawing closer and closer until they're pressing against me, entrapping me in their branches, circling me in a prison.

I crash my magic hard against the trunks as they squeeze tighter and tighter, trapping me, crushing me. The wood splinters, two of the trees sway and topple to the ground and then I sprint through the gap, hoping I'm running the fucking right way.

Those voices grow louder, taunting, calling my name. I swear I see a ghostly face peering at me from behind a tree as I race as fast as I can, the trees seeming to chase me, scratching at me, reaching for me.

I stumble once and a limb wraps around my ankle, dragging me to the ground as laughter cackles through the cold air.

I slice my magic through it and then I'm running again, swerving the trees that attempt to block me, resisting my mother's plea to stay, stay with her, stay with her, stay with her.

I cover my ears with my hands. Another face and another. I fire my magic at them. But they're like air. Barely rippling as my magic passes straight through them.

I keep running, sweat pouring down my face and into my eyes, my clothes damp.

Is this how it ends? Like this? Lost among the trees, invisible so no one will even find my body.

Will she feel it? Will she know that I'm gone? Will it hurt her?

I don't want to hurt her anymore. I'm not going to. I fire my magic out in front of me, scorching the trees and running through the flames. They burn at my face but I don't stop, I keep pushing and pushing and pushing until finally, finally, I break free of the trees, and collapse down onto my knees, panting, my chest heaving. I can still hear those voices taunting me, but they're behind me now, locked in the forest.

I stumble to my feet, refusing to look back and continue on my way.

THE PRISON IS LOCATED in an old fortress in the middle of marshland to the east of the capital. There's one paved road that stretches across the swamp, but as I don't want to be spotted, I'm forced to abandon the motorbike and make my way cross-country on foot.

My feet plunge into the soggy land, and soon my boots, my socks, and my feet are soaked through. Twice I nearly lose a boot altogether, the mud sucking hungrily at my feet, and once I sink all the way down to my thighs and am forced to use my magic to pull myself out. But finally, I see the shadow of the fortress looming in front of me. It's ringed by the old moat that's guarded it for centuries, the ancient drawbridge still the only way to cross, and sentries posted along the battlements.

I peer down into the moat, debating whether I'm going to have to swim across. Even in the darkness, I can see the water is a putrid green color and things I don't want to examine too closely are floating on its surface. Yeah, I won't be swimming in that. Which leaves the drawbridge.

Tonight, it's raised and securely fixed in place.

I consider waiting until it's lowered and sneaking my way inside unseen. But who knows when that will be. I could be left waiting for days and I don't have the patience or the inclination for that.

No, I decide to use my tried and most tested method for

solving a problem. Throwing my fucking family name at it. Yeah, it's fucking arrogant. It's also damn effective.

As soon as I decide on that course of action, I regret not coming by road on the motorbike. I'm going to look mighty suspicious turning up alone outside the prison, my boots wet and my legs covered in marshy slime.

Then again, I'm the Lord Protector's son himself. I'm sure I can convince them to let me in. Of course, someone's bound to call it in, double check I'm meant to be here. But I plan to be long gone with my friend before my dad or his forces turn up to investigate what I'm up to.

I let myself reappear, using my magic to dry my boots and clean up my pants as best I can. Then I step out onto the road and call up at the guards on the battlements.

Immediately, their weapons are trained my way and a spotlight swings in my direction, blinding me in the process. I shade my eyes.

"State your identity and your intentions immediately or we'll be forced to take you out."

"Tristan Kennedy," I say in as arrogant and bored tone as I can manage. "Here under my father's orders to see the Moreau prisoner. Lower the bridge."

"In the middle of the night?" the guard says with incredulity.

"Don't keep me waiting," I snap.

The guard eyes me, then turns and whispers to his friend.

"How did you get here?" he says, still unconvinced. "We didn't see anyone approaching."

"I'm the Lord Protector's son. I have powers and abilities you couldn't even imagine. If I want to arrive unnoticed and unannounced, that is no fucking concern of yours. Now, do you want me to report your insolence to my father, or not?"

The guard peers at the other one nervously, then waves his hand and the bridge lowers slowly, groaning as it does. It takes far longer than I'd like, wasting precious minutes, and I've jumped up on the boards and am striding across before it's fully lowered.

A more senior-looking guard meets me at the entrance of the prison, rubbing sleep from his eyes, and introduces himself as the warden.

"We weren't told to expect you."

"And I suppose you're told of all my father's plans, are you?" I sneer.

"No, but–"

"Your guards have already wasted enough of my time. I've been sent on urgent business by my father and it's important I see the prisoner now." I look down my nose at the warden, imitating my dad's cold and merciless manner as best I can.

He peers back at me full of suspicion. He knows if he gets this wrong the punishment will be severe. I can almost see the little cogs turning in his head. In the end, he nods and beckons for me to follow him.

"All the mutts are being kept in the most secure part of the jail – in the dungeon cells."

"As they should be." My own mind starts whirring. This is going to make my job harder. More difficult to release Spencer, and longer for us to get out of here. "Have they been much trouble?"

"At first some were, but we learned pretty quickly that as long as we keep them in a constant state of pain, they will remain in their human states. The trick is to never let them heal." The man smiles sadistically. "They've made very effective punching bags for my guards."

I smile back, hoping I look just as sadistic and there isn't a hint of the true disgust I feel betrayed in my eyes.

"Maybe I'll have a go myself."

"Weren't you and Moreau friends? Dueling team buddies?" the man asks and maybe he isn't as dumb as he looks.

"I had no idea what he truly was."

He leads me into the heart of the fortress. It's the middle of the night and yet the prison is alive with noise – of men shouting, some screaming. Of fists thumping walls, of hands rattling bars. The warden seems unconcerned, barely seeming to register the unrest.

I follow him along a weaving and narrow corridor with low ceilings, several of the lights out, and I make a note of the way we come. At the end we reach a heavy door and the man waves his hand, reciting a complicated security spell. The door groans open and beyond them lies a stone staircase, spiraling down into the cold dungeon of the old fortress.

"Are the cells numbered?" I ask him. He nods. "And which one is Moreau in?"

"Number six." His old dueling team jersey. I have to suppress the desire to thump the man straight in his stupid grinning face.

"Thank you. That will be all."

"I can't let you see him alone," the man says.

"This is private business. I've been ordered to ensure no one else is in attendance when I speak with the ..." I swallow, "mutt."

"It's dangerous."

I draw myself up to my full height. I'm taller than this man by several inches and bigger than him too. "Are you questioning my ability–"

"No, no, only advising–"

"I didn't ask for your advice," I say and then I'm descending the steps, ensuring the door slams behind me. It clicks locked, blocking out my escape and any light. I'm plunged into darkness, the temperature frigid.

I have that sense of foreboding again, like I did in the forest. Only this time it's much much worse.

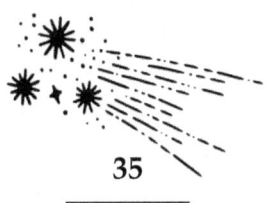

35

S pencer

It's unclear how many days have passed. I drift in and out of consciousness, the pain making it almost impossible to remain awake. I know I'm brought food and water, most of which I don't touch. I know I'm questioned and beaten, beaten and questioned. I know despite this my body is healing. But the pain, the pain remains.

Unconsciousness should be a relief from it all. But my sleep is fretful, full of dreams of the past, of the future, of nonsense. Mostly it's full of my brother – and I wake forgetting for that fraction of a second that he's gone, forced to experience the agony of losing him all over again.

In some ways, maybe it's better that he's gone. Not here to bear all this.

How many days have passed? How many endless days will pass like this? Stretching on and on forever. Until I'm beginning to lose the ability to tell when I'm awake or asleep. Both as painful as the other.

Sometimes, when I have the strength, I think of her. Of Rhi. I hope they've found her. I pray she's safe. I hope she's far far away from here.

I dream of her too. I dream of that morning in the gymnasium when I left. I dream that I don't go, that I stay. I dream that I tell her the truth. I dream that I confess how much I care about her. I dream that everything turns out different, that fate leads us down a different path, one that doesn't end with me chained to the wall of a cold and desolate dungeon.

Occasionally, when he's awake, I talk to the other were in my cell. He tells me tales of running as beasts with his pack, through the woods, through the mountains, of hunting together, of living free. Most of the time he's out cold, and I'm forced to watch as they attack his unmoving body with glee.

It's too painful. Far worse than enduring the beating myself and I slip away as often as I can, into the darkness.

I wake.

The pain hits me and I wince, my body contracting into a tight ball. I force myself to uncurl and reach for the cup of stale water resting by my side. With a shaking hand, I bring it to my lips, most of it spilling down my front and over my chin. My lips are cracked, and the water stings. I gulp it down. My leg is no longer contorted and twisted, my arm no longer hangs loose, but there are new injuries to my body. Cracked ribs that make it hard to breathe, a smashed nose, a bloody hand.

I drop the cup, to the floor, and lean back against the damp wall, panting.

I can hear footsteps behind the door. Drawing nearer

and nearer, closer to my cell. I brace myself. It could be the delivery of today's rations of food – if you can call it food. Or it could be another interrogation, another beating.

The lock clunks, the door draws open.

I blink. Am I dreaming again? Is my mind playing tricks on me? Or is this ...

"Hello Tristan," I say and he steps forward from the shadows.

"Looking good," he tells me, stepping into the cell.

I manage a smile, the expression causing my lip to split open, and I taste blood in my mouth. "You know me, I like to look my best. Have you come here to gloat or–"

He frowns. "I've come to get you the hell out of here," he says.

"Then I hope you're prepared to carry me, man, because I can barely fucking stand."

"Lucky I'm damn good at healing you then." He steps further into the cell, crouching down in front of me, and peering through the darkness into my face. "Fuck, man," he mutters, taking a grip of the back of my head and resting his forehead against mine. "Fuck, I'm so sorry."

I open my mouth to reply to him, to give him one of my usual witty remarks, but I have nothing, nothing to say, just a lump forming in my throat.

"Just get me the hell out of here, Tris," I whisper at last, "please."

He squeezes the back of my neck and meets my gaze. His emerald eyes are wet. "Of course."

Then he's closing his eyelids and muttering under his breath. I feel his magic sink into my body, warm, comforting, all the pain melting away. My own eyelids droop.

"Stay with me," Tristan says. "Stay awake."

I nod and force myself to concentrate in on the sensations of his magic creeping through my body, working to repair all the damage. Is it my imagination or does his magic seem different than it did before? In my mind's eye, his magic was always a vivid blue like the color of the sky. Now it's more purple like the sky right after sunset. And there's something wilder about it.

"Your magic's changed," I say.

"The bond," he tells me.

"How ... how does it feel?" I ask.

He frowns, his eyes still closed. "Painful."

"Because you're apart?"

He nods. "It's impacting the strength of my magic."

"Where is she?"

He hesitates, the frown growing deeper on his face. "I don't know."

I grip his wrist, leaning forward. "She's not–"

"No, no. Fuck, I'd know if she were."

"Then why aren't you out searching for her?"

"I'm going to." He opens his eyes. "But I came to rescue you first." I lean back against the wall.

"You shouldn't have done that. She's more important than me. She should be your first priority."

"There are others searching for her," he says.

"And no one searching for me," I say.

"Your parents?"

"Dead. Killed resisting arrest – according to your dad."

He nods. "I guess we're both orphans now."

"Your dad–"

"Is dead to me," he says resolutely, resting his hand over my cracked ribs and repairing them carefully with his magic. "There are a lot of injuries." I can hear anger in his voice.

"Yeah, I tried to repair them myself–"

"There are too many and you're too hurt."

I lean back against the wall. "Yeah."

He continues his work, muttering the words of the incantation, his hands resting over each injury in turn. Occasionally he pauses and glances over at the other unconscious man in the cell or over to the door.

"I'll know if anyone's coming. The advantage of wolf hearing," I say.

"Then listen out."

"I assume that means you're not meant to be in here."

"My dad sent me back to the academy–"

"The academy?"

"Yeah, he has guards watching it. They're pulling students out for questioning left, right and center. Several have vanished altogether."

"You snuck out?" He nods. "But they'll notice you're gone eventually."

"Come morning, yeah. And I'm assuming someone at this prison is going to make a call at some point to check I am here under my dad's orders like I've claimed."

"Shit, how long do you think we have?"

"Not long at all." He pulls his hand back. "But you're done. At least for now, I can repair you better when we're out of here."

I roll my shoulders and my neck, flex my fingers and shift my legs. While there are some remaining aches and pains, I feel a hell of a lot better than I did fifteen minutes ago. To prove it, I bust through the collar wrapped around my neck and break the chains tied to my wrist.

"Fuck, that's better," I mutter.

"Can you stand up?"

"Yes, I can stand up." I jump to my feet to prove it, Tristan examining me as I do.

"And can you transform?"

"Now?"

"I'm thinking your beast is going to come in handy in busting our way out of here."

I manage a grin. "And I think he'd rather enjoy ripping a few throats out."

As if he's agreeing wholeheartedly with that sentiment, the beast growls inside me. It's the first time he's stirred for days and for once I'm relieved by it.

All these years I've hated him, despised his existence and the cruel situation in which I'm caught. I've never considered what he brings me, how much I need him. How dependent I am on him. Until he was gone, I never felt that at all. Now I welcome his return. Yeah, we're going to rip those throats out together.

I peer down at the injured man slumped on the floor.

"You need to heal him too. Free him," I say.

"There isn't the time."

I ignore my friend and crouch down by the crumpled figure. He stinks of piss and shit and I suspect I smell no better. But underneath it, faintly, ever so faintly, I can smell the mountains and the forest and I can see it in my mind. Just as he described it.

I shake him gently.

"Jacob," I whisper. "Jacob. It's time to go, buddy."

His eyelids creak open.

"To the gallows," he murmurs sarcastically.

"To anywhere but here."

His eyes open fully and he looks up into my face.

"Moreau?"

"Come on." I snap through his chains and his collar and hooking my arm under his elbow drag him to his feet. "Tristan."

My friend examines the battered form of the werebeast and the werebeast examines him right back.

"That's Kennedy's son," he hisses. He spits in his direction. "Piece of shit."

"Yeah," Tristan says, "delighted to meet you too."

"He's here to rescue us."

"You," Tristan corrects.

"He's coming with us. So stop wasting time and heal him so we can get the hell out of here."

"It will take too lon–"

"It will take even longer if I have to drag him like this," I snap, and with a huff of disapproval, Tristan steps forward and lays his hands on the injured man.

Jacob groans with relief, just like I had as Tristan sparks across his body. My friend focuses on the most crucial injuries – fixing his broken arm, his sliced leg and his mangled stomach – and leaving the superficial. After a few minutes, Jacob pushes his hands away.

"That'll do."

"I should fix your–"

Jacob shakes his head. "There's no time."

Together, we walk through the open door of my cell and into the heart of the dungeon – just as damp and dank. There's no light at all but with my wolfish vision I see all the other heavy doors that line the circular space, behind which I smell my kind, can sense their pain and misery.

"Werebeasts," I mutter.

"Yes, the warden said all the werebeasts were being kept down here in the dungeon."

"We need to free them," I say, strolling towards the first door. Tristan captures my arm.

"We can't just leave them here to suffer."

"They won't be able to go anywhere unless we heal them

and I don't have enough in the tank," Tristan says, yanking me backwards towards a set of spiraling steps.

"We can't leave them," I say, tugging my arm free of his grip.

"Spencer," he says, "we'll come back for them." I scoff. "I promise you. We'll form a plan and we'll come back."

Is that usual Tristan Kennedy bullshit? Making promises he has no intention of keeping just to secure his own way? Except, there's something genuine in his tone, something I can't help believing.

"The priority is getting you out," Jacob says, and he uncurls his body, standing to his full height. He's massive, nearly seven foot.

"Me?" I say.

"Four fated mates," he says, holding my vision. "It must mean something. You need to return to her."

Tristan's gaze flicks from me to Jacob. I don't know if he's right but I see the determination in the were's face. I nod, then follow Tristan up the steps, Jacob right behind me, and at the top we face another locked door, one I can tell is fortified with complex locking spells.

"I know how to open it," Tristan says, "but you have to be ready. There'll be guards on the other side and as soon as they see you with me, they're going to know and they're going to try and stop us."

"They're not going to succeed, though, are they?" I say, slapping my palm on his shoulder. "We weren't the two best dueling players for nothing."

He chuckles. "Ready?"

"Yes," I say and Jacob growls his agreement.

He waves his right hand, brow crinkling and slowly the lock slides open. I hold my breath as the door creaks open and blink into the light.

As expected there's twenty guards waiting for us. Several faces I recognize as the men who've punched, kicked and spat at me over the last few days.

I don't even draw breath, I blast them with magic, springing forward, my body transforming as I do. They scatter, too afraid to hold their ground, but I'm on them anyway, ripping at flesh and snapping my jaw through bone, not feeling a single blow of their magic or their fists.

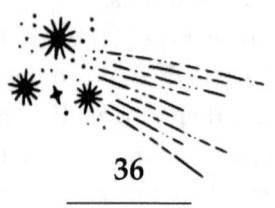

36

T ristan

THE TWO BEASTS – one black, one brown – tear through the men like creatures possessed, magic bouncing off their raised fur, men unable to hold back the force of their power. I'm barely required to do a thing – just deflect some fire and take out one or two men who make it past the raging wolves and come at me.

It takes less than a few minutes and then the men we'd faced are dead, the beasts' mouths dripping with blood. The black beast turns its great head and looks at me, its eyes the same chestnut brown as Spencer's.

Is my friend in there somewhere? Can he see and hear me? Is he in control or not?

The beast barks as if impatient and I point down the winding corridor the way the warden had brought me. An alarm blares, and red lights flash overhead. The noise from the prisoners grows a thousand times louder.

The beasts race down the corridor, their claws scraping against the stone floor and I chase after them.

Those won't be the only men we face and soon magic comes colliding around the corner. It skims over the beasts' fur and I duck, letting it hurtle over head. We slow our pace, taking the next corner with caution. More men, more fire. They're no match for the beasts. I remember how Spencer had fought at the academy – strong and powerful, determined to protect Rhianna. Tonight, the two beasts fight with an aggression and power that's almost beautiful if it weren't so destructive. The beasts tear apart the men we meet and I smash apart any locked doors we encounter. Then we're in the main yard of the fortress, the drawbridge raised again right in front of us.

The sounds from within the main fortress are louder than ever. The prisoners know an escape is in progress and sparks of magic splinter into the air, the sound of walls cracking, bars snapping clear in the night.

The chaos means there are no more guards here to face us, only the raised drawbridge blocking our exit.

The black beast stops before it, sniffing at the wood, its great shoulders heaving, its fur damp with sweat and blood.

"How do we get through?" the beast asks me, his voice deeper, older – ancient sounding.

I hurry to his side, inspecting the complicated-looking mechanism. I have no idea how to work it. I raise my arm.

"Fuck it," I say, and the bridge releases, crashing across the moat, freedom stretching into the distance beyond.

I step forward, motioning for the wolves to follow me, and as I do another group of guards come sprinting into the yard.

"Stop!" one of them yells. "Stop right there!"

Not likely.

I call on all the energy I have, forming a fireball the size of a small car to form in the air and then I fling it at them, running after the beasts, burning the goddamn bridge behind me for good measure.

As I reach the end of the bridge, my foot hitting the road beyond, I allow myself to smile.

We did it.

We fucking did it.

But then the beasts are screeching to a halt in front of me, and the smile falls from my lips.

Charging our way, surrounded by more men than I can count, is my father.

"Hello, Tristan," he calls out, his voice amplified by his magic, "I'd heard you were here."

And I've nothing left, not enough in the tank to fight him with, the pain in my gut overwhelming, making me far weaker than I should be.

The giant brown beast bares his teeth, blood and spit drooling from his jaws, and launches up into the air, right towards the mass of men.

My father simply lifts his hand, and the beast is caught in mid-air by some invisible force. It hangs there, thrashing and snarling, unable to free itself. My father cackles, flicks his wrist and a horrifying snapping sound shoots through the air. The great beast dangles limp and lifeless, then crashes to the ground, dead.

Before me, the black beast – Moreau – is bombarded with magic, hissing and smarting against his fur, the smell of it putrid, and then he too collapses motionless before me as the cold tentacles of my father's magic wrap around my neck and I fall to my knees.

"Spencer," I croak, my hands at my throat. "Spencer."

37

R^{hi}

I WAKE in the morning to find Winnie out of the bed and wrapped in a towel.

"There's a bathroom down the hallway," she says as I emerge blurry-eyed from under the cover. "You have to use your magic to make the water warm, but it's not bad really. There was even some ancient bottle of shampoo which actually smells pretty nice." She takes a piece of her hair and sniffs it.

I rub my eyes, yawning and stretching my arms over my head.

"I guess I'll go investigate then," I say, sniffing myself. "Is that toast I can smell?"

"Yeah, Azlan stuck his head in the room a half hour ago and said he was going to make some breakfast. He said not to wake you after last night." She rubs the towel over her body before picking up her discarded clothes and sniffing those too. "I wonder if I can find any clean clothes in this house."

"You might be able to, but only if you want to wear bloomers and petticoats."

"I think I'd actually look pretty fetching in a pair of bloomers," she says, tugging on her jeans. "How did you sleep the rest of the night, Rhi?" She pauses. "Any other dreams?"

I shake my head and rub my temple. "I slept fine," I say, shuffling to the end of the bed and picking up a towel Winnie's found for me.

Truth is I didn't sleep particularly well. I'd lain awake mulling over that dream, trying to work out what it could mean, debating if Azlan was right. Is the beast I'm meant to save Spencer? And if I am, how am I meant to do that? I don't even know where he is.

I pad along the hallway until I find the bathroom, stepping inside and locking the door behind me. As I'm standing naked investigating the shower, there's a knock on the door.

"Rhi, are you in there?" Stone says from the other side.

"Yes, I'm just about to hop in the shower."

In the next moment the door clicks open and Stone steps inside, his eyes running all over my naked form.

"May I join you, Miss Blackwaters?"

"What?" I hiss. "With Winnie wandering the hallways and Azlan and Renzo too."

"I'm sure we can find a way to be quiet. I'd happily gag you, Miss Blackwaters." He sidles up to me and leans down to nibble my neck, halting when he comes a few inches from my skin. "Shit, you really do stink."

He clicks his fingers, the water coming raging down, and

then he pushes me under. I scream automatically, but actually the water is a perfect temperature – scorching hot. I can't help closing my eyes and tipping my head backwards, letting the water run over my face.

Maybe if I stood here long enough, it would wash away the unnerving feeling I have lingering from that dream, a dream that's playing around and around in my head. Was there something there? Some clue, some hint, that would tell me where the beast was, how to find it?

A pair of strong arms twist around my waist and I'm pulled against the muscular form of Stone.

"I missed you, Blackwaters," he whispers. "It's good to have you back in my arms."

"Even though I stink?"

"Not for long you won't."

He reaches for the shampoo bottle, squirts the gel onto the crown of my head and then massages it into my hair, scratching his nails against my scalp.

"Good?" he asks.

"So good," I mutter.

He washes the bubbles away and then takes the soap next, rubbing it between his hands until they are foaming with bubbles. He looks down at my body and groans.

"Fuck, where to start." I raise an eyebrow at him, snatching the soap into my hands and rubbing it between them. His gaze lingers on my chest. "Your tits do look particularly filthy. Perhaps I'll start there."

"My tits are not ..." I protest but my words die away as he massages my breasts, pinching my nipples and ringing them with his thumbs.

"I'm pretty dirty myself you know, Miss Blackwaters," he says, his hands roaming over my belly and down between my legs.

I giggle. "You are definitely dirty, Professor." Damn dirty, so dirty he makes my legs shake.

"Then, are you going to return the favor?"

"Where would you like me to start?" I ask as his fingers creep between the lips of my pussy and begin to ring my clit.

"My cock, sweetheart," he growls, "start with my cock."

I peer down his body, over the ridges of muscles and trails of inks and down to his cock. It's already stiff and curled towards me like an invitation.

I bite my lip and take him in my hands, hot and hard. I rub up and down his shaft, the water spilling over our faces and our bodies, and then I cup his balls, pressing against that point I know he likes right behind them.

He growls again, his fingers working faster and when I start to moan, he snaps, "Enough." And pushes me hard up against the tiles, grinding his cock against my belly, right against the point where my bond is thrumming with excitement.

"Come for me," he orders, "come for me, sweetheart, and then I'm going to fuck you." I whimper, my legs beginning to shake. I've missed him touching me but I didn't realize how much I'd missed it until now. In fact, I'm damn needy for this, practically wild. I grind my pussy against his fingers and his magic sparks against me, making me cry out with how good he feels.

"Fuck this," he mutters, and then he's dropping to his knees under the shower and burying his mouth between my legs like he's just as needy, just as hungry, just as wild. He thrusts his tongue right up inside my pussy, groaning as he does and then he's eating me out, alternating between flicking and licking at my clit, and French kissing my pussy, his magic enveloping me and making everything more intense.

When I come, it's so powerful my legs give way, and I slide down the wall as ecstasy shimmers through my body. He rocks back, watching me, his fingers inside me and massaging me through my orgasm, and then he's kissing my mouth, pulling me up onto his lap and into his arms. He lowers me onto his cock and we both groan together, the feeling too good to bear.

"I'm never letting you out of my sight again, sweetheart," he says, one hand gripping my ass as the other pushes wet hair away from my face. And then I'm riding him, just as wild and needy and greedy as I was before. Sliding up and down him, grinding on him, working him all along my pussy.

The water falls over our faces and runs down our bodies, splashing around us on the wet tiles, and steam rises up towards the ceiling.

He drops his head and sucks on my nipples as I ride him, his fingers back at my clit and when I come the second time, it's even better than the first, especially when I squeeze and clench around him and he follows right after me, holding me tight in his arms as he does and telling me just how much he loves me.

"You love me?" I ask as we both collapse panting on the wet tiles, that confession completely flooring me.

"Yeah, I do. Of course I do."

"Me?" I say, pointing to my chest.

"You really think I didn't?"

"I don't know. I think I annoy the crap out of you most of the time."

"Yeah, you do," he says with a grin.

I whack his shoulder. "Don't do that. Go back to the love bit again, I liked that bit."

He wraps his arms around my waist and kisses the tip of my nose.

"I love you, Rhianna Blackwaters, more than anything else in this world, in this galaxy, in this universe," he tips his head up towards the ceiling, "more than all the stars in the heavens."

"Wow," I say, utterly dumbfounded.

Stone tips his head forward and smirks at me. "You know you can say it back."

"Of course, I'd have to mean it," I tease.

"It generally helps."

I kiss him, whispering against his mouth. "I love you too, asshole."

And I mean it. I really do.

I FIND both Winnie and Pip gone when I tiptoe back into the bedroom another thirty minutes later. I also find my clothes have somehow been miraculously cleaned and I am mighty thankful to be pulling on clean panties. Once I'm dressed, I follow my nose and discover everyone else already in the kitchen.

Azlan and Stone have spread an ancient-looking map over the countertop and Winnie has laid Pip out on the table, examining him closely.

"Did you clean my clothes?" I ask her.

"Nope," she says, not looking up from Pip, "he did." She points to Renzo who's sitting on a kitchen chair, his feet resting on the tabletop munching a piece of toast.

"Where did you find the food?"

"There's a freezer in the larder, working under some magical spell," Azlan says. "Eat something."

I nod, taking the chair next to Pip and helping myself to a piece of buttered toast from the stack in the center of the table. I bite through the bread, moaning a little as the butter sinks onto my tongue. It has three out of four pairs of eyes swiveling my way and I chew and avert my own gaze towards Winnie.

"Does he seem any better?" I ask her hopefully.

"No," Winnie says, stroking her hand along Pip's torso.

"It's been days," I say. "Surely he should be better by now."

"My middle sister, Petunia, once accidentally hit my youngest sister with her magic during a fight. It took Alice a week to work that magic out of her system and she was pretty sick the entire time."

"But," I say, suddenly finding it hard to swallow my toast, "she was okay afterwards, right? There was no lasting damage."

"No lasting damage. She was perfectly normal."

I tickle Pip's snout and he murmurs slightly but his eyes don't open. I continue to pet him as I finish off the last few bites of my toast and lick the butter off my fingers, glancing up to find Renzo staring at me darkly.

"What?" I ask.

"You like buttered toast."

My cheeks heat. "As much as the next person."

"And long showers." He glares at me and my cheeks set ablaze. "Very long showers."

"I don't think she was showering in that bathroom," Winnie says, taking a slice of the toast and grinning over the top of it at me.

I throw her a look I hope she can decipher means 'please be quiet Winnie', and she blows me a kiss and bites into her breakfast.

Deciding I can't handle Winnie's teasing and Renzo's dirty looks right now, I spin in my seat and peer over at my other two mates.

"And what are you two doing?"

"Deciding where we ought to travel to next," Azlan says.

"We've decided we're going to be safer if we keep on the move."

"That's what I said," Renzo calls over.

Azlan mutters something to Stone who chuckles and I recall my conversation with Winnie last night and decide I need to front this head on. The sooner we all know where we stand, the better.

"Can I talk to the two of you?" I ask.

"Go ahead," Stone says, "we're listening."

"In private." They both look up from their map and over at me. I stand up from the table and walk out of the room, the two of them following me. I find an empty room off the hallway, one whose furniture has been covered in dust sheets, yellowed by the years.

I wait for them to enter, Stone closing the door behind them.

"What is it?" Azlan says anxiously.

"We need to talk about Renzo."

Azlan and Stone both glance at each other, Azlan crossing his arms over his chest.

"I know you're feeling indebted to him or thankful or something because he saved you from Lowsky, but that's no reason to keep the dude around," Stone says. "He can't be trusted. In fact, I wouldn't be surprised if his plan is to take his opportunity when he can, hand you in and reap the reward."

"If that was his plan, he could have done it days ago when he knocked me out."

"This is my point," Azlan growls. "He knocked you out, Rhi. That's hardly sane behavior."

"And you sealed the bond without my permission," I say, addressing Azlan. "And you," I swing my gaze to Stone, "infiltrated my mind."

"What the fuck?" Azlan says as Stone's gaze falls to the floor. "You did what?"

"It doesn't matter," I say, concerned that my wonderful conversational skills have resulted in a further rift between our group. "It's in the past. My point is ..." What the hell is my point? I don't even know. I fling my head back, gazing at the ceiling and taking a deep inhale. I don't think I can look either of them in the eye when I deliver this news. "The point is you need to be nicer to Renzo."

"Nicer," Stone hisses. "Trust me, sweetheart, we're being as nice as it's possible to be."

"Then you need to try harder, because ... because ... we're all going to have to get along."

"I'll tolerate his presence if you deem it absolutely necessary. But I'm not going to be *nice*," Azlan hisses, "and we will never *get along*."

"Then we're all totally and completely fucked, screwed, doomed, because you're my fated mate," I point at Azlan, "and you're my fated mate," I point at Stone and he nods.

"And Tristan Kennedy and Spencer Moreau are too," Azlan says.

I swallow. Oh shit. I can't put this off any longer. I'm going to have to spit out the truth.

"AndRenzoBaronetoo," I mumble so quickly, I'm not entirely sure they compute what I'm saying. It certainly takes them one long minute to respond. During which time I want the ground to open and swallow me up or maybe a dragon to swoop down and carry me away.

"What did you say?" Stone says.

"Renzo is my fated mate too. Five you see. Five fated mates just like Queen Æðelflæd. I know it seems ridiculous and perhaps this is madness or maybe we're all wrong about this situation and–"

Stone throws back his head and laughs so loudly his entire body shakes. The man in black does not look amused. Not one bit. In fact, he glares at me so hard I'm surprised the ground doesn't really split open underneath me.

I cross my arms, glaring right back at Azlan as I wait for Stone to finish. Finally, his mirth subsides and he wipes at the tears in his eyes.

"Are you done?" I ask.

"Sure," he grins at me, "that was the funniest thing I ever heard in my life."

"I'm not trying to be funny, Stone, I'm serious."

"Oh, come on, Rhi, him? Renzo fucking throw-him-in-the-loony-bin-and-toss-away-the-key Barone?"

"Loony bin? That isn't funny, Stone. Least of all from you."

The smile falls from his face. "It's where he should be," he says, "that or in a shallow grave somewhere. And you're right, this isn't funny. We risked our necks to find you, Rhi – we risked your best friend's neck too. While you've been off gallivanting around the countryside with a psychopath, riding on the back of dragons, sinister forces have overtaken our country. There's nothing funny about this situation at all and it isn't the time to be messing with us like this."

"She isn't messing with us," Azlan says, staring right at me. "She's serious."

"I am. One hundred percent." Stone throws his hands in the air. "And I know it isn't ... ideal. I know he isn't the best mate out there – not one I'd have chosen if I'd had a choice.

But, let's be honest here, I'm not the girl you'd have chosen either. It's why you kept everything secret from me for all those weeks."

They can't argue with that. It's undeniable and they are both silent for a long time. Finally, Stone says, with a whine, "Are you sure he really is? You haven't just been suffering from indigestion? Or a bad case of the–"

"I'm pretty familiar with the sensation by now, Professor. I know what it is, I know what it means." He goes to ask me another question, but I beat him to it. "And before you ask, no, we haven't sealed the bond. It's only in the last couple of days that I've actually wanted to stop killing the dude."

"At least you do have an inkling of sense then," Stone mutters.

"Five mates," Azlan says.

"That we know of," Stone says, shoving his hands in his pockets, "knowing Miss Blackwaters, they'll probably end up being a hundred."

"No," Azlan says. "Five. There will only be five." I nod my head. I think he's right. It's no coincidence that fate brought my mates to me all at the same time. If there were more, I'd have met them by now. "It's the strongest number."

"Yes," I say, "fate has thrown us together – she wants us together." Stone swears under his breath but I ignore him, addressing Azlan. "Which is why we have to rescue Spencer Moreau."

38

R^{hi}

When we return to the kitchen, we find Winnie has set Renzo buttering bread for sandwiches – although sensibly, she's the one in charge of the serrated bread knife, whereas he has the harmless-looking butter knife. Of course, he probably has my very sharp knife hidden in his pocket somewhere but Winnie doesn't know that. If she did, I doubt she'd be willing to stand so close to him. Then again, I'm amazed she's willing to stand that close to him at all.

Winnie's gaze flicks to us as we enter and I can tell she's curious about what we've just been discussing, but she tries her best to look casual about it.

"Renzo?" I say.

"Here." He grins.

"Can I talk to you next?"

"You can do whatever you like to me, little rabbit," he

says, which has Stone grinding his molars. "Hey, Prof., it's only fair. You did what you wanted to her this morning in the shower."

"What?" Azlan says.

I grab Renzo's hand and drag him out of the kitchen, back to the room I just left. Inside, I pull my hand free of his, but he grips onto it with his fingers and tugs me towards him.

"You smell of him, little rabbit."

"We haven't come in here to talk about my sex life." The last thing I need is Renzo spiraling into some hissy fit because he's jealous or something. However, without warning, he buries his nose into my hair. "I like it." I have to admit, I wasn't expecting that. "Next time, can I watch?" He licks his tongue up the column of my neck and, oh stars, that has me shivering with desire.

"We need to talk," I tell him, resting my palms on his chest and attempting to push him away.

"I'm listening," he murmurs against my throat.

I don't think he is, but I also don't think I can stop him. And yeah, I am a deranged slut, because frankly I don't want to.

"I told them – Stone and Azlan – my other mates – about us."

"About what we did in that shepherd's hut?" He nips at my skin.

"Erm, no. About you being ... about you being my fated mate."

He freezes and then he's sucking on my neck, his hands finding their way inside my shirt. I moan, tipping my head back and letting him suck even harder.

"You've never said it out loud before, little rabbit. Never admitted it. But you do feel it?"

"Y-y-yes," I gasp, as he squeezes my tit and grinds his hard erection against my belly. "You're meant to be mine."

"And you belong to me."

I close my eyes, bathing in the sensations his mouth, his hands, his cock, set ricocheting around my body, feeling how his magic tingles in the air.

"I belong to all of you."

"All of us," he growls.

I don't know how this is going to work. I don't know if it will. Maybe fate is cruel and twisted. Maybe she plans to bring us together, only to watch us rip each other apart. But right now, I can't find the motivation to care, not when he makes me feel like this.

"I'm going to have you, little rabbit," he says, biting at my jaw.

"Not yet," I gasp. "I'm not ready for that."

He lifts his head and pouts at me, giving me the full-on puppy dog eyes. The look on his face should be ridiculous. He's a grown man. A killer. Yet, it has butterflies dancing circles in my stomach.

"Oh jeez," I mutter. "Don't look at me like that."

"Why?"

"Because it makes it damn hard to stick to my resolution when you do."

The corner of his mouth twitches and that wickedness glints in his eyes now.

"Wanna do it on the couch right now, little rabbit? Want me to hold you down and–"

"Stop!" I say, covering his mouth with my hand, which only encourages him to nip at my palm. "We're not doing that yet. You need to show me you can behave first. Because you know if we do–"

"Fuck like rabbits," he says against my hand.

"–it will seal the bond and that is forever. Irreversible." His eyes grow wide like I've just suggested the most magical possibility ever. "And I won't be bonded to a man I'm worried might change his mind and murder me any second."

He removes my hand from his mouth. "The only people I'll be murdering from now on are the people who try to hurt you." He glances towards the door. "Including those two if they ever–"

"This is what I mean. You can't be threatening to kill my other mates – or maim them!" I add before he thinks he's sneaking around the rules. "You have to be nice to them," I say, telling him the same thing I told Stone and Azlan.

"*Nice*?" he says, complete confusion racing over his features. "*Nice*?" He steps away, tilting his head to one side, like he's finding it hard to compute the word.

"Yes, you know, don't say mean things, don't hurt them, try to get along," I say as if I'm explaining this to a child.

"You want me to play nicely?"

"Yes."

"No one's asked me to play nice in a very long time."

His job has required him to do the opposite. I examine him, realizing he's my fated mate, someone I'm destined to be with until my dying day, and yet I know nothing about him.

"How long did you work for Lowsky? For the Wolves of Night?"

He shrugs. "He picked me up when I was thirteen, fourteen, set me to work."

"Picked you up?"

"Took me in."

"Why?"

"I showed potential. And also I had nowhere to live."

He says it devoid of any emotion as if it isn't the most heartbreaking thing I've ever heard.

"No home? No family?"

His brow creases, anger flashes across his face. "This is boring. Let's talk some more about the fucking."

"No," I say firmly.

"It's just talking," he says, stalking towards me. "We can talk about how I'm going to drag you to your hands and knees and–"

"I'm leaving," I tell him, scurrying from the room with my hands over my ears. It doesn't deter him, he's still describing in intimate detail what he wants to do to me as we step back into the kitchen.

"–and I'm going to stuff my tongue up your pussy," he says as we step back into the kitchen.

"Fucking delightful," Stone says, as Winnie snorts.

I ignore them all, coming to stand by the table.

"Now we have all that straightened out," I say.

"What exactly were you straightening out?" Stone says, throwing both me and Renzo a dirty look and I am grateful it's no longer so easy for him to wander into my mind and read my thoughts.

"We need to decide what we're going to do next."

"We have decided," Azlan announces, "Rhi's dream indicates Spencer Moreau is injured or hurt and so we're going to find him."

"The werebeast?" Renzo asks. Azlan nods. "You know how to find him?"

Azlan pauses. "No."

"Was there any indication of where he was in your dream, Rhi?" Winnie asks.

"The dream last night was different from the one before," I say, biting at my thumb. "Before I was on the mountain, running up the slope. Last night, I was some-where dark, somewhere cold. I could hardly see a thing."

"I think it's likely he's been detained. We've been listening to the broadcasts made by my uncle. He's arresting and locking up all kinds of people."

"Including werebeasts?" I ask.

"I don't know. But I suspect it's very likely."

Stone sinks down on one of the chairs and taps his fingers on the table. "He could be anywhere. Anywhere at all. It's not a lot to go on."

"There are the memories," I say, "the ones in my head. There might be something in there that could help us."

"I told you before, Rhianna, I'm not going back in there. It was too traumatic for you last time. I'm not putting you through it again."

"I can handle it, Stone."

"You can't," he says. "And, besides, there was nothing about a beast in your head."

"We didn't look–"

"Rhi, no."

I slump down on a chair as far away from him as I can find and cross my arms.

Renzo lifts the bread knife. "Want me to make him do it?"

Stone scoffs.

"No!" I say. "Nice, remember."

Renzo lowers the knife, looking exactly like a scolded puppy dog.

Azlan rubs at his chin. "I could do some investigating, tap up some old contacts, some allies I have in the authori-ties. See if I can find any information."

"You could reach out to your nephew," Stone says.

"Tristan?" I say, my bond automatically aching in my stomach. "Would he help us?"

"He's your mate," Azlan says. "He's on your side now."

I peer down at the scuffed tabletop. And yet he's not here. He's not with us. As far as I know he's making no effort at all to find us. I'm pretty certain Tristan Kennedy has once again turned his back on our bond.

"Have a little more faith in him," Stone says.

I shake my head. After all, we've been through together, after the way he's treated me, keeping the faith is damn hard.

"Investigating sounds dangerous," I say, spinning in my chair to face Azlan, "we don't know who we can trust."

Azlan walks towards me, crouching down so our faces are level. He slides his rough fingertips over my cheek. "You know I can take care of myself. And I'd be leaving you in safe hands," he smiles, that expression he rarely makes, "Winnie's."

Stone curses at him but I'm too full of anxiety to manage a smile back. I rest my hand over his.

"I only just got you back."

"I won't be gone for long, I promise you that. I couldn't fucking bear it."

He leans in and kisses my mouth.

"Promise?" I whisper, so that only he can hear, my heart now aching too.

"Promise," he says.

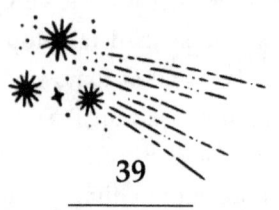

39

T ristan

I OPEN MY EYES. The ache in my gut is more painful than ever, matched only by the ache in my head. A stark light assaults my vision and everything swoops in and out of focus.

"Tristan," a voice says from very far away.

I try to move but my hands are cuffed behind me and my legs chained to a chair.

"Tristan," the voice says, louder now.

The voice is familiar but no matter how hard I strain, I struggle to place it. I struggle to place anything. Have I been drugged?

I reach for my magic. It's weak, drained and as woozy as the rest of me.

There's an unfamiliar sting on my arm. What the hell have they given me?

A hand grips my face, squeezes my cheeks, forces me to look up, up into a pair of cold sinister eyes.

My father.

"Concentrate," he says.

I speak, but the words are nonsense.

My father shakes my head, my brain crashing against my skull.

"Enough of this nonsense. Time to talk."

Talk? I don't want to talk to him. I don't want to tell him a thing. But I fear the drug circulating in my body is in control of my senses, and I feel it tugging at answers I'm keeping concealed.

"Why did you free the werebeast?" my father says.

I don't answer him and his face comes into focus, and beyond him the room. Dark except for the one interrogation lamp trained my way. I think we're alone.

"I've had enough of your insolence, boy," he says. "Answer my question."

The drug loosens my mind a little more and his magic tugs at me.

I fight it, fight to give him the answer I want.

"He's my friend. My best friend."

My father scoffs, throwing my face to the side and releasing his grip. "There's no room for 'friends' in this world, Tristan. Friends are weaknesses. You know this as well as I do. What is the real reason?"

"That is the real reason. He's my friend. He doesn't deserve to be locked up. He's done nothing wrong."

"He's a mutt. A curseded. His blood's infected and he's dangerous. In a cell is the only place he deserves to be."

I shake my head even though it costs me more pain.

My father stands to his feet and surveys me, his hands tucked behind his back.

"You disobeyed me. You were told to return to the academy and remain there. Do you know what has happened to others who have disobeyed me?" Again, I don't answer. I can guess. "You think you should be treated any differently just because you are my son?"

"When have you ever treated me any differently," I spit, remembering all those beatings, every single one, some before I could even walk.

"What are you talking about? You think great magicals are created through kindness, by mollycoddling? They are created through discipline and endurance, hard work and pain. I've made you the man you are – top of the academy, aspiring chancellor." He laughs. "Or at least I thought I had. This recent spate of insolence and inkling for weakness is most disappointing. Maybe you are more like your mother than I realized." He pauses. "Or maybe something has changed."

I grit my teeth, forcing my jaw together. I won't tell him. I won't tell him a thing, not even if he beats me senseless, not even if he threatens me with death.

Because if he knows, if he learns the truth, Rhi won't be safe. She'll never be safe. He'll make sure of that.

He has his power now. His limitless dominance, ruling without restraint or boundaries. He won't stand for any kind of threat – perceived or real. He will crush it. And I won't let him crush her.

"What is it, Tristan, tell me?"

The drug swirls through my blood, warm and misleading, making me promises, whispering in my ear.

If I just tell him, if I just explain, utter the words ...

No!

I ball my hands into fists and bite down on my own damn tongue.

No!

"Is it that girl?" my father sneers. "There's always some girl. Your uncle was the same – nearly threw away everything for a woman. And as for your cousin! Fools, the two of them!" He narrows his eyes. "Are you a fool too? Fallen for some wisp of a girl? There's nothing special about her, is there?"

I know he's taunting me. He has an idea just how special she is. He wouldn't be hunting her down otherwise. He wouldn't have me in here chained to this chair, pumped full of drugs, attempting to wheedle answers out of me otherwise. He'd have already beaten me to a pulp and sent me back to the academy, perhaps even a prison cell.

There were witnesses that night the academy was attacked. People who saw just how powerful Rhi is, who saw us fighting side by side. And then there's that interesting piece of information Summer gave him. Fucking Summer.

"Some say a girl will come ... what I want to know is, is it her?"

My father paces this room as I struggle against the combined effects of the drug and his magic. My mouth is desperate to open and spill everything to him. I clamp it shut, fighting my own jaw.

"We can do this the easy way, or we can do it the hard. You can tell me what you know willingly, or ..."

"I don't know anything," I choke out.

My father smiles coldly. "So be it."

He lifts a hand and a needle comes hurtling across the room, I try to swerve out of its path, but I'm chained to my seat and it stabs me deep in my arm, the drug plunging deep under my skin.

The room blurs, my mind loosening as I struggle to hold on, to maintain control of my own goddamn will.

"I've had enough of your disobedience, boy."

The drug pulls me under and for the first time I see it. The truth.

I'd always thought my mom's pills were an escape from her reality, an escape from him. Now I see what they were, what they really were. A leash. A way for him to control her as he now plans to control me.

I close my eyes, struggling, fighting.

"From now on, you will do as you're told. You will be the son the Lord Protector demands. From now on, you're mine."

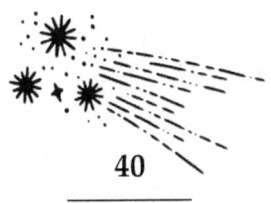

40

R enzo

THE ENFORCER LEAVES LATER that morning, setting off on
foot. My little rabbit goes to see him off at the door, accom-
panied by the professor and the smart girl with the pigtails.
I remain in the kitchen, watching over the pig as I spin my
knife around by its point on the tabletop.

The thoughts buzz around noisily in my head, and, for
the first time, among those thoughts are my future spread
out like a path in front of me. Never seen that before, never
thought about it. It's always been one day at a time.
Intrigued to see if I'd make it to the end or if that would be
the day it all ends. Like a game. Like tossing a coin. Not
caring how it lands.

Now, there are possibilities.

She said sealing the bond would be forever and forever
sounds like a long, long time. All the way in the distance

where I'm an old man with a walking stick and a fucking bad temper.

Huh! Me? Old? They always said I wouldn't make it past my 21st birthday. They said all sorts of shit.

Did I believe more of it than I realized?

The little rabbit walks into the kitchen – her eyelashes all wet, tear tracks run down her face – followed right after by the smart girl. They both stop by the pig and peer down at him. Then the smart girl scoops him up.

"I'm worried he's cold," and then she scurries away with the pig.

I take my opportunity and catch my little rabbit around the waist, pulling her onto my lap. She doesn't scuttle away, she leans against my body, resting her head against my shoulder.

I strain my fucked-up brain to come up with something *nice* to say. Because me and her, I want us to grow old together. Surrounded by litters of piglets. I like that idea.

For once my mind is empty, devoid of anything she'll consider nice. The only thoughts rattling around now are dirty, really fucking dirty.

I shake my head, trying to knock an idea free.

"I've seen the enforcer kill five men at once," I tell her. Because she's sad – I think she's sad. Sad about him leaving.

"What?" she says, sniffing.

"He fights well."

"I suppose," she says. She shifts her head backwards and looks up at me. Those crinkles all over her forehead.

"He can look after himself."

"Oh," she says, the crinkles melting away, "he can. But there's only one of him. I think it's safer when we're together. I don't like it when we're apart."

"You believe all that stuff about the five mates?"

She rubs at the wetness on her face. "Do you?"

"Five mates – six of us altogether. Six has always been the most powerful number in magic."

"Who taught you that?"

"No one," I say with a chuckle. "It's just something I know, like how I know breathing will keep me alive," I bite at her ear, "or stuffing you full of my cock is going to make you feel real good."

"Behaving, remember?" she says, although she's perching right over my cock – a cock that's now hard – so what the hell does she expect.

I flip my head back and growl at the ceiling. "Behaving is hard, little rabbit. You're asking too much of me. You can't expect me to be nice to those jerks *and* keep my fucking hands off you. It has to be one or the other."

"It doesn't."

I shake my head. "Compromise?" I say a word I've never used in my life before. "You can put your hands on me." I take her hands in mine and rest them on my cock. "And we don't have to go all the way."

"I don't trust you," she says.

"You don't?"

"You say one thing, do another."

Maybe she has a point, my cock is jerking eagerly against her hands. If it came to it, can I trust myself? Could I stop myself? It's not something I've ever had to consider before. I take whatever I want.

"You have a point," I say. Removing my hands, although encouragingly, hers stay right there.

I pick up the knife from the table and she stares at it, glinting under the kitchen light. I swivel it in my hand and offer her the handle, the blade that's made a hole in the tabletop, directed straight at my throat.

"Like before, little rabbit? You want me to stop, you have the knife to stop me."

She stares into my eyes unblinking. Then takes the knife in her hand, weighing it in her palm.

And fuck, doesn't that look good, my little rabbit with a deadly weapon in her hand?

"I missed this knife," she whispers, and her magic hisses in the air, a spark of that darker magic there too. Her eyes darken as she stares at the blade, her magic tingling against my skin.

She stands, knife hovering in front of me and then lowers herself back down on my lap, straddling me this time.

"You'd really let me do that?" she says.

"I'd let you do anything you wanted to me," I say, my voice dangerous.

"Even this," she says, and, not breaking our eye contact, she leans forward, bringing the knife closer and closer and pressing the point into my neck, the blade slicing against the point where my pulse thuds. I don't even flinch.

"You like that, little one?" I whisper, sliding my tongue along my bottom lip and tasting her magic as it sizzles.

She nods her head and then she grinds her hips against me, like she's riding me, except, there are two layers of fucking clothing between us.

And a knife.

I lift my hands to reach for her waist, but she presses the knife deeper into my throat, the pinch of the blade delicious.

"No," she says, "keep your hands by your sides."

I swallow.

The knife stings. Her core grinds against me, fondling my cock.

Pleasure and pain. Pain and pleasure. The two are forever intertwined.

She works harder. Up and down my cock. The friction doing something to her too. Her brow's all damp. Her breath panty. Her skin flushed.

I keep completely still. Let her have her control.

Moans bubble in her throat, and she moves faster. Wilder. Grinding her pussy against me.

"Oh fuck," she groans.

My fingers twitch.

I want to pick her up, throw her on the table, and bury myself between her legs.

As if reading my twisted mind, she leans forward, her forehead pressed to mine, the knife shaking at my throat.

"No," she tells me.

"Let me touch you, little rabbit. Let me taste you. Just one little bite." I snap my teeth together and the little thing comes, jolting around on my lap like I just electrocuted her. (Only without the aroma of burned flesh and the accompanying death gurgle.)

The knife slips under my skin, pain radiates through my veins. I close my eyes and groan.

Nothing ever felt so good.

Her hand rests on my shoulder.

"I cut you!" she pants.

"You did, little rabbit," my lips curl upwards, "you did. I like it when you're bad."

Then I feel something wet against my skin. I open my eyes. The little rabbit has caught the droplet of blood racing down my neck with her tongue. Holding my gaze, she scoops it up and trails her tongue back up to where the knife sliced me. Then she sucks at the wound. I grunt, grinding at her from below.

"Think you could suck that next, little rabbit."

And to my fucking delight, she slides off the chair and kneels between my thighs.

For all her words, her actions speak louder. Roar into the silence. She can't keep her hands off me. She wants me. It's only a matter of time before she has me.

With the knife still gripped in her right hand, she frees my cock with her left and then she takes the head of me into her mouth, her lips crimson with blood like the hint of that magic pulsing in the air.

This little rabbit has a dark side. One that wants to come play. One that wants to come play with me.

She sucks on my cock like something possessed. And I was wrong. A knife in my little rabbit's hand isn't the most beautiful thing I've ever seen. My little rabbit with a knife in her hand and my cock in her mouth is.

Someone should fucking paint this. Hang it in some gallery.

She swirls her tongue around my cockhead, and then takes me further into her mouth, sucking up and down my shaft, until my legs are shaking and I'm vibrating on the fucking chair, my nails deep in the wood.

I lift my hips, thrust inside her sweet mouth, and she pulls away, my cock leaving her mouth with a pop that reminds me of bubblegum.

"Deep throat me, Renzo," she growls, waving the knife dangerously close to my cock, "and I will castrate you."

"But little rabbit," I whine, because I want to stuff my cock right down her throat and have her choking on it.

"I mean it."

She rests the blade against my thigh.

"All right," I say. "All right."

I like pain. I also like my cock. And my balls. My thigh? She can fuck that up as much as she likes.

She keeps the knife resting where it is and takes my cock back inside her mouth, continuing right where she left off, only now she sucks me harder, the sounds she's making delicious and dirty.

Pleasure radiates around my body, more pleasure than I've ever experienced before. But it's not the same without the pain.

"Cut me, little rabbit." Her eyes leap up to mine and for a moment she does nothing. Then she presses the blade into my flesh and I come, grunting as loud as I can so that the fucking professor can hear wherever the fuck he is.

My little rabbit swallows all my spunk down her throat, and when she's done, she rocks back on her heels and licks her lips.

"Satisfied?" she asks.

I lean forward on my seat, taking the knife from her hand, and wiping the blood from the blade with my finger, pressing my finger between her lips in the next moment. She licks away the crimson liquid.

"Yeah," I say, eyes all over her, fascinated by this girl.

But I'm lying. She's right not to trust me.

I won't be satisfied until I'm bound to her for eternity.

Dramatic? I always have been. It's my greatest asset.

41

R^{hi}

I SLEEP with Winnie again that night because I can't be dealing with the quarrel that's likely to ensue if I choose Stone over Renzo, or Renzo over Stone. Not that I do sleep. I'm switching between my body being wracked with worries – about Azlan, about Spencer, about all our other friends out there – and my body being flooded with ... well ... lust, my mind floating back to what happened in the bathroom and the kitchen today.

I can see there may be some advantages to five mates, even if keeping the peace between them is going to be an ongoing challenge.

Just after midnight, I hear a sound from the ground floor and sit upright in the bed. Pip's migrated from the end of the bed to a position between Winnie and me on the mattress.

He's also dressed in a knitted cardigan and what looks like a baby's bonnet. Something Winnie discovered in one of the wardrobes and insisted he needed to wear.

Both he and Winnie are snoozing peacefully, Pip looking comfortable for once, and I decide not to disturb them, tugging a hoodie over my t-shirt and creeping to the door.

On the other side, I can hear Renzo snoring quietly and I pull back the door gently, finding him curled up like a dog on the other side. I step over him and pause at the banister. From below there's the sound of heavy boots, and maybe I'd be sounding the alarm if I didn't recognize those footsteps.

I pad down the staircase and find the man in black in the kitchen, standing by the window, staring blankly out of the dark window.

He turns when I enter and his face is drawn and tired.

"Are you okay?" I ask, striding quickly towards him and resting my hands on his forearms, peering at him for any signs of damage or injury.

"I'm fine, Rhi," he says, pulling me towards him and resting his chin on the crown of my head. He inhales, his chest expanding against my cheek, then blows it away with resignation.

"What's wrong?"

"It's worse than I thought."

"What is?" I gasp. "Spencer?" Tristan?

"Everything. My uncle's grip on the republic is absolute and brutal. And all of it is falling into place so fucking quickly." His words are bitter. "He must have been planning this for years."

"But it won't last, right? The chancellor and the council members, they'll fight–"

"The chancellor hasn't been seen since the night of the

attack by the West. And half the members of the council are locked up or dead. The other half have fled. My uncle has always been powerful. And there's no one to stand up to him now. I don't see how his rule can end. Not unless the West attacks again and overthrows him – and even my uncle – cruel and corrupt as he is – is better than that outcome."

"Then all we can do is hope for the best. Maybe life under your uncle's rule will be little different from life under the authorities."

"Tell that to those locked up. To those grieving. He's already restricted liberties – the whole of Los Magicos is under curfew. I don't see it getting any better."

I'm quiet as I take in this information. For me, life under the chancellor and the council was never wonderful – scraping a living, dodging the lowlifes who were after us, evading the authorities. But for many people – people like Winnie and Trent – life wasn't so awful. Now ... now Winnie doesn't even know if her grandma is dead or alive.

"How about Spencer? Did you find anything out?"

"To be honest, Rhi, I don't know how accurate my information is. A lot of my sources – allies of the chancellor – are under arrest or have gone to ground. But I did hear one rumor that both he and Tristan are under house arrest in my uncle's home." He sighs. "I'm not sure that sounds particularly likely."

"And Ellie?"

"Home with my father. Safe for now."

"Thank goodness," I mutter.

He squeezes me tight. "Come on, let's get to bed. It's been a long day." He threads his fingers through mine, and leads me up the stairs. At the top, I attempt to pull away and return to my bedroom.

"I'm sleeping with Winnie and Pip again tonight," I whisper.

"No, you're not," he says firmly, clearly bartering no argument. "Tonight, I need you in *my* bed, Rhianna."

And how could I possibly refuse that?

I let him lead me through to the bedroom on the other side of mine. It contains another four-poster bed, the canopy adorned with faded scarlet drapes and matching curtains covering the large bay windows, a crystal chandelier hanging from the ceiling. Despite the dust, it may be the most grand bedroom I've ever entered.

Azlan comes to stand behind me, lifting my hoodie over my head, and then the shirt I'm wearing, so I'm left standing in just my panties. There's no fire in this room and the air is frigid, my nipples crinkling and stiffening against the cold. Or is it because of him? His mere presence arouses my body automatically and makes my bond hum with pleasure.

He sweeps my hair over my shoulder and rests his mouth upon the nape of my neck.

"I know no matter what I say, you're going to want to try and save him. No matter how dangerous or foolish I tell you it is. I know you won't be deterred. That's just who you are." I nod. "So let me have tonight, Rhianna. Just the two of us, because, I'm not ashamed to admit it, I'm frightened of what the dawn may bring."

I spin in his arms to face him. "I'm not frightened when I'm with you." I never have been. And isn't that strange, because he's one of the most terrifying men I've ever met? But ever since that moment in the forest when I killed that man and saved him, I've known our lives would be irreversibly linked, long before I understood about the bond and fate's intentions. I always knew he'd keep me safe.

"You're so beautiful, Rhianna," he says, brushing his

knuckles down my face. "So irresistible." And if to prove his point, he walks me backwards towards the bed and pushes me down into the mattress. Then he reaches behind his head and yanks off his t-shirt, shedding his pants next, and then he's lying on top of me as I part my legs for him. And I'm not cold anymore. His body is warm pressed against mine and I love the feel of his skin. I comb my fingers through his dark hair, peering up into those midnight eyes.

"Thank you," I tell him, as he rests his forearms either side of my head, caging me with his body.

"What for?" he says, searching my eyes,

"For what you did today. I know it was a risk and I know you did it for me."

"I'd take a million risks for you, Rhianna." He kisses my mouth, then grinds his way inside me. "And whatever happens next," he says, "whatever fate may throw our way, you know I love you."

The way he makes love to me is more gentle than it ever has been before. Usually, he pounds me into the mattress, making me scream until my throat is raw. But tonight he's slower, taking his time with me, kissing my mouth, and my throat, my shoulder and my breasts, his hands all over me too, caressing my waist, stroking my thighs, touching my face.

I feel like I'm being worshiped, like he's committing every part of me to memory, and our magic spins in the air, curling around us in an embrace of its own.

I come, clinging on to him, whispering that I love him too, and he keeps grinding inside me, so that I'm lifted right up to the heavens themselves, as if I leave my body all together and am somewhere lost among the canopy of the bed, watching the two of us, entwined and moving together like we're one being and not two.

I come a second time and he follows right after, releasing a long drawn-out groan as he sinks into me.

"I liked it that way," I say, combing my fingers through his hair again and kissing his cheek.

It felt special and maybe he feels the same way, because he doesn't let me go and we fall asleep with him still buried inside me.

※

THE MONSTER IS STILL and unmoving. I try to rouse him, try to shake him awake. But he's cold. His heart silent.

Terror grips me – like before in the academy. I feel my mind unwind and I'm lost in the dark. Unable to reach him. Trapped and alone and frightened.

Why am I alone? Where are my mates? Where are the men destined to protect me?

I cry out but no sound leaves my throat and there's no magic. There's no magic.

※

"WAKE UP," a firm hand shakes my shoulder. "Rhianna, wake up."

I open my eyes and stare up into the concerned face of Azlan.

It takes a moment – a moment for me to come back to myself – and then I fling my arms around Azlan's neck, clinging to him for salvation.

"It's okay, sweetheart," he says, rocking me in his arms, my body damp with sweat. "You're all right. It was just a dream."

"It was so real though, Azlan. So real. It felt like I was there, really there."

I gulp, tears racing down my face and into my mouth.

"What did you see?" he asks me gently, "what did you see?"

I screw shut my eyes and the image springs in front of me. I don't want to look. I don't want to be back there. "The monster was dead."

"The monster? What monster?" he says. "Was it the beast – Spencer – the one you're meant to save?"

"I don't know," I say, inhaling his scent, trying to focus in on the feel of his strong arms, on the here and now. "I couldn't see his face. I couldn't see who – or what it was. I just know it was dead." A sob wracks my body. "What if we're too late, Azlan? What if Spencer is already dead?"

"He's not, Rhi. It was just a dream. If he were dead, you'd know it, you'd feel it."

I shake my head. "We're not bonded."

"It doesn't matter. I still think you'd know."

"What if this is my way of knowing?" I cry.

He takes my head in his hands and wipes away my tears with the pads of his thumbs. "We'll formulate a plan. First thing in the morning. No more delays. We're going to rescue him, Rhi. We're going to get him out of there."

I sniff and nod. I want to believe him, I want to believe that we can. That we're not too late, that there is a way. I don't want to believe in bad dreams and nightmares.

"Okay?" he says, examining my face.

I feel my racing heart rate settle, my ragged breathing return to normal.

"Okay," I say at last.

"Try to get some more sleep, sweetheart," he says, dragging me back down onto the mattress with him. "Everything will seem better, brighter in the morning, and we'll find a way."

I snuggle into his embrace, his heart beating right below my ear, his arms wrapped around me, his hands stroking along my spine.

A way. We'll find a way.

If there is one.

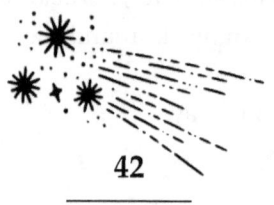

42

A zlan

To my surprise, she's back asleep within minutes and I'm left there in the dark, examining her face, the thoughts rushing around in my mind as I try to formulate a plan. One that extracts the Moreau boy from my uncle's grasp but keeps Rhi out of harm's way. Again and again the ideas I find hit a stumbling block, some impassable hurdle, and I'm forced to scrap them and start again, all the time watching her face for any signs of another dream.

The last one had her trembling and clutching at her throat, struggling for breath. It was terrifying to see, and I don't want her to suffer another one like that. The first sign she's plunging into another of those dreams, I'm waking her up and dragging her out of it.

At last the dawn filters through the curtains, the darkness chased away by the light, and I know there's only one way we can do this. Gently, I nudge Rhi awake, and after we're washed and dressed, we return to the kitchen.

The first thing I spot is the pig. He's no longer lying on his side, trembling and feverish. He's trotting around the kitchen, snorting at everyone and demanding food and affection. He's also wearing what looks like a cardigan and a bonnet.

I frown, but Rhi's already dropping to her knees and scooping him up into her lap, showering him with kisses.

"Pip!" she cries, "are you better?" She looks up at her friend. "Is he better?"

"His fever broke this morning and now he's back to his usual lively self."

Phoenix mutters something under his breath, but both girls ignore him, Winnie crouching down beside Rhi and adding her own kisses to the pig's head.

"That pig receives more affection than any of the rest of us," Stone mutters, pouring out a coffee for Rhianna.

"That's because he deserves it," Rhi says.

I shuffle on my feet. We don't have time for these niceties and distractions.

"Rhi had another dream last night," I tell the others. Rhi's body stiffens and she buries her face against the pig's body.

"The same one?" Phoenix asks.

I peer at Rhi. "This time the beast was ... dead."

Winnie gasps and falls backwards. "You don't think Spencer's–"

"No," I say firmly, more for Rhi's sake than Winnie's or any of the others. "I think Rhi would know if he were. But I think it means we have limited time. We need to act now." They all stare at me.

"You have a plan?" Phoenix asks.

"Yes," although they aren't going to like it. Hell, I don't like it. "We're going to have to hand Rhi in."

"What the fuck?" Barone says, leaping to his feet, and knocking over his own cup of coffee. "To who?"

"To my uncle, to the Lord Protector. It's the only way we'll be able to make it inside the house where I think Spencer is being kept."

"You're fucking crazy," Phoenix scoffs. "You'd hand Rhi over to him? And then what exactly?"

"Together, Rhi and I can fight him. We can rescue Spencer and Tristan."

Phoenix shakes his head.

"Even if you were strong enough to fight your uncle," Winnie says, "you couldn't fight him and all his guards too."

"We'll have the element of surprise. He won't be expecting us to attack him. Not if I'm handing her over to him."

"That's the most stupid fucking plan I've ever heard. In fact, it's the most stupid *thing* I've ever heard and I've taught twenty-year-old students for the last five years. The amount of idiotic crap they speak!"

Rhi ruffles the pig's ears and stands to her feet. "You think it's the only way?" she asks me.

"I can't think of any other way we'll be able to get inside my uncle's house. Even if he were to trust me enough to let me in alone, I wouldn't be able to defeat him by myself. With you, there's a chance."

Rhi thinks about this, her eyes flicking around us all and landing back on me.

"Okay," she says.

"Rhi!" Phoenix says. "This is madness. It's a stupid fucking idea. We can think of another one."

"I've been trying to think of one all fucking night, Phoenix. This is the best I have, the only plan I have."

"And we don't have time," Rhi says, "if we wait, if we're too late ..."

"Christopher Kennedy knows that Azlan is your fated mate. There's no way he'll believe Azlan has had a change of heart and is now handing you in to the authorities."

"There's a chance he might. My uncle has no understanding of love. His own loyalty has only ever been to himself and the family. He may believe I've 'seen sense' and am doing what's right."

"He won't," Phoenix says flatly.

"Then you'll have to do it," Winnie says to my friend.

"Me?"

"Yes, he doesn't know you're Rhi's mate too. He's more likely to believe you'd hand her in."

"And why's that Miss Wence?" he says, eyes narrowing at the girl.

"Because you're always going on about how broke you are, Stone," Rhi says, "and the reward for my capture is considerable."

"A fucking fortune," Barone adds.

"And of course, I'd do that. I'd stoop so low as to shop some girl – a student of mine, my friend's mate no less – right into his hands, all for money," he spits.

Rhi shrugs.

Phoenix begins to pace. "Okay, so maybe that works, maybe he believes me, maybe lets us in, past all his guards, maybe together we take him out, find Spencer and Tristan. It still leaves one giant problem. How the hell do we get out? I'm assuming the Kennedy mansion is now more fortified than ever."

I hesitate. Then nod, my shoulders slumping. He's right.

It's a major flaw in a plan already full of plenty. I look towards my mate, her face contorted with worry.

"I'm sorry, Rhi, he's right."

"No," she shakes her head, desperately, "there must be a way. There must be a way we can get out."

"There is," Barone says, spinning his knife, "me."

"You?" Winnie says, eyeing the assassin with suspicion.

"Yeah, I can shoot us out." He says this like it isn't a big deal, spinning the knife around like the conversation is actually quite boring.

"I don't understand," Winnie says.

"Renzo can ... travel through time and space."

"A contortionist?" Winnie says, mouth falling open.

"Yeah," he says, yawning.

"But can you take others with you?" I ask.

"I took Rhi," he says.

"That's one person. This would be four excluding yourself."

He shrugs.

"Could you shoot us inside the house too?" Phoenix asks, hopefully, clearly still unhappy with my proposed plan.

"Better not to push my luck," Barone says, and I conclude shooting four people with him across time and space is going to be harder than he's making out.

"That's decided then," I say.

"No, it's not," Phoenix insists. "How do we take Barone with us?"

"You pretend you're working together. That you captured Rhi together and you're both handing her in to collect the reward."

Phoenix laughs. "Me and him?" he says, thrusting his

thumb in the assassin's direction, the assassin peering up at him from his knife. "Working together? I don't think so. Maybe your uncle will buy the fact I'm some money-hungry bastard with no morals. But he won't believe I'm working with *him*."

"Phoenix," I say, walking towards my friend, "the entire world has turned upside down. People are desperate out there. People are leaving their morals and their scruples at the door. There are men and women who have always despised my uncle, now licking his asshole. It isn't so unbelievable."

"And we are old friends, after all, right, Prof.?" My gaze flicks to the assassin. Old friends?

"We were never friends, Barone."

"Friends?" I say. I thought I knew everything there was to know about my best friend. He's certainly revealed his deepest darkest secrets to me and I've revealed the same to him. We've seen each other at our best and at our worst, at our downright lowest. But friends with Barone? That has never been mentioned before.

"Something to discuss later," Rhi says. "Do you think that would work?" she asks Winnie. "Do you think Azlan is right, that they'd believe Stone and Renzo were working together to hand me over?"

Winnie leans on the table. Perhaps I should feel insulted that my mate doesn't trust my judgment, but actually I can see she's smart. She wants to gauge everyone's opinion – like any good leader would – and Winnie is intelligent.

"It's a crazy amount of money, Rhi. And people are motivated to do really crazy things by money like that. Plus, I think if anyone could use his charm and wit to fool Christopher Kennedy, it would be Stone."

"I'll take that as a compliment, Miss Wence."

"You can be rather charming when you're not being a complete asshole," Rhi tells him, smiling at him and, my friend, for all his bravado, sarcasm and downright grumpiness, can't help but smile right back at her.

"Fine," he says, utterly weak in the face of Rhi and what this girl wants, "fine, I'll do it – I think it's a crazy, stupid, completely ridiculous idea – but I'll do it."

"Surely by now, you've worked out that I am crazy, stupid and on occasion completely ridiculous." Rhi walks up to him, balancing on her tiptoes, twining her arms around his neck and kissing him. "Thank you, Stone," she says earnestly.

"Hey," Renzo calls out. "How about me? Do I get a thank-you kiss too?"

"No," Phoenix says, curling his arm around Rhi's waist and kissing her right back.

When the kiss goes on for a little longer than is necessary, the pig starts snorting loudly and butting his snout against Rhi's ankles.

"For fuck's sake," Phoenix mutters, glaring down at the pig as Rhi pulls away from him, "I preferred it when you were unconscious with a fever."

"Ignore him, Pip," Rhi says, "he was as concerned about you as the rest of us." Phoenix looks at me with an expression that tells me he disagrees.

"Come on," I say to them all, "let's pack up. We can finalize the details of this plan on the drive to Los Magicos. We'll take Winnie's car."

They all nod, filing out of the kitchen, Rhi cradling the pig in her arms. Only Phoenix remains.

"You do know this is madness," he says with concern

when we're alone. "And it puts Rhi right in the heart of danger."

"Yes, Phoenix, I know. But I believe this is something we have to do."

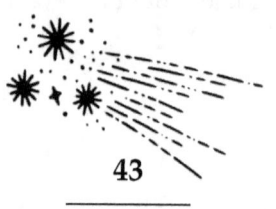

43

S tone

IT'S dusk by the time we reach the outskirts of Los Magicos and, despite spending the last few hours going over and over our plan, analyzing all the things that could go wrong and searching for potential solutions, I feel no better about it.

This is fucking stupid, and no one will convince me otherwise.

Several months back, before I met Rhianna, I would have walked away from a stupid scheme like this. Thrown my hands up and refused to take part.

But things are different now. I'm irreversibly linked to this girl – to all of them. And so I'll do it – fuck I'll give it my best damn shot – even if I think we're doomed to fail.

An unease sits in my belly and I can't help glancing at Rhi. If anything happens to her ... It's my worst nightmare. What I feared the most. Losing a fated mate. Ending up like my mom. The pain so extreme I'd be driven to insanity by it.

But isn't that why we're here doing this? To save Rhi from that fate? Spencer Moreau can't die. We can't let that happen. Spencer Moreau has to live.

Like I said, we're all in this together now, our lives woven with each other's, bound to protect one another until our very last breath, burdened by destiny. Rhi and all of them. All of us.

I take her hand in mine as Winnie weaves us through the empty streets of the city. It's past curfew and no one is out, the usual busy bustling streets devoid of people. It makes the unease worse and I squeeze her hand.

"Okay?" she whispers to me and I nod my head.

The first part of this plan is all down to me and my ability to fool Christopher Kennedy – to appear as ruthless and fucked up as he is himself. Can I do it? Or will he look into my eyes and see the truth – how much this girl means to me? Will I be able to hide it?

Azlan has Winnie driving through the back streets away from any patrols and then we're parking up.

"This is as far as we can take you," he says, spinning around in his seat to face Rhi, Renzo and me in the back seat. Then he's unbuckling his belt and climbing out of the car. Rhi leans forward in her seat, hugging her best friend and handing her the pig. He squeals and squirms in her arms, refusing to be handed over.

"Pip," she says firmly, "You can't come with me!"

But I have a feeling the pig is as unhappy with the plan as I am.

Eventually, Winnie wrestles him out of her arms, making us all promise to be careful, and then we follow Azlan out into the dusk.

"We'll be waiting for you back at the mansion," he says. "You know the plan. Make sure you stick to it," he adds to Barone who simply stares blankly back at him. The unease doubles in my stomach. We're trusting our safety – our damn lives – to a mad man. I think that somehow makes *us* the crazy ones. Azlan pulls Rhi towards him, hugging her close to his body.

"Stay safe, sweetheart, and make sure you come back to me," he whispers, his voice faltering.

She hugs him back. "I will."

Then he climbs back into the car, watching us all through the window with a pain I feel in my gut as the car pulls away.

Once they've disappeared into the coming night, Rhi steps forward, placing her hands behind her back, and with a deep inhale, I secure them together with magical cuffs. Just like that first day we met. Only these she'll be able to break apart when the need arises.

Barone looks at her.

"She looks too healthy," Barone says.

"What?" I say. I mean, she does. Unlike the last time I cuffed her hands together, she's no longer a malnourished, skinny thing. Her cheeks have rounded and so has her ass.

"If I was bringing in a person – to Lowsky or whoever – I'd have some fun first. You know, rough them up." He licks his lips. "Make them hurt."

I step towards him, pointing a finger right in his face.

"You're not laying a finger on her."

The assassin rolls his eyes. "You're so fucking funny, Prof." Then he waves his hands and when I peer over my shoulder at Rhi, her hair's all messed up, there's a bruise on her cheek and another around her throat.

"Fuck, she looks good," Barone says with wonderment

and I have to suppress every goddamn instinct in my body not to thump him in the face.

"Let's go," I say. The sooner this is over, the better.

I take Rhi by the upper arm and we set off, twice shrinking into the shadows to avoid the patrolling security forces. It takes us over an hour, but soon we're in the suburbs of the city where the great houses lie and the great families reside; the side of town I've never belonged in. Some of the houses aren't looking as grand as they did. Their gates toppled, their windows smashed and their doors kicked in. Others look just the same as they always have, as if nothing has changed at all.

The security focus becomes more plentiful the closer we approach the Kennedy residence and finally, with no other possible way through, we have no option but to present ourselves at a barrier.

As we step into the searchlights trained on the street, the line of guards sees us and they raise their hands, magic sizzling in the air threateningly. The lead officer commands us to stop.

"Who are you and what do you want?" he calls out. "There's a curfew. It's against the authorities' rules to be out on the streets."

"I am Professor Stone from the Arrow Hart Academy," I tell him, raising my hands in surrender and hissing at Barone to do the same. He looks at me like I'm dumb but raises them halfheartedly to hover by his ears. "We have one of the magicals on the Lord Protector's wanted list. We've come to hand them in."

"Who?" the officer says.

I smirk at him. "I think that's something we'd like to disclose to the Lord Protector himself."

The officer steps forward, peering at our faces. "You can

hand the prisoner to us. We'll see she's taken to the Lord Protector."

"Errr, no," I say, lowering my hands slightly and letting my own magic crackle in the air sinisterly. "We'll be handing her over ourselves. This prisoner is worth a lot of money."

"We'll see you get your reward," the officer says with obvious disgust.

"But the Lord Protector won't get the additional information we have to disclose about the prisoner," I say.

"You can tell us that too."

Barone laughs.

"And if he has questions?" I say, my smirk solidifying. "Will you be able to answer them?"

The officer hesitates and the thoughts in his mind tell me he's unsure. He doesn't want to face the wrath of the Lord Protector.

"Is that a risk you're prepared to take?" I say quietly.

"Fine," he says, "but my guards will be accompanying you and if you try anything–"

"We just want our money, man," Barone says, bored.

The guards march towards us and I step closer to Rhi's side, gripping her arm, hoping Barone has enough sense in that befuddled brain of his to do the same. I don't want anyone touching her but us.

"We need to search you for weapons before we take you any further," the commander says, stopping right in front of us.

Rhi's eyes flick to me. Renzo has his knife. A knife that once belonged to Rhi. There is no way he'll hand it over and this is where everything could turn messy.

"You realize she's a weapon, right?" I say quietly to him.

The man stares at Rhi and I can tell he doesn't believe that for one minute. He's underestimating her. People always do. We just have to hope Christopher Kennedy will do the same.

"I'm sure she is," the man says flatly, "but we still need you to empty your pockets." A soldier steps towards Renzo and I see him flinch.

Fuck!

I need to convince this man not to search us. I need him to change his mind.

I can read all the suspicious thoughts already spinning in his head. He's read the situation. He knows one of us is armed, maybe both, and he's not going to let us pass unless we hand over our weapons. I see those thoughts glistening in his head, the words clear to read, and then it hits me.

It's not something I've ever tried to do before. Sure, I've been damn tempted, especially when I was younger and more foolhardy. But even then I wasn't stupid enough to do something like that. Something that would have me carted away to the northern labor camps for life.

There's nothing holding me back now, though, and so carefully – oh so carefully – holding my breath – I rearrange the thoughts in his head, reorder the words and letters, manipulate them until they are something altogether different.

The prisoner must be taken to the Lord Protector immediately, without delay.

"We have no weapons," I tell him.

He nods. "Fine, let's go then. We're wasting time here. This prisoner must be taken straight to the Lord Protector."

The soldiers around us glance at their commander, surprised his mind has changed so quickly. Renzo and Rhi look equally shocked. But I don't hang about for anyone to unpick this chain of events. I hold Rhi's arm and walk us forward and soon everyone is falling into step.

We walk the length of the road leading up to the Kennedy residence, through the now heavily guarded set of iron gates and up the steps that lead to the great house's entrance. There are yet more guards at the door and our commander steps forward to speak to them. More questions, more suspicion, and I'm required to do some more altering of thoughts until finally we're let through and made to wait in the main entrance hall surrounded by so many guards I lose count.

Yeah, this was the most stupid plan Azlan and I have ever come up with and there have been some pretty dumb ones over the years.

A messenger is sent off to inform the Lord Protector of our arrival and I can sense Rhi's nerves beside me. I squeeze her arm, try to send her reassuring emotions through the bond, but, truth be told, I'm as nervous as she is.

I never liked Azlan's uncle. He always gave me the creeps. And that feeling has only cemented the older I've become. Maybe once men like him both terrified and amazed me. I'd stand in awe of their power and abilities. Those times have long passed. Now I see them for the jerks they are.

We wait. The house is large and sounds emit from within its depths – voices, machinery, the whirr of magic. It is clear the new Lord Protector has moved the heart of his power base from the ruined council building to this mansion.

"Is he here?" I whisper to Rhi without moving my lips.

She nods her head ever so slightly, keeping her eyes trained ahead, her chin lifted in defiance.

"Can you tell where?"

She tilts her head to the side. I follow the trajectory and spy a door in the wall, a guard standing before it. I search his mind. There's a staircase behind him that leads down to the old cellars of the house. The boy is being kept in there along with one or two other prisoners the Lord Protector deems of particular interest.

I search the guard's mind some more – for information on the security precautions down there in the cellar – for what we might face when we head down there. But the guard is ill-informed. His job is to guard the door and that is all. I skim through other minds searching for answers, finding none.

Do we risk it? There are twenty men at least in this room guarding us and who-knows-what down there in the cellar. Are the three of us strong enough to take that on? We have the element of surprise, we have Renzo's ability to travel through space. We also have his pure craziness and my ability to manipulate minds. In fact, maybe I could use that ability right now to–

But I'm too late, because the Lord Protector is already here, and we're well and truly screwed.

44

R^{hi}

A MAN STROLLS down the grand staircase, his back rigid, his hands clasped in front of him and his black robes billowing out behind him in a way that makes him look like a bat swooping down from the ceiling.

His skin is sallow, his nose hooked and his eyes full of malice.

I don't need any introductions to know this is Christopher Kennedy. I recognize him from the dueling match. Although that day, he'd been a formidable blur in the distance. Tonight, he's much closer and, despite my attempt, I struggle to see the likeness with his son.

Where Tristan is all golden and fair, his father is colorless and dark. And where Tristan disguises his intelligence behind that mask of nonchalance, his father's cunningness radiates from every pore. In one way they are alike though, both arrogant. Both powerful. The man's magic seems to fill the great hallway, even the guards cowering in his presence.

His intelligent eyes lock onto me and a wide unkind smile spreads slowly across his face.

"So it really is you, Rhianna Blackwaters. I wasn't sure whether to believe it or not. And delivered to me by none other than the academy's wayward professor and Lowsky's hunting dog. How intriguing. How very intriguing indeed."

"We've delivered her to you," Stone says, "now we want the money."

"I'm sure you do, Professor Stone," Christopher Kennedy says, continuing to stalk down the staircase. "I'm sure you do. Once a sewer rat, always a sewer rat. That desperation for money never leaves you, does it, no matter what pretty position the academy hands you?"

Stone bristles on the spot, struggling to hold his tongue.

Christopher Kennedy reaches the bottom of the staircase and crooks a finger towards me.

"Come here," he commands.

Beside me, Stone flinches ever so slightly and alarm flares through our bond. I don't flinch at all. In fact, I don't move one little bit. Instead, I stare at the man now terrorizing our country. A man, I suspect, remembering all those healed injuries deep inside Tristan Kennedy's body, has spent a lifetime terrorizing his son. A man, who I've no doubt plans to terrorize me too.

Yeah, well, he wouldn't be the first. I doubt he'll be the last. And I'm no longer so easily afraid of assholes like him.

The new Lord Protector frowns, an expression that suits his face far better than the smile, and diverts his attention back to Stone.

"Come, Professor, tell me everything. I'm sure this will make a pretty tale indeed. How did it come that you are working with a known criminal and not at your post in the academy? And how did you catch the girl, Professor? She's been a very tricky one to trace. I've had men out searching for her all over the republic. It seemed the girl had simply vanished into thin air the night of the Victory ball, the night our great republic was so savagely attacked."

Stone opens his mouth to speak. He has his answers, well rehearsed on the journey here. I'm sure he can make Christopher Kennedy believe him – Stone could make anyone believe anything if he truly wanted to.

But before he's emitted one word from his mouth, Christopher Kennedy swoops his hand through the air and the two men beside me fall to their knees, their arms snapping behind them and iron gloves clamping over their hands. I go to fling my own arms forward, to fire my magic, hot and angry at the man smirking in front of me, but cold metal curls around my hands as well, encasing them completely.

"What the fuck!" Stone cries, as he struggles to free his arms and Renzo flails around on the floor, kicking out at the men around him, spitting at them and cursing.

My magic sparks against the metal confines but no matter how hard I try, I can't blast through them.

Christopher Kennedy shakes his head.

"Did you really think I was so stupid, Phoenix Stone? Did you really think I didn't know?" He takes a step forward. "But it seems you and my nephew were far more stupid than *I* expected. Delivering her straight into my hands. How can I ever thank you enough?"

"If you hurt one hair on–"

"Take them away," Christopher Kennedy says, flicking his wrist as if Stone and Renzo are nothing more than annoying insects.

Several guards pull my mates to their feet, Stone shakes them off and stands himself, but Renzo refuses, kicking and scrapping, biting and snarling so that the men are forced to drag him along the floor.

I yank harder on the cuffs encasing my hands, blast more of my magic against the confines. It's useless, utterly useless. Whatever this damn contraption is, it's stopping me from using my magic.

"We can come to an arrangement," Stone says desperately, trying to regain the Lord Protector's attention. "We can help you. We can ... we can give you information. I can read minds. I can help you interrogate your enemies." Stone's words become more desperate and more frantic as the guards walk him towards the door behind which I know Spencer lies. "Rhi!" he shouts, as the door opens, "Rhi!" He struggles against the hold the men have on him. It's no use. He's outnumbered, they both are, and soon they're pushed through the doorway, the heavy door slamming shut, separating me from my mates.

And then it's just me and Christopher Kennedy.

"So many mates," he says, "all belonging to one scrap of a girl from the wastelands. It's extremely curious." I flinch. He can't know about my mates, can he? We've been careful. "Four mates," he adds.

I stare at his cruel face. Four. He only knows about four.

"At least, that's what they believe, anyway, isn't it, Rhianna Blackwaters? We both know that isn't true. We both know you've used magic to seduce these foolish men, to trick them into believing you're something special to them. Clever, really. But not clever enough to fool me. There's no way fate would choose an unregistered girl from the wasteland for my son, to bear my heirs. No way at all."

Bear his heirs? Is he fucking serious? Vomit burns my

throat. Of course, that's what an asshole like him would see when he looks at a girl like me. Not a person with hopes and desires, not a magical with powers that could match his own. Just a means to an end.

He steps forward, lowering his voice so only I can hear. "There are even whispers that you are the girl predicted, but we both know that can't be so. Not you."

Girl predicted? I remember what the chancellor told me that day in the office – the day he'd threatened to melt my face off. My mom had foreseen a girl with powers even greater than hers.

"Fetch my son," he snaps to the guards, and then lowering his voice, adds, "he's no longer under your spell, Rhianna Blackwaters, I've freed him from it."

I don't know what the hell he means, what the hell he's talking about. All I care about is getting as far away from here as I can. I tug again on the cuffs. There must be a way to free myself; to free myself, blast this evil bastard away and rescue my mates. I swing my gaze desperately from side to side, searching for a way out, something that could help me.

And then all my thoughts trail away because Tristan Kennedy steps into the entrance hall.

The world stops spinning on its axis. Time itself halts. My heart thumps. My bond spins.

I gasp.

I can't hold back anything anymore, anything at all, because he's there in front of me, alive, and the last time I saw him ... the last time I saw him he was slipping away. I thought he'd gone forever and the pain was unbearable, agonizing, excruciating, and now he's here, right in front of me, color in his cheeks and breath in his lungs and my bond purring, my magic sparking in every one of my cells, my body keening towards him.

I see him first, before he spies me and it takes him a moment, his green eyes sweeping around the entrance hall and all the people in it and then landing on me.

On me.

My bond spirals inside me.

He jolts, shock and pain and fear rushing across his face.

My feet carry me forward.

"Tristan!" I cry because I can't hold it in, despite knowing I should, despite knowing I'm a fool, despite anticipating how dangerous this is; I can't help myself.

For a split second an expression of confusion hovers on his face and then, then the mask of indifference slams down. His eyes glaze and he peers down his nose at me like he's always done.

"Pig girl," he says, his voice emotionless and cold. And it's like it always is, it always was. His disdain for me and his disgust. And a shard of ice hits me through our bond.

I am a fool, a stupid, stupid fool to ever believe, to ever think, to ever wish ...

Tristan Kennedy is his father's son. As cold, as heartless, as cruel. He never wanted me, he's never cared about me, he's always resisted this. Our bonding was accidental, unintentional, something he most definitely regrets with every fiber of his stuck-up body. I doubt he's even felt one drop of pain at our separation.

His dad laughs.

"Ahhh, yes, I heard that's what they called you at the academy. On the account of that revolting little pig you stubbornly refused to be parted with." The man shakes his head. "A little trouble maker right from the start. A waste of time and space, isn't she, son?"

I glance at Tristan but he's not looking at me. He's staring straight ahead into space, his eyes blank, as if being dragged here for this conversation is the dullest thing he's ever been made to endure.

"There's nothing special about her," Tristan says, his voice just as bored as his expression, almost robot-like. "I've told you countless times. She's not worth your time or your interest."

Despite my best efforts, the hurt his words cause me reflects on my face. Christopher Kennedy smirks at me.

"Now, now, Pig Girl," he chuckles, "no need to be upset. You didn't really believe my son was interested in you?"

"I'm not interested in your, or your son's, petty games," I spit, finding my tongue at last.

Anger flashes in his eyes. "Yes, I've heard about your temper and your ill-manners."

"It's your son's manners that leave a lot to be desired."

"Oh, I'm not talking about my son." He points to Tristan, motionless and quiet beside him. I peer at him. He's like a shell of his usual self. None of the usual swagger and arrogance. "I heard it from another, very reliable witness who tells me you have a penchant for attacking other students."

I growl, guessing exactly who he means.

"Summer Clutton-Brock is a spoiled little bitch obsessed with petty revenge and–"

"On the contrary, I've found my future daughter-in-law to be a very reliable informant and a most willing aid. Very keen to *serve* me." The smallest of frowns flickers across Tristan's brow and I jolt.

Daughter-in-law? Summer Clutton-Brock? Did I hear that right? I can't have heard that right!

"No," I mutter, not realizing I've said the word out loud until it falls from my lips.

"Yes. Tristan Kennedy and Summer Clutton-Brock are engaged to be married. It will make a very good match.

Joining two powerful families together. And a high-society wedding – I hate to flatter myself – but a *royal* wedding – is just what the people need after all they've been through. Some joy. Some cheer. Everybody likes a wedding. And Miss Clutton-Brock will make an especially beautiful bride."

My knees begin to shake and I can't make them stop. I knew Tristan Kennedy was an asshole. I knew all along he didn't really care about me. But there's no denying we are fated mates – no matter what his father might say – fated mates who have sealed the bond, who are bound to be together forever. How ... how could he marry someone else? How could he *be* with anyone else?

My bond pangs inside me, adamant this can't be true.

"No," I mutter again, shaking my head as my legs continue to tremble, "no, he wouldn't–"

"Tell her, Tristan."

"Summer and I are extremely happy," Tristan says, eyes still blank, voice still monotone. "And very much in love. We hope to be married as soon as the arrangements can be made."

"Ahhh," Christopher Kennedy says, "and here she is. The beautiful bride-to-be herself."

I look up and find Summer fucking Clutton-Brock sweeping down the grand staircase, dressed in a long gown that flows over the steps behind her. Her hair has been cut shorter, styled more elegantly, and she looks older, more sophisticated, like a damn film star.

She halts at the bottom of the stairs, curtsying a little to the Lord Protector like he really is royalty, and then sliding up to Tristan and curling her arm through his. He doesn't move, doesn't respond to her presence and my bond – so new, so raw – spits and claws inside me, desperate to scratch the silly bitch's eyes out for daring to touch my mate.

My mate. But not mine. Hers now.

She smiles at me with more menace than I've ever seen before.

"So it's true. She really has been captured." She leans her head against Tristan's shoulder and rests a hand against her chest. Her left hand. A massive diamond ring winking right at me. "That's such a relief. This girl is dangerous. She bewitched Trissy-Boo, and attacked me because I'm his girl-friend. She's a menace. I hope she'll feel the full force of your justice, Christopher, for what she did to us."

"I saved you," I hiss at her, "from that dragon."

"I don't know what you're talking about," she trills. "Come on, Tristan," she takes his hand in hers, "let's go. I can't stand to be breathing the same air as her."

She tugs on his hand and he doesn't move, doesn't respond.

"Tristan," his father says in a dark tone and he jerks to attention. "Go with your fiancée. I will deal with Rhianna Blackwaters."

Without looking at me, without acknowledging me at all, he lifts his feet and climbs the stairs, Summer trotting alongside him. Halfway up the staircase, she peers over her shoulder at me, smirking, and if my arms weren't bound, I'd finally blast that girl right to hell itself. After all, I'm certain that's where she belongs.

My body continues to shake while my bond screams at Tristan to come back. He must be able to feel that. He must! And yet he keeps right on walking like he can't feel me at all.

Finally, he's gone completely, and the pain is so vast, my legs crumple beneath me and I sink to the floor.

"The truth can be cruel, Pig Girl, but it can also be necessary. You don't belong in this family. You don't belong to him. You belong in a cell. And tomorrow that is exactly where you will be taken." He clicks his fingers and the soldiers remaining in the room jump to attention. "Take the girl to the east wing guest room and ensure she is heavily guarded."

Two hands grip my upper arms and drag me to my feet.

"Until tomorrow, Pig Girl," he says. "Sleep well."

"Go to hell!" I snarl, fighting the men marching me towards the staircase. But it's hopeless. I'm smaller than them, and without my magic, pretty pathetic. Christopher Kennedy knows it, smiling at me like a bat that intends to sink his fangs into my neck and suck me dry.

45

R^{hi}

I'M GUESSING the east wing is reserved for guests like me. The guests that don't matter. The ones considered unworthy, because it's not a lot better than my dorm room back at the academy. A single bed lies against the wall, the mattress and duvet bare, the windows curtain-less and no rug resting across the hard wooden floor boards. The walls too are undecorated and no other furniture stands in the room.

When the door shuts and locks behind me, I sink to the ground, curling in on myself as best I can with my arms clamped behind my back.

The pain hurts worse than ever in my stomach. It's been a day since I last drank some of Renzo's potion and seeing Tristan like that seems to have stirred everything afresh. I press my eyes against my knees and try to breathe through the agony. I don't know what's worse. The incessant ache in my bond or the splintering sensation in my heart.

How can I have been so stupid? How could I have believed in him? He never meant it. He never really cared. I was just a passing distraction, a mere amusement.

Tristan is interested in his image and his status above all else. He was always going to end up with a girl like Summer, one he considered high status like himself, one who would help him in his ambitions. Someone like me was never going to fit the mold.

My bond tries to argue, insists I'm wrong. It reminds me that Tristan didn't seem right just now. Not his usual self – not over-brimming with swagger and self-confidence. Something was wrong.

Is that true?

I'm not sure what to trust anymore. Especially when it comes to Tristan Kennedy.

Because he tells me that I'm nothing and that he despises me. He treats me like shit on the bottom of his shoe. And yet, he follows me into the wood, saves me from the werebeast – from Spencer. Then he tells me that we're fated mates, destined to be together, that he's changed his mind, that he wants me. He buys me dresses, asks me to the ball, throws himself in front of that cursed magic in order to save me. And then ... and then he makes no effort to find me. No effort to reach me, to come for me and he stands in front of his father and says I mean nothing to him. Tells me he's going to marry another girl.

Tristan Kennedy has given me serious whiplash and I'm surprised I don't have a crooked neck and a nose bleed from it.

Well, if that's the way he feels, so be it. I certainly won't let him beat me now.

I roll up straight, ignoring all the pain, and assess my surroundings. The window is barred, confirming my suspicions that this is no ordinary guest room, and there's nothing in the room that could help me. Nope, no helpful bolt cutters, no secret door. I'm locked in, unable to use my magic, and, if the shadows under the door are anything to go by, there are guards blocking my only exit.

I curse and reach through the bond for Azlan and Stone. Immediately, I'm hit by Tristan's emotions instead, and they almost have me tumbling backwards. They're confused and muddled, slow and slurred and I don't understand them at all. I try to push them aside, reaching for Stone and Azlan in the hope we can work something out, but Tristan's emotions are too loud, and in the end, I shut them down entirely and rest my head back against the mattress, thinking, desperate to find a way out of this mess.

I'm still awake several hours later when I hear a noise outside the door. The sound of two thuds. My eyes flick that way.

Bodies hitting the floor?

I frown, scurrying up to my knees as the lock clicks and the door creaks open. Just a little.

I scramble to my feet, waiting for whoever is there to enter the room.

Nothing. No one.

The door clicks shut.

I blink. Still no one there and yet my bond tugs me towards the doorway anyway.

"Tristan?" I say, not sure why the hell he is here and what the hell he can want. He emerges from the gloom, slowly coming into view, translucent at first and then more and more solid, until it's him, all of him.

Except it's not the Tristan I'm so used to seeing, towering above me, glowering down at me.

His body is pressed against the wall, his palms flat against the plaster. His face is damp, his golden hair stuck to his brow. And his breathing is labored, his body tense and vibrating.

"Tristan!" I cry this time, stepping towards him.

He screws up his eyes and his entire body trembles.

"Tristan, what's wrong?"

He struggles to open his mouth, his tongue moving behind his teeth but no noise coming out.

"What is it?" I say, coming right up close to him, peering up at his face. There's a sickly sheen to his skin, like he's ill, and his eyes are flickering widely behind his closed lids.

Our closeness has my bond humming and his body shaking more violently.

"Tristan!" I say in alarm, struggling again to release my damn hands.

"Dr ... dr ..." he says, struggling to form the words in his mouth. He grunts, his teeth grinding, his jaw hardening as if he's fighting with his own mouth to speak. "Drug," he spits out at last.

Drug?

"Dr-dr-dr-drug," he spits out again.

My gaze flits around his troubled face.

"Tristan," I say, still unsure if I believe anything this man says, still unsure if I trust him, but wanting to, really really wanting to. "Did they drug you?"

His shoulders sag slightly as if in relief and he grunts out a mumbled yes. He opens his eyes and this close I see how dazed they look, how the green of his irises is so much fainter than it usually is, how the dark irises are glazed.

Drugged. By his dad? Why?

I take another step closer, and he growls, his body shaking so violently, his head knocks against the wall.

"Not ... too ... close," he pants, slamming his eyes shut again, "don't ... want ... to ... hurt ... you." His fingers flex as if they'd like to wrap around my throat.

Alarm flashes through me. I don't know what to do. It's clear he's attempting to fight the effects of the drug but what the hell does this drug do? Why would he hurt me?

"I can help you, Tristan, but you have to release my hands. I can't use my magic otherwise."

He grunts as if struggling against some great physical force and his knees buckle. He sways, but then he's rigid again, nodding his head.

I look at his face, wondering how dangerous this is, if any minute the drug might take a hold of him and he might attack me, kill me.

"You're not going to hurt me, Tristan," I whisper to him. "You're my fated mate. We're meant to be together."

His face contorts. "P-p-piglet."

I frown. That isn't exactly my favorite term of endearment, but we'll deal with that later – as well as everything else. Like his engagement to Summer Clutton-Brock.

Right now, releasing my hands so I can use my magic is the priority.

"You need to release my hands." Inhaling, I turn around and pray whatever feelings he has for me are more powerful than the effects of the drug his father has pumped through his veins. And I realize as I wait with bated breath that I want those feelings to be real. I want what he told me about caring about me to be true. And not because I want him to release me, but because my own feelings for him have grown too.

I don't hate Tristan Kennedy like I used to. Maybe I never have.

His cold fingertips touch my wrists, trembling against my skin. He whispers words in a strangled voice. Then he presses the catch on the cuffs and they spring open.

I gasp in relief as immediately my hands spark with magic and it flows through my body freely again.

I turn slowly back around to face Tristan.

He's pressed against the wall again, and his body jolts like he's possessed, like there's another person inside him struggling to break free.

He groans, his fingernails scraping at the wall, his face contorted. Then suddenly his body jerks rigid, his eyes snap open and he glares at me with a hatred. He draws himself up to his full height and takes a menacing step towards me.

"No," I say firmly, lifting my right arm in front of me.

He snarls at me, reminding me more of the werebeast than a human, and takes another step forward.

"Tristan, it's me, Rhianna," I swallow, "*Piglet*," I say, that name tasting bad in my mouth.

He swipes for me, but I duck. He growls and lunges for me this time, trying to grab at me. I slip away and land my palm firmly on his chest, right above his beating heart.

At my touch, he freezes, and his body convulses all over again, like he's fighting to regain control.

"No," I repeat, and with my magic, I search for the drug in his blood. I find it rancid and evil, careening, lingering in his blood. It hisses at me, and a shock spins up my arm. I grit my teeth and chase the drug as Tristan's body shakes beneath my hand, his heart pounding against my palm.

"Come on," I grit out between my teeth, pushing my magic to race harder, until finally I grab a hold of that drug. It struggles in my magic's grip, stinging and scraping at me. I don't let go. I yank at it, trying to pull it from his body. It fights me, struggling back, burning me so violently I let out a cry.

"Rhi," Tristan murmurs.

"You need to help me," I pant. "Tristan, you need to help me."

His hand lands flat against mine, warm now, the feel of his skin electric in an altogether different way.

Together we tug at the drug, pulling and pulling together until finally we wrench it clean from his body and the liquid splatters against the floorboards, a neon green. It smolders on the floor, smoking and sizzling, until eventually it sinks away into the wood.

Tristan slumps against me, his head falls forward, and he gasps, his shoulders heaving as he catches his breath.

"Is it gone?" I whisper. "Is it all gone?"

He lifts his head, his damp golden hair falling back around his face, his emerald-green eyes now vivid and clear.

"It's gone," he whispers.

I let out a sigh of relief, unable to drag my gaze from his eyes. They are no longer overflowing with hatred, now they are brimming with heat.

I go to withdraw my hand from his chest, but he holds it firmly in place, pressing it right against his frantic heart.

"Piglet," he says and I scowl at him. He frowns too. "I'm so sorry, so fucking sorry."

I examine his face. My bond strains towards him. His emotions are clearer through the bond now and I can feel his remorse.

"What are you sorry for, Tristan?" I whisper.

He stares down at the floor. "Everything."

"Everything," I repeat with a sigh. And maybe it's the shock of what's happened, or all my emotions bubbling up to the surface like an erupting volcano, but the tears start to roll down my cheeks. I sniff, wiping them away with my fingers. "You know the worst of it, Tristan. I don't know what to believe anymore. I don't know whether you were lying to him or to me."

"Him, Piglet, him. Always him. If he knew the truth ... I had to hide it from him."

"Why? Because you're ashamed, ashamed of me?"

"You don't know what he is like. How dangerous he can be. If he thought you were powerful, if he thought he could use you ... I wasn't prepared to let that happen." He lifts his gaze to mine. "I'll never let that happen."

"But you told him about my mates – didn't you? It was you."

"I tried not to, Rhi. Believe me, I tried with all my might but that drug and his magic–"

"You stood there, right in front of me, and said you loved Summer Clutton-Brock. Let her fawn all over you. Do you know how that felt?"

"It was the drug. I was under his control. I didn't mean any of that stuff I said. I'm not in love with Summer. I'm not going to marry her."

"Did you sleep with her?" I say, intending to spit the words in his face. Instead, they leave my mouth as a feeble sob. Because as much as I hate to admit it, the thought of him with Summer breaks my goddamn heart.

"Summer?" he scoffs. "No, no. I can't stand the girl."

"There was a time, Tristan Kennedy, when you couldn't stand me!"

"That's not true. There was never a time I didn't want you."

I frown. "I'm not sure that's really the same thing. You

didn't come looking for me, Tristan. You didn't try to find me."

"Because I was trying to free Spencer." He grimaces. "And I fucked it up."

"Right, because Spencer is your best friend and I'm just—"

"Because Spencer is your mate too and you need us all," he snaps.

I stare at him aghast and in the next minute, he tugs me right up close against his body. It's hard to think straight. It's hard to think at all.

His body is warm and hard and strong and my bond makes me giddy, it's so freaking high, elated to be this close to him, to feel his skin against mine.

"I've always wanted you." He spins me around, crushing me against the wall. "Only you. I can't stop thinking about you. Day and night. All the time. I'm losing my mind."

"It's the bond. It's like that when you first seal it."

"I've been crazy about you since I met you. Long before the bond between us was sealed. You're like no one I've ever met. You're fucking entrancing." He leans closer, staring deep into my eyes. He's pretty damn entrancing himself, especially those eyes, penetrating and beautiful. "You mean the world to me, Piglet. And I'd do anything for you."

Then his mouth is on mine and I can't resist him, can't resist this. He's always made me feel things I shouldn't and when he says things like that, I could almost believe them.

I kiss him back, my hands tugging at his shirt, finding his warm skin beneath, letting my hands trail across all the ridges of hard muscle I find there.

We sealed the bond. We relented to Fate's desires. And ever since we've been apart, ignoring her demands and she has punished us for it.

Now we are together and neither of us has the willpower to ignore her any longer, despite our circumstances, despite the goddamn stupidity of it.

He growls and I know my touch feels as good for him as his does for me, our magic already spinning around us, glinting and glimmering in the darkness.

"We should go," he murmurs, his hot lips finding my throat, "we should really get out of here, but stars forgive me, I can't ... I can't ..."

He reaches up inside my t-shirt and squeezes at my tit, his other hand sweeping down my body, caressing my waist and my hips.

And I don't think we need to beg forgiveness from the stars. I think this is exactly what the stars want, especially when he grinds into me and I realize just how needy I feel, my bond going crazy in my belly.

He pinches my nipple and I moan.

"No, little piglet," he says, his fingers fumbling at the waist of my pants. "You have to be quiet. Like before, quiet for me."

I shake my head, his fingers dipping into my panties and stroking through my folds. "I can't," I pant.

He freezes, the beat of his heart leaping in his throat. "You can't do this?" he says, emotions crashing across his face.

"I can't be quiet," I say, grinding myself against his fingers.

He smirks in that way that's oh so familiar to me, like the Tristan Kennedy I know so well, and then he winks and my pants are a pile on the floor. He removes his hand from my panties, causing me to pout at him, and undoes his fly, lowering his jeans and his boxers and giving me my first view of Tristan Kennedy's cock. It's better than I imagined, and yeah, I guess I have imagined it more than I'd care to admit.

He grips his thick shaft in his hand, rubbing his fist up and down his length. The fuzz on his groin is slightly darker than the locks on his crown, and his cock curves upwards in a way I have enough experience to know by now is going to feel damn good.

With his free hand, he hooks his two forefingers through the front of my panties and yanks them to one side.

"Wet," he says, and I can't deny it. I am. Wet and needy. My heart is beating just as frantically as his, and my bond spins with anticipation.

But as giddy as I am, I still have a little of my sense and so I land my palm firmly against his chest once again.

"If you're using me," I warn him, "if this was all about claiming another notch on your bedpost ..."

He shakes his head, the arrogance falling away from his face and something more real resting in its place.

"You still don't get it, do you, Piglet? I'm yours. Entirely. Forever."

And then he's covering my mouth with one hand and hooking his other under my backside, lifting me against the wall until his cock lines up with my hole. Then I watch, transfixed and giddy, as he pushes his way inside me. He's big but I guess I'm used to that now. The stretch isn't as uncomfortable as it was, there's no sting, just pleasure, all pleasure as he grinds his way inside my pussy, hitting every sensitive place inside me.

I moan against his palm, unable to help myself, and once he's bottomed out, he leans his forehead against mine, peering deep into my eyes, panting again.

"Fuck, Piglet, fuck," he mutters.

But as good as it feels, it's not enough. I need him to

move. I need him to fuck me. I nip at his hand with my teeth, wind my legs around his waist and push my heels against his backside, tug at his shirt.

"Shit," he says, and for a moment I'm a little desperate, concerned he hasn't gotten the message. But then, in the next breath, it's like a fire has been lit between us and we're all flame and all passion; all that heat – all that heat that's been sizzling away, sparking and flickering between us – finally combusting, consuming us both. He fucks me hard against the wall, my head knocking on the plaster, his hand tight across my mouth, his fingers sinking deep into my backside.

I forget where we are. I forget this is fucking dangerous. I forget everything but the feel of him, the sound of him, the scent of him and, as his hungry mouth claims mine, the taste of him. I dissolve into him completely, our magic entwining so completely it's no longer possible to know where mine ends and his begins.

"So good," he mutters against my mouth, "so fucking good, Rhi."

"Uh huh," I moan, as the sensations become too much, too good, too overwhelming, my body winding tighter and tighter, higher and higher, until I come, writhing against the wall, screaming silently into his hand.

"I love it when you come, little mate," he whispers, "it's all I've been able to think about. How I made you come on my fingers. How beautiful you looked." He sucks on my throat. "Come again!"

His magic sparks against my clit and it happens again, this time his thrusts becoming erratic, wilder, until, with one loud grunt, he comes deep inside me.

He stays that way as we both float back to earth, catching our breaths.

"Fuck," he says at last, "fuck, Rhi that was ..."

I float in that giddy cloud of passion, in the feel of him. I float so high, loving the press of his skin and the embrace of his arms.

But soon, I'm falling, dropping down to earth, tumbling back to reality.

And now it's over, now all that raw passion is fading away, the flames of it withering, I realize how dumb this is.

I push his hand away from my mouth.

"We need to go." He makes no effort to move, his cock still buried inside me. "Tristan, we need to get out of here." He doesn't move. I push against his shoulder. "We need to find the others and go."

"Shit, Rhi, just ..." He leans his hand against the wall above my head. "Just give me a moment."

And stars, I must be a fool, because every fiber in my body wants to grant him that moment, wants to soak, bask in it with him. But we can't.

"My bond feels so ..." he says. "I don't want to go. I want to stay here in this moment with you forever." I search his face, peer deep into those emerald eyes and try to discern whether Tristan Kennedy is telling me the truth, whether this is as real as it feels. "Please," he adds.

I rest my hand against his cheek, then stroke back the damp golden locks that have fallen into his face.

"Tristan," I say. "We have to."

He meets my gaze, his eyes a green I won't ever be able to forget, and then he nods, pulling out of me and carefully lowering me to the ground. Taking my chin in his hand once I've found my feet and kissing me, this time deep, slow.

Reluctantly, I pull away from him and find my pants on the floor. I pull them on, his eyes on me, mine on him as he buttons up his fly.

I'm sticky and breathless, my bond desperate for me to place my hands on him again, but I need to snap out of this spell, and focus.

"Is there a way we can sneak down to the others?" I ask him. I'm sure together the two of us could blast our way out of this house, but I'd rather avoid the Bonnie and Clyde scenario – it didn't end well for them. I'd rather opt for a way that is most likely to ensure we remain in one piece.

"Down to the others?" he says. "We need to get you out of here, Rhi. As far away from my father as it's possible to be."

I lift my chin and glare at him. "I'm not going anywhere without Stone, Spencer and Renzo. And I'm surprised you want to. Isn't Spencer meant to be your–"

"Renzo?" he says, dumbfounded. "Renzo fucking Barone? What the ... why the ..."

I stare him right in the eye. "Renzo Barone is my fated mate."

His jaw falls open. "Renzo Barone tried to kill you."

"And you humiliated me in front of the entire school and fucked other girls in–"

"Okay, okay," he says, throwing his hands up. "I get your point." He tilts his head. "But, seriously, Piglet, him?"

"We're not discussing that now." I jab my finger at him. "I'm rescuing the others and getting out of here. So are you going to help me or not?"

"Of course, I'm going to help you, Rhi. I'm going to follow you to the ends of the earth from now on if that's what you want."

I nod, still a little taken aback by Tristan's desire to aid me, rather than belittle me.

"Is there a way to sneak out or not?" I ask. "I can't make myself invisible like you can."

"Ahhh," he says, reaching into his pocket and pulling something out. I step forward as he opens his fist, staring down at my locket – at my mother's locket. "I knew it was yours so I retrieved it for you."

I smile, taking it from his hand and lifting it over my head.

"It's a cloaker, right?" he says. I nod. "Can you make it work?"

I stroke my fingers over the silver locket, allowing my magic to do its job, "Yes," I say. "Yes, I can make it work."

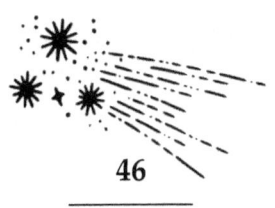

46

T ristan

MY HEAD IS WOOZY. My bond thrumming. My magic buzzing.

And I don't know if it's from the after effects of that damn drug or because I just fucked Rhianna Blackwaters.

Fucked her. Made her come twice. And now her cunt is all sticky with my come.

Shit, all I want to do is push her down on the mattress, spread her thighs and gaze at how fucking messy I've made her. Suck on that stiff sensitive little nub of hers and make her fall apart all over again.

Yeah, maybe the drug has affected my senses.

Or maybe it's the bond.

Or maybe it's just me.

Doesn't matter. All that is going to have to wait. We need to get out of here. We've already wasted precious time –

yeah, not wasted, those minutes were fucking well spent! However, I don't know what my father has in store for her, what he has in store for my friend, fuck, what he has in store for me. One thing's for certain though, it won't be good.

She runs her fingers over the locket, her magic flaring and her lips moving in a silent spell. I wait. Nothing happens.

"I can still see you," I say, anxiety stirring in my blood. Escaping from this hell hole is going to be much easier if we can't be seen.

"Because I want you to see me. Because you're my mate." I frown. She's making no sense. "Trust me," she says, "if I don't want someone to see me, they won't be able to."

"You're sure?"

She lifts an eyebrow, telling me exactly what she thinks of that comment. I'm being a jerk. "Yes, I'm sure," she says.

"Good." I take her hand in mine and let myself disappear from view. "Don't let go."

"I won't," she says, threading her fingers through mine for good measure.

By the door, we listen for any sounds and, when we're sure the coast is clear, we open it, stepping over the two guards I knocked out earlier. The hallway at this end of the mansion is empty and dark, and I lead Rhi through this wing pausing when we reach the family section. Here there are more guards. One stationed outside my father's room, two more patrolling the hallways.

"Quietly," I whisper to her, and then squeezing her hand in mine, we tiptoe along the landing, holding our breaths as we pass the guard. He can't see us. I doubt he can hear us either. But he senses us, nonetheless.

He stands to attention, swinging his gaze around.

"Who's there?" he calls out. I pull on Rhi's arm, increasing our pace. "I know you're there!"

He throws magic down the hallway and I yank Rhi to the side, watching as the angry bolt crashes into a far wall.

I keep pulling Rhi along.

We're almost at the staircase when my father's door swings open and he steps into the hallway dressed in a black silk dressing gown that makes him look like a pimp. He never did have any taste.

"What is it?" he asks in irritation to the guard.

"Someone in the hallway."

My father peers into the gloom as we descend the first step, all the lights suddenly ablaze.

"I can't see anyone," my father says.

Someone else steps out of my father's room and onto the landing.

Someone dressed in a scarlet nightgown that hugs her figure.

Summer.

I halt in shock, nearly stumbling over my own feet, Rhi bumping into me from behind.

Summer? Is my father sleeping with Summer Clutton-Brock?

Yeah, he definitely has no taste. I guess I shouldn't be surprised. By either of them. Of course, Summer wouldn't be content with me. Of course, she'd have her sights set higher. And as for him ...

"Your family really is fucked up," Rhi hisses by my ear and I pick up my pace, dragging her down the staircase as I hear my father start to issue orders.

"Check the girl's room. Check Tristan's too," he says.

"You don't think they've escaped," Summer says, reaching out to cling to his arm like she's some helpless maiden. My father shakes her off in irritation and strolls to the top of the staircase just as we reach the bottom.

"Come on," I hiss at Rhi, pulling her across the grand entrance towards the doorway that leads down to the cellar where I'm sure the others are being kept. We're halfway across when the giant chandelier above our heads, all lit up and made from glittering crystal, snaps from the ceiling and crashes towards the floor.

My grip slips from Rhi's as we dive in opposite directions, glass splintering all around us.

"I know you're there," my father thunders from above and I jump to my feet, pulling Rhi to hers, blood on her skin, as my father sends a rain of fire down upon us.

"The door," I cry in her ear and we sprint in that direction, no longer caring if we can be heard or not.

The guard at the door spins his gaze around desperately as my father yells at him to stop us. But I knock him out and we're through the door and racing down the steps.

Somewhere behind us, my father roars with anger. It's only a matter of time until he catches up with us, and too late I realize, as the two of us take out the guards rushing up the steps to meet us, that I'm going to fail to rescue my friend all over again. I'm going to fail to rescue Rhi too. Because even if we reach Spencer, we're going to be trapped down here like rats in a drainpipe with nowhere to go. No escape. Just like the prison.

"Rhi," I say. We need to stop. We need to rethink this. But she's racing down the steps in front of me and I have no choice but to follow her.

At the bottom, she lets out a howl of pain, swaying on her feet. Professor Stone and the assassin, Renzo Barone are both chained to the wall.

And so is Spencer. Looking just as beat up, just as hurt as before.

"Spencer!" she gasps.

He looks unconscious, his body hanging limply from the chains. At the sound of her voice, though, he raises his head, his face a mess of dried blood, his nose smashed in.

"Oh my–" Rhi cries.

"Sweetheart," Stone says. The professor looks surprisingly well. The assassin on the other hand sports a black eye, a cut lip and he's missing a front tooth. "We've no time for reunions. You need to get us the fuck out of here."

"There is no way out," I tell them all flatly.

We're doomed, all of us. I can hear my father's footfall across the hallway. He'll be here any minute with his infinite number of guards, and there'll be nothing we can do. Sure, we can fight, and fuck I will fight. I'll fight with everything I have. But it will be no use. We're going to lose.

"Of course, there's a way out," Piglet snaps in irritation, racing towards the assassin. "Just hold them off, okay?"

I consider explaining to her that she's wrong. I know this house. I know every hiding place. Every escape route. The only way out of this cellar is back up that staircase. And at the top of the staircase, blocking our exit, waiting for us, will be my father.

"One thing you're going to need to learn quickly, Kennedy," Stone says, "is not to argue with the woman." The assassin snorts, rubbing his newly freed wrists and Rhi turns her attention to the professor next. "Not if you want an easy life."

"And what the hell is that meant to mean?" Rhi asks.

"That you're always right, sweetheart."

She throws him a dirty look but then our attention is diverted to magic crashing down the staircase.

"Shit," Stone mutters as the assassin joins me and together we hurtle our own magic back up towards my father.

Behind me, I hear more snapping of chains and cuffs and then Spencer moaning in agony.

"Okay," Rhi says, "we're ready."

"Ready?" I say. "Ready for what? What the hell is the plan now?"

"Time to go," Barone says.

"I'm telling you, there's no way out. We're trapped."

"And I'm telling you there is," the assassin says, his eyes – mismatched and manic – gleam. "Me."

Then he grabs my arm as Rhi reaches for his hand and I don't know what the hell they have planned but my father is here, racing down the steps, shooting powerful magic our way.

Immediately, Rhi flings her hands forward and fires her own magic, meeting his with a crash of sparks.

Rage rolls through her body in hot, hot dangerous flames and she makes no effort to hold it back. She pushes her magic at my father with the full weight of her body.

His own magic withers away and he holds up his arms, shielding himself, although the force of her magic has him sliding backwards.

"There!" he says. "Powerful. But not quite crimson magic. Seems Miss Clutton-Brock was a little over excited in her description."

He goes to strike Rhi back, and no fucking way.

No. Fucking. Way.

No way is he laying one single finger on my girl.

I dart in front of her and crash magic his way before he can retaliate against her. His face curls with rage and he raises his arms to strike me back.

"Renzo," Rhi shouts, this time firing far darker magic at my father. He raises his arms again, shielding himself a second time, only this time I can feel his defenses are no match for hers. I can feel them creaking.

"Ready?" the assassin calls.

"No." Rhi shakes her head. "Tristan!"

The assassin tuts his tongue. "Really?" he mutters. "The dude's kind of a jerk."

I'd take offense if I knew what they were talking about. Instead, I'm too busy battling my father.

"Renzo, please," she insists.

"Fine," he says sulkily. "Grab the beast," he says to Stone, then takes a hold of Rhi's arm and Stone's. "When I count to three," he tells Rhi, "you stop firing and grab the jerk, okay?"

Rhi nods, battling as the Lord Protector attempts to push back her magic.

"One, two, three!"

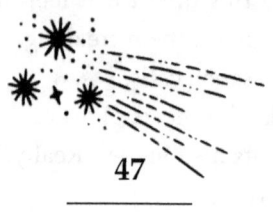

47

R enzo

I BEND the strings of time, force them to part, and slip the five of us through.

But fuck me, that's tricky stuff. Really fucking difficult. Much harder than I expected. Or maybe I knew. Yeah, maybe I knew it would be this hard.

Maybe I did it anyway. For her.

And now I am out.

Completely empty.

Tank drained.

So this is the End.

Curtain down.

Lights out.

Sayonara.

Shame, felt like I was only just getting started ...

48

R^{hi}

PRESSURE SQUEEZES against the sides of my skull, and the sound and light around us bends and warps. I hang on to Tristan's arm with all my might, feeling Renzo's fingers tight in my hand, and praying with everything I have that the other two – Stone and Spencer – are with us too.

The oxygen in my lungs runs out and there's no air to breathe and just when I think I can stand it no longer, we land with a thump on the hard kitchen floor of the mansion.

"Rhianna!" I hear Azlan call and then a pair of strong arms catch me as I sway on my feet.

I blink open my eyes and as my vision swims into focus, sweep my gaze around the room, desperately counting, checking everyone is with us.

Renzo stands in front of me, swaying too. Tristan is

hunched over his knees, retching, and Stone cradles Spencer in his arms, Winnie already hunched over him, examining his injuries.

"Spencer!" I cry, struggling in Azlan's arms.

"It's okay, Rhi," Stone says. "He's going to be just fine. We're going to sort him out."

I go to step towards him, to help them, but Azlan holds me tight.

"Just take a minute, Rhi. Just breathe." I do as he says, my racing heart rate slowing in the warmth of his embrace. "You did it," he says, kissing my crown. "Although what took you so long? I was beginning to worry."

"Things didn't quite go according to plan," I admit.

"I hate to say I told you so," Stone mutters, lifting Spencer's face to take a look at his nose. "But I most definitely did tell you so."

"And I definitely told *you* she could do it," Azlan says with pride in his voice.

"With Tristan's help," I say, and Azlan glances towards his cousin. "Where's Pip?" I ask and I hear a squeak from Renzo's ankles. I swing my gaze that way, in time to see the assassin sway left and then right.

"Fuck," he mutters before slamming down backward onto the floor, his head hitting the ground with a thwack that makes me wince.

"Renzo!" I cry as Pip butts his snout against the man's cheek.

I struggle free from Azlan's arms, rushing down to his side.

"Renzo, are you okay?" He stares up at the ceiling. His eyes unblinking and unmoving. Blank. His chest still. And I can't feel his magic – usually so vibrant, so chaotic, so alive. It's not there. I can't feel it at all.

"Renzo?!" I cry again, this time with more urgency, shaking at his shoulder.

Nothing. No response. And though I search for his magic, I can't find it. He's drained, completely drained.

"Azlan!" I scream. "Azlan!" I shake Renzo harder. "He's not moving. He's not moving." I lay my head above his mouth and will his breath to hit my cheek, to feel it rustle against my skin. Nothing. "He's not breathing. Winnie! Winnie! What do we do? Oh my god, what do we do? His magic's gone."

Which means ...

Renzo is dead.

I scurry backwards, away from him, away from his lifeless body.

The world swoops and swerves and I can feel it spinning away from me, tipping me over into despair, like it did before, like it did when ...

No, no, this can't be happening. Not to him. He's unstoppable. Im-fucking-mortal.

Faces spin in front of me, voices rise and fall. I don't understand. I don't know what's happening. I curl myself up tight into a ball, pain coursing through my body.

Not again! Not again!

"Rhi!"

A voice in my head. A hand at my shoulder.

"Rhi, stay with us."

Stone.

"Can you hear me?" he says, inside my head.

"He's gone," I say, unsure if I'm speaking out loud, the despair seeping through every part of my body. "Renzo's gone."

"You can save him, Rhi."

Save him?

I grab hold of the world with both my hands and force it to stop spinning. It comes to a screeching halt and then I'm back in the cold, silent kitchen with the body of my mate lying lifeless by my side.

"Save him?" I murmur. "Me?"

"Yes, Rhi," Azlan says. "You know what to do," he hesitates, "if you want to."

I stare down at the assassin's face. I know he's committed hideous crimes. I know he's killed and tortured and maimed for fun. I know a man like him should pay for his sins and maybe giving his life to save us all was the ultimate atonement. Perhaps that is justice.

Perhaps I don't give a shit!

I crawl forward, resting my hands above his heart and staring down into those empty eyes – the green one and the brown, staring straight back up at me, unseeing. Beneath my palm, his usually strong heart lies dormant, silent, waiting, and his face isn't frightening anymore. I see the boy he was. The lost boy. The boy without a family, without a home.

I let myself fall into his eyes and let my magic fall with me into his body, curling around his heart, caressing and cradling it, willing it to beat again. My magic seeps into his veins, binds into his being.

I give him my magic – just like Azlan gave me his – and I save Renzo Barone's life – just like Azlan did mine.

And in doing so, I seal the fated mate bond between us – permanently, irreversibly, forever.

Beneath my fingers, his heart murmurs, the faintest of twitches. Then another and another until it's thudding against his ribs. He sucks in a lungful of air, his eyes focusing in on my face.

For a heartbeat, he simply stares.

Then he smiles. He smiles like someone who just won the lottery.

"Fuck me, little rabbit," he laughs, "I fucking died."

And I fall backwards onto my behind and sob with relief into my hands.

49

R^{hi}

I GUESS someone wraps a blanket around my shoulders and forces a cup of something strongly alcoholic into my hands as Pip curls up by my side. With shaking hands, I lift the rim to my lips and tip back my head. The amber liquid stings my nose, before hitting my lips, making me cough as it slides down my throat, warming my gullet.

I let the alcohol seep through my veins, calming my racing heart and my quivering limbs, and then I lower my cup and find Winnie attempting to look Renzo over for injuries, although he's resisting every attempt she makes, still a mile high from his brush with death. Helping her, with a look of extreme trepidation on his face, is Trent.

"Trent?" I gasp.

He spins around and grins at me. "Hey Rhi."

"When did you get here?"

"Your friend insisted on a little detour on our way back from Los Magicos," Azlan says, crouching down beside me. "She can be pretty damn persuasive when she wants to be."

"I said I wasn't driving him anywhere unless we stopped by to pick Trent up first," Winnie says over her shoulder, attempting to grip Renzo's wrist in her hands and count his pulse.

"Good for you." I peer up at Trent. "She's been really worried about you."

The top of Trent's ears burn red. "I've been pretty worried about her too. You know she's on the wanted list. You all are."

"Yeah," I say, "we know." I glance back over to Winnie. "Is there any news on Rosa?"

Winnie stops what she's doing, rocking onto her backside and shaking her head. "She hasn't been seen. I don't know if that's a good thing or a bad thing."

"It's a good thing," Azlan says reassuringly. "That woman is tough. She can take care of herself. I'm sure she's lying low someplace safe."

"You think so?" Winnie asks hopefully.

"Definitely," my mate says, nodding his head, and I can see his confidence eases Winnie's worries a little, exactly what he intends. My heart warms for him and I take his hand in mine and squeeze it. He may be this big tough enforcer, built like a brick house with eyes as dark as night, but the more I know him, the more his softer side is revealed.

"How is he?" I ask Winnie, motioning my head towards Renzo whose eyes are locked on my and Azlan's linked hands.

"If he'd hold still and let me check him over, I could tell you," she snarks with irritation.

"I'm fine, little rabbit. Never been better."

I roll my eyes. Only Renzo, dead literally five minutes ago, would describe himself as 'never better'.

"What?" he says. "We're bonded now. And it feels fucking fantastic." He lays his hands on his taut belly and I can feel all his exuberant emotions spiraling through the bond. It's like an actual whirlwind, making me dizzy and euphoric at the same time. I predict being bonded to Renzo is going to have me feeling that way, plus a little afraid, the entire time.

I don't regret it though. Not when he smiles at me with such genuine affection, it makes my heartbeat skip.

"How about Spencer?" I ask, turning my attention back to Azlan. He's no longer in the kitchen and neither is Tristan and Stone.

"How about *you*, sweetheart?" Azlan asks, cupping my face and peering into my eyes. "How do you feel?"

I manage a half smile. "Pretty tired."

He strokes his thumb against my cheek. "Then go get some rest. We can take care of Barone and Spencer."

"But shouldn't we keep moving?" I ask, unable to help glancing towards the darkened window. "They're going to be after us, aren't they? Your uncle doesn't seem like a man who would happily let us slip away."

"He won't be the only one," Renzo says.

Azlan twists around to face him. "You know who else is looking for her?"

"Magicals from the West," Renzo says.

Azlan twists back to me. "There was no attack from the West. It was some clever trick of my uncle's. A coup."

Renzo scratches his cheek. "Nah, those dudes were from the West. But I don't think they were here to invade the republic or any of that bullshit. I think they were after little rabbit."

Azlan shakes his head. It's obvious he thinks Renzo's talking nonsense.

"We're not going anywhere tonight," Azlan says. "You need time to recover and so do the others."

"Is it safe to stay here, though?" I say.

"I think so. Winnie, Trent and I cast some protection spells on this place while you were gone."

"He was pacing about like a caged tiger," Winnie says. "I thought it was sensible to give him something to do."

"Will they hold?"

"I think so," Azlan says with that same confidence.

"I can add some of my own," Renzo says, jumping to his feet and nearly knocking Winnie over in the process.

Azlan eyes him, clearly wary of any spells Renzo might cast.

"That would be really helpful," I tell Renzo, ignoring Azlan. Renzo's magic is more chaotic, more unpredictable and less practiced than ours. He wasn't taught in the same way the rest of us were. I think a lot of his magic he taught himself. And I think that may give us an advantage when it comes to Christopher Kennedy and his forces.

"Wanna help me, little rabbit?" Renzo says, holding out his hand. In response, Azlan clutches my hand more tightly.

I stand up, tugging my hand from Azlan's grip but not taking the hand Renzo offers.

"I tell you what," I say, "why don't the three of us do it together?" Renzo frowns at me and Azlan goes to open his mouth but I ignore them both. "I think we could build something pretty darn strong and impregnable between the three of us, don't you?"

My two mates look unconvinced but Winnie – always

ready to take my side – nods eagerly. "I think it would." She grabs a hold of Trent's arm eagerly. "We'll leave you to it." Then she pulls her boyfriend out of the kitchen and we hear her giggling as they race up the staircase.

"They're going to fuck," Renzo says helpfully.

"Yes, thanks," I mutter, "I think we figured that out for ourselves."

"That's what we should do after we've done this spell," Renzo continues, Azlan scowling at him. "What?" Renzo says, grinning at the man in black. "We're freshly bonded, and it's the only way to ease the pain, right, Az? Isn't that what you told her?"

"I didn't tell her anything," he growls between gritted teeth.

I clear my throat, regaining both their attentions. "Can we focus on the job at hand please?"

"You can take triggerwot for the pain," Azlan says, "there doesn't have to be any fucking."

"The spell!" I say. I'm relieved beyond belief that we're all together, safe for the time being, but this situation between us is going to be tricky. There's work to be done.

"Right," Azlan says, throwing one last dirty look Renzo's way. "The spell."

I take Renzo's hand in my right and Azlan's hand in my left.

"Now you hold hands too," I say motioning with my head.

"This isn't fucking kindergarten," Azlan mumbles, but I give him a no-nonsense look and he takes Renzo's hand loosely in his.

Renzo winks at me. "He has big hands, little rabbit. Big strong hands."

I swallow. Yep, that's something else I don't need Renzo to tell me. I know.

"Okay," I say, "are we ready?"

Azlan mumbles a "yes" and Renzo nods his head enthusiastically.

"Let's do this then."

I close my eyes and start to recant the protection spell my aunt taught me. The one she would cast over the house every night before we headed to bed. Beside me, I hear Renzo and Azlan do the same and immediately I see how different our three spells are. Renzo's chaotic and hissing and sparking just as I predicted. Azlan's strong, solid and dependable. And mine? Beautiful – like a web spun around us.

At first our magic is separate and distinct, but soon, they melt into one another, combining and weaving together. It's not quite like it is when I combine my magic with Tristan's. It's different from that, but it still has the blood in my veins thrumming, and my bond spinning. A smile plays across my lips and I can't help bouncing up on my toes.

We're better together. Cleverer. More complex. Stronger.

Maybe I am beginning to see why fate wants us together after all.

I'm lost in the magic and the sensations pulsating through my body, that is until a sarcastic voice pops our magical bubble.

"Am I interrupting something?" Stone asks.

Immediately Azlan drops my hand and Renzo's too. His cheeks are flushed and, with his gaze fixated on the ground, he marches out of the kitchen, pushing past his friend in the doorway.

"What was that about?" Stone says watching his friend go.

"We were casting protection spells," I say.

Stone swivels his gaze back to me. "Are you sure? It looked like you were playing nursery games."

"I'm sure."

Stone nods. "I thought you might like to know that we've finished healing all Spencer's injuries." He rubs a hand against his beard. "He was in a pretty bad way. A really fucking bad way. Those people really are sick."

"But he's okay now?"

"Physically, yeah, but emotionally ... I think you should go talk to him, Rhi."

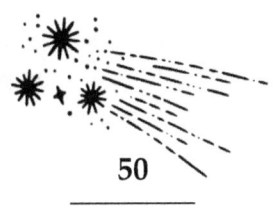

50

S pencer

THE DOOR of the bedroom creaks open and Rhi stands in the doorway. Tristan lounging on the end of the bed where I'm laid out, jumps to his feet.

"Rhi," he says.

"I need to talk to Spencer," she tells him, then turns her head to look at me.

"Yeah," Tristan says. "I think you should."

She steps into the room and the overhead light catches her face. I think about Jacob, what he asked me.

Is she pretty?

Fuck, she's damn pretty, far prettier than I even remembered. Those plush pink lips, those honey eyes, her soft skin. I'd hardly noticed her when she first arrived at the academy – this small, scrawny thing who seemed to hide in the shadows. I didn't appreciate how pretty she was until that first day on the mats when I'd gazed down into her face and the thing in my gut had tugged me towards her, tugged me hard.

Tristan hesitates, then walks towards the doorway, stroking his hand down her arm as he passes her, making her body shiver. He steps outside, closing the door behind him and then it's just the two of us.

For a moment we simply stare at each other, both knowing there are things that need to be said, neither knowing how to say them.

Although my body's mended, I'm tired, drained by everything that's happened. Yet, being in her presence revives me, has me alert and attentive.

She takes a step forward, then another, then seeming to make up her mind, walks around to the bed and lays herself down alongside me on the mattress, resting back against the cushions, her hands resting in her lap.

"Thank you," I say finally, "thank you for rescuing me. I hear it was your idea."

"You left," she says.

"Wh-what?" I say, taken aback by the aggression in her voice.

"You left. You turned your back on our bond and you left."

I hang my head in shame.

"You know the truth now," I mutter. "You know what I am."

"A werebeast."

I cringe at the word. A werebeast. A mutt. A curseded. I swallow. "So you must see, you must understand. I had no choice but to leave."

"No choice?!" she says, shifting on the mattress to look round at me.

"Yes, no choice," I say, my jaw setting. There was no choice. I had to keep her safe. "You want to be bonded to a werebeast? Do you know how fucking dangerous he can be? Do you know what he could do to you?"

"But you didn't even tell me," she says. "You didn't even give *me* that choice. You just assumed. You just made the decision on your own. And you left me ... left me feeling ..."

She swipes at a tear trailing down her face and I feel utterly wretched and so damn stupid.

"I never meant to hurt you," I say softly. "I thought it was for the best."

"But you did hurt me, Spencer. Over and over again."

I screw up my eyes. "I had to make you hate me. I had to make you stay away from me. I was trying to protect you."

She shakes her head. "You could have simply told me the truth."

I open my eyes and look at her. "And what would you have said? What would you have done? We've always been hated, despised, outcasts. That hatred has always been there, bubbling beneath the surface. But now it's out in the open. And now they've locked us all away to rot."

"You don't think I felt like an outcast the entire time we were at the academy? You don't think you and Tristan and all your dumb friends made me feel that way all the time?"

I hold her gaze and then I nod.

"I had a lot of time to think about stuff in that cell." I swallow. I don't want to think about that cell. I don't ever want to think about it again. "I had a lot of time to mull over everything that's happened. There were a lot of things I regret, a lot of things I've done that I am ashamed of, a lot of stupid, fucking horrible things." She chews on her lip. "The worst of it was the way I treated you. And I'm sorry, truly fucking sorry for it. If I could turn back time, if I could undo my choices and my actions ... Because I know, believe me, I know, what it's like to be on the receiving end now."

Her eyes flicker back and forth over my face.

"What did they do to you, Spencer?"

I lean my head back against the cushions and take a deep inhale. I don't want to talk about it. I don't want to relive it.

There's something else I need to tell her.

"There were these moments when the abyss was calling to me, tempting me down, down into its depths. And I knew if I let myself just slip away, fall into its cold embrace, never wake up, all the pain would stop, it would all end. And fuck, when it was unbearable, when I could hardly endure it, it was so so fucking tempting." My body shakes at the memory. Bile rises into my throat and I swallow it down. "But there was this one thing, this one thing, keeping me from that temptation. That kept me hanging on."

Her eyes are fixed on me. "What was it?"

"You, Rhi," I say, "you. The thought of you was the only thing keeping me alive."

"You have so much to live for, Spencer Moreau." She smiles at me. "Captain of the dueling team. Winner of the transatlantic cup. Son of council members."

"No, the only thing that matters is you, Rhi."

She considers me for one long, long minute. Then she shuffles up on the mattress and I wonder if she's going to stand up and walk away. Whether my words are meaningless and empty in the face of all I've done to her.

She doesn't. Instead, she presses her mouth to mine. This crazy, fearless girl, who risked her fucking neck to come save me, even though I've been a giant ass to her, kisses me.

I close my eyes. Sometimes in that cell, I dreamed about

kissing her. It was like another kind of torture. I didn't think I'd ever have the chance to kiss her again. And now I am, her lips soft and wet against mine.

Deep inside me the beast purrs with satisfaction. Satisfaction and relief.

I go to tug her closer, but she's already pulling away, shuffling back down the mattress and resting her head against my shoulder.

And I know we're not done here. I know there's still so much to fix between us, so much *I* need to fix. But this is a start. A start at least.

I take her hand in mine and close my eyes.

51

R^{hi}

I WAKE up curled against Spencer Moreau's warm body, morning light spilling across the bed. I glance around the room finding Pip laid out by my feet and my other mates sleeping in the room too; Renzo comatose on the floor, Stone and Tristan stretched out on chairs and Azlan leaning against the wall, eyes closed, arms folded against his chest.

I look at each one of them in turn, puzzled at how dramatically my feelings for these five men have changed over the course of the last few months. I've gone from hating nearly every single one of them, to emotions that are much softer, much deeper, much more complex. Maybe I don't love every one of them, but I think I could. In fact, I can feel myself falling for them that little bit more each day and I certainly care about them.

Carefully, so as not to disturb the sleeping giant beside me, I roll up to sit. Pip, spotting I'm awake, comes crawling into my lap and I stroke his ears, kissing the top of his head and whispering how much I've missed him.

When I finally look up from our little love in, I find the five men in the room are all awake and watching me.

"Good morning," I say, unashamedly. I may like these men, I may find them hot as hell, I may find it hard to keep my hands off them, but Pip will always, always come first. And that is something they are simply going to have to live with.

If, that is, we're sticking together from now on. I frown. Are we? This is the first time we've all been in the same room together and haven't either been fighting for our lives, or mortally wounded? We haven't exactly had the chance to talk.

"So ..." I say, chewing on the inside of my cheek with unease.

"So," Stone says, leaning forward on his seat, "here we all are. Rhianna Blackwaters and her five fated mates."

I swallow. When he puts it like that it sounds pretty intimidating. *Five.* Nine months ago, I'd never even had one boyfriend. Now I have five mates. And not just any old mates at that.

"But why?" I say. "Why me? Why you?"

"Because you're special, Rhianna Blackwaters," Azlan says with no trace of sarcasm or tease.

"Don't tell me what I am, Azlan. I know who I am."

I glance at Renzo and he tilts his head, curious. He has his theories as to who I am. But I don't even know if that's true. I do know who raised me. I do know the woman I am.

Maybe Renzo is right about my father. Maybe he's not.

Maybe my mom was some great seer, fought over by both sides. Maybe all I am is a girl brought up in hiding by her aunt out there in the wastelands.

Maybe I don't care where I came from. I know who I am.

There are other questions I have now.

"What I don't know is why fate has tied us together. The six of us. Why she's determined that we should be together. Us?" I say, spreading my arms wide and looking at each one of my fated mates in turn, my bond tugging forcefully towards each one of them as I do.

The Enforcer.

The Professor.

The Assassin.

The werebeast.

And the Lord Protector's son.

It makes so little sense. Especially when we seem so good at hurting each other. At making one another suffer. What purpose could there possibly be in bringing us together?

"There must be a reason for it," Stone says, reading the thoughts in my mind.

"But what is it?" Spencer asks.

"I don't know," I say, locking my sights on Stone. "But there's one way to find out. We're going to reopen those memories in my mind."

Read the final book, book five next,
Destined Dawn

Want to read a bonus scene from this story? You can find all my bonus material on my website here

For sneaky previews, spoilers and all the latest news, join Hannah's reader group

Thank you so much for reading. If you enjoyed this book, please consider leaving a review or rating — it's a great help to indie authors like me!

ALSO BY HANNAH HAZE

All available on Amazon and Kindle Unlimited.

Fantasy Romance RH
The Arrow Hart Academy
Fractured Fates
Twisted Ties
Shattered Stars
Burdened Bonds
Destined Dawn

The Firestone Academy
Storm of Shadows
Spark of Sorcery
Taste of Thorns
Lure of Lightning

Contemporary RH omegaverse
The Rockview Omegaverse
Pack Rivals Part I

Pack Rivals Part II
Pack Choice
Pack Gamble Part I
Pack Gamble Part II
Pack Education Part I
Pack Education Part II

In With The Pack
In Deep - Rosie's story
In Trouble - Connie's story
In Knots - Alexa's story
In Doubt - Giorgie's story
In Control - Sophia's story
In Stockings (Christmas Novella)

Contemporary MF omegaverse series
The Alpha Rock Stars
The Rockstar's Omega
Rocked by the Alpha
Fourth Base with the Alpha

Contemporary MF omegaverse standalones
Oxford Heat
The Alpha Escort Agency
Omega's Forbidden Heat

Contemporary MF omegaverse novellas
The Omega Chase
Online Heat
Christmas Heat

Alien omegaverse MF romance series

The Alpha Prince of Astia
<u>Alien Desire</u>
<u>Alien Passion</u>

ABOUT THE AUTHOR

A recovering cynic, Hannah grew up swearing she would never marry. Then in 2001, she met her husband and has been a card-carrying romantic ever since. Despite being an avid writer and reader, Hannah decided to do the sensible thing and study science at university, putting authoring ideas to one side.This all changed when she discovered the joys of a good romance book and came to the realisation that love stories are always the best ones.

She now uses her knowledge of chemical bonds and reactions to ensure her books are full of sparks. In fact the electricity between her characters is sure to set your pulse racing and your heart fluttering.

Hannah loves reading to her three children, including doing all the silly voices, and going for long walks in the country-side (the muddier the better). Her head is always full of new story ideas and you are most likely to find her avoiding the demands of her very naughty cat as she attempts to write them all down.

Sign up to my newsletter:
www.hannahhaze.com/about

Join my reader groups:

https://www.facebook.com/groups/hannahhazehotro
mancereads

https://www.facebook.com/groups/softandsteamyomega
verse

Visit my website:

www.hannahhaze.com

Catch me on TikTok:

www.tiktok.com/@hannahhaze_author

ACKNOWLEDGMENTS

As always, let me start by thanking all you wonderful readers for giving my words a chance, diving into my worlds and loving all these characters as much as I do. You are the best!

Another big thank you to my amazing beta reader team who always help me to make the story better. Thank you Courtney, Sara, Jessie, Leandri, Aimee, Jenna, Melissa, Lili and Kiki.

Thank you to Christian for another beautiful cover and James for editing my smutty words.

And finally, thank you to Mr. D, Stephy, my children and the rest of my family for their ongoing encouragement, love and support — and for letting me ramble book ideas at them! Love you all x

www.ingramcontent.com/pod-product-compliance
Lightning Source LLC
Chambersburg PA
CBHW070757120726
47910CB00001B/208